ACCLAIM FOR KELLY IRVIN

"*Tell Her No Lies* is true romantic suspense at its best! Kelly Irvin has penned a heart-stopping, adrenaline pumping romantic suspense with an unlikely heroine that tugs at the heartstrings. Highly recommended!"

—COLLEEN COBLE, *USA TODAY* BESTSELLING AUTHOR

"In *Tell Her No Lies*, Kelly Irvin has crafted a story of wounded characters overcoming and fighting their way to the truth. In a world where so many present one facade externally and another inside their homes, this novel shines a light on the power of truth to cut through the darkness. Wrap that inside a page-turning mystery and some sweet romance and it's a story perfect for readers who love multiple threads. This is a keeper of a story."

—CARA PUTMAN, AUTHOR OF THE HIDDEN JUSTICE SERIES

"I think I've found a new favorite author! What an exciting read—tense, suspenseful, and masterfully written!"

—CARRIE STUART PARKS, AWARD-WINNING
AUTHOR OF *FORMULA OF DECEPTION*

"A moving and compelling tale about the power of grace and forgiveness that reminds us how we become strongest in our most broken moments."

—*LIBRARY JOURNAL* FOR *UPON A SPRING BREEZE*

"Irvin's novel is an engaging story about despair, postnatal depression, God's grace, and second chances."

—*CBA CHRISTIAN MARKET* FOR *UPON A SPRING BREEZE*

"A warmhearted novel that is more than a romance, with lovable characters, including two innocent children caught in the red tape of government and two people willing to risk breaking both the Englisch and Amish law to help in whatever way they can. There are subplots that focus on the struggles of undocumented immigrants."

—*RT BOOK REVIEWS*, 4-STAR REVIEW OF *THE SADDLE MAKER'S SON*

"Irvin has given her audience a continuation of *The Beekeeper's Son* with complicated young characters who must define themselves."

—*RT BOOK REVIEWS*, 4-STAR REVIEW OF *THE BISHOP'S SON*

"The awesome power of faith and family over personal desire dominates this beautifully woven masterpiece."

—*PUBLISHERS WEEKLY*, STARRED REVIEW OF *THE BEEKEEPER'S SON*

"Storyteller extraordinaire Kelly Irvin's tale of the Amish of Bee County will intrigue readers, who will want to eavesdrop on the lives of these characters on a regular basis."

—*RT REVIEWS*, 4$\frac{1}{2}$ STARS REVIEW OF *THE BEEKEEPER'S SON*

"Irvin writes with great insight into the range and depth of human emotion. Her characters are believable and well developed, and her storytelling skills are superb."

—*CBA RETAILERS + RESOURCES* FOR *THE BEEKEEPER'S SON*

TELL
HER
NO
LIES

TELL HER NO LIES

KELLY IRVIN

THOMAS NELSON
Since 1798

Tell Her No Lies

© 2018 by Kelly Irvin

Published in Nashville, Tennessee, by Thomas Nelson. Thomas Nelson is a registered trademark of HarperCollins Christian Publishing, Inc.

Thomas Nelson titles may be purchased in bulk for educational, business, fund-raising, or sales promotional use. For information, please e-mail SpecialMarkets@ ThomasNelson.com.

Scripture quotations are taken from the Holy Bible, New International Version®, niv®. Copyright © 1973, 1978, 1984, 2011 by Biblica, Inc.™ Used by permission of Zondervan. All rights reserved worldwide. www.zondervan.com. The "niv"and "New International Version" are trademarks registered in the United States Patent and Trademark Office by Biblica, Inc.™

Publisher's Note: This novel is a work of fiction. Names, characters, places, and incidents are either products of the author's imagination or used fictitiously. All characters are fictional, and any similarity to people living or dead is purely coincidental.

Library of Congress Cataloging-in-Publication Data

Names: Irvin, Kelly, author.
Title: Tell her no lies / Kelly Irvin.
Description: Nashville, Tennessee : Thomas Nelson, [2018]
Identifiers: LCCN 2018028548 | ISBN 9780785223115 (paperback)
Subjects: | GSAFD: Romantic suspense fiction.
Classification: LCC PS3609.R82 T45 2018 | DDC 813/.6--dc23 LC record available at https://lccn.loc.gov/2018028548

Printed in the United States of America

18 19 20 21 22 MG 5 4 3 2 1

To Becky Monds. Thank you for making this dream come true.

HONOR YOUR FATHER AND YOUR MOTHER, SO THAT
YOU MAY LIVE LONG IN THE LAND THE LORD YOUR
GOD IS GIVING YOU.

EXODUS 20:12

Someone needed to make a perfume from stop bath and developer. The photo chemicals smelled like *come-hither* to Nina Fischer. She inhaled their biting scent and studied the image that appeared as she swished the sheet of paper in the deep, gray plastic tub. A homeless man with a toothless grin rewarded her efforts. The man smiled as if he'd invited her into a palatial home and not a squatter's makeshift campsite. His black-and-white surroundings materialized in sharp contrast around him. A graffiti-covered Dumpster dwarfed his skeletal frame. A shopping cart loaded with a tattered coat, mismatched sneakers, and a pile of blankets was parked on the broken cement like a car in a driveway. Despite the alcohol-induced trust in his bloodshot eyes, he stayed close to the cart as if he feared she would steal it away.

The photo told a story. A story that the world needed to see and Nina needed to tell. In many ways it was her story. The story of a child who'd lived in that world and survived. The words to the poem that would accompany the photo fell into place.

"Nina? You're doing it again."

Rick Zavala's irritated baritone boomed in the small darkroom.

"Sorry." Nina snatched the phone from the counter, hit the speaker button to turn it off, then tucked the phone between her ear and her shoulder while using her free hand to move the photo to the stop bath. She glanced at the illuminated face of the sports watch on her wrist. Thirty seconds and the photo moved to the fixer.

"You could at least pretend to pay attention when you're on the phone with me."

"I *am* paying attention." Now she was. Suppressing a snort of laughter, she gripped the tongs and slipped the photo into the next tub. "It's three o'clock in the morning. I'm not going to a party with you. I only have a week left to get ready for the exhibit."

"All work and no play make Nina a dull girl. Have a cup of coffee and get your second wind. Jackson hired a great band for this fund-raiser. Everyone's here. It's actually fun." Despite the loud conversations in the background accompanied by raucous Dixieland jazz, Rick's silky voice dropped another notch the way it always did when he wanted to coax her into doing something they both knew she didn't want to do.

"There're some people I need to talk to here. Having you by my side would help. It's a perfect opportunity—"

"To schmooze, I know." Glancing at her watch again, Nina laid the tongs on the counter. Thirty seconds. She flipped the switch and the small room was bathed in a soft overhead light. She had five minutes before she could move the photo to the water bath. "My favorite thing."

Not.

A chorus of whiny yowls outside the darkroom door made Nina pause for a second. The cats never bothered her when she was working. They knew better. She opened the door. A black furry streak hurled herself into the room. Nina managed a quick two-step as Daffy whirled and threw herself at Nina's legs, emitting a meow that was more of a hiss than a whine. Mango, an orange tabby whose girth prevented her from winning any race with Daffy, followed at a surprising clip. "What's wrong with you?"

"Something's wrong with me because I want my girl at my side—"

"I'm not talking to you. The cats are having a hissy fit at my feet. They have the run of my family's entire three-story home, and they have to congregate here. Jan must've forgotten to feed them before she and Brooklyn took off. And I'm not your girl."

Just to keep the record straight.

"You could be if you'd stop putting me off." His aggrieved tone reminded her of all the times she'd beaten him in one-on-one basketball games and he'd insisted she cheated. "I'm ready to take it to the next level and you know it."

His idea of the next level didn't jive with Nina's. "I'm not putting you off."

"Then what would you call it—playing the field?" Now he sounded like the sulky kid she'd first met when his mother let him tag along while she cleaned the Fischer house a hundred years ago. "Playing hard to get? Playing with my feelings?"

"I'm not playing at all. I take relationships seriously. You're the one out past midnight on a work night. You're almost thirty years old."

"This is work and I'm asking you to be here with me."

"As a prop."

"I would never use you as a prop. I would never use you period. I love your company."

In typical Rick fashion, he stopped short of saying he loved *her*. "It's late and I'm tired. Let's not do this now."

"If you have your way, we'll never have this conversation."

The opposite was true. They'd had the conversation over and over again in the years since they both returned to San Antonio after college. Always with the same outcome.

Ignoring the pique in his voice and the herd of two cats clamoring at her feet, Nina focused on a dozen photos clipped overhead with wooden clothespins on a rope strung the length of the room. She liked the progression. Early afternoon sunlight slipping into dusk as the day went on. It would be interesting to see how they compared to the video Aaron shot for their joint exhibit.

Daffy nipped at her bare ankle and yowled. "Ouch. Seriously, what has gotten into you?"

"Nothing—"

"Sorry, not you, Rick. Daffy just attacked me. You don't need me. You do fine without me."

"That's not true. I need you in more ways than one and you know it."

No, she didn't. Rick's efforts to line up supporters for his fledgling campaign for state representative would no doubt go better without her. She didn't schmooze well and she didn't have a political bone in her body.

"I'm hanging up now. I want to have this series done before Aaron comes over with the video. We have to figure out how to loop it on the wall opposite the photos, and the photos still have to be mounted and the poems finished."

"Aaron's coming over? At this hour? Doesn't he have to work tomorrow—later today?"

Nina held the phone away from her ear. Rick wanted her to come out to a party at three in the morning, but she couldn't have a colleague over to work at that time? She and Aaron McClure had been in school together at the University of Texas–Austin. He was her closest friend in ways Rick could never be. They walked a careful line that preserved that friendship, which she valued beyond measure. "Unlike you, he's taking a vacation day tomorrow—today. We're running out of time and he's just now doing the final edits to the video."

"Whatever. Let's have breakfast."

His way of ensuring she didn't share that meal with Aaron. "You'll be up by nine?"

"Probably not. Peter knows about this party tonight, and I don't have anything on the court docket. He'll cut me some slack."

Peter Coggins hadn't become senior partner in his own high-powered law firm by cutting anyone slack. "If you decide to get up, bring me a whole wheat bagel with blueberry cream cheese."

"Come with me to see the Aaron Neville Quintet play at the Empire Theatre this weekend." Rick managed to skip right over the breakfast invitation. He was not a morning person. "The guy's in his seventies. You never know if you'll get another chance."

Nina glanced down at her jazz festival T-shirt. How did he know? She wouldn't be able to resist a concert featuring her favorite non-rock artist, the soul–R&B–funk–doo-wop man with New Orleans roots. "Call me later."

"I thought your name was Nina."

Chuckling despite herself, she disconnected and tucked the phone in the hip pocket of her jeans. Rick could be sweet when he wasn't trying to figure an angle to make a situation work to his advantage. Including dating the daughter of a well-connected family whose roots went back to Sam Houston and the Alamo. Or maybe that was her imagination. Her insecurity. Couldn't he be interested in her regardless of her family's genealogy?

Their paths had meandered in wildly differing directions, then reconnected because of her dad's generosity. Giving a maid's son a helping hand with college tuition was like her dad. Exerting his influence to get Rick a job at a local firm after law school. Whether intentional or not, her dad's kindness served to keep Rick in her life. Which kept her off-balance and wondering.

With a sigh, Nina turned the volume on the radio back up on her favorite classic rock station. Vintage Bruce Springsteen's "Born to Run" poured from the speakers. Wishing she could take a long run to shake off her fatigue, she moved the print to the water bath and spent a few minutes swishing it around before hanging it next to the others. Fatigue made her light-headed. She gripped the counter and closed her eyes for a few seconds. She needed food. And caffeine if she was going to pull the necessary all-nighter.

She slipped on her flip-flops, turned off the radio, scooped up Daffy, and headed down the stairs to the most important room on the first floor. The kitchen. Mango followed, nipping at her heels as if to say, "Hurry up." Daffy struggled in her arms, her back claws digging into flesh. "Hey, that hurts, you little poop head."

Nina let go and the yowling cat leaped to the floor. Mango immediately joined in. "Hush up, you two. You can't be that hungry. I'm getting the food right now." She examined the scratch on her arm. The cat had drawn blood. "Seriously, Daffy, what's wrong with you? I want both of you to find the dogs, annoy them for a while. Okay?"

The cats ignored her instructions and followed her through the kitchen in a nip-and-tuck pattern. Thunder boomed in the distance. Maybe it was the weather. They'd forgotten what thunder sounded like after the long drought.

"Nina."

She froze, sure she'd imagined the hoarse, whispered two syllables wafting into the kitchen from the hallway. She took a mental inventory. Grace was at a writers' conference in Indianapolis. Dad had gone to bed hours earlier. Jan and Brooklyn were camping. Nina was alone on the first floor.

She cocked her head, listening. The house creaked and settled, no doubt swaying in a stormy September wind.

"Nina, please."

A screamed whisper.

A chill spread across her bare neck above her T-shirt. She eased toward the kitchen door and put one hand on the solid wood frame. "Dad?"

No response.

Concern mixed with dread made a sour concoction in the pit of her empty stomach. She strode down the hallway that led to the living room and formal dining room on one side, her parents' offices on the other. "Dad, is that you? Are you okay?"

Daffy shot past her and squeezed through the first door on the right. Mango held back, impeding Nina's progress as she stared. The door to her dad's study.

"Help me . . ."

Now a breathless whisper.

Nina touched the door with one finger. It swung open. "Dad? What's wrong? Why are you whispering?"

A low whine told her Peanuts, Dad's cocker spaniel, had beaten her to the room along with Daffy. Nina bent and picked up Mango, who weighed more than a small child. Her warm, tubby body offered comfort against a sudden chill. "I'm here. Dad, did you want something?"

No answer.

A petite Tiffany desk lamp cast just enough light for Nina to see that nothing seemed out of place. She cleared her throat. "Dad, where are you? You're scaring me."

Shadows created pockets filled with blackness. Books lined built-in shelves that covered an entire wall up to the eight-foot ceiling. The gold-and-auburn brocade drapes were pulled back and held with tasseled ropes, revealing the steady stream of rain running down two floor-to-ceiling windows. Fire bushes in the side yard scraped the windows in an annoying rustling sound.

The mammoth mahogany desk bore all the signs of a workaholic. A desktop computer, a laptop, and an iPad. Piles of papers. Law books stacked six and eight deep. Court briefs.

Her perusal of the room skidded to a stop. Behind the desk, one glass door to her dad's gun cabinet gaped open. He never left it open. He always kept it locked and the key on his chain. Ever since she and her sister, Jan, had moved into a bedroom down the hall from Trevor's room all those years ago.

The office smelled of old paper and books and something else. Something not good. Something that made her stomach turn over and her arms tighten around Mango. The cat squirmed and leaped from her arms.

The room smelled like blood.

Another whine. Behind the desk.

She started around it. Daffy sped past her and out the door as if her work were done. Peanuts crouched next to a long leg stretched out on the floor.

Her breath a hitch in her throat, Nina shot forward. "Dad?"

No answer.

The cocker spaniel whimpered, a sound that made Nina's own throat ache. "It's okay, boy, it's okay."

A bare foot next to a brown corduroy slipper. A silky, beige pajama pant had ridden up, revealing a leg covered with thick, black hair. Nina edged past Peanuts until she could see the rest of the body.

Her father sprawled on his back, hands clutched at his stomach.

Her legs trembling, Nina knelt. Blood stained his pajama top a deep scarlet. It pooled under him. A gun lay near his right elbow. Nina knew less than nothing about guns. This one was big and black. "Oh, Daddy." His eyes didn't blink and his face didn't acknowledge her presence. "Dad? Geoffrey!"

She touched his throat. His skin was warm. Almost hot. Sweat streaked his face and something else. Tears? She pressed her fingers harder, seeking a pulse. "Daddy, talk to me, talk to me."

No pulse. The voice that had spoken only seconds before had been silenced. Why hadn't she come sooner? Why hadn't she heard the shot? Daddy had always said she played her music too loud. *"You'll end up deaf."* He would never say those words again.

"No, no, no." She tugged her phone from her pocket, surprised to see bloody prints on it when she tapped those three numbers they'd all been taught to see as lifelines. "Help, I need help."

The 911 operator's voice was kind. Yes, she would send someone. Yes, Nina needed to stay on the line.

Nina hit speaker and tossed the phone on the thick carpet he'd insisted on, saying wooden floors were cold even in a climate like San Antonio's. The cold aggravated his arthritis. His joints ached and his fingers wouldn't cooperate when he tried to hunt and peck on his laptop. Had that pain seeped away with the blood that ran from his wounds?

Nina bent over, getting close to his mouth, to hear his breath. He had to breathe. She'd lost enough people in her life.

She touched his neck again. Still no pulse. Skin cooling.

Come on, God. Come on. Hasn't it been enough? Can't I keep this one person? Can You see why I don't trust You?

The pounding of her heart in her ears served as the only answer. As usual.

She gently moved his hands, sure any small adjustment would cause him pain. She began to push, up and down, up and down on his chest. Wasn't that what a person did when someone's heart stopped beating?

One should perform CPR. *One, two, three, four,* she counted silently, then aloud. "Five, six, seven, eight, nine . . ." As if counting aloud would make her efforts more powerful. His heart would start and he would open his eyes and tell her all about how this happened. How he ended up on the floor of his study. A gaping hole in his gut.

Sirens sounded in the distance, music to her ears for the first time in her life. Help was coming.

Nina paused, her head over her father's, her long hair touching his still, white cheek. The only real father she'd ever known. The man who had taken Jan and her in and made them his daughters. He liked to say he'd chosen them, which was much nicer than the truth. The ugly truth. He'd been the one to tell her it was okay to call him Daddy, a word so foreign to her vocabulary it could've been another language.

"Breathe, Daddy, breathe. Please."

His head lolled to one side, features slack. The sirens screamed. Whirling lights pierced the windows, lighting up the dark and ping-ponging on the walls in a crazy, unpredictable pattern.

It didn't matter how fast they arrived. They were already too late.

2

CSI: San Antonio. A new location for the popular TV show franchise? Nina slipped past the Evidence Unit investigator who squatted, gloved hand on the chair railing, staring at something on the base molding along the wooden floor of the entryway. Dad wouldn't like it. Pedestrian TV fare had no place in a district judge's life. Nina didn't intend to escape. She simply needed a breath of fresh air. Tuesday had dawned a gray, sunless day that promised more rain. She needed to clear the stench from her nose. She needed to clear from her ears the sound of voices murmuring words such as *caliber* and *angle* and *entry wound.* The clicking sound of a photographer taking photos made her long for her own camera. While at the newspaper, she'd learned to use the camera as a buffer between her heart and the accidents and homicide stories she'd photographed. She ached for that buffer now.

They wandered in and out of his study in such a casual manner. They couldn't know she stayed out of this room as much as possible. The room where her father had always brought her to discuss transgressions and punishments. To get called to the study was to be in trouble. A-B honor roll meant ice cream sundaes and banana splits on the veranda. A grade dipped below a B, and it was time to discuss her study habits in his office. It didn't happen often, but when it did, she never failed to feel she'd let the most important man in her life down. She shuddered. Even their last conversation in this room had been fraught with his disappointment and her stubborn refusal to acknowledge it.

The front door stood open. Half afraid someone would grab her shoulder and jerk her back in, she peeked out. The first detective on the scene, an older man with white hair and a craggy face, had asked her a few questions and then suggested with a gracious air that she should rest for a few minutes in the living room. Someone would be back to question her. Nothing in his manner suggested he would cuff her to a chair if she stretched her legs. She needed to do something, anything, not to think about Dad sprawled on the floor in another room and the indignities to which his body would be subjected now that he'd been the victim of the greatest indignity of all—murder.

She breathed in the rain-cooled air and rubbed eyes that burned with fatigue. Trying to ignore the marked media units and live trucks that lined the narrow street, she focused on the spacious front yard filled with antique yellow rosebushes and purple and pink petunias and other flowers her mother tended in a sporadic way that depended entirely on where she was in writing her latest book. Did she need time to think? She weeded. Was she mulling a sticky plot point? She dug out old plants and replaced them with new annuals.

"Nina Fischer. Nina!" Lou Briggs from News 4 screamed in that high-pitched voice that said she would never make it to a top-ten market no matter how aggressively she pursued her I-team investigations. "Can we ask you a couple of questions?"

Nina drew back, not wanting her face with its dark circles beneath her eyes and ratty, uncombed hair to show up on their noon newscast.

She understood better than most that they were just doing their jobs. They'd come out of the woodwork, their desire for the story no doubt driven by the announcement that a venerable four-term state district court judge had been killed in his own home a few hours earlier. She couldn't give them fodder.

She turned and slipped along the hallway and out to the sunporch that ran along the side of the house. It was screened but gave her a view of the second rose garden her mother had planted. The porch was a perfect place to read in the evening or simply sit and watch the light fade over the masses of pink, yellow, and red flowers that mingled in massive disarray, tumbling up trellis after trellis, seeking sun and air.

"Nina, are you all right?"

Even if she couldn't see him, Aaron McClure's East Coast accent gave him away. No amount of time in Texas could mute it. His yellow rain slicker gaped open in the front, revealing a UT–Austin T-shirt tight across his broad, muscular chest. The hood had slipped down his back, allowing rain that had turned into a drizzle to dampen his hair, already an untamable mass of auburn curls coveted by every woman he'd ever met.

Her best friend knew about her second-favorite spot in this house, second to her darkroom. He knew to pull along the side street and traipse through the alley if he wanted to avoid the police officers posted in the front yard, keeping his colleagues at bay. He had an advantage. He knew the layout.

Aaron strode through the wet grass, his boots making sucking sounds in the mud. A rain cover protected the camera he held on his shoulder.

Nina shrank back against the wall. He kept coming but slowed, his wet hair hanging in blue-gray eyes that reminded her of Cancun waters under a cloudy, late-afternoon sky. He had round cheeks and fair skin that spoke of an undiluted Irish ancestry. She always planned to grab some action shots of him working, but he did a good job of evading her lens. Like most photographers, he preferred to stay behind the camera. "You're working."

"The assignments editor called me in." He stopped walking, rain from the porch roof dripping on his head. "She figured I'd know my way around on this story, and I figured the exhibit would be on hold anyway."

"Claire knows we're friends."

"Yeah, she does, but she's all about the story." He shifted the video camera on his burly shoulder. "I'm sorry about your dad."

"Thank you."

Aaron put his massive free hand on the dark screen that separated them. His eyes told her how much he wanted to be on the other side of that screen, hugging her, comforting her. She loved those eyes. His gaze dropped to her shirt. She glanced down. Dried blood. Dad's blood. "I'm sorry, but it's my job. I gotta ask. What happened?"

She gazed over his shoulder at Melanie Martinez. The model-slumming-as-a-reporter held back, letting her photog take the first swing, knowing he had a better chance of getting a sound bite because he knew a member of the victim's family. They were about to get the scoop on their colleagues who lined up outside the black wrought-iron fence out front.

Nina turned her back on both of them. "I'm not making any statements at this time."

"Okay. I understand." His husky voice filled with concern reminded her of the honey and lemon she liked in her tea when she had a sore throat. "Are you hurt? Did they let you call someone? I tried to call you, but it went straight to voice mail."

"I'm fine." She cleared her throat. "Like I said, I'm not making any statements."

"Just between you and me, are you okay?"

Wiping at her face with the back of her hand, she swiveled and stared at him. He stared back. An electric current of warmth seemed to swell between them.

This couldn't be just between them, as much as he might want it to be. He had a job to do. Tonight it would be just between him and a top-thirty-five TV market that covered the San Antonio metro viewing area, stretching from Fredericksburg to Del Rio to Lytle to Victoria. As a former newspaper photographer, no one understood that more than Nina did. Journalists did their jobs, no matter the circumstances. The story was sacred.

"Nina Fischer, in the house. Now."

A tall, lean man, head bare, brown hair gleaming with raindrops, strode onto the sunporch. He wore a black, stylishly cut raincoat that made him look like a spy who hadn't come in from the cold. He planted himself in front of her. "Y'all need to get back out front now."

"He's a friend." Someone she counted on. Who was this guy in her family's home, giving orders? "Who are you?"

The man swiveled and slid open the front of the coat. His badge flashed on his belt. "Detective Matt King. You're not supposed to be out here. Carter told you to stay put."

"I needed air."

Detective King jerked his head toward Aaron and Melanie, whose olive skin darkened with a blush. "You needed to get your fifteen minutes of fame?"

"I told you, he's a friend. A good friend."

Even if he had no choice but to put his job first.

"Well, there's no honor among journalists." Detective King gripped Nina's arm and steered her toward the door. "I'm surprised you didn't know that. Your family's in the news all the time."

"Hey, don't touch her!" Aaron looked as if he contemplated crashing through the screen to back up his words. He had twenty pounds of brawn on the detective. "A badge doesn't give you the right to mistreat a family member of the victim."

Nina tugged from his grip. "My father is . . . was a judge. He sat on the bench on some controversial cases." She glanced back. Aaron hadn't moved. And his camera was hot. "Don't cause trouble, Aaron, please."

Aaron backed away, still rolling. Melanie at his side back-stepped and scribbled in her skinny reporter's notebook, a multitasking phenomenon. What did she have to write down? Aaron eased the camera back. "If you need anything, call me."

"You're on duty."

"I'm still—"

"She said to beat it." Detective King jerked his head. "Get behind the crime-scene tape now. If I have to tell y'all again, I'll arrest you for interfering with a homicide investigation."

Melanie raised her hand, fancy silver pen waving, as if in class. "So it is a murder? Not natural causes? What was the cause of death?"

"Contact the PD PIO."

"Come on, Detective." Melanie tried out that famous red-lipstick ten o'clock–newscast smile. "I asked nicely. Throw us a bone."

"You'll end up in the cell down the hall from this guy if you don't go."

Aaron eased toward the corner of the house. "Call an attorney, Nina. Don't say anything to these vultures without an attorney. Call Rick."

If he was suggesting she call Rick, Aaron was really worried about her.

"Hey, no reason to resort to name calling." King's grin held no humor. "There's a photo of a vulture in the dictionary next to the word *journalist*, I know. I looked it up."

He opened the screen door for Nina. "You're like your mother, aren't you?"

He looked as if she should be able to follow his train of thought. Too little sleep and not enough caffeine made that impossible. Her mother was famous. Nina was not. Her mother . . . wasn't even really her mother. "Like my mother?"

"She's in the news on a regular basis too, isn't she?"

"She's a bestselling novelist, so yes, she's occasionally in the book section of the newspaper."

"Lots of photos of you two, social-scene shots at parties."

Her mother liked company when she went to Junior League events, Library Foundation fund-raisers, and book talks. Nina obliged her because it was the only way to spend time with Grace, who was always in the middle of writing a book, editing a book, marketing a book, or attending writing-related events. "What's your point?"

"No point." He flicked an index finger at a man in a gray suit with a spectacularly hot-pink tie and lighter pink shirt that contrasted nicely with his brown skin. "This is my temporary partner Manny Cavazos. Manny, why don't you take a run at the neighbors, see if anyone heard anything or saw anybody. Surely there's one nosy, old retired lady like they always have in the TV shows."

Manny, who might be a year or two older than King, mumbled something about interviews. Nina caught her name.

"Newbies get all the plum assignments."

King grinned at his partner, who gave a "whatever" shrug and headed for the door.

He ushered her into the living room as if he were the butler and she a guest. "Just speculating." He picked up their conversation as if there'd been no interruption. "Little rich girl likes to be in the news."

White heat burned through her, erasing the earlier chill. Her body went rigid. She'd been accused of many things in her life, but not that. She was neither rich nor a little girl. Nor did she enjoy being in the spotlight. People who knew her could attest to all three facts. "You obviously don't know me."

"I'm about to rectify that, Miss Fischer. Have a seat." He pointed to a paisley print love seat. "I know you have a degree in journalism and creative writing—those two should fit together like hand and glove.

You worked at the newspaper for a couple of years and then bailed to go freelance. You're twenty-seven and you live at home with your parents."

His tone was neutral, polite even, yet she saw something in his expression. He didn't respect her choices. He didn't know her, and he already didn't like her.

"My father died this morning. I need to make arrangements. Call people. I need my cell phone."

"Sit here. Don't move. I'll be back."

"That's what the last detective said. He has yet to make a reappearance."

"Carter went home."

"At the beginning of an investigation?"

King paused in the doorway. "Night CID turns cases over to the day Homicide. Budget cuts. No overtime allowed. Even for big-time, high-profile cases like state district court judges. This isn't *CSI*."

"It's your public safety legacy costs that are eating up the general fund."

An amused look spread across his face. "Little rich girl reads the newspaper."

The assumptions he made about her could fill a wastebasket. "There's no passing of the baton? No ceremonial high five?"

"No baton, but Carter did tell me two things."

"And what were those two things?"

"Number one," he held up one long finger, "there was no sign of forced entry." A second finger immediately followed. "Number two, you were the only other person in the house when your father was murdered."

Fear trailed its icy fingers down her spine, followed by a blast of anger.

He disappeared through the door before she could frame a retort.

3

The disembodied voice at the other end of the phone screamed in Rick Zavala's ear. He threw his bare legs over the side of the king-size bed and rubbed his eyes. His boss might exude an icy calm in the courtroom. He might seem educated, well-mannered, even distinctly classy. But get Peter Coggins angry, like now, and the man spewed venomous obscenities like the lowlife he'd once been before the law degree, the high-society wife, the Mercedes, the diamond-studded Rolex, and the time-share in Cancun.

"Slow down, Peter. You woke me up out of a dead sleep." Rick hazarded a glance at Chuy Lara, who stood inside the bedroom door, his beefy arms resting on his solid chest. He looked cheerful. He just busted up a perfectly good door to get into Rick's condo. "What's going on? I was at the fund-raiser until five a.m." He glanced at the clock again. "I barely got two hours of sleep."

"I don't care if you were meeting with the president of the United States. Next time I call, answer the phone. I shouldn't have to send a guy over to wake you up. Get your butt out of bed and get over to the Fischer house."

Nina.

"What happened? Is Nina okay?"

"You need to be more concerned about her father."

"What happened to the Judge?" It was always a capital *J* in Rick's head. He wouldn't mind being Judge Zavala someday. A Supreme Court Judge if a future senatorial run didn't work out. "Is he hurt?"

"He's dead, you idiot. Nina's your girlfriend. You've got a perfect reason to stick your nose in the cop's business. My sources tell me Matt King caught this case. I don't do criminal, but my friends who do say he's a major pain in the butt."

Rick stood. His stomach lurched. One too many shots of tequila chased by icy cold Modelo Negra. Woozy. The smell of stale beer and cigarette smoke—not his, he never touched tobacco—wafted from his white wife-beater undershirt. Nina was sensitive to smells, especially ones that reminded her of the time before she came to San Antonio. In other words, of her mother.

The heavy metal drummer in his head started his solo. "I have to grab a shower."

"Make it quick. Get there before your girlfriend is transported downtown or you're fired. No more quick trip to the top for you."

"I—"

Peter disconnected.

Rick stumbled toward the closet. He tripped over a pair of seven-hundred-dollar Hugo Boss Italian calfskin oxfords. One was stained with something greasy. He swore.

Chuy chuckled and leaned against the wall. "Need some help?"

"You want to wash my back?"

The big man straightened. "I ain't like that."

"Then make yourself useful and brew us both some coffee. The Keurig is on the counter. Can you handle that?"

"I prefer an espresso, but I can live with that. You got skim milk?"

"No. Live with it. And while you're at it, find a way to close that door and make it stay closed. I have a kick-butt surround-sound stereo system and an outrageously expensive Mac computer setup. I'd like to keep it."

"Yah-yah-yah. Hear me playing the world's smallest violin for you, homie?"

Where did Peter get this guy? Rick raced into the bathroom. He'd have to live with it too. His future was on the line.

Not to mention that of the woman who was his ticket to a certain social group in San Antonio. One he would very much like to be the mother of his future children.

And besides, he loved Nina. He planned to have his cake and eat it too. No one—not Chuy and not Peter and not some dumb, poor photographer—would get in his way.

4

Foster kids learned to get good at waiting. This was no different. Nina tucked her hands under her arms to warm them and concentrated on breathing in and out. Time stretched and snapped. She longed for a fire in the mammoth stone fireplace that filled one wall of the living room. Anything to still the shaking of her hands.

So she had been the only one in the house when Dad died. How could she have not heard the gunshots? Was the darkroom that far away?

It didn't have to be an intruder. It could've been someone Dad knew. Someone he let in. But at three in the morning? And why did the shooter leave the weapon? Why not dispose of it? To make her appear guiltier? Why?

The shaking increased until her body might vibrate from the chair. *Breathe. Breathe. In and out. In and out.* "One, three, eight, two, five, ten. One, three, eight, two, five, ten. One, three, eight, two, five, ten."

Counting aloud out of order helped stave off the panic attack. She concentrated on the numbers. Remembering the order. Not the horror. Not the panic. She couldn't afford a full-blown attack. Not now.

"Breathe in, one, two, three, four. Hold, one, two, three, four. Out, one, two, three, four. Again." Doctor Wallace's kind voice echoed in

her head as it had been doing for the past sixteen years. Her therapist deserved a medal. Or to be reported to whatever board certified her as a psychologist.

Aaron would tell her to pray, but no words came that didn't start with *how could you* and end with *why.*

Geoffrey Fischer had been a believer. He went to church every Sunday. But so did many people for many reasons. It was easier, somehow, for Jan to believe. As a Christian she saw nothing strange about trusting a God everyone called Father. Two different fathers had abandoned them. Fathers left. How could she be sure a God people called Abba Father wouldn't abandon her too?

Gone. Gone. Gone.

Detective King, his raincoat absent, returned, shed a pair of rubber gloves, and stuck them in his pants pocket. He towered over her, his lean body tense, his expression thoughtful.

"Miss Fischer—"

"Nina."

"Nina, I'm sorry for your loss."

Better late than never. Not that she needed empty platitudes from anyone. She'd also learned that adults said they were sorry as if it made a difference in what happened next. It never did.

She needed her camera. She needed that lens between her and King. That buffer. If she could observe him as a subject, she could keep the tears and the disbelief at bay. He had high, sculpted cheekbones and a classical-shaped nose over full lips. His face clamored to be photographed. He had a small scar on his chin and another over his eyebrow. Tiny flaws that kept him from having a pretty-boy look that didn't go with his demeanor. All cop.

His accent said he came from that part of East Texas that really should've been Louisiana, with its gumbo and hunting and backwoods mentality. Her mental camera pictured him outside, on a pontoon in a lake. Or a camouflage deer blind deep in the piney woods. Someplace rustic and earthy with mosquitoes and chiggers.

"Nina? Is that short for something?"

She started. Lack of sleep and the sense that her life had taken a sudden, irrevocable left turn made it hard to keep her mind on the subject at hand. It was preferable to focus on the way the enormous gray clouds scudding outside the bay window behind him filtered weak, patchy sunlight that came and went, casting shadows on his face. "No. My mother was a blues fan. You know, Nina Simone."

"I'm more of a country music fan. Like Miranda Lambert." He smiled. Good teeth. "Or Carrie Underwood. Or Toby Keith, if I'm in the mood for attitude."

Which quite likely was often. She shrugged and waited.

"Let's get started. You're tired. You've been up all night. You've been through something traumatic."

Something traumatic. He didn't say she'd lost a loved one or discovered the body of a loved one. He hadn't decided yet what that something was. Or her role in it. "Yes, I have. Why is your partner temporary?"

"What? Oh, my real partner is out on workers' comp. He got shot."

"Because of you?"

"No, not because of me." His mocking tone didn't match his puppy-dog eyes. "I'm a good detective, maybe even an excellent one, as you're about to find out. So, did you call someone?"

"My mother is out of state at a conference. I called her agent, who's there too. He'll break the news. I thought it was better that it be done by someone in person—"

"Does the agent have a name?"

"Conrad Strobel. Why?"

King was busy writing in his notebook. He glanced up. "How long has he represented your mother?"

"Her entire career. Twenty years at least." Nina got it. Everything now—and everyone—could lead to a motive for murder. "He's a nice man with an excellent reputation. He has a dozen clients whose books are bestsellers."

"But he takes care of booking flights for your mother and holding her hand in times like these?"

"Like I said, he's a nice man. He's taken on more of a role of logistical support in recent years. He attends these conferences anyway to hear pitches from potential clients, so he holds her hand while he's there. Figuratively, of course."

"Of course. Umm-hmm. We'll come back to him later. So your mother wouldn't be the one to—?"

"Hold my hand?" She'd learned to stand on her own two feet a long time ago. "I'm a big girl. My sister is camping with her daughter. I don't want to tell her long distance. I texted my brother, asking him to call me before your colleague took my phone. I don't know if he answered."

His gaze went to her hands still gripped in her lap. Her knuckles were white. She loosened the tension in her fingers. His gaze returned to her face. "No husband or boyfriend?"

The jury was still out on that question. Rick thought he was her boyfriend. She'd texted him before they took her phone. Who knew if he replied? Most likely he turned it off to get his beauty sleep after the party that was to have lasted all night. "I've texted a friend."

"What about your sister's husband? Is he in the picture?"

"Army. He's deployed in Afghanistan."

"And the photographer out there . . . what's his name? McClure?"

"He's a good friend."

"In his head it's more than that."

"That's between him and me." As their friendship had grown over the years, the curious space between friendship and something more had shrunk to a minuscule line. More than once she'd wavered, longing to stick her toe over that imaginary line. She always shrank back, unwilling to risk a friendship that would be lost if the relationship didn't work out. Sometimes she caught him staring at her with this strange expression. She'd ask him what was wrong, and he'd grin and tell her a stupid joke or reel off an inane piece of trivia that made her laugh. "He's special to me."

King's dark eyebrows rose and fell, but nothing changed in his neutral expression. He eased into a matching paisley chair across from the love seat and pushed back the ottoman to make room for his long legs. "Let's take it from the top. What's your relationship to the deceased?"

"The deceased has a name." Nina pried her hands apart and heaved a breath. *Easy. Easy.* "It's Geoffrey Fischer."

"I know." His tone softened. "I really am sorry for your loss. Sometimes it's easier to put some distance—"

"Easier for whom? The man was the only father I've ever known—"

"He's not your actual father, your biological father?"

He jumped on the implication quickly. Detective Matt King was sharp, which explained how he'd made detective. He couldn't be more than thirty. Not much older than herself. He looked older in the eyes, just as she surely did.

"Not my biological father."

"You're adopted?"

"Yes. Geoffrey and Grace Fischer are my biological aunt and uncle." He didn't need to know any more. The route she and her sister had taken to living in this house with Geoffrey and Grace was not germane to his death. She refused to drag it all up for some stranger. "Not that it's any of your business."

"When it comes to homicide, everything is my business." King leaned back in the chair and laid his leg over his knee as if they were chatting about the weather. "Let's talk about what happened."

"I already told Detective Carter. In detail."

"Now tell me."

Her throat closed. Air would not come. No. Not now. Not in front of him. She clenched her jaw and willed herself to breathe. *Think of Grace. She'll be home soon. She'll need help. In and out. In and out.*

Theirs had never been a typical mother-daughter relationship. Her adopted mother lived in a world of fictional characters of her own making. Which was handy in times of crisis—for her mother. Nina closed her eyes and breathed, in and out, in and out, fortifying herself with the oxygen filling her lungs.

"Miss Fischer. Nina?"

"What happened is I found my father in his study." She swallowed bile that burned the back of her throat. Images crowded her. The brown slipper sticking out behind the desk. Peanuts's worried whine. The blood on his pajama top and her hands. "Dead."

"What made you go into the study?"

She explained the cats' strange behavior and the trip to the kitchen to make something to eat at three in the morning. At the mention of her name, Daffy rose, stretched an unbelievable distance, and then proceeded to wind herself around the detective's rain-spattered black dress shoes. Such a traitor.

He leaned over and scooped her up. The cat's purr could be heard in the next county.

"You like cats?"

He shrugged and settled Daffy into the corner of the chair instead of on his lap. "They like me."

King began by asking all the usual questions about family and pets. Only Nina's cobbled-together family was different. He paused and fiddled with his pen when she got to Jan and Brooklyn.

"You have a sister who lives here?"

"Yes, Jan, when she's not deployed. It's Janis, actually." When he didn't react, Nina shook her head. "As in Janis Joplin. Blues queen? From your part of the country?"

His forehead wrinkled. "How'd you know?"

"Your accent."

"There's an alarm system. Why wasn't it on?"

"My dad had a slew of guns in the house. We only turned the alarm system on when we all left the house."

"Not at night, when you're here."

"No."

"Possessions more important than people?"

"Again, he had guns. He didn't think it was necessary. Like most Texans, he intended to defend his own property."

"You're a Texan. Do you know how to use a gun?"

"I'm not a Texan. Not by birth. And no, I don't."

"The alarm system wasn't on."

"No. And it wouldn't have mattered. It's not monitored."

"Why not?"

"Because my dad didn't want to pay for it. He was tight with money."

That was an understatement. Even after he'd started driving a Prius hybrid, he still checked gas prices online and scrambled to line up for cheap gas sales between competing convenience stores. When they made fun of it, he simply noted how much they would appreciate his frugal nature when they received their inheritance.

It didn't seem humorous now.

"Really?" King raised his eyebrows and glanced around the room. "It doesn't appear that way."

"Grace did the decorating. With her own money."

His piercing gaze returned to her face. "You call your mother Grace?"

"It's a long story."

"Where were you?"

His sudden change of subject threw her for a second. No, it wasn't a change of subject. He didn't care about the other stuff. Just her. She was the only one in the house.

"Where was I?"

"Before you heard him call your name."

Beginning to feel a certain irritation at the repetition designed to catch her in a lie, she chewed the inside of her lip, trying to keep both feet on that thin tightrope of emotional balance. "In the kitchen."

"And before that?"

"Working in my darkroom."

"Where is that?"

She sighed and stood. Time to stretch her legs. "On the third floor. It's really the attic, but we call it the third floor."

"For how long?"

She moved to the bay window where huge drops of rain slid down the glass, giving the outside world a blurred, teary-eyed look. "I'd been there most of the day and night."

"Let's just talk about the evening. You never came out of the darkroom for anything? To eat? To go to the bathroom?"

She touched a hand to the glass. It felt solid under her fingers. The rain had cooled it. She leaned her warm forehead against it, enjoying a tiny bit of relief from the feverish sense of disbelief and unreality. "Do you want a blow-by-blow or just the high points?"

"I'm trying to understand how a man could be killed and you not hear or see anything."

"I told you I was in my darkroom working."

"Is it soundproof?"

"No, but it's on the third floor." She let her mind run through the events of the previous evening. "And I like to play music while I work."

"A little classical background music?"

His disdain dripped from the words.

"Classic rock, more likely." She closed her eyes, running through the tunes in her head. Songs from her mother's era, not her own. "Van Halen, Eric Clapton, Bruce Springsteen, Bryan Adams. 'Summer of '69.' I turned the radio down to take a couple of phone calls, but up until that point, the darkroom was rocking."

"Who called you at three in the morning?"

"A lot of people. I'm a night owl. I work at night."

"Be more specific, please."

"Aaron called about a video we're working on for our exhibit. Rick Zavala called."

"Rick Zavala, the attorney? What's your relationship with him?"

Complicated. Unclear. Long-standing. Unsettled. "He's a family friend."

"With whom you have conversations at three in the morning?"

"I've known him since I was nine."

"Did he pull on your pigtails and pass you notes?"

Rick had felt familiar when everything about her big room, nice bed, clean sheets, and huge plates of food had seemed surreal. "No. We didn't attend the same schools. He was around when I needed a friend."

"When was the last time you were in your father's study?"

He was like a dog worrying a bone. Nina silently counted to ten. "It's been a few weeks."

"Are you sure? Can you be more specific?"

"I didn't make an appointment and write in my planner, if that's what you're asking me." Neither would she forget the encounter. Dad's tone had been definitive. He'd thought about her plan and he could not support her "ill-conceived" proposal to devote herself full-time to her own photography/art business. His recommendation, offered in his most lawyerly voice, was to get her real job back.

Like a lawyer delivering final arguments to the jury, he drove home his point. That poets/photographers/artists could not hope to be commercially successful. Not like her mother, the romance author. Nina measured success differently. He couldn't understand that, but he meant well. He was a man driven to be the best, do the best. He wanted his children to have that same drive.

They'd agreed to give it another six months. He would never kick her out of his home. Neither would he give up. "It was about three weeks ago. I remember because we disagreed—"

"You argued?" King pointed his long finger at her. He might as well have said, "Aha."

"We discussed. He wasn't thrilled with my business plan, but we came to a compromise. Compromise wasn't easy for him, but he cared about his children and he wanted us to be successful."

He chose compromise because he believed he would ultimately be proven correct.

"Sounds like a fair man." King rubbed his chin, his gaze fixed on her face. "We'll need some things from you. Like your phone records."

Sorry she'd let him provoke an answer that revealed more than he had a right to know, Nina nodded. "Do what you have to do."

"I will." He popped up from the chair and came to stand next to her. His cologne had a woodsy scent to it. Definitely, he should be photographed outdoors. "We need to do a couple of things. Number one, I'd like to run a GSR test. Then I'd like to take a little field trip."

She stared at the fire bushes, yellow bells, and Pride of Barbados. They danced in the wind and rain, making a riot of bright colors against a dreary backdrop of brown grass strangled by a summer-long drought. She couldn't catch that dance with a still camera, but Aaron might let her use his video camera. If she didn't go to prison. "A GSR test?"

"Gunshot residue test."

"You think I shot my father?"

"I don't know yet, but a GSR test would go a long way in eliminating you as a suspect. I could get a subpoena."

The periwinkle jazz festival T-shirt, now covered with blood that had dried a brown, rusty color, had been among her favorites. Now she wouldn't miss it. "Whatever you need."

He disappeared from the room and reappeared a few minutes later with a crime-scene tech who didn't say a word. Or smile. He simply swabbed her hands, arms, cheeks, and even the shirt. Then he fingerprinted her, gave her a wad of floral-smelling wipes, and went on his way without so much as a thank-you or a *by-your-leave*.

King, propped against the wall, his expression unfathomable, straightened. "Now your apartment. You can change your clothes and I can see the darkroom."

"The darkroom. Why?"

"Because you were the only one in the house when your father died. You have two dogs and neither of them barked, by your own admission. They likely knew the killer. Someone who was in the house, who didn't have to break in to get here. You have his blood on your shirt and hands. I think you can figure out the rest."

"He could've easily let someone in. I wouldn't have heard. What about the gun?"

"It's registered to the judge."

"Fingerprints?"

"Yes."

"Maybe it was an accident."

His lips twisted in a wry smile, King shook his head. "The killer was playing around with a gun in a judge's study and accidentally shot him? Then dropped the gun and fled? Why?"

"I don't know." An answer would certainly be nice, she agreed.

For herself. Who wanted her father dead? And who wanted Nina to take the fall for it? "I really don't."

"Your dad was a judge so he had enemies. Anyone specific come to mind? Did he mention any problems at work recently?"

"No. Nothing specific." He'd spent more and more time in his office recently, rarely sitting down to dinner with them. "He seemed tired and talked about having a lot of work, but that wasn't unusual."

"Did your dad always keep loaded weapons in his office?"

"This is Texas, after all. He had a license to open carry."

"What about you? Do you have any enemies?"

She thumbed through photos in her mind. The more belligerent folks at Haven for Hope. She was careful not to share personal information when she chatted with them in the cafeteria after serving lunch. Many suffered from mental health and addiction issues, among the most common reasons for homelessness. "None that come to mind."

King chuckled, a dry, humorless sound.

"What's so funny?"

"Usually the most obvious answer is the right answer."

"Not this time."

"You're the one with the victim's blood on your shirt."

No good deed went unpunished. "I tried to help him. Why would I kill him?"

"You know the one thing prosecutors don't have to prove in a court of law?"

She should know from all the endless discussions at the supper table when Dad's colleagues were invited. Times when her mother was away. Her mother who said such discussions would give them all indigestion. Nina's mind was in lockdown mode, unable to recall a single word of those conversations. "What?"

"Motive. You know why?"

Of course. Motive. Prosecutors couldn't read minds, and a defendant could never be made to testify if he didn't want to do so. To self-incriminate. "Because sometimes murder is a senseless act done in the heat of the moment. There is no logical, rational reason."

King cocked a finger at her, an approving smile on his face. "You're your father's daughter."

"He sat on the bench in a civil court."

"And he was an attorney. I can get a search warrant, or you can show me the darkroom. Your choice."

"Anything to catch my father's killer. Do I need an attorney?"

"I'm thinking you probably will, but right now we're just talking." Yeah, just talking. "I'm not stupid."

"I have no doubt of that. If you want to call an attorney, go ahead."

"I have nothing to hide. Geoffrey Fischer rescued me and my sister from foster care and gave us . . ." She waved her hand at the spacious, perfectly furnished living room with its original Jesse Treviño artwork, a hutch filled with expensive crystal, perfectly matching paisley furniture, and a rug that cost more than she would make in a year. "All of this. He adopted us. He is—was—our father. I would never hurt him."

King slid his hand in his pocket, pulled out a phone, and held it out. "Call your attorney and tell him to meet us at the station."

She took the phone—her phone. "The station?"

"I'd like you to make a formal statement."

"This isn't a formal statement?"

"This is you and me talking. We need to get into an interview room where we can tape your statement, do a written transcript, and get you to sign off on it."

The only attorney she knew personally was Rick. Her dad had a family lawyer. Beyond that he had to be careful who he had contact with outside the courtroom. He never knew when a lawyer would come before him in a case. He'd recommended Rick to Peter Coggins. They'd gone to law school together, maybe that was it. She always let the shop talk between her dad and Rick go in one ear and out the other. Could his phone call at three in the morning be considered an alibi?

She thumbed in her password and checked her messages. Rick hadn't responded to her texts. Neither had her brother. Four texts from Aaron. All asking if she was okay. Could he do anything to help? Find a way to hit rewind on the last twenty-four hours. She would answer him later. After the noon newscast.

Gritting her teeth, she hit favorites and listened to the ringing. Voice mail again. She glanced at her watch. Almost eight. Partying or sleeping, one or the other. "Rick, call me. Soon. Please."

She inhaled and let the air out one beat at a time. She turned to King and gestured toward the hallway. "This way."

He pounded up the stairs behind her without complaint, unlike Rick who couldn't understand why she embraced two flights of stairs to have her own space. He'd never been in foster care with half a dozen other "paychecks" crowded into small bedrooms filled with bunk beds. He'd never lived in a tent city.

"This house is old?"

"Why?"

"Curiosity. I've never been in one of these King William houses before." He didn't sound the least bit out of breath despite the pace she kept, borne of much practice hauling herself up and down stairs that wound themselves toward the top of the three-story house. "It's . . . big."

"Eight bedrooms, four bathrooms, two studies, a living room, formal dining room, kitchen, breakfast nook, sunporch. The style is colonial revival." It was a relief to talk about something other than the issue at hand. "It was designed by Alfred Giles and built in the 1870s. The Fischer family has always lived in it."

"I guess you'll inherit it."

She hesitated at the top step. Every question led somewhere. "I doubt that. My father had a wife. I also have a sister and a brother." A brother who was the true heir to the Fischer fortune, not an adopted daughter. "To be honest, I don't know. My dad was sixty. He was in his prime. We didn't sit around talking about wills."

"Being in the legal profession, you'd think he would want all the t's crossed and i's dotted."

At the top of the stairs, the detective surveyed her living space with its low-hanging ceiling and jutting walls that ended in knee-high windows. "You live up here?"

"I do."

"If it's such a big house, why do you live in the attic?"

"When I moved back into the house last year, I knew I would need my own space and I wanted a darkroom in that space. This floor is perfect for my work."

"Which is?"

"Photography. Writing. Creating."

"Why a darkroom? Don't most photographers shoot digital now?"

"I don't want a computer or technology between the subject and me. Shooting with film is more personal."

He moved to study the first poster size–framed photo on the long, low living room wall painted an off-white as a backdrop to her pieces. Despite herself, Nina tried to see it through his eyes. It was enough to see it through her own, without the lens of her camera between her subject and herself. Painful enough.

A woman faced the camera wearing a tattered, faded housecoat buttoned wrong. A roll of belly fat peeked through at her waistline. She flashed a bright smile, revealing dirty silver-capped teeth. The sores on her lips and face suggested prolonged meth use. She looked forty but told Nina she was thirty. She held a filthy Chihuahua clutched against her chest with chapped and swollen hands. Her feet bare, she stood in one of Main Plaza's fountains. Nina had caught the water as it spurted up and wet the hem of the woman's housecoat. Behind her rose the majestic spires of San Fernando Cathedral, the second oldest cathedral in the United States.

"Must make for some interesting talk at dinner parties."

"Does it look like I have dinner parties here?"

He glanced around. Again, she saw her apartment through his eyes. Heavy, dark, mismatched furniture she'd found when she first began to explore this space. Most of it had belonged to her grandmother. It might be old, but the Fischer family always bought quality and it lasted forever. She hadn't dusted or vacuumed in a long time. The room had an unlived feel to it.

"Now that you mention it, not really. I take it you shot this."

"Yes."

His opinion didn't really matter, but like any artist she found it difficult not to care what he thought. This particular photo was framed and hung in her living space. Her private life. She didn't need anyone else's opinion. It belonged to her. It was private.

He leaned in and studied the four lines of poetry under the photo, her own calligraphy captured on white cardboard cut into black matting around the photo.

"You wrote that?"

"Yes."

"You don't like to talk about your work?"

"It speaks for itself. And this isn't an art gallery opening and you're not a reporter for the arts section of the newspaper. My father is lying dead on the floor downstairs."

"I'm well aware. Why would a wealthy girl like yourself take photos of homeless people?" He moved on to another photo. This time she'd caught three men around a trash can in which they'd made a fire. They were passing a quart bottle of beer from hand to hand, sharing without complaint. "You feel sorry for them? Did you slap a twenty in that woman's hand to appease your conscience, knowing you'll make much more than that when you sell her picture?"

"I don't plan to sell that particular photo. And I'm not a girl." Nor was she wealthy, but the Fischers didn't discuss finances with strangers. Proceeds from the sale of her other homeless photos went to Haven for Hope. Which was none of his business. "What does this have to do with my father's death?"

"I'm just trying to get some context." He made a show of examining the photo again. "I remember reading that you were involved in a fund-raiser at Haven. Do you spend time there?"

"Yes. I volunteer each week."

"Any of those folks have reason to track you down at home late at night?"

"Just because they don't have homes, doesn't make them more likely to commit murder. They're at Haven because they're trying to improve their situations. In a tourist town like San Antonio, a lot of people live paycheck to paycheck. The hospitality industry doesn't pay much above minimum wage." She tried to keep irritation from her voice. Misconceptions about people experiencing homelessness were common. "When someone like that loses a job, there's no cushion to fall back on. Plus this is a military town. We have a lot of veterans with PTSD. Then there's the people with alcohol and drug—"

"Gotcha. I didn't mean to offend. Cops are well aware of the psychology of homelessness. Believe me."

She took a breath and evened her tone. "Even so, I'm careful with my personal information, as I would be regardless of where I volunteer."

His nose wrinkled, and his body language exuded skepticism. That and some trace of something . . . Like he didn't approve of her. More than that, he didn't approve of her family. He didn't even know them.

He turned to the other wall. Photos of highway construction. Towering cranes flinging mammoth steel beams into place, the sun peeking from behind metal and cement making shadows across asphalt and gravel. Sprawling graffiti offering strange abstract designs across the metal. Urban nature.

One by one, he studied each framed piece. Each poem underneath each photo. "You get paid to do this?"

"Sometimes." Hence the attic apartment in her parents' house. "Not much. But I do it anyway."

"These are . . . unsettling . . ." Frowning, he lifted his hand and let one fingertip touch the corner of the no-frills black frame. "They're dark, somehow."

He got it. Surprised, she nodded. He was among the few who did.

He stood. "Where's the darkroom?"

She led him into the room. With his big ego, his woodsy aftershave, and his oversized feet, he filled up more than his share of space.

No one but Aaron had ever come into this room. The only person she trusted to understand. Because he felt it too. Somehow. For different reasons, maybe, but he got it.

Now a police officer took up air and space in her sanctuary. Because Dad had died.

King studied the photos hanging from the line. "You don't talk much."

"Should I?"

"Some people when they're nervous, they run at the mouth. Makes my job easier."

"I don't have anything to be nervous about."

"You don't seem too broken up about your father either."

"Do you have a meter on which you measure your suspects' grief to help determine culpability?" Try as she might, she couldn't keep the quiver from her voice. She swallowed and breathed deep. The Fischers were all about keeping a stiff upper lip in front of company. "Is there anything else?"

He pulled the door shut, making the space even smaller. For the first time in her life, Nina felt a growing sense of claustrophobia in a darkroom. She swallowed against tears that made the ache in her throat unbearable.

King cocked his head, his gaze pinned on her face. "Hmmm."

"Hmm what?"

"Where's the radio?"

She pointed to the old-fashioned boom box squeezed onto a shelf next to photo paper and containers of chemicals. "I like the radio at night. The chitchat is white noise. During the day I use my playlists on Spotify."

He flipped the On switch. Music blared. Billy Idol's "White Wedding." King shook his head and silenced it again. "How can you work with that noise playing?"

"Regardless, it's obvious why I didn't hear the gunshot."

"Nothing is obvious yet, Miss Fischer."

He'd reverted to using her last name again. Playing games with her? Or simply keeping a professional distance from a suspect?

He smiled for no apparent reason. It made him look like a shark. "You can be sure, I will do whatever I need to do to find your father's killer. You can take that to the bank."

He made it sound more like a threat than a promise. Or both. "Good. That's what I want."

If he didn't, she would. He could take *that* to the proverbial bank.

"Starting with a trip downtown." He opened the darkroom door. "After you."

5

Time for his game face. Aaron eased the camera out from under the Expedition's hatch. He kept his back to Melanie. The woman wasn't a reporter for nothing. She had the instincts of a bloodhound, which made his job as a photographer much easier. He preferred working with a reporter who had more than a TV smile to offer. The downside, however, involved her legendary curiosity and insatiable appetite for information, even if it was personal stuff that was none of her business. Or anyone's business.

He slipped the rain cover from the camera, turned to shake it out, and showered the reporter with raindrops. Squealing like a toddler who didn't want to take a bath, Melanie danced back on heels that added three inches to her five-foot-eight, skinny frame. "Hey, this is a four-hundred-dollar Brooks Brothers suit and it has to be dry-cleaned. You did that on purpose."

She was her grandpa's trust-fund baby. Most reporters couldn't spend that kind of dough on clothes even if they wanted to. Which they did. He turned back to the SUV. "Did not."

"You got it bad, A-Plus."

A-Plus. A nickname that had dogged him ever since the news director had let it slip at a newsroom meeting that Aaron had a perfect grade-point average at UT. For all the good it had done him. Grades didn't mean squat in the world of TV news photography. "Don't call me that and shut up."

"Does Nina know?"

"Know what?"

"You have to follow the story, no matter how it turns out."

"She was a photojournalist. She knows. She would do the same if our roles were reversed."

Melanie studied her notebook as if she could find a Pulitzer Prize–winning story there. "I'm just saying. Even if your girlfriend did it."

"She's not my girlfriend and there's no way she killed anyone."

Melanie took another step back in the wake of his irritation. Lou Briggs and a couple of other reporters clustered near the wrought-iron gate turned their way, their faces curious. "This is what I'm talking about, dude. If you're involved—girlfriend or not—you can't be objective. Let Claire assign me another photog. Sit this one out."

"In your dreams. I'm fine."

"Yeah, I can see that." Melanie's dry tone matched her wry expression. "You're about to self-combust."

He dug his cell phone from his jeans pocket. No response to his texts. If she needed his help—wanted his help—she'd say so. He jerked his tripod from the SUV and leaned it against the bumper.

Nina was alone in there. With cops who would stop at nothing to solve a high-profile homicide and catapult themselves up another step in the chain of command using the width of Nina's shoulders.

He was already involved. He called information. He didn't have Rick Zavala's home phone number. Maybe someone would answer at the law firm offices.

"McClure!"

No need. He disconnected and turned to face Rick, who strode toward them, umbrella in one hand and a tall Starbucks cup in the other. "It's about time you showed up. For an alleged friend, you sure took your time. Where have you been?"

Rick tucked the unopened umbrella under one arm and scrubbed at a five-o'clock shadow allowed to run past midnight. His bloodshot eyes gave him a distinctly hungover look. That wouldn't keep the women from fawning all over him. He was a walking tall, dark, and handsome cliché with high-powered lawyer firm money adding to his charisma or charm or whatever it was called. Slime might be another possibility.

"I turned off my phone to get a couple of hours of shut-eye. I just checked my messages. What do you know?"

"The judge is dead, and they've got Nina in there. She's by herself. Her mother's—"

"Out of town, I know. I talk to Nina too. Every day. Sometimes two or three times a day."

"You don't seem broken up about it. I thought Judge Fischer was your buddy."

An expression Aaron couldn't identify skittered across the other man's face. His shoulders hunched. "Judge Fischer was a good guy. He assisted my mama and me. He didn't deserve this." He wrinkled his perfect nose. "But I'm all about the living. And that means Nina."

Where had Zavala been when Nina needed his help? "You must get in there and represent her."

"You covering the story? That'll go over big-time with Nina."

It didn't make Aaron happy either. At least Nina understood that reporting was more than a job. It carried with it a responsibility to objectively report the news to viewers.

Even when it might be damaging to a loved one.

Zavala wouldn't understand that. "Why aren't you in there helping her?"

"I can't date her and be her attorney, idiot." Rick took a cautious sip from his coffee and smacked his lips as he surveyed the crowded street and empty front yard. He looked like a tourist viewing an attraction he only had half an interest in. "Besides, I'm a civil litigator. She'll need someone with criminal trial experience."

"You think she's a suspect?"

"She was in the house, dufus, and she's family. They always consider family first."

"Name calling isn't necessary." Melanie stepped forward. She squeezed Aaron's shoulder with slim fingers that ended with shiny red fingernails long enough to impale a person. Her touch reminded him he needed this job, and getting arrested for assault while on a story would not sit well with the boss. "Your firm can't do anything for her?"

Zavala planted his feet in a wide stance and leaned toward her feathered, highlighted-blonde-from-a-box hairdo. "Nice scent. As usual."

"You always did like Christian Dior." Smiling, Melanie inclined her head and Zavala planted a kiss on her cheek, old-world style. "Did Nina leave you any messages telling you what's going on? How she's doing?"

"Are you asking for your story or because you're pals with Nina?" Zavala's gaze slid up and down Melanie's figure. It lingered at her well-endowed chest. "You guys never worked together, did you?"

"I saw her at a few stories when she worked at the newspaper. We had lunch." Melanie turned up the wattage on her smile. "Mostly, I'm just curious."

"You know what curiosity did to the cat, right?" Even Zavala, who was accustomed to women crawling all over him, seemed dazed by the power of that orthodontically corrected perfect smile. The way she stepped into his personal space suggested she'd been there before. "We tried cases in front of Judge Fischer. I don't see how we can represent his daughter in a criminal case."

Aaron banged his fist against the Expedition. "Surely there's something you can do, since you're a bigwig attorney and all."

"As a matter of fact, I did. I called one of the partners. He has connections all over town. He'll make some calls. I want to hear her story first."

"Hear her story? Her *story*?" Adrenaline blew through Aaron. Nobody could believe Nina would do something like this. No one who really knew her. "Are you insinuating—?"

"Chill, dude." Rick edged closer. His body language said something completely different. "You may be working with Nina, but she's my girl. I've been taking care of her since she moved into this neighborhood. I'll find her proper representation."

"She's *not* your girl." Of that Aaron was certain. He held on to that fact as Nina's and his relationship developed in an intricate choreography of several steps forward and back over time.

Zavala frowned, his dark eyes burning a hole in Aaron's forehead. "What did she tell you about me?"

Enough to know she considered herself single. Also enough for Aaron to understand that Rick Zavala had been there for her when she was a little kid plopped down in a new house in a new town with relatives who were virtual strangers. Zavala's mom had brought him with her when she cleaned the Fischer house. A scared kid with no friends and no social skills had connected with a kid from the housing projects. She could understand Rick's neighborhood. King William District, she couldn't.

Rick understood her need to stash food in her room in case she needed it later. He understood why she didn't trust a guy who drove a fancy car and lived in a big house. He spoke her language. She was too nice to blow him off now. He'd been a friend when she most needed one. That was worth a lot. Now she needed him even more.

Aaron took a breath. "If you can't be her lawyer, go be her friend. Get in there before they chew her up and spit her out."

Zavala's slow grin made Aaron want to rip his face off. "I know her better than you do. She can hold her own."

Aaron had known Nina since their days in the UT Radio, TV, Film program. She'd been polite but distant for their entire junior year. Gradually, by simply doing the work and not asking anything more of her, he'd been able to move from project partner to friend. To have pizza from the box in her dorm room or splurge on root beer floats after a project had been finished. To see a Fellini retrospective when they needed to get away from the work. By not calling it a date, he'd managed to walk a careful, thin line that allowed him to be a part of her life.

The most beautiful, talented, self-effacing, private woman he'd ever met. Long, straight, blonde hair, pale-blue eyes, peaches-and-cream complexion, not quite too tall for a burly guy like him. Nothing stood out about her looks until she smiled. That smile did him in.

"Just get in there and help her."

Zavala held his coffee cup out in one hand, umbrella in the other, and took a short bow. "You're smarter than I gave you credit for. Step back and watch the master at work."

Aaron grabbed his tripod and jerked the legs apart. "Just don't mess up. She's depending on you."

"Better me than you." Rick threaded his way through the throng of reporters, shaking hands and kissing the cheeks of female reporters who gushed as if they'd just met the next president of the United States. On the porch he exchanged greetings with the uniformed officer now posted at the door, then handed him a card. The officer disappeared into the interior and returned a few minutes later to escort Rick inside.

"He does love himself, doesn't he?" Melanie's gaze was glued to Rick's backside. "But then, what's not to love?"

"Did you two have something going on in the past?"

She grinned. "Nothing worth talking about."

"Seriously. The man is sleazy. And he claims to be Nina's boyfriend."

Melanie shrugged. "You really think a guy like Rick hangs around waiting for her crumbs? He's working every angle. I was his media angle. He used me. I used him."

She tapped her notebook on Aaron's shoulder as if to draw his attention away from the door Zavala could pass through, but he couldn't. "He's always been one of the judge's biggest fans. His law firm loves Judge Fischer. I mean like champagne and chocolates kind of love."

"Every judge has supporters and detractors."

"So why did Fischer run on a hard-as-nails, crime-doesn't-pay-in-my-court platform and then cozy up with the biggest law firm in town known for representing fat-cat clients trying to get around the law in order to make more money?"

"Seriously? You're saying Nina's dad was dirty? He only heard civil cases, dealing with people suing each other over business deals, divorces, land disputes, and liability stuff. How dirty can you get?"

"I'm not saying anybody is dirty. Let's try being investigative journalists for a second instead of lovesick puppies. Let's start with a worst-case scenario. After all, somebody was angry enough to murder the guy. Sometimes those business deals and liability suits involved millions of dollars. People have everything to gain and everything to lose financially. It doesn't make great video, but civil court can make a judge plenty of enemies."

Melanie had a good point. Several good points. Nina would want the person who did this brought to justice. If the police were focused on her, they might never find the person who really killed Geoffrey Fischer. "Maybe we should do some digging. Ask some questions. For the story, you know."

She grinned and patted his shoulder like an animal lover rewarding her dog. "For the story, of course. I'm the reporter. I dig. You stick to photography. Time to get to work, Camera Boy."

He had a college degree same as Melanie did. He wasn't just the guy with a camera on his shoulder. If he had to clear Nina of this crime himself, he would.

And maybe God would see fit to let him have the love of his life as well.

*   *   *

Nina trudged down the stairs. Putting one foot in front of the other seemed to get harder and harder. Detective King and a crime scene investigator met her in the foyer. She handed her clothes to the woman, who slipped them into a large brown sack and wrote on the outside. Her smile barely creased her face as she turned and walked away.

Nina smoothed her crisp white blouse with damp palms. What did a person wear to the police station? Did one consider this a formal occasion? *If Dad were here, he'd say something silly like, "Put your best foot forward, Nina. You're a Fischer. Chin up."*

Nina lifted her chin. "What now?"

"Now, we take a ride—"

"We got company." Manny Cavazos strode into the room. For a second his tall frame blocked her view. Then Rick sauntered past him.

"Rick!" She slid past King and darted across the room. "You're here." She wrapped her arms around his lean waist, leaning into his familiar scent of Polo. A friendly face. It seemed as if it had been years.

Rick's arms slid around her in a quick, hard hug, then fell away. "Are you doing all right?"

"I'm fine." She backed away, suddenly embarrassed at the display of affection. A display of weakness in front of King. "You got my messages?"

"I did. Sorry it took so long. I turned off the phone when I hit the sack." He turned to King and held out his hand. "I'm—"

"Rick Zavala. I know." King made quick work of the pleasantries. He turned to his partner—temporary partner. "Anything good?"

"A few maybes. I—"

"Meet you downtown. We'll compare notes there."

"I—"

"One of the units will give you a ride. You can start working on subpoenas for phone and financial records. Whatever we'll need from his court cases. Can you handle that?"

"I can handle that." Cavazos's face reddened under his dark skin. His glance traveled to Nina and Rick. "Fine. I'll have an interview room ready for Ms. Fischer."

An interview room? Nina opened her mouth, but Cavazos whirled and stomped away, anger in the tense set of his shoulders.

King turned to Rick. "Are you representing Miss Fischer?"

"No—"

"You're not?" Nina took another step back. "I thought—"

"Hang on, hang on." Rick squeezed her bare arm, his fingers warm and strong. In his crisp white shirt and silky gray suit, he was the only man she knew who could pull himself together that well after a night of hard partying and a couple hours of sleep. His dark hair was carefully coiffed with just the right amount of product. The man always made her feel half put together. "We're civil. We don't do criminal. You know that."

"I know." She did know but somehow she'd thought he would help. "But you understand how all this works. You could walk me through it."

He let go of her arm and turned to King. Rick's dimpled face was carefully arranged in what Nina liked to call his shyster mode.

Cocky smile, lifted eyebrows, you-know-you-like-me jasper eyes. "Is she under arrest?"

"She's a person of interest." King cocked his head toward the door. "She needs to come downtown with me to make her statement."

"I've been talking to Detective King since the crack of dawn—"

Rick held up the hand that sported his Harvard law school class ring. "It's part of the drill, honey. It's important to be cooperative. After all, you have nothing to hide, right?"

He did *not* just call her honey in front of King. "I have nothing to hide." She crossed her arms around her middle. "Can you drive me to the station? I mean, that's okay, right? I don't have to ride with him, do I?"

"I don't bite, I promise." King cracked a semi-smile, but his eyes remained hard and watchful. "If Mr. Zavala wants to take you down, that's fine. He's an attorney."

Rick shook his head, his dark eyes cool despite the attempt at a genial smile in return. "Sorry, sweetie. It's best if we aren't seen together before this gets ironed out. I mean, I have to be careful about people drawing the wrong conclusion. They see me. They'll see Coggins, Gonzalez, and Pope. We tried cases in front of your dad. We don't want people to misunderstand. We'll have an attorney meet you at the station. Have you talked to your mother?"

Always worried about image. She bit back a nasty retort and concentrated on the question. "Her agent is arranging for her to borrow one of her New York friends' Lear jet."

"Then I'll pick her up at the airport."

"You'll pick up Grace?"

"You don't want her to take a taxi, do you?"

"Her agent makes all the arrangements. Why would you—?"

"Your mother just lost her husband. Don't you want someone there to meet her and bring her home?"

Of course she did, but knowing Mom's agent, she would be arriving home in a black chauffeured limousine. Conrad went for romantic cliché in a big way. Nina always suspected he had a bit of a crush on his most famous client. "I left Trevor a message. It would be better if it were a family member—"

"I'm almost family, aren't I?" Rick sounded hurt. "Besides Trevor is terrible in a crisis."

Rick had never had much patience for Trevor, who lived in an academic world filled with deep questions of universal importance that kept him awake late at night. Fortunately, Trevor didn't have much use for Rick either, and he was happy to let him take the role of being groomed by Geoffrey Fischer for big things in the world of truth, justice, and the American way. "Trevor does fine if you give him half a—"

"I'll take care of it. Trevor will be a basket case when he hears. He'll be the one needing help and he'll want your mother to provide it."

"She should be landing in a couple of hours. Tell her I'll be home as soon as I can. Tell her I'm sorry."

"You can tell her yourself when you get here." Rick leaned in and planted a kiss on her cheek. She put her arms around his neck and hugged him, wanting to hang on to his familiar scent. He tugged her arms away, smiling. "I've got this under control. I promise. You'll be fine."

His expression turning cool, Rick glanced at King. "You're familiar with what my firm does, right?"

"Ambulance chasers, sure."

"You know that if you step out of line in any way, we'll be all over the department and the city of San Antonio."

"Threats are unnecessary."

"Just making sure we're clear."

"Clear. Let's get this over with." King opened the door. "I'll go first, Miss Fischer. You're welcome to hang close if you've suddenly developed an aversion to the spotlight."

"I have nothing to hide. I've done nothing wrong."

A man with a jacket that read MEDICAL EXAMINER on it shoved through the study door, then turned to hold it open. He waved at King. "Hey, Matt. How's it going? We're ready to move the body."

"No problem, Tito."

King glanced from Nina to Rick, then moved to talk to the ME, his back to them so Nina had to strain to hear the exchange. The only words she caught were *autopsy* and *soon as possible*. Rick stood next to her, looking for all the world as if he were waiting for a taxi. "Don't you want to know what they're talking about?"

"Tito Chavez usually sends his investigators, but this will be a high-profile case. I imagine they're discussing when he'll do the autopsy. Your man King will want to be there. They'll move fast on this one. Lots of pressure from the powers that be to find the perpetrator and close the book on this."

Nina had never met Chavez in person, but she'd heard about him when she worked at the paper. He was well respected in the law enforcement community. King, she'd never heard of before. "He's not my man."

King turned as if he'd heard his name. "Sorry about that." He moved into her space, forcing them both back along the wall as the ME and another man pushed a gurney toward them. "Let these folks do their thing first. We'll follow them out."

They'd covered Dad's body with a white sheet, but his bare feet stuck out the end. Someone should tug the sheet down and cover them. She put her hand out and Rick tugged her back. Her stomach roiled. Acid burned her throat, and she put her hand to her mouth. Purple dots danced in front of her eyes.

This would be Geoffrey Fischer's last trip from the home where he lived as a child, where he courted his wife, and where he brought her home as a newlywed. This home where he raised his children and pursued his career as an attorney and judge. He would never grace these doors again.

Nina corralled tears.

"Stiff upper lip, Nina. Fischers don't cry in front of others. We lick our wounds in private."

Yes, Daddy, I know.

"Sorry about that." King did sound sorry. "Bad timing."

"It's okay. I'm fine." Her voice sounded strained in her own ears.

Rick wrapped an arm around her shoulders and squeezed. "Hang in there, babe."

Babe? He'd never called her names like that before. Why now? Because, like most men, he didn't know how to handle a woman in crisis? She wouldn't succumb to vapors or start wailing like a banshee. He reeked of discomfort but seemed determined. He was trying. She gave him a sterling score on effort. "See you on the flip side."

His smile seemed forced. "Yep. Don't worry about a thing. Gotcha covered."

He held back, while she followed King through the door and out onto the porch behind the gurney. A chorus of voices hurled questions at Dr. Chavez and then at King. And at her.

"Nina Fischer, did you kill your father?"

A ludicrous question. At least the reporter hadn't asked her how she felt about her father's death.

"Dr. Chavez, do you have the time of death?" Melanie's voice rose above the clamor of the other reporters. "What's the cause of death?"

The medical examiner didn't respond. Nina supposed no one really expected him to make a statement to the media. That only happened on TV. He would do an autopsy and report his findings to the appropriate authorities. The next time anyone heard from him or his staff would be in a court of law.

It didn't matter. All cameras swung toward her. Aaron's included. *He's doing his job. He's doing his job. To show the viewers the story. Without video, TV becomes radio.*

She would be a suspect and that made this one juicy story. The viewers would love it. A judge the victim of homicide at the hands of a daughter he rescued from foster care, brought into his own house, and raised as his own out of the goodness of his heart. The story would come out. How Geoffrey Fischer had taken pity on the poor, abandoned daughters of his drug-addicted sister.

No good deed went unpunished. That's what they would say.

6

At least it wasn't the perp walk of shame. Nina kept her head up as she trudged from the interview room ahead of Fred Teeter, her new attorney. After four hours of interrogation, she needed a shower. A long shower to scrub the smell of that room off her and the remnants of their suspicion. And Dad's blood.

It had been forty-eight hours since she'd last slept. At Teeter's insistence, the police were releasing her. The fact that the GSR test had come back negative didn't seem to faze Detective King. He suggested she might have cleaned up before calling 911. A stretch, Mr. Teeter argued, his little goatee bobbing up and down.

No one mentioned that her lawyer smelled like he'd made a stop at El Tropicano bar on his way to HQ. If they knew whose prints were on the gun, they weren't saying. King and Cavazos had taken turns voicing the cliché heard in thousands of movies. *"Don't leave town."*

Where would she go? Into hiding? Mexico? Canada? She was innocent. Innocent people didn't flee. They stood and fought. Her dad had believed in this country's legal system. He dedicated his life to it. She had to believe what he believed. She stumbled into the lobby, head down, focused on making it to Teeter's car before her legs gave out.

"Nina!"

Jan bounded across the lobby, hands in the air, her face stained with tears. Feeling a wave of protective love so fierce her heart

55

clamored against her chest, Nina rushed to meet her. "I'm sorry. I'm so sorry. I didn't want you to find out this way. I wanted to tell you myself." She wrapped her arms around her little sister, who returned the favor. "I'm sorry."

"It's not your fault." Jan's voice was muffled against Nina's blouse. "I can't believe he's dead. I can't believe you found him. You must be in shock."

Nina pulled back. "It's settled in a little. How did you find out? Why aren't you at home with Grace? She must be there by now. And poor Brooklyn, how's she doing? How's Grace taking it? Why didn't she come here with you?"

"Whoa, chill, girl. Let's see, Rick contacted the Girl Scouts office. They sent a staff member out to Camp Mira Sol to tell me. Poor woman. I suspect when she got up this morning she didn't figure her day would include telling a woman her father had been murdered."

Jan swiped at her face with a crumpled tissue. "A detective was waiting at the house when I drove up. He asked me to come in to be interviewed. And Brooklyn is fine. I don't think she really understands, not yet anyway. Mom is . . . Mom. You know how she is. She's already writing another book in her head. I imagine it'll have a widow as a main character."

When she and Jan had moved in with an aunt and uncle they'd never met, since Jan was younger, she'd adapted more quickly. It hadn't taken long for her to start calling Grace "Mom." But Jan wasn't the oldest. She wasn't in charge. She didn't have to find food day after day or a safe place for them to sleep. She didn't have to try to stay awake to make sure someone didn't hurt her little sister night after night.

"Mrs. Shelton, if you'll come with me."

Nina swiveled. She hadn't realized King had followed her out to the lobby or that he had been listening to this exchange. What would he think of Grace? "Are you serious? What do you want with Jan? She wasn't even home at the time."

"We interview all the family members." King swept his hand out in a flourish. "I asked Detective Martinez to bring your sister here so we could knock out the interview quickly and let y'all get home to your mother. It's just a question of thoroughness. We'll wait until tomorrow to talk to your mother, give her a chance to absorb it all."

Of course, thoroughness. Like the endless parade of questions he'd asked her repeatedly, trying to get her to trip herself up. She didn't kill her father, and she had no idea who did. Neither did her sister or her mother. "How considerate of you."

She turned back to Jan. Dressed in shorts, a Carrie Underwood rodeo concert T-shirt, and red cowboy boots, her sister looked much younger than her twenty-six years. Humidity made Jan's short, dark hair a fuzz ball while it turned Nina's long, blonde hair into a limp mess. She wore no makeup, yet her blue eyes were huge. She barely reached Nina's shoulder and she had curves in all the places Nina had always wanted. No one would've guessed they were sisters. Half sisters, really. But sisters in every way that counted. "This is Fred Teeter, my attorney. Do you want him to go with you?"

"I'm sorry, I can't represent you both." Teeter smoothed stumpy fingers over his shiny, bald pate. "I can make some recommendations."

"I don't need representation. I wasn't even in town." Jan jerked her thumb toward King. "I'll be out in two shakes. Do me a favor. Go home and rescue Brook from Rick and Mom's clutches. Mom's feeling clingy. I don't blame her, but it's starting to freak Brook out."

"Rick is still at the house?"

"Yep. He finally got hold of Trevor. He's in Dallas at some sort of philosophy professor conference. He'll get back as soon as he can, but he drove. Mom is already trying to make arrangements and let everyone know. Rick is standing around, trying to look like he's helping."

"Like he'd have a clue."

"Exactly."

"Everyone is falling apart except you two. Interesting." King didn't seem the least bit impatient. In fact, he seemed far too interested in their conversation. "I guess that comes from fending for yourselves from such a young age."

Nina chose not to respond. She'd answered all the questions she could answer for one day. Jan shrugged. "We can take care of ourselves. Where's the interview room?"

"This way." He jerked a thumb toward a door. "We'll get her a ride home, Nina. Don't worry about her."

"I'll get my own ride."

That was Jan. The one person Nina no longer had to worry about. Until Jan boarded a plane and headed back overseas in two weeks. Short and with all the attributes that made men pay attention to her and Dad sorry he hadn't locked her in her room in high school, she had enough vinegar to make her the perfect sergeant to get a platoon of men to slog five miles through mud and rain up a mountain in Afghanistan's treacherous terrain.

And enough gumption to become a military-trained sniper.

Jan jerked her head toward the doors. "I'll be with you in a second, Detective."

Did King know about Jan's prowess with firearms? He seemed to know everything else, right down to the exact date they'd been jerked from the last of a series of progressively worse foster-care homes and flown first class to San Antonio, where her uncle had tucked them into a silver Lexus and taken them to their new home.

By unspoken consent they moved away from King's big ears and eagle eyes. Jan squeezed Nina's hand and leaned close. "Take care of

Brooklyn for me, okay? If Will shows up on Skype, don't mention this to him. He has enough on his mind. I'll tell him when I get back."

"Don't worry about anything. Just get back to the house as soon as you can."

"Aaron's out there."

Nina tugged her hand free. "Working or waiting for me?"

Jan wrinkled her cute, freckled, upturned nose. A nose Nina always wanted. It surely came from Jan's father. They used to lie awake at night and make up stories about their dads, trying to outdo each other with their attributes and their occupations, making the unknown into the super heroic. Batman's brother. Superman's son. It seemed like a very long time ago.

"I got the impression he's waiting for you."

"He should keep his distance. He has a story to shoot."

"Aaron's a professional. He knows where to draw the line. Besides, I have a sneaking suspicion that you're way more important to him than his job. Let him take you home."

Nina glanced up at Mr. Teeter, who waited patiently in his old-fashioned blue-and-white-striped seersucker suit, his expression neutral, as if he couldn't hear any of this conversation. "I have a ride."

"Aaron needs to help."

"It's hard. He needs to do his job, but that doesn't mean it doesn't stink that his video is being used to tell the whole world about our tragedy."

"Just the San Antonio TV market. This isn't New York."

Nina couldn't help it. She rolled her eyes. "Funny."

"Let him help you."

"Why?"

Jan patted her arm. "Because it doesn't cost you anything and the man has waited patiently for you for about a hundred years."

"Don't worry about me. Worry about King."

"I'll make mincemeat out of that guy." Shoulders back, chin up, her military training apparent in every step, her sister marched over to King and craned her neck to stare up at him. "You're too cute to be a cop, you know. I always tell my husband he's too cute to be an MP, but that doesn't stop him from trying to arrest me a couple of times a year."

"I can see why he might be tempted." King held the door for her. "Let's see if we can find a reason to get it done once and for all."

"Be nice to her," Nina called after King.

He let go of the door. "I'd be more worried about watching my own back."

Again, he left her no time for a retort.

Nina blew out air and shoved through the doors into brilliant sunshine. At some point the clouds had cleared. A fierce sun beat down on her head. It felt good after the chilled air of the interview room with its dark windows and signs that read INTERVIEWS MAY BE VIDEOTAPED.

Shielding her eyes with her hand, she picked up her pace, eager to get home to Brooklyn and her mother. Jan might not have patience for Grace's eccentricities, but Nina understood them. She had a few of her own. Grace had a sensitive heart. It made her creative and the kind of mother who sewed costumes for family plays and let them build castles in the living room with boxes and chairs and blankets, and make mud pies in her fancy kitchen. She'd given them a household with a father and a mother who worked together to make a family—the first they'd ever had.

Grace encouraged them to write down their stories and paint pictures of the tent city, the last place they'd seen their real mother—their biological mother. Grace Fischer had been their real mother for the last eighteen years. She'd given Nina her first camera and challenged her to tell stories with her pictures. She'd given her a way to be who she really was.

Jan was more like Geoffrey. Which meant they mixed like oil and water. When she'd gotten pregnant at nineteen, it had been the scandal of the century in Dad's eyes. Like mother like daughter after all he'd done to give her a different life than the one her mother chose. Jan further horrified him by being happy about it, marrying the guy, and joining the Army six months after Brooklyn's birth. Geoffrey never really forgave her. Still, he insisted they live in his house so his grandchild had a stable home life.

Jan agreed because she wanted what was best for her child.

An uneasy truce that had lasted Brooklyn's entire life.

"Nina, over here."

Aaron strode toward her with all the grace—and power—of a Dallas Cowboys linebacker. Her shoulders relaxed. "What are you doing here? You should be working."

"I was supposed to be off today. I took care of business and headed here."

The business of editing video of her father's body being loaded into the ME's van.

"You shouldn't have come."

"I'm here to drive you home."

Nina pointed at Fred, who hovered over her like a six-foot, pale, white angel in last year's three-piece blue seersucker suit. "Meet Fred Teeter. My lawyer."

Aaron shook the man's hand. "Do you need her for anything else right now?"

"No. We'll set up an appointment." He had the tremulous voice of a man past his retirement date. "After Miss Fischer gets some sleep."

"Melanie's been doing some digging." Aaron turned back to her. "Let me take you home. We'll meet her later after you've had a chance to decompress."

"I'm sure she wants to have another angle on her story for the ten o'clock newscast."

"No. She's off duty now. Like me. There's something I need to tell you. Before you hear it someplace else."

"What?"

"Melanie made the rounds at the courthouse this afternoon with another photog. Getting sound bites about your dad's career—you know, a retrospective sidebar to the main story. Word has it your mom filed for a divorce last week."

7

The circus had left town. Nina raised her head from where she'd rested it on the SUV window and stared. Most of the media trucks were gone, headed back to file stories for the five and six o'clock shows. Big news for an average Tuesday. The house appeared no different than it had the day before when no one had expired in a violent manner within its historic walls.

Aaron slowed. The engine of his 4Runner heaved and sputtered. "It looks like Channels 4 and 5 are camped out. They're probably hungry for an interview with your mother. I'll pull around back so you don't have to deal with them."

Nina nodded, laid her head back, and inhaled the familiar scent of Aaron's stuff. He'd driven the same vehicle since their senior year in college when his Datsun pickup truck died, and they held a small, sad ceremony for it at the junkyard where he sold it for parts. She still had photos of that junkyard. This car smelled of french fries, motor oil, and newspaper, just like the old one. For some reason, that fact comforted her.

This had been the longest day ever and it wasn't over yet. Facing Grace would be the worst part of it, next to finding her father dead on the floor of his study. They should take off, keep driving and driving until they reached the ocean. But it wasn't done. Fischers didn't run. They didn't hide. Nina had no intention of being the first.

As the wide drive curved around the house, the backyard came into view. In the growing dusk, her mother knelt in a flower bed next to several flats of purple, pink, and white pansies. Peanuts lay nearby, keeping her company. His head popped up and he rose to his feet, prepared to greet newcomers. Always the friendly cocker spaniel, but not much of a guard dog. Grace didn't glance up at the sound of the car, either engrossed in her task or ignoring it. With Grace, it could be either. She was good at ignoring those things she didn't want to face.

"What's she doing?" Aaron braked to a crawl, then stopped. "It's too wet and muddy to be gardening."

"Nothing keeps Grace from gardening."

Especially when she was upset. Why would she be upset? She wanted out of a thirty-five-year marriage. She'd gotten her way without a messy divorce or division of property. Did they have a prenuptial? Probably not. He'd been fresh out of law school and she'd been a middle school English teacher when they met. She would've had to fight for the earnings from her three dozen or more novels and the three Hallmark movies.

Stop it. Stop it. Nina shoved away the parade of ugly thoughts that had marched through her head since Aaron made his announcement. Her parents loved each other, and they had taken vows. They would never break those vows. Aaron was wrong. He'd made a mistake.

"Nina?"

She glanced at Aaron. His concern flowed over her like a warm hug. Nina shrugged. "It's how she copes. You can drop me off. I'll take it from here."

Aaron put the car in Park. "I'm not leaving you. When will you figure that out? I'm not that guy. I don't leave."

He'd stuck around for seven years. Sure, he'd dated over the years. He used to regale her with tales of first dates and blind dates gone wrong. When had he stopped telling those stories? It had been a while. "I'm fine."

"You're not."

"I'm sure you have work to do."

"I thought we finished that discussion. I'm sorry about this morning."

He'd apologized a dozen times on the drive home. "That's not what I meant. I know it must be hard for you to compartmentalize."

"I would never do anything"—his husky voice dropped another notch—"to . . . hurt you."

Doing his job might demand that he hurt her. The murder of a district court judge was big news in any TV market, but especially in San Antonio where "if it bleeds, it leads" was the number-one rule of journalism. "It's an unusual situation. Let's leave it at that."

They sat without speaking, watching Grace putter with her trowel, the chirping of crickets punctuated by the ticking of the hot engine. Aaron pulled the key from the ignition. "I've always wondered. Why do you call her Grace? She adopted you, too, like Geoffrey did."

"I have a mother. A mother I remember." The old familiar pain lodged between Nina's shoulders and made her neck and chest hurt like a terrible cold. "I didn't know how to be around a mother who acted like a real mother. The word didn't have good connotations for me. So Grace told me it was okay to call her by her name. I liked it. Grace. She was Grace."

"Did you ever in your wildest imagination think she'd leave him?"

"Never."

"My parents were like that. One minute we were a model family getting Yard of the Month Award in our subdivision in Norfolk. The next we were visiting Dad in base housing every other weekend when he wasn't deployed on some ship in the Persian Gulf." His voice held a note of surprise as if he still couldn't believe it after all these years.

"My mother couldn't take being a military wife anymore. That's what she said. He was gone more than he was with us. Their relationship died a long-distance death."

"I can't fathom it, really." Nina put her hand on the door, then let it fall back in her lap. "They never fight. I can't remember a single fight. They were polar opposites, but he doted on her and she loved him. He gave her free rein to write, and he supported her career. She went to his fund-raisers and smiled until her face hurt."

"Maybe they drifted apart because their interests were so different."

Maybe. Maybe they fought behind closed doors and put on a good front the rest of the time. Maybe they acted like Christians devoted to their spouses because that's what they wanted people to see. People often did while living lives that fell far short of the ideal.

Maybe.

She should get out of the vehicle. She should talk to Grace. Nina didn't move. Her muscles were weighted by the sheer exhaustion of the past forty-eight hours.

Aaron's hand crept across the seat toward her. His enormous fingers were long and brown from a summer of stories shot outdoors. He had a scar across the back of his thumb and baby-fine, carrot-colored hair on his knuckles. The knot in her throat grew. She didn't dare look at him or the tears would start and there would be no denying them.

"Nina?"

Her gaze glued to her own fingers, twisted together in her lap, she nodded.

His hand covered hers. "Can you look at me?"

She shook her head, her focus on the strength of his grip and the warmth of his fingers. Her heartbeat did an odd little dance number, a double time that sped up until her heart pounded.

"I want to help."

"I know."

"Do you know why?"

She did know. How could she not? Every female TV reporter in town jockeyed to get close to him at stories, but he never seemed to notice. These days he had eyes for her only. His touch sent a tremor through her body. She swallowed, debating how much she could safely say. Giving voice to such a thought would change their friendship forever. It would set them on a road from which there was no return. She couldn't bear the thought of what would happen if it didn't work out. In her experience it almost never did.

She couldn't bear the thought of losing that daily wake-up call that generally included the weather, Spurs or Missions stats depending on the sports season under way, and his calendar for the day, followed by the third degree regarding her own plans.

She couldn't lose his corny jokes or his astute observation on San Antonio's steady rise on the national political scene. She couldn't lose the way the sun brought out the highlights in his auburn hair when they hiked on the Salado Creek Greenway in search of nature shots to offset the grim pessimism of her other obsessions, or the way he snored when he napped in the rocking chair outside her darkroom, Peanuts at his feet, Daffy on his lap, waiting for her next masterpiece to present itself.

She had lost so much. She couldn't lose him too.

She shook her head.

He sighed and gripped her fingers in a tight squeeze, then let go, leaving a shocking chill behind. "Trust is a choice. Do you believe that God is good?"

"Do we have to do this now?"

"You can trust Him. I promise you."

She snorted. "How can you say that? Let's review. My mother

dragged my sister and me around Miami to cheap motels so she could meet up with strange men. We lived in a car. Then we lived in a tent city where she abandoned us. We got picked up by social services and spent a year living in foster homes."

"And then you came here and things got better."

"And you want me to believe that was God at work?"

"I believe He works for our good in all things. Scripture says so." Aaron scooted around in the seat to face her. "Do you ever examine why you feel such a passion for helping people who are experiencing homelessness?"

The fact that he used that phrase "experiencing homelessness" said he paid attention when she talked about the labels everyone pasted on people who were without homes for myriad reasons. It didn't define them as human beings.

"I've been there. I know how it feels. It doesn't take a rocket scientist to figure that out."

"God allows us to go through the fire because it equips us with the tools we need to help others. With compassion and empathy."

"There's got to be an easier way."

"I wish there were." He used one finger to slip her hair from her face. "I wish you could've been spared that pain and the fear. But I also know you wouldn't be who you are now if you hadn't experienced life on the street. You wouldn't be the person I . . . care about."

Nina leaned into his hand for a second. When Aaron talked about his faith, he made so much sense. He made her want to believe. His words gave her hope that someday all of this would make sense.

She cleared her throat. "I need to talk to Grace."

He withdrew his hand and smiled. "Okay, but do me a favor. Don't shut me out."

"I won't." To her relief, her voice didn't quiver.

"Do you want me to stay?" His voice had returned to its usual husky timbre with that underpinning of East Coast he couldn't shake no matter how many years passed.

"Please." Knowing he was close by would give her the guts to get through this. She shoved open the SUV door. Her mother didn't look up. Nina closed it with a soft click. "Grace? Grace!"

Peanuts hopped up and dashed across the yard to meet her. Grace glanced around, her expression like that of a woman awakening from a long sleep.

"Nina, sweetheart." She stumbled to her feet, the picture of a country mistress of the house in her sunflower-covered dress with a full skirt and a skinny belt around her slim waist. Except for the mud that caked her dress and streaked her face. "I've been waiting for you. I would've come to the police station, but Peter Coggins insisted I stay here. They're inside talking and making some legal arrangements. I'm amazed at how kind people are in situations like this. Rick picked me up from the airport. Mr. Coggins stopped by to say he'd engaged legal representation for you. He said you'd be back in no time and here you are."

Nina bent down and scratched behind Peanuts's ears. The dog's tail wagged a hundred miles an hour. "I'm here—"

"Come. Plant some flowers with me. There's nothing like getting dirt on your hands to ease sorrow and soothe the soul."

Her mother wore gloves. Nina straightened. Peanuts headed to Aaron, who obliged with more ear scratching. "Where did you get the flowers?"

"I sent Abel to the nursery."

The gardener's workdays were Saturday and Wednesday. "Abel's here?"

"I sent for him." Grace pulled a tissue from a huge pocket on the dress's bodice. She dabbed at her cheeks and nose with a dainty touch. "The yard needs some sprucing up. People will come to the reception after the funeral service." Her voice faltered on the last two words.

Nina picked her way through the sprawling yellow bells and red lantana, fading with the fall weather, sidestepping the flats until she reached her mother. "It's okay. You should leave this for Abel. You know how irritated he gets when you mess around in his flower beds."

"I'm a Fischer by marriage only." Grace's voice quivered. "I don't have to keep a stiff upper lip. Or my chin up or whatever nonsense Geoffrey fed you and Jan from the minute you came into the house."

"I know. A cry is also good for the soul."

"That's right—"

"There you are, Nina. Are you okay?" Rick shoved open the back door and bounded down the porch steps. He had her in a tight hug in the middle of the garden before she could move. "I'm sorry I couldn't be there with you."

"I understand." His hug had a proprietary feel to it. His hands wandered down her back into forbidden territory. "It wasn't bad. Detective King kept badgering me about—"

"Rick, we need to go." Coggins, the founder and lead partner in Coggins, Gonzalez, and Pope, stood on the porch looking as if he'd just stepped from *GQ* magazine. His dark-blue suit cost more than six months of Nina's salary at the paper. He glanced at a gold diamond-encrusted watch most certainly of even greater value. "I have a social engagement with my wife. I trust Fred Teeter is on top of your legal needs, Miss Fischer."

"Yes, he was very helpful. I think Detective King might have held me there if it weren't for Mr. Teeter."

"Excellent. Keep us in the loop on your situation."

"That's kind of you."

"Your father and I went back a long ways. He was a good man and a good judge. We always knew we would get a fair shake in his courtroom." Coggins glanced at his watch again. "We really do have to go, Rick. My wife hates being late for these fund-raisers."

"I thought I'd stay here—"

"You're scheduled to be at the Bexar County Republican Party mixer, aren't you?"

Rick's tanned skin darkened. "That's right."

Coggins's gaze skipped to Aaron, who'd slid from the 4Runner and stood, keys jingling in his hand, several feet from Nina and Rick. "Who are you?"

"Aaron McClure."

"You work at one of the TV stations. I've seen you at the courthouse."

"I do."

"You need to clear out."

"It's all right, Mr. Coggins." Grace intervened before Nina could. "Aaron is a friend of Nina's. He's here all the time, mixing chemicals and making photos in that darkroom and eating Pearl's chicken enchiladas in green sauce. I do appreciate your concern, but Aaron is welcome here."

The appearance of tough-businesswoman Grace made Nina's bones melt in relief. To know she was still in there with the southern-belle mistress and the absentminded novelist was a good sign.

Coggins and Rick frowned simultaneously. Nina caught a glimpse of what Rick would look like twenty or thirty years from now. Coggins lifted one manicured hand and smoothed his close-cropped silver hair. Rick did the same in an unconscious imitation of his boss. For some reason, Nina found herself holding her breath. Her mother hadn't suggested that Rick stay. Yet she'd come to Aaron's rescue. Her mother never weighed in on Nina's romantic choices. Not that there had been many.

"Of course." Coggins marched down the steps and over to Grace. He held out his hand and Grace took it like a queen accepting homage from a subject. "I assume you'll be in touch with your family lawyer shortly. If we can assist in any way, we're happy to be of service. We can handle contacting the ME's office to handle the transfer of Geoffrey's body to the funeral home as soon as possible. If the police come around, let them know they can contact Mr. Teeter's firm for criminal legal counsel, should you need it."

"Thank you for stopping by. Your assistance is greatly appreciated." Smiling, Grace picked up her trowel. "Please give your wife my regards. We've met a few times at public library foundation events."

"Of course." Coggins jerked his head toward a blue Mercedes parked next to the garage and tossed a set of keys at Rick. "You drive. I'll have Chuy pick up your car later."

Rick caught the keys and turned to Nina. "Sorry." His hands gripped her shoulders. He planted a long, hard kiss on her mouth. His hands moved to her cheeks and held her still. His lips tasted like cherry lip balm and his breath smelled of coffee and Life Saver mints. Heat curled up her neck and burned its way across her face. She jerked back.

His eyes opened, and he let one finger trail down to her neck above the collar of her blouse. "I mean it. I'll call you later."

He strode after his boss, doing double time to catch up.

Breathless, Nina stared after him, her hands on her scorched cheeks. Rick hadn't kissed her on the lips since they parted ways to go to their separate colleges. Plenty of heated scenes had occurred in the front seat of his old beater in high school, followed by more of the same at the front door under a porch light with a high-powered bulb installed by her dad. But when they'd both returned to San Antonio and their friendship had resumed, she'd intentionally kept him at arm's length so she could examine her feelings for him with a clear mind. Which had brought no resolutions and resulted in heated exchanges of a different kind.

Aaron shifted behind her. She turned. He was headed for his SUV. "Don't go."

He glanced back but kept walking. "I don't want to get in the way."

"Aaron."

He paused, one hand on the door handle.

"Could you stop being a horse's patootie and stick around?" She needed him to stay. She needed him. "Please."

"When you put it so elegantly, I suppose so." His hard gaze followed the Mercedes as it rolled away, its engine making a silky rumble in the quiet evening. "If you're sure."

"Aaron, dear." Grace's voice sounded almost timid. The lady of the manor had disappeared with the Mercedes. "Could you do me a favor?"

"Yes, Mrs. Fischer."

"I've told you a million times, it's Grace."

"Yes, ma'am."

"Could you ask Pearl to fix us some of the Mexican hot chocolate with cinnamon and nutmeg that I like? I know it's early in the season for hot chocolate, but I've had a chill all day."

"Yes, ma'am." Aaron cast a last glance at Nina. She nodded and he tromped into the house, Peanuts on his heels, tail still wagging.

"I'm so sorry you had to find him. It must've been horrible." Her mother's arms lifted in a wide-open gesture that said, "Come in, be hugged, be warmed, be comforted." "I know you've had a terrible shock, just terrible. Rick told me all about it."

Nina couldn't move. Her feet were stuck to the ground. Her mother's arms dropped, but she moved forward, her fair face creased with undiluted sorrow. Her eyes bloodshot and her long, regal nose bright red. "Your father had all his affairs in order—burial plot, his plans for his service—his wishes were explicit. It will be simple. He left nothing to chance because that's the way he was. We'll go to the funeral home and finalize arrangements for when his body is released, but for now, I was just waiting for you to get here. You and Jan. Trevor will be here tomorrow. Then we'll talk, all of us, about what to do next."

"I know what you did."

"What do you mean?"

"I know you filed for divorce."

Grace's hands covered her ashen cheeks. Neither of them moved for a two-count. Her hands dropped. Her shrug had an elegant touch to it. "I asked Pearl to come a day early too. Those police officers made such a mess in the house, tromping in mud on the wood floors, leaving powder everywhere and mussing up the furniture. We need to have the house ready for the reception afterward. She's cleaning and taking care of the food people keep bringing. Why do people bring food when someone dies? Like we suddenly forget how to cook, and we suddenly run out of groceries because there's a death in the family. She'll spend the night for a few nights—"

A death in the family? "Grace, stop. Stop!"

"I filed." Grace dropped onto an ornate wrought-iron bench snuggled between two crepe myrtles. "I would've told you, too, when I returned from Indianapolis. I never had the chance."

Nina collapsed into the space next to her. The bench was wet from the earlier rain, but it didn't matter. "Why now? Why after thirty-five years of marriage?"

"Why? Why does any couple separate?"

"That's not an answer."

"I suppose not." Her expression pensive, Grace plucked at a wet, limp leaf stuck to her skirt. "At first I thought we'd simply grown apart. Your father and I were very different people. From the beginning. But in many ways that is what made our marriage work for so many years. We had our own lives, but we always came back together here at the house. For family dinners, for church, or just him reading the paper and me working on edits in the same room. But all that changed."

"I know he stopped coming out for dinner more and more."

"It wasn't just that." She shivered. "I'm so cold. Why am I so cold? It's eighty degrees out."

"Shock, I guess." Nina took her mother's hand between her own two and began to rub. Grace's fingers were icy. It had to have been more than that. Her parents loved each other. They believed in the sanctity of their vows. They had vowed before God to become one.

"Until death do us part."

A tremor ran through her. Death had parted them in a terrible, violent, irrevocable way. "Why was it more than that? Did something happen?"

Grace's chin quivered, but her voice held steady. Whatever her protestations, she, too, was well trained in the Geoffrey Fischer creed. *Chin up.* "It seems your father had another life he forgot to tell me—us—about."

8

Upstanding citizens of the community did not lead double lives. Nina dropped her mother's cold hand and moved over on the bench. A breeze rustled the tree branches overhead, casting leftover drops of rain on her warm face. Not tears. She would shed no tears. Geoffrey Fischer had been a judge and an officer of the court and a father and a husband. What other life could he possibly have or want? "I don't believe you. Do you have proof?"

"I was searching for a printer cartridge one day. I went into his office to raid his supplies." Grace's smile was bittersweet as if the memory brought her a bit of joy. "He was always so much more organized than me. He always had an extra everything. Cartridges. Pens. Reams of paper—"

"Grace."

"No, it's funny, really. He liked to hide his office supplies from me. It was a running joke." She tugged a tissue from a pocket embroidered with large stitched sunflowers and blew her nose with great gusto, not like the lady she so often pretended to be. "I'm supposed to buy my own supplies and keep the receipts for tax purposes, but I never remember to buy things until I run out, so I'm always stealing his stuff. Especially printer cartridges. We have the same printers. So he would hide them."

"He hid them and one day you went looking for a printer cartridge?"

"Yes. In the closet in his office. I always thought it was cute that we had his-and-hers offices down the hallway from each other. We could pop in and say hello. I could steal his stapler or take his scotch tape—"

"You found some receipts instead?"

"I moved boxes of files and all sorts of junk around. I just knew there had to be a cartridge in there somewhere. And in the back was a box that should've had reams of paper in it."

"But it didn't."

"No."

"What was in it?"

"Credit card receipts, among other things."

"Receipts for what?"

"Plane tickets. Hotels. Las Vegas."

Geoffrey Fischer, the staid judge who ushered at church on Sunday and belonged to the Rotary Club, went to Las Vegas without telling them. There had to be a logical explanation. "People go to Vegas all the time for fun. They enjoy the shows and the restaurants. It's not just a place to gamble."

"So why did he hide it?" Grace snorted, this time in a delicate, ladylike way. "When I thought he was hunting with his buddies, he was in Las Vegas. I found paperwork for a condo. He bought a condo in Las Vegas and never told me."

Everything Nina had ever known about her adopted father took a hike into never-never land. She didn't know any more about him than she did the biological father her mother had never told her about. In some ways it was worse. To think she knew her father, to love a curmudgeon with a penchant for overstatement, only to find he had tricked her into believing something totally untrue. Fathers couldn't be trusted. *Are You surprised I can't trust those who call themselves father, God?*

"Are you saying he was leading a double life? Are you saying there was another woman?"

"I wouldn't call it that. I think he was just having some fun on the side."

"Was there another woman?"

"It wasn't a woman."

"What do you mean?"

"He wasn't cheating on me with another woman. He was gambling."

The idea didn't mesh with any image Nina could conjure of Geoffrey Fischer. He grumbled if one of them left a room without turning off the light. He bought a Prius. He trolled the internet for the cheapest places in San Antonio to buy gas. He bought clothes at the outlet malls in San Marcos. He was tight. Frugal. Downright cheap. Under no circumstances did he waste money. They joked about it. "How do you know?"

"He admitted it."

"Just like that. He said, 'Hey, dear wife, I've been gambling and hiding it from you'?"

"Not exactly. He broke down when I told him I couldn't stay married to a man who kept secrets from me, who lied to me, who was cheating on me. That even God would understand if it was obvious we were unevenly yoked."

"So he told you he had a gambling problem. That's not the same as cheating."

"It is when it becomes more important than anything else in your life. More important that your wife and children. So important you have to hide it."

"Did he say why he hid it from you?"

"He said he was ashamed."

If Geoffrey was gambling, he either won or lost. Most people lost.

How could Grace not know? Hadn't their finances suffered? "Didn't you notice that money was missing?"

Grace's pale-blue eyes filled with tears. "That's what I can't understand. It scares me, because I can't understand it. As far as I could tell no money *was* missing. When I asked him about it, that's when he clammed up and refused to talk anymore. Even when I told him I was filing for a divorce. He wouldn't tell me where the money came from or where it was going. If he won, where was the money? If he lost, why didn't it show up in our accounts?"

Some sort of finance trickery? A second set of books? "You have joint accounts, right?"

Grace stood, took a step, then stopped as if she couldn't remember where she intended to go. "We've always kept the money I make from my books in separate accounts. I have a checking and a savings account in my name only. For tax purposes."

"But you make more than he does—did—don't you?"

"In more recent years, yes. But he never seemed to mind. If he did, he never expressed it. He always supported my writing career."

He never thought she would become rich and famous from it. Most novelists didn't. But Geoffrey had underestimated his wife's talent and how much women across the country loved to escape in a good romance, especially in hard economic and political times. Her sweet romances never failed to make *New York Times* and *USA Today* bestsellers lists. "But there are joint accounts."

"There are and the balances are always good. I pay the household bills from those accounts. I have no idea how it's possible that the amounts of money I saw being spent in those receipts didn't drain our joint accounts."

"So maybe he had his own accounts too. Secret accounts you didn't know about."

"Maybe. I suppose that could come to light now that he's . . .

gone." Grace choked on the word in an effort to stifle a sob. "I have no intention of crying over him. He doesn't deserve it. Yet I can't seem to stop."

"Dad was a good man. You loved him." So did Nina. She contemplated this new scenario. "Did you tell anyone else?"

"Who would I tell that my husband, a district court judge, had a secret gambling fetish and a source of money to supply it?"

No one. Absolutely no one. Geoffrey Fischer had counted on his wife's discretion. Who else knew? His staff at the courthouse? His hunting buddies? People in Las Vegas? Who went with him on these trips?

Had he owed someone money? Had someone owed him money and they killed him for it? Questions crowded her, fanning her exhaustion and a surreal sense of falling into a deep, black hole. The only facts in evidence were that someone confronted her father in the study and killed him.

Aaron shoved through the screen door with his shoulder. He held a tray with two mugs on it. "Pearl says you need to come in and eat some real food. She sounds serious about it."

Nina shook her head. He eased the tray onto a small rattan table with a round glass top between two Shaker rocking chairs on the back porch and retreated. Nina stood and put an arm around her mother. "We'll figure this out."

Her mother's face blanched even whiter. "To be honest, I'm not sure I want to figure it out."

"Don't you want to know who killed Dad?"

"I suppose. It won't matter. He'll still be dead. I still won't be able to change the last words I spoke to him."

"Which were?"

"I don't love you anymore."

"Did you?"

"Of course I did. I was simply hurt and angry. I gave Geoffrey Fischer my heart more than thirty-five years ago. I thought our arrangement worked for us. Until I found out he wasn't who I thought he was. There was no getting it back even if I wanted it."

"Then we'll figure it out."

"Whatever he has done, he doesn't deserve to have his reputation shredded in the media now that he's dead." Tears trickled down her mother's face. Geoffrey might have been a Fischer, but Grace wore her heart on her sleeve. "Not only his name, but our name. Yours, Jan's, Trevor's. If this comes out now, it's all he'll be remembered for and we'll be destroyed."

"His murder may have nothing to do with the gambling." The words sounded naive said aloud. "I'll see what I can find out quietly."

Somehow she had to walk the line between removing herself as number-one suspect in her father's murder and keeping his secret life out of the news. For Grace's sake. For their family's sake.

More of a high-wire act.

Grace sniffed and wiped at her nose with a tissue. "What do I do?"

"You take care of the funeral arrangements and Trevor and Brooklyn." If the secrets were dirty, they had to be kept away from Grace as much as possible. She had opened the door and walked through alone. Now Nina would take her place. "Did you keep the paperwork?"

"I dumped the receipts back in the box and returned it to the spot behind the other boxes."

Nina squeezed her mother in a quick hug. "Drink your hot chocolate. I have to talk to Aaron."

Leaving her mother in a rocking chair, she slipped into the house and found Aaron in the kitchen, sitting on a stool at the mammoth island, Daffy on his lap, a mug of black coffee in one hand. "Is she okay?"

"Let's find out who killed my dad."

He set the coffee aside. "Now you're talking. When do we start?"

"Right now." She touched the ring his coffee cup had made on his napkin. "This is off the record."

Hard lines etched his face. "Your private life has always been off the record."

"I understand what a huge story this is. You get the jump on other stations and you can springboard into a top-ten market."

"Have I ever expressed a desire to go top ten?"

He hadn't, which always surprised her. Aaron was an East Coast guy who'd ended up in Texas because his mother returned to her family when she divorced his father. He was smart and ambitious. He had the best eye for a shot that she'd ever seen in a commercial photographer. He would take LA or Chicago or New York by storm. "You're good at what you do and it's important to you. The story is important."

"Not as important as you are."

"Aaron—"

"Don't sweat it. I know where to draw the line and if it gets fuzzy, I'll tell you. I will be here for you no matter what it means. A job's a job. I can always get another one. I'd flip burgers before I'd give you up. Friends—true friends—are worth way more."

His words rang true. As crushed as she'd been time after time by simply trusting people, Nina couldn't help believing in those blue-gray eyes and that genuine smile that had curled her toes the first time she saw it in a photo-lab class at UT. "How do you feel about removing potential evidence from what's left of a crime scene?"

9

"What are you doing?"

So close yet so far. At the sound of Jan's voice behind her, Nina dropped her hand just short of the study door.

Her sister scowled. "You're not going in there are you? Surely you'll have enough nightmares as it is?"

"We were just—"

"Revisiting the scene of the crime? Seriously?" Her face white with fatigue, Jan smoothed back her dark hair and shut the front door. "I thought you were the smart one, Sis."

"We wanted to search for—"

"I need closure." Improvising, Nina shook her head at Aaron. Jan didn't need to know about her father's secret life. Not today. Not after spending hours being interrogated by Detective King. Not two weeks from deployment. "I wanted to visit his office one more time."

"You're delirious. You need to go to bed." Jan strode down the hall, her cowboy boots clacking on the tile. "Is Mom okay?"

"She's asleep. So is Brooklyn. She was asking for you when I tucked her in. I told her you would check on her when you got home." Nina turned to Aaron. "I'm really tired. Let's talk tomorrow."

Aaron's eyebrows rose and fell. "Sure, sure. I'll call you in the morning."

He called her every morning. With the weather. With the sports stats of the day. With his verse of the day, even though he knew she found it hard to believe. "Just come over. Thanks for everything."

"I didn't do anything."

"Yes, you did and you know it."

He stepped forward and hugged her. A bear hug that should crush bones but, instead, made them melt. He smelled of Irish Spring soap. His five o'clock shadow scratched her cheek. She held on longer than she intended.

Finally, he loosened his grip. "Be safe," he whispered as he stepped back. His gaze enveloped her. "Be careful." He turned and headed toward the door. "Bye, Jan."

The urge to follow him, grab his hand, and make him stay billowed through Nina. Along with the heat of his sure touch. She folded her arms across her chest and bit her lip. "Text me when you get home so I know you got there safe."

"Will do."

Two words, but he made them sound like a promise.

The door closed behind him. Jan sat on the bottom stair step and pulled off her boots. "That King guy is a case. He actually said the words, 'Don't leave town.' He sounded like a bad TV show."

A rerun too. "What did you tell him? Why did it take so long?"

"He wanted our life story. I'm sure he wanted to see if our stories matched."

"You weren't even here."

"Yeah, but I know my way around guns, and he figures a sniper knows how to be stealthy. Waring's a forty-five-minute drive at the most. Each way." She hoisted herself from the steps and padded barefoot down the hall. "I need water. Do you want anything?"

Nina trailed after her. "He really thinks you're a suspect?"

"I suspect he thinks everyone is a suspect." Jan snorted at her play on words. She pulled two bottles of Dasani from the stainless-steel fridge, handed one to Nina, and sat down at the island. "Somehow he knows I didn't get along with Dad. Did you tell him that?"

The hint of accusation in her tone stuck in Nina's craw. "Of course not. We don't air our dirty laundry in public. Ever. Besides, if anything, I got along with him worse."

How had that happened? When they were children, they loved going to the courthouse with him on days when he wasn't presiding over a case. He would take them to Brackenridge Park for a picnic lunch and to feed the ducks. Or to Milam Park to play on the playscape.

Then they became teenagers who had minds of their own.

"Neither of us chose careers he approved of, but I'm the one who got knocked up."

True, but that unfortunate circumstance had resulted in a beautiful, funny, smart, sensitive little girl who charmed the socks off her grandpa every time she skipped into his office and asked for a knock-knock joke. Babies were never mistakes.

Nina popped the lid from her bottle and tossed it on the counter. "He forgave you. He never forgave me for refusing to go to law school."

"At least he thought you were smart enough to become an attorney."

Jan had always been certain Dad liked Nina more. She didn't understand that Dad's favor meant expectations that couldn't be met. He wanted his girls to be successful. He wanted them to be able to stand on their own two feet in a difficult world.

In other words, he didn't want them to be like their mother.

He had high hopes for Nina, but she had no interest in law or even academia. She went to college to please him, but she chose her course of study to please herself. Dad begrudgingly recognized that it was better than having a college dropout for a daughter. "And what about Trevor? His own flesh and blood living in academia. It might as well be la-la land as far as Dad was concerned."

"Trevor did take the love-hate relationship to a whole new level, but he's outgrown it."

Nina's phone's ringtone told her someone not in her contact list was calling. Media had been calling all evening. People who were once colleagues had her number. Now she was a story to them. Ten o'clock news fodder.

Ignoring the ring, she pulled the phone from her back pocket and plugged it into the charger on the kitchen counter. Exhaustion rolled through her. "Trevor never had a chance."

"He wouldn't have lasted a day in the tent city."

Nina rubbed her aching neck. Trevor would've toughened up just as she and Jan had. "Did you know Mom filed for divorce?"

"Yes."

"And you didn't tell me?"

"She begged me not to. She said she would when you finished your exhibit. She wanted me to know before I deployed."

"Will you still go?"

"No choice."

"You could ask for a bereavement leave until Will gets back."

"We both know I'm not bereaved." Jan's tone was flat, her face expressionless.

"You loved him."

"Yesterday, before Brooklyn and I left for camp, he called me into his study."

"No, not *the study*." Nina couldn't stifle the hysterical giggle. "Even as adults we couldn't seem to say 'no, not going.' We could've stood our ground and said, 'You want to berate me, do it here in the kitchen or the living room or the patio, but don't call me into your office like a principal or a boss.' We just went. Pavlov's response."

"Yep. I went like a good little girl." Jan drew circles in the condensation on her water bottle. Her lips curled in a sardonic smile. "I knew what was coming. I should've recorded the last argument and replayed it. Saved both of us our breath."

"He didn't want you to deploy."

"He said what he has been saying for seven years. I'm a bad mother. A terrible wife. An awful daughter."

"He didn't say that, and if he did, he didn't mean it."

"I'd rather play with guns than take care of my baby. Women like me shouldn't have children."

"Regardless of what Dad said, his action showed something different." Nina chose her words carefully. "He didn't want me to give up my job at the newspaper, but it was his idea for me to move back into the house. He didn't want you to enlist in the Army, but it was his idea that you and Will live here so Brooklyn would have that stability while you two make a career out of the military. He groused and he lectured and he shook his head, but he never stopped loving us. Never."

Jan's lips trembled. She took a breath and straightened. Her gaze locked with Nina's. "I really hated his guts."

"No, you didn't."

"No one pushed my buttons like he did." Her voice shook with remembered or renewed anger. "He said he was Brooklyn's saving grace, just like he was for you and me. Without him, she'd have no real family."

"What was he trying to accomplish with this harangue?"

"I plan to reup when my contract ends next year."

"How did he know that?"

"I suppose Mom told him. She's against it too. More because she's afraid for me than she thinks it's wrong. She's known all along I intend to make a career of the Army."

"What about Will?"

"Will was married to the Army when I met him. We're much better apart than we are together. We're both in it for the long haul."

"And Brooklyn?"

"Now you sound like Dad."

"I know you love the Army. You've done two years in Germany, a tour in Iraq, and another one in Afghanistan. You've given a lot in service to your country. It's just hard—"

"Hard to understand how proud I am to serve. How the military gave me a sense of purpose. A sense of belonging. A sense that I'm worthy of something."

"You could die. Every time you go, we wait and worry. That's what Dad was thinking about."

"No, he was thinking about a girl he adopted who didn't know her place in his world. After all he'd done for me, I dumped my kid on him and took off."

"What did you tell King?"

"The truth." Jan's despairing stare dared Nina to interpret those words any way she wanted. "We fought the day he died. He was an overbearing man who wanted to run his adult children's lives. That I sometimes wondered if he adopted us to make himself look good in the eyes of his church and his community."

"Please tell me you didn't say that. It's not true. You butted heads, but he loved you and you loved him. You gave King a totally untrue picture of our dad."

"You've always been a daddy's girl. You wanted him to be your daddy. You've always worn blinders. You've always made excuses for him. You wanted to please him. You never could. I promise you."

"I know he loved us. He pushed so hard because he did love us. He wanted us to be everything we were capable of being."

"You know what he said before I walked out on him yesterday?"

Nina didn't want to know. She fought the urge to put her hands over her ears. Or shove a sock in her little sister's mouth. "Just shut up. Please, shut up."

"He said he didn't know which was worse. You trotting around town with a camera around your neck, pretending to be an artist and writing bad poetry or me running around the world playing soldier, wanting to be one of the boys."

"Stop. Stop." Nina stood and knocked back the stool. It crashed to the floor. "You're just being hateful now."

"I'm just being truthful."

Brooklyn's soft voice called for her mommy. The noise had awakened her.

"I'll put her back to sleep." Jan stalked across the room. At the door she paused and turned back. "I told King I didn't kill Dad, but I wasn't sorry he was dead. We may not air our dirty laundry in public, but Fischers don't lie either."

Geoffrey Fischer had lied and deceived. He'd also saved their lives by plucking them from destitution and adopting them. They owed everything to him. Their health, their education, the roof over their heads. He didn't deserve to die in a pool of his own blood.

"You didn't see him." Nina whispered the words, but Jan was already gone. "I saw him."

10

Not all attorneys were created equal. Rick shook his head and took a long sip of Crown and water. No ice. It had been a long day, starting with the murder of a man who had been a steadying influence in Rick's life for as long as he could remember. Despite his flaws, an outstanding attorney and even better judge.

Fred Teeter had been assigned the duty of representing Nina because he owed Peter a favor, and Peter could use him to find out what the police knew. Or didn't know about the judge's murder. Not because Fred was the best criminal lawyer in town. He had been at one time, but now he was a decrepit has-been who spent more time in a bottle than in court. His firm kept him on because his name still meant something. His reputation had outlasted him. To add insult to injury, he wore those inane seersucker suits with blue-and-white stripes that made him a twin of that old guy who played the TV lawyer Matlock.

His curiosity piqued, Rick set his glass on the bar, picked up his phone, and googled it. Yeah, Andy Griffith.

"Are you planning to join us?"

Peter's voice had all the ice Rick needed. He turned to face the other four men in the law firm's conference room. Peter; Fred; Jerome Solomon, the judge's bailiff; and Chuy. Chuy didn't count, really. He was simply the muscle. If a fat gut could be counted as muscle. Or a mouth. Rick did a double check to make sure he hadn't said those words aloud.

Peter had his back to the others. He was writing on a dry-erase board that ran the length of the wall on the other side of the conference room's ridiculously long cherrywood table. "King and his partner will go after family first. Grace has an alibi, but she has the money to hire an assassin. She found out about his gambling and life of debauchery in Las Vegas and decided to seek revenge."

"Do you think that's true?" Rick couldn't see it. Miss Romance Novel lived for the happy ending. "It's more likely it was Jan. She hated the old man. He demeaned her every chance he could because she embarrassed him by getting knocked up and joining the Army. She's a great shot. A sniper."

Peter wrote Jan's name under the suspect list. "What about your client, Fred? Nina was in the house alone with Geoffrey. She has to be the primary suspect."

Teeter's hand shook as he gently set his empty glass on a coaster. He cleared his throat twice and stood as if preparing to address an imaginary judge. Unfortunately, the illusion dissipated when he passed gas and excused himself. "At first glance, perhaps. But Detective King had to concede several points. That's why she was allowed to leave the station a free woman. She called 911. She administered CPR. She stayed with her father until the police came. No GSR on her clothes. No prior record, no prior experience with guns. No episodes of domestic violence ever reported. Good work record. A volunteer at Haven for Hope. A respected photographer and artist."

Teeter cleared his throat yet again. "Her father allowed her to live free of charge in his house. He paid for her groceries and frequently made her car payments after she quit her job at the newspaper. Why kill the golden goose?"

"Maybe she inherits a load of *dinero* and she's tired of begging the old man to dole it out?" Chuy's contribution to the discussion. Peter's frown made the big, fluffy man step back toward the door where he took up a guard position. "Just sayin'."

"Chuy's point is well taken." Jerome's black leather chair squeaked. The judge's bailiff took a long swig from his bottle of Bud. "Who drew up the judge's will?"

"Not us, obviously." Still staring at the board, Peter added Trevor's name and the name of Grace's agent, Conrad. "Rick, can you find out?"

"Sure, I'll just say, 'Hey, babe, who did your daddy's will?'" Rick snorted. He'd give his left arm for a single line of coke or one hit off a joint. He'd given all that stuff up before law school, but he still jonesed for it some days. Nina could never know. She would never associate with someone who did drugs. "We want to know if you had a motive for murder."

"I suggest you be a little more delicate in your approach." If Peter's eyes were bullets, Rick would be dead now. "Tell them you want to help make the necessary transitions—paperwork, contact the attorneys of record to set up the meeting."

"I know what to do."

"What about Trevor? What's his story?" Teeter offered the new topic in the weird sizzle that followed the exchange. "You put his name on the list. What's his motive?"

"Dad didn't approve of his career choices, made him feel like a sissy for choosing academia. Dad was grooming Rick for greatness instead of him." Peter dropped the marker in its slot and picked up his Dewar's. "But he's such a book head, I can't imagine him killing Geoffrey in cold blood."

"Anybody can do it under the right circumstances."

Rick swiveled. A newcomer stood next to Chuy. Someone Rick had not met before. He was tall, five o'clock shadow, black jacket with a hood. He wore black Nikes and black jeans. Mr. Mysterious Man in Black. Johnny Cash's cousin. "Who are you? This is a private meeting."

"I invited Mr. Miles." Peter motioned for Miles to have a seat. "I don't know what the police are thinking, but we need to be proactive. If there is any chance any of these family members know what Geoffrey was up to, then they know about us. Either they'll take the same route as he did, or they'll choose to be law-abiding citizens. We need to prepare for both eventualities."

"And what does that have to do with Mr. Miles?" Rick hated to ask the obvious question, but he didn't like the smirk on the man's face. Too sure of himself. Too much like the gangbangers from his old neighborhood.

"He's going to do some reconnaissance for us. He'll also serve as our insurance as the situation unfolds. His company provides a myriad of services."

"What kind of services?"

"Let's just say not the kind you can google." Miles grinned and picked up the beer Chuy brought him without asking. "You got a much bigger problem than the cops. Or the family. Now you got reporters snooping around trying to figure out who did it. They all want to break the story first. They'll harass the cops every day trying to have something new for the ten o'clock newscast."

"The cops won't give them info in an ongoing homicide investigation." People liked to bad-mouth the media. Rick found them extremely useful. Politicians needed to know how to finesse them. Lawyers could use them to get information. "They're not stupid. Not much anyway. And if they do tell them something, we'll know what it is."

"Maybe." Miles's gaze swung to Jerome. "Then you got staff members who are scared. Thinking maybe they'll be next. Or thinking maybe this is their chance at a moment in the sun. Fifteen minutes of fame, you know. They'll talk to the media."

Jerome settled his beer in his lap, both big hands around the sweating bottle. "If you think I'm talking, I've got as much on the line here as any of you do."

"What about the court reporter? What about the court coordinator?" Peter rolled up the sleeves of his salmon-colored dress shirt. He loosened the matching tie, the cords in his neck bulging with anger and stress and whatever cocktail of drugs he'd imbibed. "What about his paralegal and his clerk? Do they all have as much on the line as you do?"

"I saw that skinny little reporter from Fox 29 making the rounds this afternoon. She talked to a bunch of folks, but she spent about fifteen minutes making nice with the court coordinator Serena Cochrane." Jerome stood and poured another drink for Peter. "If you have concerns, I can touch base with them, starting with Serena. She worshipped the ground Geoffrey walked on and she was his right hand. If he confided in anyone, it would be her. I'll commiserate. I'll remind her how the media hounded them during her judge's big cases. She was his front line on stuff like that. She'll see it my way."

"That's what you get paid for. To be our eyes and ears. Do the same with the court reporter and the others too." Peter picked up the eraser and eradicated his list with quick, efficient strokes. "Rick, you know that reporter, what's her name, Melanie Martinez, don't you?"

Melanie was on a list of women he'd dated during those brief interludes when he gave up on Nina and swore he would never beg her for crumbs again. As much as he enjoyed the liaison with Melanie, he couldn't scrounge up a single iota of feeling for the reporter. "I know she's fond of crawling through sewers to get stories."

"Find out what Serena told her. Get close to her."

Fat chance of that. Melanie never revisited old flings. Neither did Rick. He did, however, know his way around her house. And he knew her daily routine. "I'll figure out something."

"Be quick about it. We need to stay ahead of this. You have your assignments. We'll meet back here at four tomorrow." Peter glanced at his watch. "Four p.m. today."

Finally. Rick headed for the door. He ducked past Miles, who nodded, his expression inscrutable.

"Mr. Miles, stay a minute. There's a couple of things we need to go over." Peter's tone was equally unfathomable. "Chuy, go bring the car around. I'll meet you there."

Rick glanced back before the door shut. Miles stood next to Peter. Their voices had dropped to near-whisper level. Both were smiling now. Peter looked distinctly pleased.

A chill rolled up Rick's spine. Peter pleased was good, right?

So why did he have a nasty feeling in the pit of his stomach?

11

Most of the hot air in the world came from women and their insistence on arguing. Aaron leaned back in his chair, plunked both feet on Melanie's newsroom desk, and crossed his legs at the ankles. A pile of skinny reporter notebooks teetered, but nothing fell. "You're wrong."

"I'm not wrong." Melanie had written five names on the dry-erase board in her curlicue script that mimicked something a teenage girl would write in her diary. Just short of hearts instead of dots over the *i*'s. "The obvious suspects are Nina, her sister Jan, Grace Fischer, Trevor Fischer, conceivably the agent since you think he's in love with Grace. Those are the first people King and Cavazos will go after. They'll interview them like crazy, talk to the neighbors, talk to all their friends, go through all their financials, their computer records, phone records. Then they'll start to realize they're going nowhere. Then they'll examine the bigger picture. The judge's cases. The enemies he's made."

"King is a smart man. He's intuitive. He'll see right away that none of them are killers. He'll start with the judge's cases and work up a list of folks who left his court unhappy. Those big settlements you talked about. It has to be something related to his job."

"Sure they'll look at it. Eventually. But first they'll leave no stone unturned regarding your sweet girl. She was home alone with Daddy and he was a hard man to live with."

"She's not my girl." Aaron let his feet drop to the floor. Not anyone's girl. She had trust issues, but someday. Someday soon he would find himself on the other side of those barriers. By being the one man she could trust. By showing her she could trust him and God. *Please, God, let me be that man.*

"By the time they get done with Nina, her reputation will be in tatters. She'll be remembered as that woman suspected of killing her adoptive father after he rescued her from a life of abject poverty and abuse.

"So, for the sake of this story, we'll pretend she's not your girl so the boss doesn't pull you from it." Melanie took a straw and stuck it in a twenty-two-ounce Styrofoam cup of Diet Pepsi. For such a young woman, Melanie was wise. "I'll start researching his cases from the last five years." She started a new list. "First thing tomorrow morning, I'll do follow-up rounds to see if anyone bites. They won't want to talk at work, but I may be able to arrange something off-site. Coffee. Lunch. On me. Well, on Fox."

"It's twelve thirty. It's already Wednesday morning."

"When the courts open."

"You'll be up at eight?"

"We'll see, A-Plus." She rumpled his hair. "Don't take it so hard. She'll be okay."

"Don't call me that." He ducked his head. "Leave me the list of names. I'll make the rounds in the morning."

"My sources. They'll talk to me. They see you coming and they'll hide behind their desks. They're camera shy."

"They like me. They know I'm always neat and presentable and respectful and I don't put jurors on TV. They trust me."

"They love me."

Melanie was sure everyone loved her. She was the "Gotta Love Me" of San Antonio TV news. The camera loved her so everyone else must too. She headed toward the door. Her phone jangled a Justin Timberlake tune. She popped it to her ear. "Serena? Yeah, thanks for calling me back. I know it's a tough time for everyone." An excited grin on her face, Melanie gave Aaron a thumbs-up and headed toward the door. "I know. I can't believe it either. I don't think anyone is sleeping tonight."

The sound of her voice dwindled and then dissipated as she slipped through the double doors without telling him what the thumbs-up meant. The woman liked to play her cards close to her vest. They were a team, but she was the quarterback and she never let anyone forget it.

Not a problem. As long as they cleared Nina's name, he didn't mind getting the story too. The girl first, and then the story. With Melanie, it was always the other way around. Until now that had been true for Aaron.

Never had so much been at stake. Personally or professionally. He should go home. He should sleep. He should pray. He should do all three.

Instead, he trudged to an edit bay. He could do what he did best. Edit video for the exhibit he and Nina would share when this was all over. When night ended, he'd go back to his other job—and saving the damsel in distress.

He flipped on the light and chuckled for the first time that day. Nina a damsel in distress?

Very funny, McClure, very funny.

Nina might be an artist and a poet, but she could take care of herself.

One of the many things he loved about her.

*   *   *

A floorboard creaked. A window rattled. Or a door squeaked.

Startled from a light, restless slumber, Nina rolled over. She was falling, falling. She opened her mouth and shrieked. No sound echoed in the night.

Heavy footsteps sounded in the hallway.

Someone was in the house.

It's a dream. It's a nightmare. Just wake up. Wake up.

A veteran at fighting nightmares, Nina forced her sleep-deprived, burning eyes open. Darkness broken only by moonlight that seeped through the half-pulled drapes created strange, skinny shadows on the walls, like bars. Her hands groped in the dark. Floor. The rug in the living room. She'd fallen from the couch. Images grouped and regrouped in a strange kaleidoscope of memories. Dad dead in his office. Blood. Detective King. Divorce. Grace among the flowers. Aaron with his auburn hair and blue-gray eyes and warm touch.

Nina had curled up on a couch and pulled a comforter over her exhausted body after she talked to Aaron. She had to call him. The fight with Jan had been too loud in her ears to sleep, despite having been up forty-eight hours straight. He could come over and they could search for the papers in Dad's office.

"*Wait until morning,*" he said. "*If you still want to do it then, we'll do it. I'll be back. I promise.*"

But sleep first.

As if she'd ever sleep again. *Tick-tock, tick-tock.* The *dong-dong* of the grandfather clock had marked the passing of each hour. Nine o'clock. Ten o'clock. Eleven o'clock. Midnight.

Noise. Footsteps. Her heart revved. Her lungs constricted. The muscles in her legs and arms turned to water. Her pulse pounded in a crazy *rat-a-tat-tat.*

It's just the wind. God, let it be the wind. Can't You see? I can't take any more of this. Just once, give a break, will You?

They lived in an old house. Sometimes it seemed alive. It wiggled and settled like an old lady trying to get comfortable on her bed.

Just a dream. Just a nightmare. Nina forced herself to her knees. She leaned on the couch and hoisted herself to her feet. Her legs wobbled. *Breathe. Count one, two, seven, five. One, two, seven, five.* Her therapist's directions kicked in. Count. She couldn't panic and count out of order at the same time.

Breathe. Breathe. She had to check for herself. Act. She wiped her slick hands on her sweats and felt around on the table next to the couch. No phone.

She didn't want to talk to anybody, especially not people calling to give their condolences but really wanting the rest of the story. Her cell phone was still plugged into the charger in the kitchen where she left it after she talked to Aaron

Go to the kitchen and get the phone.

What if it was nothing? What if it was her overactive imagination fueled by a lifetime of ugly scenes—some she remembered, some tucked away in the part of her psyche that protected her from too much too fast for a little girl to assimilate?

Just look.

She stumbled barefoot to the door that led to the hallway and her dad's office. The tiny lead-glass window in the front door allowed a shaft of light from the front porch security light to shine on the tile in the foyer.

Nothing. She cocked her head and listened. A scrabbling noise. One of the cats probably. "Daffy? Mango?"

The scrabbling noise stopped. It had been coming from Dad's office. An intruder. Or her imagination?

The study door stood open. Not her imagination this time. Nina's stomach roiled. She eased into the hallway. The intruder would hear her fearful breathing. Everyone in King William would hear it. She inhaled and held her breath. One step, two steps, three steps.

A black ball of fur streaked past her toward the door.

She shrieked and clapped her hand to her mouth.

The guns in the gun case.

The key was in the kitchen on the key rack with the extra house and car keys. No time to run for it. Nina didn't care about her own life. It was piddling. But Brooklyn and Jan? Trevor and Grace? The animals? Doubt disappeared. She'd kill for them without blinking.

She could go for the phone. The police would come. What was hidden in Dad's office? What did the intruder want? And what about the box of receipts that would destroy Dad's reputation? She needed to get to it first. The intruder couldn't have it. Nor could the police.

Acid burned the back of her throat. She swallowed and gritted her teeth. *Chin up.* She touched the door with one finger. *Easy. Easy.* She pushed it farther back, a bare eighth of an inch. Another half inch. She eased through the door until both feet were in Dad's office.

A fist came at her, square in the face. Then another.

Pain shooting through her nose and mouth, she lost her balance and fell backward. Her head banged on the tile. More excruciating pain. "Ow, ow, ouch!" Purple dots and white stars danced in her vision. Blood spurted from her nose. Trying to quell the bleeding with one hand, she propped herself up with the other.

A dark figure dressed in black shot down the hall.

"Stop, stop!"

He—or she—paid no heed to Nina's breathless command.

The front door slammed shut. The intruder was gone.

He. No woman hit that hard.

12

The frantic, incoherent call from Nina at four thirty in the morning had aged Aaron ten years. The kitchen light made his head hurt. He rubbed his forehead. "Let me call the police."

"Not yet." Her voice was a whisper. She'd been adamant that she didn't want to wake up her mother or Jan. She always wanted to carry the load. She was wired that way. "We have things to do first."

"You need a doctor."

"Be quiet, please. I'm okay." Seated on a stool at the island, she held a bag of frozen peas wrapped in a dish towel to her nose. Dried blood decorated her swollen upper lip. Her nose was so swollen she sounded like she was getting a cold. A livid purple bruise spread over her right cheekbone. Her eyes were red rimmed. "I'll live, I promise."

Who hit a woman like that? Whoever it was, Aaron couldn't wait to hunt him down and return the favor. He never considered himself a violent man, but one look at Nina's bruised and bloody face had him pounding his fist on the table. He took a long breath, and then another one. "How did he get in?"

"I don't know. It doesn't make sense. The lock on the front door hasn't been jimmied. As they say on the cop shows, there's no sign of forced entry."

"Someone has a key?"

"Everyone who has a key is in bed asleep right now, besides me.

102

And Trevor, I guess, and he wouldn't hit me. He hasn't hit me since we were little and we used to wrestle. He hits like a girl."

She was definitely sleep deprived. "As far as you know."

"What do you mean?"

"There was so much you didn't know. Your dad led a life you didn't know about. Who's to say he didn't give a key to someone? Or they took it? Maybe he got rolled in Vegas and someone took his keys and his wallet."

"And I thought *I* had a wild imagination."

"There's so much we don't know at this point."

"So let's get in there and find out some things."

"Let the police do it."

"If there's evidence of Dad's gambling in there, we can't let the police find it."

He picked up a clean washcloth and dabbed at the blood on her face. "Are you sure you want to conceal evidence from the police?"

Silence. She winced, closed her eyes, and allowed him to clean her face.

The desire to kiss away her pain flowed through him. He cleared his throat. "At least take a quick shower and change your clothes. You don't want your mother to see you like this. And it'll give you time to think about it."

She opened her eyes. Her lips trembled. "How did you get so smart?"

"From hanging around you."

"I want to know what evidence is in that box of receipts. I'll get cleaned up and then we take a quick look. Then we decide what to do next. The crime scene is already messed up. King won't be able to tell."

"I'll make coffee. I can't make any decisions without caffeine."

He already knew what he would do. What he was willing to

do. Whatever it took. First, Nina found her father murdered, then she found out he's living a double life. Now some guy broke in and popped her in the face. How much could a woman take? A beautiful woman who made him crazy and made him want to do all sorts of man-of-steel, knight-in-shining-armor stuff.

Rick Zavala's kissing Nina had been like a sucker punch. Like watching a pit bull maul a kitten. Time to put up or shut up.

A half hour later she was back and looking more determined than ever. She took the large mug of dark roast Costa Rican coffee and offered him a pair of purple latex gloves. Fortified with two cups of black coffee, he took them. "You sure you're up for this?"

"It was my idea, remember?"

The bite in her tone warmed him. She might appear fragile, but she'd always had a steel beam for a backbone.

"Just remember, everything I've told you is off the record. You can't tell anyone."

Counting to ten twice, then once backward, Aaron waited for the sting to subside. "Either you trust me. Or you don't."

"Sorry. When it comes to trust, I'm a work in progress." She ran a hand through her still-damp hair. "Let's just get it over with."

"It's still illegal, whether someone else did it first or not."

"This is my parents' home. My home. I live here. It's not like *I'm* breaking and entering."

"This is a crime scene—twice over."

"You want to tell me about that? I was the one who found him—"

"I know, I know." He held up a gloved hand. "Let's just make it quick, okay? Don't touch anything unless you absolutely have to."

"I got it." She squeezed past him, her lips pressed in a thin line that told him she was trying hard not to show how gut-wrenching this really was for her. "Are you coming?"

He'd never been in the judge's study before. Furniture was askew.

The EMTs had left the remnants of their lifesaving efforts on the carpet. Law books and the pages of *Wall Street Journals* were strewn across the floor, mixed with legal briefs with blue covers. It looked like a fierce wind had raced through, followed by a sudden, still quiet.

"Is it the same as yesterday, or did the intruder mess it up more?"

Her eyes brimming with tears, she shrugged. "It's worse. More stuff moved."

The computer had been knocked over. The laptop was gone. "Did the police remove everything, or was something stolen from his desk?"

"King said he would be back with a warrant for the computers and the files. He said they would show probable cause that the computers might have information on cases he presided over that might get him killed."

"A federal judge who oversees civil cases. Who would have thought it possible? What about the guns? I'm surprised they didn't take those."

"No probable cause if they already have the murder weapon."

"If not, they'll be back for them too."

It had to be the murder weapon. Left just beyond reach of her dying father's hand.

Nina took a few steps toward the middle of the room. Her fair skin was so white it seemed translucent. Her hand fluttered to her mouth.

Aaron stepped between her and the desk. "You don't have to do this. I can find the box and bring it out."

She whirled and strode toward the far wall and an open door. Away from the desk and the spot where she'd found Geoffrey, bled out from being shot twice, and tried to resuscitate him. "Grace said the box of receipts was in the back of the closet."

"What makes you think the police didn't take it?"

"They couldn't take anything they couldn't connect to the crime."

As the daughter of an attorney and judge, Nina knew more than he did about these things. More than she wanted to know, most likely. She tugged open the closet door, flipped a switch, and disappeared inside. "Let's get this over with."

Aaron followed. The walk-in closet was almost as big as his apartment bedroom. It smelled musty, like dust and old papers. A single bare bulb lit the space. Boxes full of files were squeezed into corners. Shelves had been added. They were crammed with books, mostly law tomes, but there were a few legal thrillers by a local author and even some books of poetry. "Your dad is full of surprises."

The words hung out there. How Aaron wished he could take them back. He never managed to say the right thing at the right time.

Nina, who already squatted by a box, both hands on the lid, released a small burble of a chuckle, then guffawed. He didn't dare laugh with her. Did he? "What are you laughing at?"

"You. You have a penchant for stating the obvious." She stood and stepped over another box, squeezed between two more, and wiggled her way to the back of the closet. "You make me laugh. That's one of the many things I love about you."

Love. Many things. Heat coursed through him. He longed to hear more. But this wasn't the time or place. *Breathe.* "So my corny jokes are what keep me in the running?"

"The running for what?" She looked back. Her pale cheeks stained a pink color like roses at odds with the bruises. "Don't answer that. Are you just going to stand there, or are you going to search for the receipts?"

"Right." Sure his head would explode if he kept looking at her, he averted his gaze. *Concentrate on the job at hand, McClure.*

He popped the lid off a box and pawed through the contents. Old tax returns neatly arranged by year. Going back three years. Good boy. "Nothing here."

They worked in silence for several minutes, methodically going box by box.

"Whatcha' doing?"

He jumped three feet. Nina shrieked and slapped her hand to her heart. "Brooklyn! What are you doing up?"

"I'm hungry." The girl, feet bare, dressed in an oversized Dallas Cowboys T-shirt that apparently served as pajamas, frowned. She rubbed her face against Daffy's head, light against the dark. The cat, ensconced like a baby in her thin arms, yawned and burrowed her petite face into the girl's chest. Next to her stood Runner, an oversized brown and white greyhound that never spoke unless spoken to. At least that had been Aaron's experience. "Grandpa told me I couldn't come in here. He said it was off-limits."

She emphasized *off-limits* as if it were a direct quote. No doubt it was.

"I know. He told me that too." Nina slid a box from the top shelf in the back of the closet. The muscles in her upper arms flexed as she eased it on top of another stack and popped off the lid. "I'm looking for some papers I need."

Aaron straightened. Brooklyn was the oldest seven-year-old he'd ever met. Having two parents trade deployments to faraway places a person could barely find on a map would do that to a child. She handled it with an aplomb he admired. Now this. "I'm sorry about your grandpa."

"Me too."

"Where's your mommy?"

Brooklyn ran her free hand along Runner's knobby back. The dog emitted a low sound like a hum. "She's in my bed. She squeezed in next to me in case I was sad during the night. She thinks I'm a baby."

"But you're not."

"Nope."

"It's still early. You still shouldn't be up yet. You should go back to bed."

"I'm hungry. I want breakfast." The expression in Brooklyn's blue eyes, so like Jan's, grew pensive. She rested one hand on Runner's back. The dog was nearly as tall as she was. His head bobbed closer to hers. "Pearl said she would make pancakes for breakfast. Mom said she should heat up the sausage-and-egg casseroles. Why do people give you casseroles when someone dies?"

"So you don't have to cook." Nina sounded as if she'd lost the thread of the conversation. She shuffled through the box's contents, then held up one sheet. Eyebrows lifted, her gaze traveled to Aaron and back to the paper. "And because they feel bad and they want to do something nice for you."

"Nice would be chocolate chip ice cream. I don't like sausage." Brooklyn tugged a rubber band from her hair, letting a wild tangle of blonde curls spring up like a mane around her freckled face. "Can you make pancakes, Aunt Nina?"

"I can make pancakes." Aaron answered when Nina didn't. Her gaze was glued to the contents of the box in front of her. "When your mom gets up, we'll have pancakes with chocolate chips. How about that?"

"Runner can't eat chocolate. It's bad for dogs."

Brooklyn's legion of pets enthralled Aaron. His mom had been allergic to cat dander and to the mess dogs made. He had a gerbil once, but it died. Brooklyn planned to be a veterinarian. She'd told him so on numerous occasions and wasn't above practicing on humans, should they need a bandage for a paper cut or minor surgery, such as removal of a splinter.

"I'll make his without. I saw an apple-cinnamon strudel cake on the counter. We'll have that for dessert." Aaron high-stepped over the boxes blocking his path so he could squeeze in next to Nina and pick up the prize box. "Why don't you go see if your mom is ready for breakfast and take her order. When we get done with all this adult stuff, we'll make breakfast together. Okay?"

"There's ice cream in the freezer. Pearl gave me ice cream for breakfast once when Daddy was in Iraq and Mommy went to Fort Hood for training."

Good for Pearl. "We'll see if we're still hungry after the pancakes."

Brooklyn trotted away, Daffy still reclining in her arms like a doll, all four paws limp, Runner two steps behind.

Wishing he had his camera, Aaron tore his gaze from the small parade and focused on Nina. "Is this it?"

Nina held up the sheet of paper. "Credit card receipt for a room at the MGM Grand Las Vegas."

"Why would he keep all this stuff?" Grunting, Aaron picked up the box, trying not to think about her fresh scent of spearmint and eucalyptus. The soap she used in the darkroom to relieve her stress and cut the chemical odor. "Why didn't he get rid of the evidence?"

"My father was incapable of getting rid of a piece of paper. I imagine he thought he could figure out a way to use the purchase of another home to his advantage on his taxes."

"Only if he could figure out how not to claim his winnings."

"If there were winnings. Do you really have to claim winnings as income?"

Aaron, who'd never been to Las Vegas or gambled in his life, for that matter, had no idea. Melanie would know. She knew everything. "We better get this box up to your apartment."

Nina nodded, but her gaze was fixed on the contents of a smaller Reebok shoebox wedged underneath the bottom shelf. Scrawled across the side in black magic marker were the words MISCELLANEOUS LETTERS. "This might be something."

"Your mom said one box, didn't she?"

"Hmmm." Nina tugged the shoebox from its resting spot and settled it on top of the receipt box. "I'm just curious what letters he would keep. They'd have to be old. Most correspondence occurs via email or text. No one writes snail mail anymore."

She popped the lid off and peered inside. Her face hardened as she lifted a slim stack of envelopes from the box. "I can't believe it. He was such a liar. Such a liar."

"What is it?"

"Letters from my mother."

Pretty romantic for a guy like Geoffrey Fischer. He didn't strike Aaron as the type. Why did writing letters to his wife make him a liar? "When were he and Grace ever apart for more than a week or two?"

Nina held out a yellowed envelope. "Not Grace. My mother. My biological mother."

13

The letters that weren't. Nina ran her fingers over the crumbled, yellowed envelopes that Geoffrey told her, more than once, didn't exist. She didn't recognize the loopy handwriting, but why would she? As far as she knew, her mother had never written to her. According to Dad, her biological mother had never tried to contact him or her two children. Yet there was her name—Liz Fischer—on the return address. Dad always called her Lizzy. Short for Elizabeth. Apparently she preferred Liz. Nina didn't remember that. Why didn't she remember that?

"Are you okay?"

She forced her gaze to Aaron's concerned face. He stood frozen, the box of receipts in his arms.

"It's just . . . one more thing my dad lied about." She shuffled through the envelopes with shaking fingers. Sixteen lies. "He said she never tried to get in touch with us after he brought us here. We would run out to the mailbox on our birthdays and at Christmas, just thinking, hoping, like little girls do . . . but we never found anything. And whenever I asked Dad about it, he said he didn't know where she was. That he hadn't heard from her. He said she ended up in prison and he didn't want us mixed up in that."

"Only he did hear from her."

Nina flipped the last envelope up. "Sixteen times." Her fingers touched something else. Something slick. She glanced down. A photo.

111

She dropped the box on the shelf and tugged the photos from the bottom of the box. Faded color prints. Poor composition. In the first one, her mom sat on a bed somewhere—a cheap apartment or a motel room, probably in Florida—with Jan on her lap, a cigarette in one hand, and Nina standing next to her. Scrawny, hair unkempt, face surly. She might have been six or seven. Before they landed in the tent city, but not long before. Her mom wore a dirty white T-shirt, which bore the words BIKER MOM in purple letters, and blue jeans. She was so thin, her arm around Jan seemed like a child's. Jan grinned for the camera, but Nina looked miffed. She'd never liked getting her picture taken. She preferred to be on the other end of the camera. Even then. She had no recollection of this photo being taken. Or who took it.

"Is that you and your mother?" Aaron leaned closer, his scent of aftershave mixing with the smell of his mint toothpaste. "You were a cute kid. That could be Brooklyn at that age."

Brooklyn looked like her grandma, with her petite nose, her dimples, her blue eyes, and her curly blonde hair. If God was as good as Aaron insisted, she wouldn't inherit anything else. Addiction ran in families, which was why Nina and Jan had made a pact—when they were old enough to understand such things—to never drink.

Nina cleared her throat. "I've never seen a photo of me with my mom."

"You don't have any photos of your mother?"

"Not one."

"You should take the box up to your apartment. You can read the letters in private." Aaron picked his way through the boxes as he talked, his biceps bulging with the weight of the one he carried. "You can have Jan with you."

"I need to read them first . . . without Jan. Just in case, you know, there's something in them . . ."

Something hurtful, like a request that Dad adopt her girls because she had a new life and it didn't have room for them. Like she'd finished drug rehab, met a great guy, married, and started a new family. Or she was dying and wouldn't ever be around again, so go ahead and adopt them. The scenarios rumbled through Nina's head, each one a little more hurtful than the one before.

Aaron paused at the doorway and looked back. "I can work on breakfast in the kitchen while you do it, you know, to give you some privacy."

She imagined the empty apartment with its dusty dinette table, smell of burnt coffee and chemicals, and unread mail. "I'd like for you to be there, if you don't mind. I'll ask Jan to get breakfast started. By now Brooklyn has gone off on one of her quests. She'll take a rain check."

"I don't mind. I'll take this box up and we'll go through it together."

"What's in the box?"

Aaron nearly dropped his burden. Nina did better. She managed to slip past Aaron into the main office where sunrise began to shed light through the huge east windows. She tried to wipe away the night's trauma from her expression. Mango snuggled in his arms, Trevor stood outside the door of the study. Only his head breached the door frame.

She dropped the shoebox into Aaron's box and strode across the room to wrap her brother in a hug. "You're here. At the crack of dawn. I'm so glad to see you."

Mango whined in protest and wiggled from Trevor's grasp. Trevor stepped back as well. "What happened to your face?"

"Collided with the door in the middle of the night."

"I don't believe you."

"Trevor—"

"Don't lie to me. I always know when you're lying."

It was true. Dad used to say Nina would never be able to play

poker. Every emotion, every thought played out on her face. Trevor
removed his wire-rimmed glasses with careful precision. He wiped at
his pale-blue eyes with his shirtsleeve. With even greater precision,
he returned the glasses to his nose, hooking the wires behind his big
ears. "Tell me."

She ran through the events of the previous night, glossing over her
injuries. "It happened in a split second. He was here. He was gone."

"So instead of calling the police, you're cleaning up Dad's office?"

Aaron's snort turned into a cough.

"Something like that." To her chagrin, her voice broke.

"Ah, come on, Nina, don't get all goopy on me."

"You're the goopy one, and dopey too." She never thought of
Trevor as her stepbrother. He was the big brother who accepted two
prickly, street-smart, foul-mouthed kids, who didn't know how to
bathe themselves or brush their teeth, into his life as if he got new
sisters from Florida every day. "I'm sorry you had to hear about this
from Rick. It must've been an awful drive back from Dallas. How are
you doing?"

His nose was as red as his bloodshot eyes. He'd lost weight. Not
having Pearl to cook for him, most likely. He probably lived off micro-
wave dinners and Chacho's tacos.

He looked over her shoulder and fixed Aaron with an accusing stare.
"What are you doing here so early?" He scowled at Nina, who barely
reached his shoulder despite her above-average height. "How could you
let a TV person in our father's study? The place where he . . . ?"

His Adam's apple bobbed under the straggly black hair on his
chin. Trevor always wanted a beard. He thought it would make him
more distinguished when he finally got that professorship he desired
at one of the local universities. His genes wouldn't cooperate. He
couldn't grow a decent beard to save his life.

"Aaron's here as a friend. I asked him to come." Nina tugged her brother away from the door and into the hallway. Aaron followed with the box. "I just wanted to look at some old papers."

"Ouch!" Trevor jerked his hand from hers. He cradled it against his chest. "No need to pull on me."

The knuckles of his left hand were raw and red. "What happened to your hand?"

He glanced down at his fingers as if they belonged to someone else. "I smacked it on something yesterday."

"At a philosophy conference? What were you doing? Arguing with someone about the theory of nothing?"

He let his hand drop. "What papers are you looking through?"

He wouldn't allow her to change subjects. Nina took a breath. Grace hadn't shared her story with Geoffrey's only son. Nina didn't blame her. She could barely breathe thinking about it. Trevor had just lost his father. He didn't need to lose his respect for him as well.

His expression uncomfortable, Aaron edged toward the stairs. "I'll let you two talk—"

The doorbell tinkled a bright, airy song that had always grated on Nina's nerves. Or maybe that was the tension that wrapped itself around adrenaline and coursed through her body. "It's six o'clock in the morning. If it's a reporter, I will call the police."

Trevor's scowl suggested he agreed. "I'll see who it is."

Nina nodded and turned to Aaron. She waited until Trevor made it to the door before she spoke. "Take the box upstairs. Put it somewhere. I'll be up as soon as I can."

"Maybe we should go to the police with all this." Aaron hesitated. "Or not."

"It may have nothing to do with his death." It wasn't her intent to impede a murder investigation. She wanted the murderer found. And she wanted to prove she didn't do it. These papers would only serve to point a finger at Grace instead. Nina simply needed a little time to figure this out. Someone had wanted her dad dead and it might or might not have something to do with his gambling. "Why ruin his reputation if it's irrelevant? I can't do that to Grace. Please, take the box upstairs."

"Okay."

"It's some guy in a suit. I don't recognize him." Trevor peered out the skinny windows that ran down the sides of the mahogany door. "He's holding up a badge. He has a gun on his belt."

"King." Adrenaline shot Nina's heart rate into orbit. The detective was the only one with the guts to show up at this hour. She ran to the door and peeked out. "It's him. Hurry, Aaron. Go. Now!"

14

Nina opened the door a crack. Detective King bulldozed his way past her, forcing her to swing the door wide open. He looked freshly shaved and far too chipper for six o'clock in the morning. He held two extra-large Starbucks cups—which explained the self-satisfied grin on his face—and a manila envelope under one arm. Mango took one look at him and disappeared into the interior of the house.

"It's a little early for house calls, don't you think?"

"I'm a morning person with a full agenda today." His grin faded. His glance went from Nina to Trevor and back. "What happened to your face? And who is this?"

She should simply call a news conference and announce it to the world. At least then she wouldn't have to keep repeating herself.

Ignoring the first question, she introduced her brother.

"Yeah, what happened to your face?" Trevor ignored King's extended hand. "And don't say you walked into a door."

"I'll tell you, but I need more coffee first."

King held out the cup. "Talk."

She repeated her story just as she'd told it to Aaron earlier.

Neither man spoke for two long beats.

"And you didn't call 911?" A low growl emanated from Trevor's throat. He sounded like Runner when Peanuts wanted to play.

"And you didn't call me." King's hand went to the cuffs on his belt. "I should arrest you for obstruction of justice or impeding an investigation. Something."

"There's no law that addresses impeding an investigation. That's a TV bluff, if I ever heard one. Besides, I thought you were a homicide investigator. This was a burglary."

"I'm the lead investigator on Geoffrey Fischer's homicide. Someone rifled through my victim's office and stole a laptop, I need to know." King raised a Starbucks cup to his lips and sipped. "I'm positive you're intelligent enough to discern a connection."

"I do. The guy ran off. He was dressed in black head to foot. I didn't see his face. None of that is different at six in the morning than it was at three in the morning."

"Somebody smashed you in the face and you called no one?"

"I called Aaron."

"Of course. The guy who's just a friend." King's gaze raked over Nina. He moved on to Trevor. "Where were you? Why didn't you hear anything?"

"I didn't get here until this morning. I drove all night."

"Are you left-handed or right-handed?"

"Why?"

King cocked one index finger at Trevor. "You hurt your knuckles. Left hand."

Trevor examined the hand as if he'd never seen it before. "I'm left-handed. But I did that trying to fix my bathroom sink. It was stopped up and I—"

"Yeah. Okay." King brushed past him down the hallway to the study, his black Ropers barely making a sound on the rug. He paused at the open door, swiveled, and stared at Nina. "What would make a woman go back into a room where she'd found her father dead on the floor?"

Nina studied her bare feet, considering the responses. "I was looking for closure."

"That won't happen until the murderer is caught and brought to justice, and probably not even then."

Silence seemed the best response considering the Fischer code of ethics mixed with almost twenty years of regular church and Sunday school attendance that kept her from outright lying to a police officer—or anyone, for that matter.

King shot her a hard look, his lips pressed in a thin line. He jerked his head toward Trevor. "Go wait somewhere. You're on my list of people to talk to today. Along with your mother." King consulted a small notebook tucked in the same hand as the oversize envelope. "And a cook/cleaning lady named Pearl Safire and a gardener named Abel Martinez."

At least he hadn't mentioned Brooklyn.

"Can I get a cup of coffee?" Trevor sounded like a high school kid asking permission to go to the bathroom. "We haven't had breakfast yet."

"Yes. I need to speak with your sister alone."

Trevor hightailed it out of sight before the sentence was finished. Nice of him to have her back. Nina folded her arms over her chest and waited, trying not to look toward the stairs.

Aaron would take care of the box.

And the letters. The letters her father hid from Jan and her. No matter the reason, it had been wrong. So wrong. She wanted her father back so she could ask him why he hid something so important from them. How could he let them go through life thinking their mother didn't care enough to bother to write a simple letter? Or send a card? For eighteen years?

She would never have an answer to that question because someone had taken her father's life before she could ask. That person needed to be held accountable.

She needed to know what Detective King knew. She focused on his perplexed face. He'd obviously been talking and she hadn't been listening, to his irritation.

"You're sure the person who hit you was a guy?"

"Yes."

"How tall?"

"Tall. Taller than me." She stuck her hand above her head. "Like that tall."

"Right-handed or left-handed?"

"I don't . . ." She stopped. "Why do you ask?"

"Your brother's knuckles are raw. Like he hit someone."

"Trevor has never hit anyone in his life. He's a professor of philosophy. He spends his days thinking deep thoughts."

"I'm sure your dad was very proud."

"Not really, but then we all disappointed him."

"Even your sister?"

"Women don't become Army snipers."

"She's really good with guns."

"What's your point?"

"Just thinking out loud." He smacked the study door with his boot. It swung wider. "What were you doing in there?"

"Looking for some paperwork."

The truth. A half-truth, but the truth.

"And you're a person of interest in a murder that occurred in this room." King's dark eyebrows drew up under a creased forehead. If he thought any harder his head would explode. "We have to connect some dots in order to get search warrants on some of these things, so don't be messing with them until we do that. I can't make you leave stuff alone, but I can ask you with great force."

"Or you could ask nicely."

"Not my style."

"I noticed." Better not to antagonize him any more than she already had. "I'm sorry."

Sorry she'd been caught. Sorry her dad had died. Sorry Brooklyn's grandpa was gone. Sorry he hadn't been the man everyone thought he was. "Is there something we didn't cover yesterday?"

"Come in here."

She followed him into the study. Had he been in the closet the previous day? Would he realize a box was missing?

She turned her back on the closet door and focused her gaze on the bare desk. She felt like a child in a game of hide-and-seek. *Don't look. Don't look. Don't look.*

King dropped the envelope on the desk and strode around it to the gun cabinet. Remnants of a light-gray powder clouded numerous places on the glass doors that covered at least sixteen racks. At least ten of those racks had been full as long as she could remember. Her dad liked his hunting rifles and handguns as much as the next eighth-generation Texan.

"Do you remember how many weapons Judge Fischer kept in this case?"

"Ten maybe, I guess, more or less."

"You don't know for sure?"

"I'm not a gun person. I didn't pay any attention. In fact, I try not to pay attention."

"You don't like guns?"

Surely as a homicide detective, he could imagine why a person might not care for guns. "Do you?"

"When it's on my hip or in my hands? Yes. Otherwise, not so much." He took another long sip of coffee and set the cup on the corner of the desk. "You don't have much of a social-media presence."

"I don't have the time or the inclination. Is that a crime?" Facebook, Twitter, Instagram, and on and on. They sucked time out of the day in a way Nina couldn't afford. She had opened accounts and then forgotten to visit them for days and weeks. "People are desperate to connect so they put all their private stuff online for strangers to read."

"But not you."

"I can see how it might be useful for families who are spread out around the country to stay in touch by posting photos and updates. Jan posts photos so her husband can see Brooklyn growing while he's gone. And vice versa. But even they have to be careful because terrorists have threatened to target military families."

"You have a mother somewhere."

"Maybe." Did he know something she didn't? "I just can't see myself putting a photo on Facebook and begging people to share it until poor little me finds my mommy."

"You're pretty cynical for someone so young."

"Not much younger than you."

"Even your mother is on Facebook. In fact, she's all over social media: Twitter, Instagram, Pinterest, you name it. She's the Tweet-Tweet queen."

"That's marketing for her books. It's her demographic. Women who read romances. She has a virtual assistant who takes care of a lot of that for her."

"What about your adoptive brother? He's all over social media. Is that marketing?"

Trevor had underdeveloped social skills. Connecting online might be easier for him. "Brother. I don't think of him as an adoptive brother."

"Sometimes Facebook helps us catch people in lies."

"I suppose it does. According to the news, some people videotape themselves committing crimes or admit to it. I always assumed those people weren't very bright."

"Your brother said he was at a conference in Dallas."

"He's a professor. He goes to a lot of workshops and conferences. He's trying to get published and get tenure."

"He wasn't in Dallas."

"Okay." Why would Trevor lie? Because he was an idiot. Because he was afraid of something. Trevor was always afraid. "So what?"

"He was tagged in a photo in a bar here in town. His girlfriend posted it."

"He doesn't have a girlfriend."

"That's not what the girlfriend says. She says they live together. Have for six months. She's a tattoo artist. She has a beauty that runs from midcalf all the way to the top of her thigh. Nice work. She also has a rose on her collarbone that she had done in San Diego when she was in the Navy."

"That's not possible." Of course it was. Trevor wouldn't want Dad to know he was living with a woman. Especially a tattoo artist. He'd never had a girlfriend in his life. That she knew of. "What does this have to do with anything?"

"He lied. He wasn't in Dallas. He was in San Antonio. He could have come over here and killed Judge Fischer. Your dad would've let him in. Or he had a key. The dogs know him. He could skip out scot-free."

Her dad wouldn't have to let him in. Trevor had a key. "I thought you thought I did it?"

"Until I saw the scrapes on his knuckles. It looks like he hit somebody."

His point hit home like the shot from a high-powered rifle. "He would never hurt Dad and certainly wouldn't hurt me. Why would he?"

"Why lie about where he was? Why not come home immediately?"

"My dad would never approve of a tattoo artist. He already disapproved of Trevor's career choice."

"He aspired to be a tenured professor and your dad didn't approve. I thought my parents set high standards."

"A professor of philosophy. My dad wanted him to be a lawyer." Nina studied the detective's face. He hadn't lived up to his parents' standards either. "What did your parents want you to be?"

"My dad was hoping for doctor. My mom wanted anything but a police officer. Something safe and close to home. She wants grandkids she can see every day."

"You don't have brothers and sisters who can fill that order?"

"I do. Five of them." His tone said that subject had closed as quickly as it opened. He picked up the envelope and opened it. Nina shivered despite herself. She didn't need to see photos of the crime scene. She remembered every aspect of it in vivid detail. "Come here, take a look."

Reluctantly, she started around the desk. The sight of the dark, almost-black bloodstains on the carpet stopped her in her tracks. King followed her gaze. He shoved the photos to the front of the desk. "Sorry. I'm not usually this insensitive." He stepped back to the other side of the desk. "At least I try not to be."

"It's fine. Really." She tore her gaze from the stains and followed. "I want to help."

"Check out the rack from here. Are any guns missing?"

She studied the gun case. Hunting rifles, handguns, they mostly seemed the same to her. Silently she counted. Eight weapons. More than any one person could ever need. They hadn't done her dad an iota of good two nights ago. "I don't know. I thought there were ten, but I could be wrong. I didn't pay that much attention. Why? What does it matter?"

"Look closely. It matters."

She followed his terse command. "I thought there were ten." She pointed to the second row. "I think that empty spot had a little gun in it."

"Like a handgun."

"I suppose. What is this about?"

"Would there be an inventory, a record of the guns your father purchased over the years?"

"I suppose so. My dad never threw anything away. He kept lists of everything."

"Would your mother or your brother know?"

"I doubt it. Grace has as much interest in guns as I do. Trevor is a pacifist and a vegan, so you can imagine what his thoughts are on Dad's collection. Jan did some shooting with Dad. You should ask her. She's the gun expert."

"I'd rather not."

The significance of King's statement sank in. "Jan's fingerprints are on the gun?"

"No."

"Then why not ask her? You've got the murder weapon and she obviously didn't fire it."

"Turns out we don't."

"It was right there. I saw it. On the floor."

"That's called jumping to conclusions or making assumptions based on faulty observations."

Nina backtracked, trying to understand. She'd seen the gun. A gun. "The gun wasn't the murder weapon? Where is it?"

"You tell me." His smile had a cold edge to it now. "The weapon recovered on the floor only had one person's fingerprints on it. Geoffrey Fischer's. It hadn't been fired."

"He was trying to defend himself?"

"Possibly. Maybe he intended to shoot someone and that person defended himself." His grin broadened. "Or herself."

"Are you suggesting I shot my father because he was trying to kill me?" She held up her hands. "You said yourself I didn't have GSR on my hand or face."

"Maybe you did a good job of washing up before the EMTs got to the house."

"I still had blood under my fingernails."

"You missed a spot."

"What about my clothes?"

"Too much blood. Maybe the whole thing was a setup. You muddied the crime scene while your sister, the gun expert, slipped away with the murder weapon she fired."

"That's ridiculous. Neither one of us would hurt my father and he would never hurt us."

"There has to be a gun missing and you were the only one in the house when EMTs and police arrived. There was time for your sister to get out and dispose of the murder weapon."

"She was camping in Waring, almost an hour away."

"We'll need to talk to her daughter."

"No."

"That's not up to you." He shook one long index finger at her. "Let's try this scenario. You grabbed a gun from this case, shot your father, and then disposed of it."

"Before the EMTs arrived? Before I performed CPR? Before I called for help? While I was doing all that hand washing you think I did?"

He pulled opened the envelope and handed her the contents. A search warrant for the guns. "The crime scene folks are on their way to pick up the guns. I'll have them revisit the scene to see if our intruder left any prints."

"Fine. None of those guns have been fired recently." She studied the gun. "What about DNA? Will you test for that?"

"If there is any. But it's not like *CSI*. It'll take six weeks, maybe longer to get those results." Scowling, he chewed his lower lip. "I'd like to search the rest of the house and the garage."

"Add that to the search warrant if you think you have probable cause."

"Or you could give your consent to search the house."

"This isn't my house. You'll have to ask my mother."

Who'd been married to a judge far too long to do such a thing. She would make King jump through the legal hoops.

"A judge's wife? I have to go to the . . ."

"What? You have to do what?"

"The autopsy is scheduled this morning. I sent the newbie, but I need to go make sure he doesn't hurl on the . . . sorry." His grin disappeared. He ducked his head and stared at his shiny black Ropers. "I'm not really as insensitive as I come off sometimes. It's how we deal. Morgue humor."

"Actually, I understand. That's how journalists deal with it. Crispy Critters. DOTR, DRT, floaters."

"Burn victims. Dead On The Road. Dead Right There. Drowning victims. Morgue humor." His tone commiserated. "I'm sure you, as a photographer, use the camera to separate you from the images you're shooting. You didn't have that luxury the night of the murder."

He didn't want her imagining her dad's body in the morgue. One point for the detective's humanity. "Once that's done, will they release his body so we can bury him?"

"As early as tomorrow. Once the autopsy is done, there's no reason to hold the body."

"I imagine you're getting a lot of pressure to put this one to bed quickly."

"Sure, but I want to do that every time, every case—not just one involving a well-known judge and pillar of the community."

"Either way, I appreciate it."

"You won't by the time I'm done. I'll ask for an officer to be posted outside so there's no more funny business. We'll also be subpoenaing all the judge's bank, computer, and phone records." He picked up the coffee cup and sipped. "Sure you don't want to save me the hassle and tell me what you or your sister did with the murder weapon?"

Those records would most likely reveal her father's trips to Las Vegas and the habit he'd tried so hard to conceal. "Do what you have to do."

"Tell your brother I'll circle back with him later today. As well as your mother and Brooklyn."

"My mother was out of town when my father died. Brooklyn's seven years old. She was most likely asleep in a tent at a Girl Scout camp."

"Your mother can afford to hire someone, and it was storming that night. Little girls don't sleep through storms.

"And their mothers don't abandon them in a tent in the middle of a storm."

Of course they did. Liz Fischer had abandoned her two daughters in a tent city.

"I promise I won't traumatize her. Mrs. Shelton will be permitted to stay with her throughout the interview." King tapped the envelope on the desk, his gaze never leaving her face. "I hear your mother filed for divorce."

He'd been waiting to drop that bomb on her at the perfect moment. Nina stuck her hand on the edge of the desk and held on, her sense of equilibrium gone. If the police knew, it was only a matter of time before the media got hold of it. "More than 50 percent of all marriages end in divorce. Usually folks just let their lawyers fight it out for them."

"And sometimes, they don't." Detective King saluted her with the envelope. "There's a thin line between love and hate." He paused at the doorway. "Tell your buddy Aaron I'll want to talk to him too."

"What makes you think he's here?"

"That's his bucket of rust out back isn't it? See you in a bit."

"Why do you want to talk to Aaron?"

"You said the two of you talked not long before your dad was murdered."

"And?"

"If the two of you were planning to kill him, that's conspiracy to commit murder."

Now the detective was delusional. He was grasping for straws. He had a million scenarios and not enough evidence to support any of them. "For what reason would Aaron possibly want my father dead?"

"There's always a reason, Miss Fischer, not always a good one, but it's there. Money, lust, revenge, for fun. I just have to find it. Wait here."

The last two words were not a request.

She'd been ordered to stand down. She eased onto the step and propped her elbows on her knees.

Waiting for the other shoe to drop.

15

Grave robbers probably felt less guilty. Aaron paced the length of Nina's apartment. Not much room for pacing. She had less space than he did, but he always found her place cozy. Daffy, who was curled up in a ball on the couch, obviously thought so too. And Peanuts, who'd been beside himself since finding the judge, had finally passed out in the sunshine that burst into the room from the two windows on the far wall. He'd gone as far from the study as he could.

Aaron understood that desire. He eyed the darkroom where he'd hidden the box of receipts and the letters. King would know he was in the house. The 4Runner with its Channel 29 badge hanging from the rearview mirror would be a dead giveaway. So what? He had a right to be here. He and Nina were friends and colleagues. Let King chew on that.

Aaron eyed the closed door. He could take a run at those receipts. No. It didn't seem right to go through its contents without Nina. Besides, nothing said King wouldn't come up here looking for him.

He could print some photos. No. His job was video. Act normal. He'd just taken a box of papers germane to a murder investigation from a dead judge's study. Act normal?

He blew out air, once, twice, then tugged his phone from his pocket. Maybe Melanie had learned something. At the very least she knew what the other stations were reporting.

The phone rang five times. He was about to give up when her irate voice squawked in his ear. "What are you doing calling me at the crack of dawn?"

"It's not anywhere close to dawn. It's almost seven o'clock. What did you find out?"

"I overslept. I never oversleep. Quite a bit."

"Like what? Spill it!"

"All in good time." The sound of a lighter popping followed by sucking told him Melanie had lit the first of what would be a pack of cigarettes before the end of the day. "We need to meet."

"Why?"

"Because I did some digging and there's some stuff you need to know. It's not good and your girlfriend might not be all that happy about it. You might not want to be the one to tell her."

The line between what he knew from helping Nina in her hour of need and what he knew because of his job would be a plank he would have to walk each day. "She's not my girlfriend. What kind of stuff?"

"I don't want to talk about this on the phone. Besides, I told Serena Cochrane we'd meet her for a late breakfast. I need to take my morning run and shower first. You remember her. Fischer's court coordinator."

He did. A sweet lady with a large bowl of candy on her desk. "She says he's on the take?"

"Not in so many words. She loved her judge." The sucking of nicotine filled the line. "But she scheduled his cases and guarded the door to his inner sanctum like a she-lion. She'd been with him for his entire judgeship. He trusted her. She'd been up pacing the floor last night trying to decide what to do. She knows something."

"About what?"

"She says the judge gave her something to keep for him."

"And she'll give it to you."

The nicotine hissed out. "She's thinking about it. She says I did a decent job on the cases I covered in her court."

"When did you ever have the occasion to be nice to a coordinator in a civil court?"

"Remember that helicopter crash case that ended up settling?"

"I do, actually."

"I covered it. Serena is a very sweet lady, and she's all broken up about the judge's death, but that's not to say she wouldn't love her fifteen minutes of fame. She says the judge told her if anything happened to him, she was to give it to Mrs. Fischer. She doesn't want to give it to the lady because she heard about the divorce. Mrs. Fischer is not in her good graces, she says."

"What was it?"

"She didn't want to say on the phone."

"But she told you about this something. A reporter."

"I told her I was helping Nina clear her name. Serena loves Nina because the judge loved Nina. She wants to help her. She's known her since she was a little girl. Her and Jan and Trevor too. I told her I'd buy her breakfast and hear her story. Can you meet her at Jim's on Broadway about eight thirty?"

"I think I can swing that, depending on when the detective downstairs leaves."

"Downstairs? Where are you?" Her chortle nearly blew out his ears. "You're with Nina, aren't you? Are you in her apartment? You can't be working on the exhibit, not when her father just died—"

When Melanie found out he hadn't told her about someone breaking into the Fischer house and assaulting Nina he would be off this story. So be it. He'd given Nina his word. "Shut up, will you? I came over to help her look for some paperwork. I'm helping out a friend who is in trouble, remember?"

"You want to help her, get over to Jim's by eight thirty. I may be running late."

He hung up and checked the time on his phone. An hour. Nina would want to go with him. Which was fine. Serena Cochrane might be even more forthcoming with the beloved judge's daughter right there.

"He's gone." Nina trudged into the room. She looked done in. She needed to sleep. But she wouldn't. "He's coming back with a search warrant."

"I have to go to Jim's restaurant in a little bit." He recounted his conversation with Melanie. "Maybe Serena can tell us something that helps make sense of all of this."

"Serena is a wonderful lady. Dad loved her. She wouldn't say a bad word about him. He couldn't be bought."

He'd give anything to wipe away the pain on her face. "I'm sorry. But we need to find out. He had a gambling problem he hid. Maybe someone blackmailed him."

"I don't know what I was thinking."

"What do you mean?"

"Trusting him. As a kid I learned not to trust anyone. Yet I let him in."

"He was a good father."

"I'm beginning to wonder if good fathers are extinct."

"God is a good Father. We can't always understand what His plan is, but we have to trust He has one."

"Can't always understand? Try never. Dad was a hypocrite and a liar."

The bitterness in her voice reverberated in the room. Restoring her faith in God the Father was on Aaron's daily prayer list. The judge certainly hadn't made it easier. "Let's just see what Melanie found out before we pass judgment. Let's see what Serena has to say, okay?"

"Knowing Serena, she'll have plenty to say."

"She's a talker?"

"A big talker, but she's a hard worker too. She's been Dad's court coordinator for more than fifteen years. She's loyal, a quality Dad valued above all else."

"He trusted her to keep something very important. I'm curious to see what it is."

"Me too." Nina plopped onto the couch next to Daffy, who didn't budge. "King's coming back with a search warrant. Trevor is about to self-combust. Mom thinks we need to clean up. She doesn't want the police to think she's a bad housekeeper. Jan wants to take out King with a sniper rifle."

"She probably shouldn't express that sentiment too loudly." Grace hadn't done her own housekeeping in years. "You have nothing to hide."

"Except a box full of receipts I don't want him to see."

And the letters from her mother. Aaron glanced at his watch. "There's still time. If you want to look at the letters before he comes back, and before I have to meet Melanie."

She closed her eyes and opened them. Her hands clutched at her knees, then loosened. "I'll look at the letters while you dig through the receipts and let me know if you see anything that . . . helps."

Aaron brought out the boxes. He handed her the letters and settled next to her on the couch, leaving a discreet space between them. Their fingers touched when he handed her the letters. She felt warm, almost feverish. "You sure you want me here? You don't want Jan?"

"Stay." She unbundled the letters and smoothed her fingers over the top envelope. She glanced over at him. "According to the postmark, this is the first one. Can I tell you something?"

"Anything."

"I've always dreamed of having some communication from her,

and now that it's here, I'd rather have the stuff I made up. That Jan and I made up. Somehow, I know I'll be disappointed. It's all she ever did. Disappoint. Jan more than me. I was older and . . . more realistic."

Nine years old. Not that old. "Reality can really bite."

"Yeah, it can."

Her face was so full of pain, he had to duck his head and focus on the receipts. Neat envelopes each bearing a date in black magic marker. They went back five years. Five years of extended hunting and fishing trips with his buddies so he could take a hike to Las Vegas. He apparently believed the adage that what happened in Las Vegas stayed in Vegas.

At first it was mostly hotel rooms and car rentals. A small, incongruently neon-green notebook held rows and rows of Judge Fischer's elegant penmanship. A true patron of cursive to reflect his growing addiction to gambling. He started small with craps and slot machines. Graduated to blackjack and poker. The amounts grew accordingly. Lost and won. Often more winning then losing at first. Then he added betting on football games and boxing matches to the smorgasbord.

Each envelope contained its own notebook in different colors. Somehow that appealed to the judge. Neon green, electric blue, stunning turquoise. The numbers inside weren't as bright. He lost more than he won. In the second year, he started a new, separate notebook recording sums of money that apparently had nothing to do with gambling.

They were fat, round numbers next to dates. Nothing else. Dates across a span of two years. No hint of what they represented.

The last year held a receipt for the purchase of a condo: $750,000. Another receipt showed he had purchased a new Jaguar. No Prius for Vegas Fischer.

How did he lose so much at gambling and still afford to buy a luxury condo and a fancy vehicle? Receipts for fancy restaurants, roses, clothes, jewelry from high-end shops on the strip. Aaron went back to the dates and sums of money. Where had a district court judge gotten that kind of money?

Melanie's voice lingered in his head. *"He's on the take."*

Melanie. "We need to go."

Her expression pensive, Nina held a creased piece of Chief tablet paper in her hand.

"Nina?"

Heaving a sigh, she folded the letter and returned it to the envelope. Her blue eyes were wet, but no tears fell. "She wanted us back." Her voice quivered. Still, she smiled as she tapped the envelope. "In this letter she's talking about a Christmas when we went to a shelter, and there was a Santa Claus and we both got Strawberry Shortcake dolls. They were used, but we didn't care. We were so excited. We got stockings with candy and apples and oranges and nuts in them. She said it was a great day." Nina ran her fingers over the envelope. "She got a bottle of cheap perfume and some toiletries. It was a great day."

"Where were you?"

"Either Tampa or Pensacola. I think it was Pensacola. We walked down on the beach waiting for the party to start. We took a city bus to the shelter. We were all sandy when we got there. They gave us both new sneakers."

"A nice Christmas."

"The only good one I remember. That's why she remembers it. She probably doesn't recall what happened after that."

"But you do?"

"She had a Salvation Army voucher for a hotel room. As soon as we got there, she took off. She left us watching *A Christmas Story* on the TV. Told us to play with our dolls and eat candy. Jan ate too much and barfed on the bedspread. I had to clean it up."

"Where did she go?"

"A bar, I guess. She came back in the middle of the night, all giggly and stinking like beer. She had a guy with her. She woke me up all irritated because the room stank like vomit. The guy left. He said he wasn't up for a lady with two kids. She shook me and screamed at me and woke up Jannie, who cried."

"You didn't cry."

"That's what she wanted. Even when she left bruises on my arm from squeezing so hard, I wouldn't give her that one thing she wanted."

"I'm sorry."

Nina held up a Polaroid photo that had been wrapped inside the tablet paper. Aaron took it. Two little girls in faded blue matching jumpers and an emaciated woman with hair the color of red that came out of a box smiled up at her. The girls clutched dolls to their skinny chests. Nina had been a towhead. Jan's dark hair was caught up in a ragged ponytail. Both her front teeth were missing.

"How could she not love two girls with smiles like that?"

"My dad said she gave us up without a fight." Her face filled with pained bewilderment, Nina shook her head. "Social services and the cops swept the tent city. They wanted to dismantle it. Which is absurd. The homeless have to go somewhere. We got picked up as unaccompanied minors. We went into the foster system while they tracked her down. I guess she still had some tiny bit of decency left. She called Dad and asked him to take us so we wouldn't get lost in the system forever."

"She loved you enough to know she couldn't take care of you and her brother could."

Her gaze wandered over his shoulder to some distant spot. "She abandoned us and gave up on being our mother."

The hurt in her voice filled Aaron with the intense desire to do something, anything, to take it away. He wanted to smack someone

around, and he wasn't the barroom-brawl type. Judge Fischer hadn't
known much about the tender hearts of little girls. Or grown-up ones.
"Are you going to read the rest of them?"

"Not right now. I need time." She smoothed the stack of envelopes with gentle fingers. "I want to make a collage of these. Preserve
them. They're all I have—all Jan and I have—of her."

"After you and Jan read them."

She bundled the stack with its thick rubber band and laid it gently
on the coffee table. "I shouldn't have involved you in this."

"We needed to see the receipts. I think they're important to what
happened to him. I'm just not sure how." If she wanted to change the
subject, Aaron would oblige. He summarized what he'd seen in the
notebooks, noting the unexplained sums of money and the Las Vegas
bank account registry. "Your father had another source of income.
That's how he financed his other life, his gambling and the high life
he lived in Vegas. The big question, among many, is where did the
money come from?"

"If King gets Dad's financial records, he'll eventually ask the
same question."

"And he'll start looking around for other evidence." Aaron joined
her in staring at the box. "We could mail it to him. Or I could tell
him I found it."

"He already thinks you had something to do with all this because
of me."

That was bound to happen. Her explanation of King's interest in
him made Aaron do some snorting of his own. Conspiracy to commit
murder. For what earthly reason? He'd covered enough murder trials
to know there didn't have to be an earthly reason. Or any reason at
all that made sense.

Murder was generally senseless.

He stood. "I'll be back as quick as I can. Hold down the fort."

She looked up at him with those liquid blue eyes, pain etching lines around her swollen mouth. She'd seen so much. Been hurt so much. It had to stop. A person shouldn't have to bear quite this much. He leaned down and kissed her uninjured cheek. A soft, quick kiss. No staking of territory. A question. Or an invitation.

Her skin was soft and warm. She smelled like spearmint and eucalyptus. He closed his eyes and breathed her in. Now was not the time for this. She was too vulnerable. He wouldn't take advantage of her emotional state.

He straightened. "Sorry."

"Why are you sorry?"

Her hand came up and touched his face, drawing him back. Her eyes were big and her mouth slightly parted, an invitation that couldn't be ignored. He sat and leaned into her. The kiss began softly, so softly. An exploration, all the sweeter because it had been so long in coming.

Her lips tasted sweet. He let his lips linger there. He kissed her forehead and the bruise on her cheek. He trailed his fingers across her silky hair, then traced her jawline. Her lips sought his. They felt exactly as he had imagined. Only better. He eased back. "My timing stinks."

"I disagree." Her hands fluttered. She touched her lips with two fingers and let them drop. "It's confusing, I'll admit, but sooner or later, we have to figure it out. We've both known that for a while."

"I don't mean to take advantage." He stood, backed up, so he wouldn't be tempted to kiss her all over again. "You're going through so much right now."

"I stopped letting people take advantage of me a long time ago." Frowning, she pushed her hair behind one ear, making herself seem even younger. "You're my best friend. I don't want to do anything to change that, or I would've kissed you a long time ago."

He let her words sink in. He had to be grinning like an idiot. His face hurt. She had the same concerns that he did, but he wanted to build that friendship into something that would last a lifetime. And he wanted a partner in Christ. Scripture was clear about the whole unevenly yoked thing. "You'll always be my best friend."

And more.

"You say that now, but my experience with . . . stuff like this is that someone always ends up hurt."

"I would never do anything to hurt you." That, she could bank on. "I'm sorry. This is something that should wait."

"Stop saying you're sorry."

"We'll talk later."

Certain if he didn't go now he would swoop down for another kiss, this one longer and deeper, Aaron strode to the top of the stairs without looking back.

"Aaron, stop. I told you, I'm going with you."

"That's not a good idea." He put his hand on the ornate banister and swiveled halfway. "It'll make King even more suspicious."

"We'll be back before he gets his warrant." She popped up from the couch and grabbed her beautiful Leica M6 from the table. It was her most prized and valuable possession. One that had cost her an entire summer's wages before her sophomore year at UT. She used it when she wanted to shoot black-and-white film. "Besides, I'm not under house arrest. It's a free country."

He didn't bother to ask why she needed the camera. Nina took at least one everywhere she went. The workhorse Pentax from her high school years or the Mamiya RZ67 that shot both digital and film. They had a calming effect on her. Gave her a sense of control. Through photography, she kept the panic attacks at bay. He understood that. Besides, photographers never knew when something would catch their eye and need to be memorialized. He hated missing that shot and so did she. "Sort of."

"I'm coming."

Aaron nodded.

He pounded down the stairs, out to his car, and shot from the circle drive onto the street. Nina hung on to the door handle but didn't ask him to slow down.

In fact, she didn't say a word.

16

Idiot. Aaron took his gaze from the road for a split second to take a peek at Nina. She stared straight ahead. She hadn't spoken in the six miles between the house and the restaurant. She was vulnerable. She'd just lost her father in a horrible, violent crime. She was the subject of a murder investigation. She had unresolved issues with Rick Zavala. She didn't trust God with any of this. All reasons he should give her room to process. *Be a friend. Don't take advantage.*

God, help me walk that fine line. Don't let me blow this now.

Yet she didn't look offended or upset. She hadn't tossed her cookies on his shoes. She'd responded to his touch, to his overture. Not like a friend. More like someone who'd wondered about it. Who was curious. She'd kissed him back. An exploration. The kisses had been an exploration.

No more exploring. Not until this was over.

"Why are you shaking your head?" Finally. Now she decided to speak with a decided note of laughter in her voice. What was so funny? "I can almost hear the rocks rattling."

"Ha. Ha. Just thinking." He drove through the parking lot, running his gaze over the cars. "I don't see Melanie's Charger."

"Maybe she texted you."

Aaron parked close to the street and checked his messages. "Nada."

142

He punched her name under favorites. No answer. He glanced at the time on his phone. "We're two minutes early."

"We don't have a lot of time." Her camera hanging from a strap around her neck, Nina shoved her door open and looked back at Aaron. "Unless King has trouble getting the warrants."

The guy needed to be taken down a peg or two. His attitude toward the media was ridiculous. "That would be nice, but I wouldn't count on it."

Together they pushed the restaurant's double glass doors. A middle-aged black woman with a middle-age spread dressed in a neat two-piece green pantsuit sat alone in a booth meant for five. "That's Serena." Nina waved.

The woman waved back. A toothy, wide smile turned into a sudden frown. "Nina Simone? What happened to your face, pumpkin?"

"It's a long story. How are you doing?"

"I'm fine. No offense, honey, but I never agreed to talk to you. I can't talk about your daddy in front of you. He may be dead, but he's still my judge." Her double chin trembled, and her pudgy cheeks wrinkled when she talked. Her gaze raked Aaron. "You must be the photographer. I told Melanie. No video. Background only. Off the record."

"We're not doing this for a story." At least Aaron wasn't. He jumped in before Nina could. "I want to help Nina. We only want to figure out why this happened to the judge. We only want to talk."

"I hate talking ill of the dead. I hate talking about my judge at all. He was a good man. A good judge." Serena's trembling hands smoothed her perfectly straight cornrows. Her blunt-cut nails were painted silver with green rims. "I loved your dad. I know you did too. You used to come into his chambers when you were little and sit in that big leather chair and write in your diary like such a big girl. You always had that Pentax camera around your neck. The one your mom gave you for your tenth birthday."

"I remember that too. It was so frustrating. No point and shoot for me. Manual all the way." Nina slid onto the Naugahyde seat and laid her hand on top of Serena's. "That's why I know you want to help us. You know me. You know Daddy better than anyone, besides family. Maybe better than family. What happened? Any ideas?"

No one commented on her use of present tense.

"I can't." Serena started to rise. "I have to go."

"Okay. If you can't tell me, please, please tell Aaron. The police think I may have done this."

"That's crazy."

"Exactly." Aaron squeezed in next to Nina. Even though the restaurant smelled of bacon and sausage frying, all he could smell was the older woman's perfume. She smelled like his mom's lilac bushes. "Which is why we need your help."

"You poor baby. I'm so sorry for your loss. Your dad asked me to do one thing. One thing. But I don't trust your mama. I don't know who to trust anymore." Serena twisted an emerald ring round and round her plump finger until the skin underneath turned red and puffy. "Can we wait for Melanie? I'd feel more comfortable."

"Sure, sure." Nina exchanged glances with Aaron. He shrugged. They didn't have time for this. "Melanie promised you breakfast. We'll get breakfast. I'm sure she'll be right here."

He checked his texts. Nothing.

They perused the menu. Aaron ordered a cup of coffee and a cinnamon roll. Serena ordered a full-blown American breakfast. Nina asked for a glass of water. They made conversation about the weather, the bad traffic, and the latest bad decision by the city council. Nina snapped a few photos. Serena didn't seem to mind. When she pointed the camera, Aaron crossed his eyes and held up both hands in the hook 'em horns sign all UT graduates recognized.

Five minutes later, his coffee came along with a large, warm cinnamon roll. Still no Melanie.

Five minutes later Serena's breakfast arrived. By that time they'd exhausted all topics of mutual or nonmutual agreement. Serena was a widow with three children, all of whom lived elsewhere, none of whom had produced the requisite grandchildren. She was a Republican, a Baptist, and she loved *Dancing with the Stars*. Still no Melanie.

"Hey, fancy seeing ya'll here."

Serena's fork dropped to her plate with a bang. Aaron swiveled. Jerome Solomon approached. The lean African-American had a smile plastered across his face. He'd never given Aaron the time of day at the courthouse. Nor had he been actively hostile. Aaron stood and extended his hand. Solomon shook it and nodded at Nina. "Sorry for your loss, Miss Nina."

"Thank you. I appreciate that."

His gaze roved from Nina to Serena and back. "Y'all just run into each other?"

"Serena just wanted to let me know what a great joy it was to work for my dad." Nina jumped in when Serena didn't answer. "We're just sitting here remembering all the good things about him."

"He was a good man." Jerome tugged on his Texas Rangers ball cap. "It's hard to believe he's gone. Are you doing some kind of follow-up story? I would've thought you'd be on to the next crime of the day."

Aaron shrugged. "We're hoping to have more details from the police today. Maybe the autopsy results. We like to balance that with more comments from the people who worked with him."

"Balance is not a word I associate with the media." Jerome made a show of glancing around the restaurant. He scratched his chin. "Where's your camera? And that skinny little reporter who was always bugging us during the helicopter trial?"

"She's running late." Aaron cocked his head toward the door. "As soon as she gets here, I'll get my camera."

"Yeah, yeah. Well, I'd be happy to give you a sound bite, too, if you want. Just let me know."

He tugged on his hat a second time. "If you need anything or need someone to talk to, you can always call me, Serena." The emphasis on *me* was unmistakable. "You know Judge Fischer was a private man. He would've hated all this publicity."

Her double chin wobbling, Serena nodded hard. "I know, I know. But this is something special to remember him by." Her voice trembled. "It seemed like it would be okay."

"Sure, sure. I have to get home to the missus. Good seeing y'all." Hands in his pockets jingling keys and coins, the man ambled away.

None of them spoke until the double doors eased shut behind him.

"He'll tell everyone at the courthouse I was consorting with the media." Tears brightened Serena's eyes. "You know what, I don't care. I really don't care. I'm retiring. I've put in my time and I could never work for anyone else after Judge Geoffrey."

Nina tucked her arm around the woman and squeezed her in a hug. "He loved you so much. That's why he trusted you with his secrets. You can tell us whatever he told you."

"It wasn't much. He just sat down in the chair next to my desk one Friday afternoon. He looked tired and in a funk. He got that way sometimes. He said to me, 'Serena, I'm not who people think I am.'" She shook her head. "I had no idea what he was talking about. My phone rang and he got up and walked away."

"That was all he said? But—"

Nina's smartphone vibrated. She scooted back from Serena and touched the screen. "Jan says King is at the door. He's spitting nails, he's so angry. He says I better get my behind back there now before he puts out a warrant for my arrest."

"You better go, honey." Serena tossed her napkin on her plate. "I'll get this."

"I'll get it." Aaron dug a crumpled twenty from his pocket. "We need to find out what happened to Melanie. I'll pick her up after I drop Nina off at her house. We'll come see you at the courthouse. Is that all right?"

"Whatever you say, Nina." Serena struggled to hoist her amply padded frame from the booth. Nina turned and accepted a hug from the woman, who made two of her. "Take this." Serena shoved a small brown envelope at Nina.

Nina turned it over. Both sides were blank. "What is it?"

"Just take it. You have to run. Be careful, baby."

"I will. We will."

"Thank you, Serena." Aaron stifled the urge to pat a grown woman's shoulder. She looked so sad. Heartbroken. Lost. "You're doing the right thing. Nina will do right by her dad. We all will."

"I know. Whatever Jerome says, not all media are bad. I always knew you were one of the good ones. Just take care of her."

That was the plan.

Together they raced to the 4Runner. Nina stayed close. He opened her door for her. "What did she give you?"

"An envelope. What happened to Melanie?"

"I don't know." He careened around to the driver's side and slid in. Nina opened the clasp on the envelope. A small silver key slid out, along with a Frost Bank card.

Nina peered into the envelope. "That's it. Just a key. Looks like a safe-deposit key."

Aaron shook his head and started the car. "One thing at a time. Buckle up."

Nina did as she was told. "What happened?"

"I don't know." He could only worry about one thing at a time.

Melanie was never late to a story. Dinner, yes. For station meetings, yes. But not a story.

On the other hand, she was no shrinking violet. She had a gun and she knew how to use it.

She could handle herself.

17

Melanie hated running behind. A late reporter missed the story. She never did that. But somehow, she'd managed to oversleep. Probably because she'd stayed up past midnight partying on North St. Mary's—breaking her cardinal rule never to drink on a work night. For a reason.

She unlocked her front door and padded down the hallway, peeling off her tank top as she walked into her bedroom. She threw it on the floor and glanced in the mirror. Yep. Dark circles and bags under her eyes. TV reporters couldn't afford that stuff. They also couldn't afford to gain an ounce. Which was why she refused to miss her morning run followed by a hot shower to sweat out all the toxic stuff. She'd cut it short, but at least she got some sweat time in. Aaron would keep Serena Cochrane busy until Melanie could swoop down and capture the mystery key.

Key to what? Key to solving the mystery of who killed District Court Judge Geoffrey Fischer? Key to the biggest story of Melanie's career?

Key to a slot in a top TV market like LA, New York, Boston, or DC. Houston and Dallas–Fort Worth were closer, but she was done with Texas. She wanted a station on either coast—back to civilization.

She belonged in a top-ten market. She had the voice, the look, the hair, and she had all the moves and the savvy to go with them. She'd given up a fiancé for her career.

Nothing meant more to her.

The thought propelled her to the closet. Her go-to Liz Claiborne red slacks and matching jacket. Power color. White silk blouse. Makeup she could do in the car. Five minutes and she'd be out the door. She would make up for lost time with her Charger. Rush-hour traffic would have cleared by now.

A creak, loud in her three-bedroom, two-bath, too-big-for-one historic house brought Melanie to a halt. She tilted her head and listened.

Creak.

Like someone walking on the new faux wood floor in the living room. She didn't even have a dog or a cat.

Have no fear. That was her motto. She tugged on a tank top. She didn't plan to meet an intruder in her underwear. Far too intimate. She tugged open the dresser drawer next to her unmade queen-size bed and grabbed the baby Glock.

Anybody who messed with her was in for a surprise. One of the best things about Texas—open carry. A reporter who made enemies—and overzealous fans—couldn't afford to be without one. She cradled her little friend in her hand. Nobody messed with Melanie Martinez. She came from a long line of hunters. She didn't just own a gun; she knew how to use it.

She enjoyed using it.

It was loaded. No need to check. Why have a gun in the house if it wasn't loaded and ready to be used?

Breathe. It could be Josh, here to surprise her. The photog from Channel 4 had become something of a fixture lately. No, he would call first. He would knock. He knew about the baby Glock.

Confront the intruder? Maybe it was a burglar who didn't bother to check the garage and see her silver Charger tucked inside. Maybe he'd steal her TV and her computer and call it a day. Neither were worth dying over. Electronics could be replaced. Idiot probably wouldn't recognize the value of the paintings. The Jesse Treviño. The Amado Peña. Or the quality of Robert Lebsack's emerging art. She loved *Perils of Indifference*.

She hoped not.

She considered praying. It had been a long time. It seemed rude to check in with the Big Guy only in emergencies, but wasn't that what He was there for? *God, sorry about this, but I'd rather not kill anyone today. If You could get this one, I'd appreciate it. If not, forgive me for what I'm about to do.*

The gun heavy in her hand, she fought her way through the overstuffed clothes in her walk-in closet and pushed aside boxes of shoes to make a spot where she could collapse, cross-legged, and pull the slatted French doors shut.

She touched Aaron's name in her phone's list of favorites.

"It's about time. Where are you?" Aaron's East Coast accent was hard to understand when he got agitated. His voice sounded far too loud in the eerie silence. "She wants to tell her story to you—"

"Someone's in my house." No squeak in her whisper. No quiver. Just reporter excitement, not fear. Good. Melanie had a reputation as the best reporter in this market. It had to be upheld. "I think he's going through stuff in my living room."

"Where are you?"

"I'm in the closet in my bedroom. I've got my baby Glock."

"Call 911."

"I will. Get here. I want you to shoot this. Think of the story. Reporter catches burglar in the act. Holds him at gunpoint until police arrive."

"Are you nuts? *You'll* get shot. Call the police."

"I'll make him clean up the mess, and if he decides to do something stupid, I'll shoot *him*. Just get here."

She hung up. Her breathing was loud in her ears. *Easy, easy.* She inhaled, exhaled through her nose. Who was it and why her house? Had to be a burglar.

A random burglary. She wouldn't cower in the closet while a two-bit, penny-ante thug took her stuff. Stuff she'd worked hard for. Not worth dying over, but still. The idea was irritating.

Melanie peered through the slats. No sign of the thug. With the gentlest of touches, she nudged the door open. *Squeak.* She cringed. What she wouldn't give for a can of WD-40. She tucked the gun in the back of her pants and crawled out. Crawled to the door and peered down the hallway.

She couldn't see anything, but she could hear him. He was tearing up her study. Creep. He wasn't stealing anything. He was searching for something. What? She rose to her feet and inched along the hall.

A tall, lean man dressed in black jeans and a black T-shirt stepped into the hallway. He wore a matching ski mask.

Frozen, they stared at each other. Cussed in unison.

How could they be so in sync?

He backed away, one step, two steps. No way. She darted forward.

The intruder whirled. She couldn't shoot him in the back. She needed him to talk. She wanted her story. Then she would shoot him.

Melanie launched herself at his back. Her arms curled around his neck. Her legs wrapped around his waist. "No way, you thug. You're not getting away from me."

His fingers wrapped around her hands. He was strong.

Too strong.

He reared up and down and peeled her fingers from his neck. Gutter Spanish poured from his mouth. His voice sounded so familiar. She grabbed at the ski mask. It slid off.

"Rick?"

That did it. She might be three generations away from her Mexican ancestors, but she understood the cuss words. Rick didn't just run—he worked out with weights to stave off the fat from all the fund-raiser meals and alcohol he consumed. He had four inches and sixty pounds on her. He bucked her off. She fell backward on the tile. All air whooshed out of her. With a grunt of pain, she rolled over. Her cell phone. It was gone. Bedroom floor?

Gasping for air, she crawled toward her bedroom.

"No you don't." He switched to English. Not law-school-educated, sophisticated Rick. This guy was a throwback to the barrio. "Get back here."

He grabbed her hair and jerked her head back. Her neck popped. Then he had the back of her shirt, then her pants.

Then he had the gun.

Rick, on track to be the youngest partner in the history of Coggins, Gonzalez, and Pope, up-and-coming politician, and Judge Geoffrey Fischer's first choice for son-in-law pointed a gun at the back of her head. This day couldn't get any more surreal.

"Get up."

She acquiesced. "What are you doing here?"

"I was just looking for information. You showed up from your run early."

The guy had nerve. Melanie snorted. "Showed up in my own house. If you wanted to talk to me, you could've just called. You know my number. You could've rang the doorbell."

"Somehow I don't think you'd share your notes with me. Or that handy-dandy digital recorder I'm betting you used when you talked to Serena Cochrane yesterday. They're not in your office. Where are they?"

"We chatted, that's all. Why would you care? What's going on?"

Serena hadn't wanted to talk at first. But she'd changed her mind and called Melanie in the middle of the night. Why was this important to Rick? What would drive a respected attorney to commit breaking and entering? Had he killed the judge?

The questions amped up Melanie's adrenaline, as if struggling with an intruder wasn't enough. A big story was her drug of choice. "Tell me what you think she knew or told me. Come on, Rick, give me the story. Be my inside source. I won't tell a soul, you know that. I'd go to jail before I gave up a source."

"You were seen talking to Serena at the courthouse yesterday. What did Serena tell you about Judge Fischer?"

Someone was spying on the judge's staff in the wake of his death and reporting back to CG&P. Why? "I talked to everyone who worked for him. She told me he was a great man, that she loved him."

"And that he was on the take, right?"

"She'd heard that, but she didn't believe it."

"Where's the digital recorder?"

"What kind of reporter shares her story notes with someone who breaks into her house to get them?" Her story suddenly grew exponentially. One of the most reputable law firms in town with millions of dollars in billable hours was somehow involved with a district court judge's death. "Why didn't you call me up, ply me with drinks, and then ask me?"

"Because you wouldn't hesitate to lie through your teeth."

"And you know I'd end up getting more information from you than you would from me." Melanie forced a laugh. "I'm good at what I do. Why don't I make some coffee and we can talk?" She halted in the living room. "I haven't eaten. I could go for some breakfast tacos. We can eat and then head to the bedroom. After all, you always liked my bedroom, didn't you?"

"You aren't very good at following instructions." The gun jabbed her again. "Keep walking."

"At least tell me why you're doing this."

"What if I said it was to protect a man's reputation?"

"The only reputation you care about is yours."

"That's not true." He sounded hurt. "I always liked you."

"You used me and I used you."

"That's exactly what I like about you." He actually chuckled. The sound sent chills rippling up Melanie's spine. "We're just alike. Upwardly mobile. All about our careers."

"I thought you were in love with Nina." She turned to face him. "Have you thought about what embracing a life of crime will do to her?"

For the first time he hesitated. His gaze ricocheted around the living room. "You've added some artwork to your collection. I bet they took a chunk out of your trust fund."

Her money was none of Rick's business, but the conversation bought her time. Melanie edged toward the hallway. "Come on. All this adrenaline has me worked up. Do you want to see the redecorating I did in the bedroom? I have a new painting there."

And her cell phone.

"I don't have time to mess around. I want the digital recorder."

Which was tucked inside her purse. Sitting next to the Keurig in the kitchen ready to go with her to work. Once he had the recorder, what would he do to her? He couldn't think he would get away with this. She was a reporter, for crying out loud.

The only way out of this for Rick now was to kill her.

He was a lawyer and a candidate for higher office. None of this made any sense. "Why would you kill Judge Fischer?"

"I didn't kill the judge." Anger raged in his face. He no longer looked like a handsome up-and-coming politician. The depth of his emotion drew lines on his face and turned his eyes into smoldering coals. "That's what started this whole thing. If he hadn't been killed, none of this would've happened—"

"None of what would have happened? What was the connection between the judge and your firm?"

"Knowing you, you were working on the story in your bedroom last night. Your stuff's in there, isn't it? Your laptop and the recorder? Let's go."

"Fine, you're so hot to go to the bedroom, let's go." She drew a breath and gave him her best top-ten market smile. She needed her phone. They were moving in the right direction. "And while we go, you can tell me what this is all about."

"You don't need to know."

She did. If she was going to die today, she'd at least like to know why. She wanted the story. Not even her gun in her killer's hand could change that.

18

Aaron glanced in the rearview mirror. No sirens screamed.
No red lights flashed. The drive from Jim's restaurant to Melanie's
neighborhood north of San Antonio College took less than ten
minutes. He punched the accelerator and hung a left. The 4Runner
swerved around a corner. Tires squealed. They made the first two
green lights. No such luck at the next stoplight. He jammed on the
brakes. The back end slid. He steered left. The SUV straightened.
The guy in the Chevy Traverse next to him rolled down his window
and gesticulated. His expression said it all. Aaron ignored him.

Two more blocks. Two more blocks.

Nina shoved her phone in her pocket and grabbed the door handle
with both hands. "The dispatcher says a unit is already on the way."

"Their response time is pretty good."

"Maybe there's already a unit in the area."

"Maybe."

The light changed. He took off. The 4Runner shimmied. The
engine whirred and whined. "Don't quit on me now."

Nina threw both hands up as if to prepare for imminent contact.
"Take it easy. We can't help Melanie if we die in a one-car rollover."

He plowed around another corner and hit the entrance to her
neighborhood.

"You need to chill." Nina's placating tone only riled Aaron more.

He sucked in a breath and tried to stave off the effects of adrenaline and fear for Melanie. She was an irritating woman, but she'd grown on him in the three years they'd worked together. Nina leaned over and squeezed his arm. "If this guy really is still in her house, we don't want to walk into the middle of something. We need a plan of attack."

"Maybe it's just a random burglary."

"Her car's probably sitting in the driveway. Would a burglar break in if he thought she was home?"

"Depends on whether the burglar knows her routine. Does she park in the garage—which of course she does, given that she drives a new Dodge Charger. Does she have more than one car? Does more than one person live in the house? Does she work days or nights? Maybe he's stupid." Not likely. "Try her number again."

Nina punched in the number and waited. She shook her head.

"Try texting her. Maybe she doesn't want to talk while the guy's in the house."

"You think he's still there? Every second he lingers he risks getting caught." Nina thumbed the screen with the dexterity of someone who didn't have fat fingers. "Maybe he took her hostage."

"Pray."

She didn't answer. He didn't dare take his gaze from the road. If she couldn't pray, he would pray enough for both of them.

Aaron slowed and turned onto Melanie's street. The one-story colonial-style house was in the middle of the block. No car in the driveway. Melanie loved her silver Charger. It would be parked in the garage. She lived alone. She said she liked it that way. No fuss, no muss. People from the news station had been invited over many times for parties. She liked to cook and always served good eats. A big draw for the TV crowd. Nobody got paid squat, so free food and good shop talk meant all-nighters.

He didn't drink, but he ate plenty and he never tired of shop talk. He liked serving as a designated driver to make sure his buddies arrived home safely. A DUI would kill a photog's career. Had to be able to drive to stories.

He pulled over to the curb two houses down, put the 4Runner in Park, and surveyed the neighborhood. Quiet during the day. Nice cars, mostly SUVs, in the driveways of two-story, historic brick-and-wood homes with big front yards and no fences like San Antonians preferred in the newer gated subdivisions. Nice landscaping. Basketball hoops on the edge of driveways. Tricycles parked next to front doors. At least the older kids were at school.

He turned off the ignition. "You stay here."

Nina snorted. "In your dreams."

"She has a gun. The intruder may have one too." He undid his seat belt and shoved his door open. "I don't want you getting caught in the cross fire."

"You either." Nina opened her door and hopped out. "When did Melanie get a gun?"

"A couple of years ago. She has a license to carry. She does a lot of stories that irk people who have long memories and long arms."

But mostly she liked guns.

Aaron ran to the back of the 4Runner and pulled out his camera. He stuck the camera on his shoulder. Her Leica still dangling from her neck, Nina met him at the curb. "You're really going to shoot this?"

"I have to. I'll help her and get the story for her." His voice sounded breathless even though he hadn't exerted himself. He always got an adrenaline rush on big stories, but it had never involved someone he cared about. "That's what she wants. Get in the car."

"No way."

"I don't have time to argue. Stay put."

"I'm not a puppy."

"I don't have time for this."

"Then move." Everything about Nina's posture and tone said he'd lost this argument before it started. "I've got your back."

Using a neighbor's car for cover, Aaron surveyed Melanie's yard. Perfectly manicured. A crepe myrtle and a rubber tree in the front yard. Fire bushes under the windows. He ran to the next car and stopped. His heart pounded in his ears. He'd shot stories at active crime scenes many times. Guys holed up in their houses with children as hostages. He'd done ride-alongs with the cops. News photographers lived for those moments. The juice flowed. Getting as close as possible to the first responders was a welcome challenge.

He'd never known the victim before. Not a victim. Melanie was a reporter. His reporter. Aaron stayed low and ran toward the front door. It was closed, pinecone wreath still in place. The little cement porch, just big enough for a Christmas cactus and a welcome mat, looked undisturbed. Normal. He paused and glanced back. Nina kept pace. He shook his finger at her and pointed at the 4Runner.

She shook her head so vehemently her long ponytail flopped. "Wait for the police or I'm going with you."

"I can't wait. It's Melanie."

"How are we getting in?"

He turned the knob. Nothing. "Around back."

The camera bumped on his shoulder as he ran. Melanie kept a spare key hidden under the deck. She was the queen of losing her keys but refused to do the predictable and leave the spare under a potted plant by the front door.

He opened the gate and slipped through, aware of Nina close enough to be his shadow. She touched his shoulder. "We won't need a key." Her voice was high and breathless. "Someone beat us to it."

The back door stood open. A crowbar lay on the red-cedar deck.

Strips of wood hung from the door around the jimmied lock plate. Aaron grabbed Nina's hand. "Go back." His whisper sounded loud in his ears. "Call for help."

"I'm not going back unless you do."

"I have to help her."

"Are you going to knock the guy out with your camera?"

A shot rang out.

*   *   *

Nina flattened herself against Melanie's house. Adrenaline pumped through her body, making it hard to suck in a breath. She swiped at her face. Sweat burned her eyes. Her heart beat so hard it hurt. They edged forward across the deck to the door. It stood open. Aaron peeked in. He leaned back again and nodded. "Here we go."

They moved in to the kitchen. It was spotless. A reusable water bottle sat on the counter next to a Keurig. Melanie's Louis Vuitton purse lay on its side. The room smelled of fresh coffee.

Aaron's hiking boots clomped against the tile. She touched his arm. He looked back. She put a finger to her mouth. He nodded.

Nothing like seeing a big burly former linebacker try to tiptoe.

"Melanie?" he whispered the name. He might not even know he said it aloud. "Melanie."

They moved through the kitchen, the breakfast nook, and a formal dining room that held a modern-looking dining room table and six chairs. Nothing had been touched.

Into the foyer by the front door. To the right, someone had knocked over a chair in the living room. Magazines and books were strewn across the tile floor. Paintings hung at odd angles.

Nina put one hand on Aaron's back. His T-shirt was damp with perspiration. Without looking, she knew he'd started shooting. Her other hand closed around her Leica. It felt solid warm in her hand. Others had guns. She and Aaron had cameras.

She jerked her head toward the hallway. He nodded. They moved in sync.

First door, guest bathroom. Empty. Second door, a computer desk, chair, bookshelves, computer. Office. Again, papers were strewn in all directions. Third door, empty bedroom.

The last door stood open. Aaron's arm came back across Nina's chest, knocking her against the wall. "Stay."

His voice was the barest whisper.

She shook her head, but he never looked back. His arm dropped and he charged forward. "Melanie?"

She followed as close as she dared.

A figure dressed in black jeans, a black ski mask over his face, darted into the hallway. He shoved Aaron, who slammed backward into Nina. His camera banged into her sore face. Pain blossomed across her cheekbone. She flailed, desperate to keep her balance. No dice. Her head banged on the tile. She rolled and the Leica slammed into her chest.

Aaron tripped over her, righted himself, and raced after the intruder.

Idiot.

Nina opened her mouth and tried to scream. *Stop. Don't do it.*

Nothing came out. The fall had knocked the wind out of her.

She rolled over and dragged herself to her knees. Blood from her nose dripped on the tile. She crawled forward, one hand on her camera.

Her ragged breath filled the air. It was so loud in her ears, she wanted to clap her hands over them.

Sirens screamed in the distance.

Finally.

"Help." One syllable. Barely a whisper. Her lungs ached for air. "Here. We need help here."

Look. Just look.

A powerful sense of déjà vu buffeted her. No cats or dogs this time. No darkness. An intruder, though, a powerful one. Built differently. Dressed differently. Jeans instead of sweats. She crawled through the doorway. Her hands encountered carpet. Soft. Nice on her aching palms and fingers. She let the camera drop and used both hands to move forward.

Melanie sprawled across the carpet, her arms and legs askew. She wore a tank top and leggings. Her feet were bare. Her toenails had been painted a bright red. So festive. So Melanie.

Her eyes were open.

A neat bullet hole decorated her forehead. A pool of blood soaked the once-tan carpet around her wet, tangled hair.

"Melanie?"

Silence filled only with Nina's panting.

She sat back on her haunches. She put hand over mouth. Acid burned the back of her throat. Her stomach, empty except for water, heaved.

Throwing up at a crime scene wouldn't be good.

Melanie Martinez, the model turned reporter with her perfect makeup and high heels, was gone.

She looked so surprised.

Nina gritted her teeth. She crawled forward to do that thing a person must do in this situation. She touched the woman's throat. No pulse. CPR. She should do CPR. Every second counted.

A small, black gun lay just beyond her long, red fingernails.

"SAPD. Everyone down. SAPD!"

Heavy footsteps pounded on the hallway tile.

The room filled with bodies then. Uniformed officers, guns drawn, screaming.

"On the ground. Hands over your head."

Nina hit the deck. "CPR. She needs CPR. Help her." A police officer squatted and grabbed Nina's arms. "What are you doing?"

"Handcuffing you, ma'am."

Reality faded into a surreal world where anything could happen and did. The cuffs bit into her wrists. At least she could still feel pain. "What about Melanie? She's hurt."

Another officer knelt next to Melanie. "If this is Melanie, she's gone."

19

Aaron couldn't let go of the camera. His shoulder hurt and one of his fingers might be broken. Adrenaline had flown the coop, leaving him drained. Still, he couldn't let go. Had he shot video of Melanie's killer? Maybe. Tears choked him. He swallowed them, swiped at his face, and gritted his teeth. The camera had definitely been hot when the intruder came at him from the bedroom. In that split second Aaron had been sure he would die. That Nina would die. Like Melanie had died. He closed his eyes, trying to block out the distorted video that ran like a movie on an endless loop in his head.

Running, running, the camera heavy on his shoulder.

Panting sound in his ears.

The smell of something rotten in his nose.

His stomach heaved. *Breathe.*

"Even though I walk through the valley of the shadow of death, I will fear no evil, for you are with me; your rod and your staff, they comfort me."

Silently, he repeated his favorite verses over and over. The desire to hurl receded.

He breathed and leaned his head back on the warm cloth upholstery. *God, I'm sorry I didn't get here sooner. I'm so sorry. Tell Melanie I'm sorry.*

Melanie's faith had been hit or miss. He should've done more. Friend evangelism was his forte. He'd been working on her for three years. *Lord, please have mercy on her soul. She meant well. She didn't deserve to die like this. Too soon. I'm sorry I didn't do more. I needed more time.*

He opened his eyes. The video started again.

The open door. The figure in black. Black ski mask.

The race down the hallway.

By the time he reached the front yard, the intruder was gone. He disappeared just as the cop cars arrived. Three of them skidding to a stop. All parked at weird angles. Guns drawn, they exited the marked SUVs.

He had to get back to Melanie and Nina. But the drawn guns stopped him in his tracks. A second later he was flat on his face, his camera on the grass next to him.

They didn't handcuff him. After he produced his media ID, an officer escorted him to the backseat of the cruiser. He'd gotten Nina into this. He needed to get her out.

Long, drawn-out minutes passed. Then she appeared in the doorway, handcuffed.

They were crazy. His protests fell on deaf ears.

Now she sat on the back of an ambulance parked directly across from the cruiser. Her camera still hung from her neck.

A paramedic examined the back of her head. She leaned over. "One, two, seven, four, eight, nine." She counted in a high, breathless voice. "One, two, seven, four, eight, nine."

Aaron poked his head out from the car.

"Hey, I told you to sit tight." The uniformed officer standing guard outside the vehicle looked familiar. Too many stories over too many years. "They'll get to you eventually."

"Is Nina all right—the woman over there by the ambulance?"

The officer shrugged. "From here it looks like she's having a panic attack."

"I need to talk to her. I can calm her down. I can help."

"Nope. Suspects don't get to coordinate their stories."

"I'm not a suspect."

In his mind.

The officer scowled. "Media doesn't get to interview a suspect before law enforcement. We have rules about stuff like that."

"Has she asked for a lawyer?"

"None of your business."

"She's with me."

"So you keep saying. Just sit tight."

Easy for him to say.

"Aaron, Aaron! Over here!" Louis Aragon, a reporter for Univision, yelled from beyond the crime-scene tape the officers had strung from the mailboxes along the curb. "Is it true Melanie's dead? What happened? Lovers' quarrel?"

Marked media units started showing up about ten minutes after the first responders. Word had spread fast that it was Melanie's house. She would hate this. Hate being the story. She would want her station to have it first. He ignored Aragon.

"Aaron, are you okay?" The high, familiar voice of Diana Mitchell cleared the chatter of the rest of the media. They'd worked together for his entire tenure at Channel 29. Aaron swiveled and craned his head.

Diana was squeezed between photogs from Channel 5 and News 4. She'd been crying. She'd attended plenty of parties at Melanie's house. She knew. "Should I ask Greg to call the station's lawyers?"

News director Greg Stevens would be having a cow about now. Aaron scooted toward the door again. "Can I talk to her?"

"Are you kidding?" His grin derisive, the officer chuckled. "No talking to the media."

"She's a friend."

"She'll have to wait like the rest of them."

A dark-blue Crown Vic rolled up to the scene and parked at an angle. Detective King exited the driver's side. He ripped dark Ray-Bans from his face. He looked as if he was itching for a fight. The guy with him was almost an exact replica, but he wore cheap sunglasses and kept trying to loosen a navy-and-red checked tie with two fingers.

"Detective King, what can you tell us about Melanie Martinez's murder?" A reporter from the *Express-News* got the first question in. Others followed in a cacophony of strident inquiries. They jostled against the tape and an officer waved them back. To be on the other side of that tape. It looked so good. So familiar. Getting the story, not being a part of the story. Sometimes a guy had to take a chance. He had to step up. Nina was worth it.

King ignored Aaron's buddies. His gaze rested on the officer next to Aaron. "Who's in charge of the scene?"

"Lopez."

King, followed by his sidekick, swaggered over to an almond-skinned, plainclothes officer standing on the sidewalk talking to a CSU tech who wore cowboy boots and jeans. The three engaged in conversation that looked more like an argument. Lots of hand waving and gesticulating. The Hispanic man's face darkened. He stuck a cell phone to his ear and talked.

More gesticulating.

King turned and stalked toward the ambulance. His buddy tromped inside with Lopez.

"King, wait." Aaron stuck both legs out the door.

The officer tried to shut the door on Aaron's legs. "I told you to stay put and I meant it."

King changed directions "It's okay. I need to talk to him anyway."

"Media always think they should get special treatment."

"Ain't that the truth. They stink like three-day-old fish." King leaned over and stared into the cruiser. He had the evil-eye thing down. He pinched his nose for a second. "Aaron McClure, right? You were in the house with Nina. What were you doing? Aiding and abetting?"

"Melanie called. She was in trouble. We came to help." Aaron wanted out of this car and he wanted Nina out of the handcuffs. "Nina had nothing to do with her death."

"Instead of calling the police?"

"Nina called 911. The dispatcher tapes will prove it."

King wrinkled his nose as if he really could smell fish. "Let him out of the car."

The officer rolled his eyes. "Seriously? Lopez said to keep him separated from the suspect."

"I'm the lead investigator on the Fischer homicide. These two are persons of interest in my case." King's voice remained cool, but his expression said, "Don't mess with me." "Lopez has the scene, but I have these two."

"You're King? The one who got his partner shot—?"

"You should shut up now." King whipped into the other cop's space. The words were clipped and icy cold. "Not the time or place for historical chats."

The officer smirked, but he took a step back.

Still clutching his camera, Aaron slid out and stood.

"Over here."

They walked over to the shade of Melanie's crepe myrtle. Aaron kept Nina within sight. She seemed lost in her own misery, unaware of anyone around her.

King eyed the camera. "Shoot any video?"

Aaron held on tighter. "Melanie called and said someone was in her house. She wanted me to come."

"To shoot the story?"

Aaron nodded.

"I want the video."

"Is Nina really under arrest? We heard a gunshot. We ran inside. Melanie was already dead."

"How do you know?"

"Because the intruder ran out after the shot."

"But you didn't see it happen and you ran after the intruder, leaving Miss Fischer alone with the victim."

"Do a GSR test. It'll show Nina never touched the gun."

"We will. I want the video."

"Let me talk to her."

King held out his hand. "Video. I can get a warrant. You know I can."

"You won't need a warrant. My bosses will want to help find Melanie's killer. She was one of us." His bosses would agree to hand over raw video to law enforcement. No sources were at risk and Melanie was family. "But I'll make a copy at the station. I can send you an electronic file or bring you an MP4. Just let me talk to Nina."

"I'll have an officer take you to the station to make the copy. Then he'll bring you downtown to headquarters."

"I want to talk to Nina first."

"Did you and Miss Fischer meet a woman at Jim's for breakfast this morning?"

How could he possibly know that? "What does that have to do with this?"

"Yes or no?"

"Yes. We met Serena Cochrane for breakfast. She's—"

"Judge Fischer's coordinator."

"How did you know?"

"Shortly thereafter we got a call for a hit-and-run accident, an MV-Ped, not far from the restaurant."

A motor-vehicle-pedestrian accident. Aaron's stomach roiled. The cinnamon roll and coffee threated to come up. "Was someone hurt?"

"Mrs. Cochrane was hit. She died at the scene."

*   *   *

King's approach didn't help with Nina's anxiety attack. She inhaled, counted, exhaled, exactly as her therapist had taught her. The attacks had almost disappeared when she left San Antonio for college. Now they were back with a vengeance. *Get a grip.* The image of Melanie's face floated in her mind. The blood. More images of Dad. Inhale, exhale.

The morning's event was like a rerun. Different location. Different time of day. But the same results. A body on the floor. Gun next to the body. A gaggle of reporters screaming at her, begging her for comment. Asking her if Melanie had been murdered. Asking her if she'd killed the reporter.

Why would she do that? Melanie was helping Nina prove she didn't kill her dad.

Instead, she was finding proof that he was a corrupt judge.

Enough reason for Nina to kill her in some people's minds.

Melanie had cursed like the old men who gathered around cans burning trash in the tent city and she drank more than most of them. She smelled much better, however. She smelled like Chanel No 5. During Nina's short tenure at the newspaper, Melanie had been nice to her at news conferences and gaggles outside the courthouse or impromptu lunch gatherings before city council meetings.

"Take the handcuffs off."

Fury raged in the detective's dark eyes, but his tone was even. She held out her arms. The uniformed officer removed the cuffs.

Rubbing her wrists, she stood. "I know you're mad."

"Mad has nothing to do with it." He turned to the paramedic. "Does she need to be transported?"

"No. Minor bump on the head. The cut on her cheek is worse than it looks because of the existing injuries." He ripped off his latex gloves. "She should probably see a doctor about the panic attacks if she's not already."

"Don't talk about me like I'm not here." They didn't need to know about her therapy sessions or her medical issues. "You want to question me, do it. I'm a big girl."

"What were you doing here?"

"I'm sure Aaron told you." Aaron was slumped in the backseat of a police cruiser again. He had to be devastated about Melanie. "I saw you talking to him. I'd like to make sure he's okay."

"He's fine. Let's talk about what you were doing here instead of staying at home and waiting for me to serve the warrant as previously instructed."

"It's still a free country. I wasn't under arrest."

"That could change since you decided to leave your home and bust in on another crime scene."

"Am I under arrest?"

"You were found kneeling next to a gunshot victim. What do you think?"

"I think she was dead before Aaron and I reached the hallway to her bedroom."

"How did it happen you were here at all?"

Nina recounted the phone call from Melanie, the open door, and the man dressed in black.

His expression doubtful, King rubbed his chin. "Black jeans. But still black."

"It felt different. He was . . . taller, leaner than my intruder.

He looked like someone who works out. I don't think it was the same man."

My intruder. It sounded so personal. It was personal.

"With a black ski mask over his face?"

"I'm not an idiot, Detective." She stood and brushed past him. "Melanie was dead when we got here. An intruder shot her and killed her right before we walked through the door. Believe me. Don't believe me."

King kept pace with her. "Why didn't he shoot McClure? Or you?"

"My guess is the gun belongs to Melanie. You'll know soon enough, right? He threw it down and came charging out, not realizing we were there."

"He didn't come to kill her?"

"I don't know."

"Did you take pictures?"

"What?"

He pointed at the Leica. "Did you, like your ghoulish photographer friend, take pictures during this alleged event you're describing?"

Nina's hands clutched the Leica to her chest. Images flashed in her head. The Jesse Treviño painting. The overturned chair. Papers strewn everywhere. The blood. Open eyes. Had she taken those photos or were the images simply memories? She swallowed a hard lump in her throat and shook her head. "I'm not sure."

"You don't know?"

"Everything happened fast. You may be used to situations like this, but I'm not."

"Can't you tell by looking?"

Nina checked the dial. Fifteen. How many shots had she taken at Haven for Hope last Friday? Had she put in a new roll? "Maybe. I'll have to develop the film."

Disbelief mingled with impatience bloomed in King's face. "How well did you know Serena Cochrane?"

The change of subject gave Nina whiplash. She tried to regroup. "She was Dad's coordinator for about fifteen years—for as long as I can remember." Something in his tone tipped Nina off. "What happened to her?"

"You seem to be leaving a trail of bodies in your wake."

He might as well have punched her in the gut. "I talked to Serena for a few minutes. She was fine—"

"She's not fine anymore. She's dead."

"You're lying."

"I don't lie."

"What happened to her?"

His words were incomprehensible. A car accident. A hit-and-run. Sweet Serena with her fancy fingernails and designer shoes. Her love of Rosario's enchiladas and *Dancing with the Stars*.

"She can't be. I just talked to her."

"I know. My point exactly."

Tears formed. Nina halted. She gritted her teeth and closed her eyes, willing them away. Images rolled in her head. Serena lifting her into the big leather chair and handing her a Butterfinger candy bar. Serena painting her fingernails red when Daddy was busy in court. Serena teaching her to sing "I'll Fly Away." Serena laughing, her cheeks wobbling as she roared her signature line, "Lord give me strength!"

King stuck his Ray-Bans on his face and stepped in front of her. "I'm going to get a CSU tech to swab you for GSR. You know the routine."

"I can't believe she's dead." Her legs buckled.

King grabbed her arm. "Easy."

"I'm fine." She jerked away and staggered toward King's Crown

Vic. "Let's go. I'll do whatever I have to do. I want Serena's killer found. I want Melanie's killer found. My dad's killer."

"Then we want the same thing. But first I need to see the video your friend shot. I'm going to have my colleague drive you downtown if you're willing to go."

"I'll do whatever I can to help."

"Good. We'll talk at headquarters."

Another uptake of adrenaline and Nina's back straightened. "I also know my rights."

King smiled and saluted. "Tell Mr. Teeter he is always welcome."

"Like you could keep him away."

The bodies were piling up. People she loved were dying. The killer was there. "The longer you mess with me, the less time you spend finding the real killer."

"Don't worry. I'm good at my job."

Not as good as he seemed to think. If he didn't want to look for the real killer, she would.

20

The second Jack Daniel's straight went down smoother than the first. Rick figured three or four more and he would forget the moment he was face-to-face with Nina in Melanie's hallway. Nina and her sidekick, Aaron. She wasn't supposed to be there. No one was supposed to be there. But least of all the woman he'd loved since he was ten. The ski mask saved him. Having the wherewithal to put it back on before he left the bedroom had to be God looking out for him.

Nina could never know he killed a woman. No one could know, but especially Nina. She was good. She wouldn't understand he did it for them, for their future, for their life in DC, away from their crummy pasts. He would be a respected representative, one day a senator, or maybe even a cabinet member. Who knows? The first Hispanic president if one of the Castro twins didn't beat him to it. She would be a famous photographer. As famous as Ansel Adams. Maybe she'd work for *National Geographic*. They would have beautiful kids. He simply had to hang tight and let this blow over.

Hang tight. Get a grip. Suck it up.

Rick wiped his face and turned to face his boss. Peter was angrier than Rick had ever seen him. Except maybe the morning Fischer had been murdered. They had Fischer right where they wanted him. It had been a perfect arrangement for both parties. Jerome's presence was likely the only thing that kept Peter from a total meltdown. Chuy,

176

the door breaker and all-around bouncer, had been sent on a sand-wich run.

"It was a simple job. Simple instructions. They did not include killing a reporter." Peter slugged back a scotch and soda. He banged the glass on the table and paced in front of the windows in his over-sized corner office that overlooked Travis Park.

At a loss for an explanation, Rick joined him. Silence reigned for one, two, three, four seconds. Around the park three churches vied for downtown churchgoers—the Fischers' conservative Presbyterian church, an Episcopalian church, and San Antonio's most liberal Methodist church famous for its homeless programs. Nina would like that, but she always toed the line, always went to her father's Presbyterian church because he'd insisted.

Maybe Peter had it out of his system just like that.

"I said find out what she knows, that's all. Have a drink, pump her for information, that was it. You idiot, moron, buffoon."

"She went for a run. That usually takes half an hour, at least." Rick dove in before Peter ran out of synonyms. Everything had gone wrong. "She came back early before I could find her notes or her recorder. I thought I would sneak out, but she heard me. And she had a gun. I had no choice but to take it. But Melanie wouldn't let it go. She came after me. And even after I had the gun, she refused to tell me anything. She lunged for her phone and I thought she was coming at me. The gun went off."

"The gun went off? You killed her and got nothing."

"McClure and Nina showed up before I had a chance to finish searching."

"Killing her was your only choice?"

"Once she saw my face." Rick couldn't control an involuntary shudder. So much blood. He'd hunted deer, wild hogs, and turkeys. But this was different. One minute she was sassing him. The next she lay a corpse, her smart mouth silent. "I needed to know what Serena had told her before it showed up on Fox 29's newscast."

"Like she would tell you."

"She claimed Serena didn't tell her anything. She claimed her story would be autopsy results and stuff she got from digging into his biggest cases. Second-day junk."

Peter shrugged off his jacket and laid it across a leather swivel chair behind an oak desk as big as Rick's office. His pits were wet. "What any reporter worth her salt would say."

"Except I had a gun pointed at her." Melanie might think she knew how to handle it, but like many women who became victims of their attackers, she forgot to factor in size and strength. She was so sure of herself. The story was more important to her than her own life. If she'd pulled the trigger, he'd be dead and she would be alive.

"Thank God. I'm pretty sure if she thought she had her story, she would've shot me and went out for breakfast tacos afterward. I got out of there without being seen by McClure and Nina. The cops could treat it like a home invasion. She interrupted a burglary. It doesn't have to be connected to her job. She's not usually home at that time of day."

"And we've cleaned up any loose ends with Serena Cochrane." Miles leaned against the wall and crossed his arms. His presence gave Rick the creeps. He wore the cat-ate-the-canary look permanently. "Everybody needs to chill."

"Serena would never have soiled the image of her boss, the great and glorious Judge Fischer." Rick's eyes burned. Serena was a nice lady. Too much collateral damage. He never signed up for this. All he wanted was a life of service. Sure, money too. Enough that he never had to eat beans and rice again. He needed sleep. He needed time to think. He needed a shower. And a jug of bleach to wash away his deeds. "You didn't have to kill Serena. She was harmless."

"Every time we plug one hole in the dike another one spurts open." Peter paced the floor, his leather loafers silent in the thick navy carpet. "You have to get over to the Fischers' house and talk to Nina. Find out what Serena told her and McClure this morning. Find out what Nina told King. But don't kill anyone."

"I would never hurt Nina."

"I hope you don't have to." Peter's icy-blue eyes glittered. "Just don't forget whose political career is on the line."

A chance to rub elbows in DC. A chance to leave behind a childhood that stank of cheap beer, beans, and burned corn tortillas. "There's no chance of that. Just don't forget whose firm is on the line."

Peter took a step forward. "We both know who'll come out on top if push comes to shove."

Jerome stepped between them. His lean frame smelled of body odor and garlic. "Nobody's pushing or shoving anybody. We're all on the same team. As long as we stick together and keep our mouths shut, we're fine."

Attorneys were not known for keeping their mouths shut.

"That includes Nina." Rick turned his back. He poured another finger of Jack and chugged it. "She's off-limits."

"Do your job and your girlfriend might survive." Peter's tone could cut glass. "But I wouldn't place any bets on it."

Rick slammed the glass on the bar and whirled. Jerome shoved him back. "Get out of here. Now."

He had no choice. He squeezed past the bailiff and stormed to the door.

"Rick."

He glanced back. Peter's expression had returned to its normal neutral stare. "Take a shower. You stink."

He mumbled a response and kept going. He should've kept the Glock. If it were in his hand right now, he'd use it.

"If Nina knows too much, she's a liability."

Rick gritted his teeth and kept walking.

"If you can't do it, I've got someone who can."

He let the door slam behind him.

He would have no regrets about killing Peter Coggins.

None like he felt when he stood over Melanie's body and watched the blood drain from her wound. The look on her face had been almost comical. Midsentence, she stared at him as if trying to make sense of something. Still trying to get the details for her story.

Melanie saw the bullet coming, but she knew there was nothing she could do. She had that split second of horror before death enveloped her.

He never wanted to see that look on Nina's face. How much was he willing to give up for her?

That was the question.

21

The newsroom—usually filled with the noise of people talking, half a dozen TV screens blaring at the same time, and the scanners squawking—went quiet. Eerily so. Acutely aware of Detective King on his heels, Aaron took a breath and walked through the cubicles. Most "civilians" didn't get to see the inner workings of a newsroom. King probably didn't know that and wouldn't care. Rows of cubicles, some messy, some neat, a bank of TV monitors tuned to news channels, the scanners, the news desk. Not much to see really, but it was home. And right now Aaron needed home.

Her chubby face streaked with tears, Claire Chagra stepped from her desk next to the scanners and opened her arms. "Aww, A-Plus. Sorry it had to be you."

"Thanks. Don't call me that." He leaned into her hug. She was a fluffy woman who favored embroidered Mexican dresses in bright aqua or pink and huarache sandals. She smelled like cigarette smoke and bubble gum. She quit a least once a month—smoking and her job. Being an assignments editor at a top-thirty-five news market TV station was one of the toughest jobs in the industry. She juggled scanners, spot news, photographers, reporters with delicate egos, irate calls from viewers, news tippers, and schedules with aplomb. Only occasionally did she slam a receiver on the desk and cradle her head in her hands.

Today would've been one of those days.

"I can't believe it," she whispered as her hands rubbed his back. "What do you need?"

Others had gathered round. Joey, one of Aaron's photog colleagues who worked the afternoon shift; a couple of interns; Smitty, the equipment guy; Sherri, who did the noon weather; and Chuck Dillon, one of the five o'clock sports anchors. A laptop in one hand, Greg Stevens, the news director, strode toward them. Their faces were pinched with disbelief and wariness. People in the news business saw the worst up close and personal. They understood that bad things could and would happen. Even to them. It was still a shock when it did.

Aaron introduced King. The detective said nothing. Aaron's colleagues nodded. Claire sniffled. King offered her a tissue from a box on top of a cubicle wall. She took it with a mumbled thanks.

Those outside the business liked to think the media was cold-blooded, immune to the misery they saw, intruding on the most painful moments of loss and horror in people's lives. In truth, some reporters were like that. But most believed in what they were doing. They believed in telling stories the world needed to hear and see. They also needed to put food on the table for their families, just like everyone else. Aaron had never considered any other job.

He wiped at his face with his sleeve and cleared his throat. Claire squeezed his arm. "Take your time, love."

"Someone shot Melanie. They think it was with her own gun."

Sherri gasped. Chuck put his arm around her.

"It's all over social media. Channel 5 has it on their website." Greg held up his laptop. "I'm sorry to be so abrupt. I'll call a newsroom meeting for six o'clock tonight. We'll take time to talk about Melanie then." His Adam's apple bobbed. His voice cracked. He cleared his throat. "Right now, we have jobs to do. If anyone needs to go home, go. We'll all understand."

No one moved.

"Okay, hang tough, guys." Greg turned to Aaron and King. "Let's grab an editing bay in the back. We can watch the video together. Diana is getting sound at the scene with Joey. They'll bring back the interviews and b-roll."

He talked and walked. Aaron let King go first, then followed. The grim silence of his colleagues continued until they went into the editing bay and closed the door.

"Grab a seat."

Aaron took the swivel chair in the middle, popped the tiny STM card from his camera, and stuck it into the card reader connected to the computer. A few seconds later they were staring at his video on the dual twenty-two-inch monitors.

What had seemed likes hours had lasted a few minutes. He sprayed the broken back door, the kitchen, and dining room. Nothing out of place. In the living room he focused on the overturned chair and the broken lamp. Then the hallway. There'd been enough ambient light to make out the photos hanging on the walls. Video of the office and the spare bedroom.

Then a frame or two of the open bedroom door.

The figure coming at him. Blurred and indistinct. No time to focus. Shouting. He didn't remember shouting. "Stop. Stop. Melanie? Where is she? Stop."

A jumble of images and sounds of grunting. The arms. The shove and tilting dizzying distortion. A cry. Nina? The wall, the ceiling, the floor. A few seconds of brown tile.

Aaron's stomach rocked. He swallowed bitter bile and breathed through it.

The sound of footsteps running. The camera came up and the shot continued, blurred, the floor, the hallway. The figure dressed in black. Black sneakers. Then the figure was gone. Out the kitchen door. The back door. The same way he'd gotten in.

Sun. Red cedar deck. Across the grass. Through the gate into the front yard. Sirens. Cops.

Grass.

He cleared his throat. "That's it."

The other two men didn't speak for a few seconds. Greg's breathing sounded heavy. King leaned back in his chair and clasped his hands in his lap. "Again."

Aaron played it three more times, stopping each time on the frames that showed the intruder.

"Can you enhance it?"

"It's not like *NCIS*."

"I know." King leaned forward, stuck his elbows on his knees, and stared at the screen. "You never went in the bedroom."

"No, I wanted to stop the guy."

"You wanted to get video for your story."

"I wanted to grab him and rip that ski mask off his face. Whoever he is, he's a coward and he killed a woman."

"You didn't know that at the time."

"Melanie wasn't answering her phone. She always answered her texts. She was an addict. She couldn't help herself. She'd answer a text in the middle of her own wedding."

"She didn't have an alarm system?"

"She did, but knowing Melanie, she turned it off when she went out to get her newspaper. She always read the *Express-News*. She was old-fashioned like that. Then she went for a run and took a shower. Maybe he got in while she was running. Or showering."

"Her hair was wet. There was a wet towel on the floor." King seemed to be thinking out loud. "You think it was a man?"

"He ran like a man. His hands felt like a man's when he shoved me." Aaron closed his eyes and relived those terrifying moments. "His sleeve rode up on one arm. Hairy. Black hairy arm. It was a man."

"Women sometimes have dark hair on their arms."

"It was a man."

"You never made it into Melanie's bedroom."

"No, I told you that."

"You didn't see what happened while you went after this intruder."

"No, and I know where you're going with this. We heard a shot before we went in. There was no second shot. I would've heard it. Nina didn't kill her."

"What was Melanie working on?" King directed the question to Greg.

"Last time we talked she was digging around in Judge Fischer's life. She wanted to do some kind of follow-up on his murder." Greg stared at the computer screen where Aaron had frozen a frame of the intruder. "She was pretty secretive about her investigative pieces. She was paranoid about her ideas getting stolen. Aaron was her shooter. He probably knows more than I do."

Both men looked at Aaron. He worked hard not to drop his gaze. "She didn't tell me a lot." The key Serena had given Nina burned a hole in Aaron's psyche. Did she still have it, or had they searched her and taken it? "She said some of his staff thought the judge might be into something hinky."

"Hinky like what? Hinky with women?"

"No, like on the take."

King's face brightened as if Aaron had given him a Christmas present. "The pillar of the community taking bribes."

"Maybe. She didn't have any proof. Yet."

"If you knew more, you'd tell me, right? Or are you more concerned about getting the jump on the story like your friend Melanie?"

Aaron turned and began copying the video onto a thumb drive. He could never play poker. Everything showed on his face. "Melanie was my friend and I want whoever killed her caught and prosecuted to the full extent of the law."

"Oh, he or she will be." King leaned over his shoulder. "You can be sure of that, A-Plus. I'm headed downtown to interview your girl-friend. You need to come with me and get in line."

"Don't call me that. What I know is what I shot on the video."

"I'll make you a deal. Swing by on your own recognizance. You can talk to my temporary partner. He'll go easy on you. In and out. Get you back here in a jiffy."

"Fine."

"Fine."

"I'll get the station's lawyer on the phone." Greg stood and held out his hand to King. They shook. "You can be sure, Detective, that we want justice for Melanie. Whatever she was working on got her killed. We want that story. She would be extremely put out if we didn't go after it with everything we've got. So we will. Aaron will. I will. Count on it."

Aaron held out the thumb drive. King shook his head. "We need the original for court. We have to be able to say it's an original so no one can say we tampered with it."

Greg nodded and Aaron dumped the video on the computer and ejected the STM card. He handed it to King, who pocketed it and made a production of providing a property receipt for it. "Just so everything is buttoned up with every i dotted and every t crossed."

"Right. I hope you expend as much energy finding Melanie's killer."

"Count on it."

Aaron didn't breathe until both men left the edit bay. He wanted this story bad. He wanted it for Melanie. He wanted it for himself. What he didn't want was to hurt Nina in the process. She'd been hurt too much already. She couldn't catch a break.

Neither could Aaron.

22

Déjà vu all over again. After hours in a Public Safety Headquarters interview room, Nina expected darkness to greet her. Instead, a crowd of reporters and photographers called her name and closed in around her. She put her hand to her forehead and squinted against the late-afternoon sun. They were a patient lot, waiting all this time for her. One or two had followed her downtown from Melanie's house. Others had been sent by assignments editors glued to the scanner, to social media, and the other stations' websites. The TV stations often got their leads from the newspaper's website, mysa.com. It didn't matter now.

In a fierce, overwhelming déjà vu, she'd found herself walking out, her attorney, Fred Teeter, at her side. No GSR on her body or her clothes. No blood. Aaron's video confirmed the intruder. She was not under arrest.

Exhaustion weighed her down. For all his East Texas charm, King had been relentless. He hammered her with question after question. He knew things. Things that had nothing to do with Melanie and everything to do with her dad. Her dad liked to visit gambling sites. Did she know that?

No, she hadn't.

She needed to talk to Aaron. They needed to figure out what bank deposit box the key Serena had given her opened. She needed to dig through the receipts and read the letters.

Her feet didn't want to work. She rubbed her eyes and tried to focus. One step at a time. Just get to the car. Get home.

Those letters. She needed to tell Jan about the letters before she deployed. Nina owed her sister that.

"Nina! What happened to your face? Did you get into a fight with Melanie Martinez?" A reporter from Channel 12 who looked twelve noticed Nina first. She had a ton of blonde hair and the flat chest of a child. "Did she hit you so you shot her?"

Nina's hand went to her face. The ibuprofen the paramedic gave her at the crime scene had worn off. Her head ached and her mouth hurt every time she moved it. "No, no."

She tried to go left around the cluster of reporters. They shifted with her.

"Did you kill Melanie? Do you know who did?" Diana Mitchell, one of Aaron's colleagues, dodged Fred's arm and stuck a microphone in Nina's face. "You were in Melanie's house. Why did they let you go?"

Diana's voice cracked on Melanie's name. This wasn't just professional for her, it was personal. For all of them. One of their own had died. It hurt. They would get the story because that's what Melanie would've done. Then they would go home and cry into their pillows.

"No, I didn't kill Melanie." Nina dodged the mike and kept walking. "And no, I don't know who did."

"No questions. She's not answering questions." Fred's feeble attempts to shoo the media away had no effect. He reminded Nina of Pearl shooing flies from her fresh-baked pie on the windowsill. "Get back."

"It's okay, Fred." She halted and faced the people who'd once been her cohorts in pursuit of the story and the photo and the video. "I have nothing to hide. I wish I had more to tell you. All I can do is plead with the public. If you know anything about the death of my father, Judge Geoffrey Fischer, or the death of Melanie Martinez, or the hit-and-run this morning that killed Serena Cochrane, please, please call the police. If you saw anything, call. You don't have to use your name. Call the Crime Stoppers tip line."

The number was engraved on her brain from all the news conferences she'd covered. She never expected to need it herself.

"What are you doing? Are you nuts?" Rick plowed through the crush of reporters. Fury lined his face. He grabbed her arm and dragged her away. "You can go, Teeter. I've got this. You obviously don't."

"Rick, stop it." Nina jerked away. His grip was tighter than necessary. She rubbed her arm and looked back. A flummoxed expression on his white-whiskered face, Fred stood defenseless, the media milling around him. "I know what I'm doing. I don't need you to swoop in and save the day."

"Apparently you do. Where have you been?" Rick's normally modulated Harvard tone disappeared, leaving his southside homeboys accent. "I stopped by your house and found your mother wandering around like a lost kindergartener. She said she thought you went to take pictures somewhere with 'that sweet boy Aaron.'"

"Is that what this is about? You're jealous of Aaron?"

"This is about you skipping around town like a juvenile delinquent who doesn't know when to do what the police tell you to do. Didn't King tell you to stay put? Your mother was there alone when he came back with the subpoena. They tore your house apart."

The letters. The box of receipts. If they'd found them, King would have mentioned it in the interrogation he called an interview.

"How did you know that?"

"Trevor mentioned it on his way out the door. He apparently helped your mom through it since her daughters were too busy to stick around."

"Where was he going?"

"I'm not his keeper."

"You're not mine either. And since when are you so concerned about my mom's welfare?"

"I . . ." Rick's voice trailed away. He looked over her shoulder. The media had turned their attention from Fred to the full-blown argument taking place in front of the police headquarters at Unity Plaza.

Beyond the crowd King trotted down the steps in front of the six-story building of cast-in-place, blast-resistant concrete with its three-story glass atrium. "Hey, wait."

"I'm done. I'm not going back." Nina turned on her heel and rushed toward Santa Rosa Street where Teeter had parked his car in the city pay lot. "I've had enough for one day."

Enough for years. Finding Melanie. It was too much. She fought back hot, angry tears. *Too much, God. You expect too much.*

"Y'all go about your business. This isn't the place to loiter." King's East Texas accent did nothing to sweeten his tone as he stomped down the steps toward them. "Move along. Nothing to see here."

He couldn't make them leave. It was public property. But some scattered toward the media office housed in the building. Others headed toward their marked units parked on the street or anywhere close, legal or not.

"Miss Fischer."

"Really, all the time we've spent together, surely you can call me Nina."

"Nina, your brother Trevor was scheduled to be interviewed this afternoon. He agreed to come down on his own steam after helping your mother with some arrangements. He hasn't shown. He's not answering his cell. His girlfriend says she hasn't seen him."

"Trevor has a girlfriend—"

Nina put her hand up to stymie Rick's question, but her gaze remained locked with King's. "I've been here with you. Why are you asking me?"

"I called your mother. She seems to think he was meeting you somewhere. Apparently he told her you two were seeing about getting your father's body released."

"I saw Trevor this morning." Nina was too tired to think fast. She shook her head, trying to clear the cobwebs from her brain. "We talked about what needed to be done, but so much has happened since then I don't know . . ."

She wouldn't lie. Jan was right. Fischers didn't lie. Except for Geoffrey. The father of all liars. Another father who couldn't be trusted. *Do as I say, not as I do.*

I promise to love, honor, and cherish. Until I don't.

"When you see him, tell him we're looking for him." King's gaze went to Rick. "I'd hate to put out an APB on him."

"He'll show up." If she had to drag him downtown herself. They didn't renege on their responsibilities either. "I'll talk to him." She whirled and pounded toward the street corner.

"Where are you going?" Rick kept pace.

"To Fred's car. He's giving me a ride."

"Let me. I'm on the street at Milam Park." He gestured toward the park between Market Square and Santa Rose Hospital with its enormous dove mural by her favorite local artist Jesse Treviño. The beautiful dove that represented hope for the patients who entered the building. Which took her right back to Melanie and the Jesse Treviño painting on her wall. The one she would never look at and admire again. Her eyes were wide open, but she couldn't see.

Would her body be in a refrigerated slot in the ME's office some-where near the one that held Dad's?

Rick tugged on her arm. "Slow down, slow down. You'll give yourself a heart attack."

Panting, she slowed and then stopped. She put her hands on her knees. *Inhale, exhale. Inhale, exhale.*

Rick's warm hand tugged her into his arms. His smooth-shaven chin nuzzled her cheek. "You're okay. You're safe. You're fine. I'll take care of you."

She pulled away. "Thank you, but I don't need your help."

Rick's black BMW loomed in front of her. It was parked in front of a fire hydrant.

"I don't need a ride from you."

"I'm sorry I got carried away." He stepped in front of her, forcing her to halt. "I get a little crazy, worrying about you."

"I can take care of myself. I'll wait for Fred."

"I know you can take care of yourself. I've watched you do it for years. Maybe it's time to let someone else carry the load for a while." He touched her cheek. "Please, forgive me. Let me feed you. I'll take you to Mi Tierra for enchiladas. You love their enchiladas."

The thought of food made her stomach lurch. "I need to get home to Grace, remember?" She fumbled for her phone in her jeans pocket. "I need to find Trevor."

"You need to eat. Your face is whiter than a baby's butt."

She couldn't help it. She snorted. "You're the worst."

"You're the best."

"Just take me home. Pearl will feed me."

She slid onto the leather seats while he fired up the AC and gunned the engine. Seat belt on, she sent a text first to Fred to let him know she had a ride, then to Trevor, then to Aaron. The last two said the same thing: *Where R Yu. Need to talk.*

Aaron answered first. But he called instead of texting. Glancing at Rick, Nina answered on the first ring. "Are you okay?" His voice was soft like his lips trailing across her cheeks and forehead with exquisitely tender kisses. He felt different than Rick. Solid. Sturdy.

No slick snake oil. No hair product. No expensive cologne. Just Irish Spring soap. Had that only been this morning? "Nina. Are you okay?"

"Yes. Rick is taking me home."

A long pause. People talking in the background. Static. Scanners. TVs blaring. "You said you needed to talk."

"I do. I thought you had to make a statement to the police."

"I did. Some guy named Cavazos. King's partner, I guess."

"Hey, Aaron. Don't worry. I'll take good care of her." Rick yelled as he whipped past a VIA Metro bus and screeched around a corner onto Cesar Chavez Boulevard. "You just keep working on your story."

"Shut up." Nina slapped her hand over the phone and scowled at him. "He just lost a good friend. He doesn't need you needling him."

"Forgot. Sorry." Rick managed to sound repentant. "Tell him I offered my condolences."

Nina removed her hand from the phone. "How's everyone there taking it?"

"They're a tough bunch. You have to be to work in this business. Claire's taking it hard." His voice caught. "It must've been terrible for you—seeing her. And so soon after your dad. I'm so sorry you had to go through that again."

The round hole in the middle of Melanie's head filled Nina's vision. Her jaws ached from gritting her teeth all day.

"I can't believe Serena died minutes after we left her." The pain in her jaw radiated up to her temples. She rubbed a spot in a circle, trying to rub away the memories. "Do you think we had something to do with it?"

"I don't know. I hope not. She was a nice lady. She didn't deserve to get run over in the street after breakfast."

"She was always so sweet to me. Like the grandma I never had."

"Do you still have the envelope she gave you?"

Nina glanced at Rick. Looking predictably annoyed, he thumped his thumbs on the wheel to a musical rhythm she couldn't hear. He raised his eyebrows. *Get off the phone*, he mouthed the words. He was an attorney. He was a friend. He said he cared. He also cared about his position at the firm. He cared about launching his political career. He cared about social standing and not having it.

He cared about his BMW and his hair.

She wanted to trust him. She trusted Aaron more. "Can you come by the house?"

"Why does he need to come by your house?" Rick swerved onto South Alamo Street. "He should be there with his pals. Having a wake or lifting a glass to their dear friend."

"Are you sure? You've got Rick with you."

"There are things we need to talk about." She shifted her gaze to the enormous Steves Homestead on King William Street. As a kid she'd thought it a palace. Compared to her former abodes, all the historic houses in this district were mansions. Beyond anything she'd ever seen before. Her dad reveled in belonging to one of the historic families who started this German enclave in the late 1800s. "We need to . . . compare notes."

"It'll be late. I'm reviewing archive video files. We're doing a piece on Melanie's career for the six and ten. Then everyone's getting together at Greg's. He had to call her mother in Phoenix and tell her. He said it was the worst thing he's ever had to do."

"King should've done it."

"Greg thought it would be better from him."

"Maybe." Nothing could make the death of a child better. "So maybe not until tomorrow."

"If it can wait. If not, I'll skip the—"

"No, don't do that." He needed to mourn his friend with his colleagues. It would be selfish to make him miss that because she needed him. "Call me later, okay, when you can."

"Hang in there."

"You too."

He disconnected.

"What do you need to talk to him about?" Rick pulled into the driveway. Instead of driving around to the back where Pearl would be able to see them from the kitchen, he put the car in Park inside the fence and let the engine idle. He stared at the front of her house as if he'd never seen it before. "What were you talking to Serena about?"

"She wanted to see me."

"With a TV news photographer in tow. What, was she looking for her five minutes of fame as the court coordinator to a murder victim?"

"No, no, she wanted . . . she cared about Dad."

"What did Melanie have to do with it—with her?"

"She interviewed her yesterday afternoon, at the courthouse."

"Did the old biddy—I mean, did Serena have any insight into why someone would want to kill your dad?"

"No. She loved him. She said everyone loved him." That was true. Serena wore blinders when it came to her judge. *Tell him about the key. Tell him.*

Trust. It came down to trust.

"Come on, are you holding out on me? Don't you trust me? What did she say?"

"She didn't have a chance. Aaron got the call from Melanie and we had to go."

The key. What about the key?

"You didn't answer my question. You don't trust me. If you need something—anything—I'm your guy."

A five-o'clock shadow darkened his face, making his perfect teeth seem even whiter. His dark eyes seemed to see straight to the heart of the matter. The envelope fit snugly in her bag. She could pull it out and hand it to him. Done. Simple as that. Let him figure out what her dad was hiding.

And ruin his reputation. Rick idolized her dad. He would want to hide the truth as much as she did. But for different reasons. It would suit his plans.

She didn't trust him. Not with this. Not with her dad's reputation on the line. She'd learned long ago to be careful with trust. If a child couldn't trust her mother, who could she trust? Aaron had proven himself over and over again. Everything about his actions and his words gave her hope, gave her a sense of possibility. Which made him the most dangerous. Rick was a known quantity. "I know that. I'm just trying to sort things out."

"You're not still planning to do the exhibit at the Blue Star Art Complex, are you?"

Nina shook her head. "It'll never be finished in time now, and who knows when the funeral will be. And Melanie's funeral. Aaron has a lot to handle too—"

"Aaron this and Aaron that. What is it with you and this guy?" Rick's lips contorted in a deep scowl. His baritone deepened. "Your face is messed up. You get hauled downtown to PSHQ. He's a terrible influence."

"He didn't influence me. If anything, I influenced him."

"You have more sense than that. More smarts." He shoved his dark hair back, messing up his perfect do. "At least I thought you did. You used to have more street smarts."

"You don't have to worry about me. I know how to take care of myself."

He leaned forward and touched her face. "Apparently not. I don't like this." His hand slipped behind her neck and pulled her toward him. His lips met hers in a hard, angry kiss that hurt her lip. She struggled to move back. He didn't let up.

She closed her eyes and tried to identify the current that ran through her. It was deeper, more violent, steeped in hurt and loss and uncertainty. Familiar. Dinner and the movies or bowling or a Missions baseball game followed by time in his old Datsun, just the two of them. Restless. Unsure of how it went. How anything went. Explorers. She always drew the line. He always argued, kissed, and tried the seduction moves of a seventeen-year-old.

She held the line.

She never wanted to be her mother. She didn't want to bring children into the world she couldn't care for. She wanted to be good. *I was good, God. Look where it's gotten me.*

His hand tightened. His heat seeped through her blouse, burning her skin. The kiss deepened.

A bonfire burned. She could smell the dry leaves combust. Earthy and sweet. He tasted like earth.

He leaned back. A slow smile played across his face. "There you are."

"It doesn't work." She swallowed tears he could never see. "We don't work. I wish we did, but we don't."

They were fundamentally different animals. He lurked in the dark and lured her to places she shouldn't go. He reveled in seeing how far he could make her go. He reveled in the hold he had over her. He ignored her desire for a love that she could trust. A love that reflected light and hope.

"Yes, we do." He walked his fingers across her collarbone. She shivered and swallowed. He grinned. "When you relax and let me in, we work."

"We're not teenagers anymore."

"Or two kids trying to be something we're not."

The son of a maid and the daughter of a drug addict. Neither one of them had felt at home in the historic King William District that bordered downtown San Antonio. A few blocks away and they were in Rick's territory. The housing projects. There Nina felt at home.

A long time ago. Now Rick was an attorney, mentored by her dad, and she was a photographer, an artist, and a published poet. Two very different people with only the past in common.

She slid away from him to the far corner of the seat until the door handle pressed into her back. The frigid AC air cooled her damp face. She was sweaty all over, like she'd run a hundred-yard dash. She pressed her fingers to her throbbing lip.

"Did I hurt you?" His voice softened. "I didn't mean to. You just affect me that way. You know what I want, but you refuse to give in. Sometimes I catch a glimpse of what it would be like, and it keeps me coming back for more. You're a tease."

That was not her intention. "I have to go."

"Did King actually threaten to put you in jail?"

She straightened. This was safe ground, crazy as it seemed. "He did. He knows I couldn't have killed Melanie. He's seen Aaron's video. That's the only reason I walked out those doors."

He turned the ignition off. "I'm coming in."

"Don't."

"You need me."

She'd needed him since the first day Rick took her exploring the southside neighborhood just beyond the bubble where she lived. They escaped while his mother cleaned and her mother wrote. He showed her the house where he lived with his four older sisters and a revolving door of "uncles" who sometimes paid the rent and took it out of his backside. He showed her the good, safe places to hide out. The parks where they could swim for free at the city pools, swing, and shoot baskets until the homies took over at dark. "Right now I need to sleep."

"You invited Aaron over."

"Rick, please."

"Can I come back tomorrow?"

Her head pounded and her cheek throbbed. She could never shut him out completely. "Sure. That would be good."

He grabbed her arm and pulled her toward him. This time the kiss started below her right ear and made its way to her lips. The burn started slow, revved, and raced through Nina. She had no place to go. "Stop."

He stopped. "Always the good girl." His rueful tone stopped short of critical.

"I have to go." Hand tight on her Leica, she let herself out. The whir of the window coming down kept her from turning away.

He leaned forward and looked up at her. "I love you."

Finally, under duress, he said those longed-for words. They reverberated in the humid night air. A mockingbird sang. Car engines hummed in the distances. He would do this now. He had the car in Drive so he could make his escape. She turned. "Rick, can we just—?"

He revved the engine and drove away.

Rick never failed to meet expectation.

She shivered, clutched her camera closer, and whirled toward the house.

Grace pushed through the screen door. She wore a black silk blouse, black skirt, rubies in her ears and on her hands. Thick gold bracelets clanked on her right wrist. A heart-shaped watch encrusted with diamonds dangled from her other wrist. She still wore her spectacular diamond wedding ring. She looked like a romance novelist in mourning. "I just saw you on TV. You looked terrible. All beat up. Like one of those women who do interviews after their children have been killed in drive-by shootings. They were angels, so sweet, the best children ever. When they were gangbangers with tattoos of tears under their eyes and on their knuckles. What were you thinking?"

"I was thinking someone might come forward with useful information."

"The ME's office called." Grace's voice quivered. "Your father's body is being released in the morning. We can get on with the arrangements. I called the funeral home. We'll have the service and burial on Friday morning."

She plopped onto the wrought-iron bench and put her head in her hands. Sobs shook her body.

The romance novelist was gone, replaced by a grieving widow.

23

The police had done a number on her living quarters. Nina stood in the middle of the room and did a 360-degree turn. Books tumbled to the floor. Pillows tossed around. A stack of mail scattered across the coffee table. Heathens. Cleaning it up would help take her mind from the day's event crowned with Grace's meltdown. Getting her into her nightgown and into bed had been a torturous task filled with her mother's tears and Nina's own effort to maintain composure.

Dad would've appreciated that. *"Chin up, Nina. You're a Fischer."*

The letters and receipts. Rubbing her eyes, she stumbled into the darkroom. Her safe room, her haven, had suffered the same indignity. Bottles of chemicals shoved about. The filing cabinet drawers that held her photo archives stood open. What did it cost to shut them? Too much apparently.

She put both hands on the cabinet and lowered her head. Pain pulsed where Rick had kissed her. Rick, then Aaron, then Rick. Drive-by kisses. They were so different as to be light and dark in her life. One who knew her before she knew who she was and the other who'd helped her find herself through her photography and her writing.

To let go of Rick was to let go of her past. To open herself up to Aaron was to embrace the possibility of a future where she could be happy without fear of the other shoe dropping.

It always dropped. Sooner or later.

She touched her fingers to her lips. Exhaustion blew through her. She had no answers. Thinking about herself served no purpose. Right now, figuring out who killed Dad, Melanie, and Serena, sweet Serena, was paramount.

First things first. She straightened the darkroom, removed the film from her camera, and went to work developing it. An hour later, she had her answer. The photos she shot at Melanie's house revealed nothing about the killer. A shadowy, blurred figure in the hallway. Fuzzy, black nothingness. The photographer in her had continued to shoot, even after the struggle ended. The walls and the carpet.

Nothing. She dumped the last photo in the fixer, swished it around, and let out her breath. "What now?"

No one answered.

The letters and receipts? She hadn't finished reading the letters. She flipped on the light, whirled, and strode to the wooden table where Aaron had concealed them behind huge bottles of chemicals and boxes of photo paper. Still there. The receipts and the strange little neon notebooks. She took them out and stacked them on the counter. Read through them again, one by one. A secret life in Las Vegas. A secret source of income. Dad had been a walking sham. A feckless husband. Another man who couldn't be trusted.

Aaron insisted she could trust God. For his sake, she wanted to believe. But it didn't work that way. To trust would be such a relief. To let someone else carry the load she'd carried all these years with Jan and now Brooklyn. Light-headed, she closed her eyes and leaned against the counter. *God? God! How can I trust You when every father I've had has left me, deceived me, walked away from me, lied to me? You say You will always be there for me. Where are You now?*

No answer.

She opened her eyes and took a long breath.

What was the intruder looking for in Dad's office? These receipts?

What about the key to the safe-deposit box? She needed to get to it, find whatever Dad had hidden there. More secret life? How could there possibly be more?

The letters were still there too. She grabbed them, turned, and slid down the wall on her back. She cradled them in her lap and counted. All sixteen missives.

Fierce tears burned her eyes. They weren't important to a police investigation, but they were important to her. She swallowed. *Suck it up, Fischer.* A variation on her Dad's theme.

The top letter on the stack had a Tampa postmark over the stamp. It was mailed six years after she and Jan came to San Antonio. No return address, of course. With shaking fingers, she pulled the letter from the yellowed envelope. A photo slid out with it. Jan and her in wet shorts and T-shirts standing on a beach, the ocean behind them. Neither of them was smiling. They both held up small seashells.

Liz's crabbed writing covered a single page from a Chief notebook with its green lines. The ink was purple and faded.

I don't know if you'll ever see this. I understand if your uncle Geoff doesn't want you to read it. But you're fifteen and fourteen now. Old enough to make your own decisions. He should let you decide if you want to read my letters and write me back.

I have good news. At least I think it's good. I'm pregnant. You'll have another little sister or brother. Pretty cool, right? I already stopped drinking and smoking. Well, I'm down to two cigs a day. Not bad for me, right?

I didn't drink or smoke when I was pregnant with you either. I'm not that stupid.

I want you to come back to Florida and live with me.

Your uncle Geoff doesn't agree, I know.

I could come to San Antonio. He could see how good I'm doing.

We could go to the zoo. Are you too old for the zoo? We could do that laser quest thing. Or go to Fiesta, Texas. Whatever you want to do.

You can convince Geoff. I bet you girls wrap him around your little fingers.

You both loved Florida. You loved the beach. Nina, I remember how you spent all your time collecting seashells and building fancy sand castles. You hardly ever got in the water. The big waves scared you. Not you, Jannie. You were fearless. I had to drag you out of the water.

You both cried because you wanted to keep the seashells and I wouldn't let you. You each had to pick one. We didn't have room for a bag of shells in the car.

We could go to the beach again. You can collect all the shells you want and keep them all. I promise.

Let me come get you. It'll be great. It'll be different. I'll be different. I promise.

I love you.

She signed her name with a big heart over the *i*.

They had gone to the beach once. With a man named Duane. He smelled like burnt car oil.

They couldn't keep the seashells because they were living in a Datsun.

She had a thirteen-year-old brother or sister. What kind of life was Liz giving him or her?

Had Dad known? How could he not tell her and Jan? How could he not let them meet their sibling?

Because he knew what Nina knew.

It'll be different. I'll be different. I promise.

Love, Mommie.

Liz's promises were worth about as much as a VHS tape.

Nina folded the letter. She stuck it back in the envelope. She scrambled to her feet and went into the back room where she slept. A varnished box covered with red, pink, and yellow roses sat on the dresser. A gift from Grace the day she moved into the house. A keepsake box, Grace had said, for good memories.

Nina tipped the lid up and removed the seashell. She'd picked it despite broken, rough edges because it was hollow. She imagined hearing the ocean waves when she held it to her ear. It lulled her on dark nights full of boogeymen who were not figments of a little girl's imagination.

A long, long time ago. That scared little girl didn't exist anymore. Nina laid the shell in the box and added the photo to her small stash.

The other letters would have to wait. One at a time. Beautiful but toxic. Like life itself.

Her phone vibrated from the depths of her back pocket. An unknown number. She flopped back on the Lone Star quilt pieced by Pearl years ago and stared at the wooden beams. On the third ring she answered.

Strains of music. Crackling. Familiar. "Hello?"

Nina Simone's voice, husky, melodic, a symphony of instruments from a single source, filled her ear. "Who is this?"

The words of "To Love Somebody" wafted from the phone.

She never listened to Nina Simone, if only because the singer was her mother's favorite. She preferred Janis Joplin's rendition. "Liz?"

The music faded. The song ended.

So did the call.

"Mommie?"

Dead air.

24

His death might have left a sea of unanswered questions, but Nina's dad had left no detail unaddressed regarding how he wanted to be laid to rest. The sight of his body in a casket only days after finding it on the floor of his study seemed only slightly more surreal than being a murder suspect in his death.

The release of his body had propelled Grace into a frenzy of activity that alternated with bouts of unrestrained crying. Nina's duties had been to plan and carry out all tasks related to the reception. A daunting task, given the number of people expected to attend. Grace wanted a harp player, a smorgasbord of her husband's favorite beverages, servers, extra tables and chairs. A montage of photos representing his life—most of the later ones taken by Nina.

Not an hour to slip away to the bank to reveal the contents of the safe-deposit box. Not a minute to grieve in private. Not a second to envision a future without her father. Only the time spent mounting the display of photos had given her an opportunity to reflect on his life and the hole his death left in hers.

Teeth gritted, determined to hold back tears, Nina stood at the pulpit at the First Presbyterian Church and stared out on the mourners who filled the pews on a sunny Friday morning. The fierce urge to hold her camera surged through her. She'd been forbidden to take photos at her own father's funeral. People looked so noble in moments such as these, the darkest times in their lives. She wasn't allowed to step behind a camera lens to separate herself from their anguish.

Nina stared at the paper in front of her. Her hands shook as she smoothed the wrinkled pages of the eulogy. Even knowing Nina's horror at public speaking, Grace had insisted Nina deliver her father's eulogy. "You're a poet," she said, "and what is a eulogy, but a poem written to memorialize someone you love?"

Dad's desires for his funeral had been clear. None of that calling people up to tell their funny little stories, little anecdotes from his life. A dignified affair with the appropriate music. "In the Garden" and "How Great Thou Art" sung by a member of the church choir.

And a proper eulogy. Not poetry. Nina tucked in a piece of hair that kept falling out of her bun and cleared her throat. Could they see the bruises and cuts on her face? Jan had tried to cover them with makeup, but they were there, right next to the cuts and bruises on her heart.

People began to wiggle in their seats. Someone coughed. Ladies used memoriam booklets to fan their warm faces. *Breathe. Just breathe.* "Geoffrey Fischer was a hardworking man dedicated to the law and to his family." The words blurred. She swallowed and fixed her gaze on Brooklyn for a second. Her niece held a stuffed giraffe her grandfather had given her when Will deployed the last time. Another animal for her collection, he said.

"He was a man. He wasn't perfect. None of us are. But Geoffrey Fischer did his best. He rescued my sister and me from a horrible situation and welcomed us into his home. He didn't just adopt us. He was the only father I've ever known. Jan and I were the only daughters he had. He didn't just put food on the table and clothes on our backs. He didn't just pay for our educations, proms, and vacations. He protected us, he chided us, he pushed us to do better and be better people.

"Sometimes we disappointed him. And he let us know it. Because he cared. That's the bottom line. Whatever he did, he did because he cared. That's why he spent more than twenty years as a district court judge—because he considered it his duty. Some might choose to remember his failings. I choose to remember his love. I forgive his shortcomings, just as he forgave mine. He never gave up on me or his desire for me to do well. Because he loved me. And I loved him."

She stepped down from the lectern and found her way to her seat despite tears that made the steps impossible to see. Grace folded her into a hug.

One more song. One more benediction.

Finally, it was over.

Grace tucked her hand under Nina's arm and wiped her face with a dainty embroidered hankie that was an incongruous, brilliant white against a black flowing dress that reached midcalf.

The sound of Brooklyn's bewildered sobs followed them. Nina slowed and took the little girl's free hand. Jan held the other. Together they made their way down the aisle. Geoffrey Fischer's girls. Followed by Trevor, looking lost in an ill-fitting suit.

Two rows back Nina's gaze locked with Rick's. His sculpted face morose, he sat next to Peter Coggins and several other members of the firm. He'd attempted to sit with her in the family pew, but the look on her face led him to seek another spot without a word. Appearing contrite, he raised one hand and waved. Her heart refused to stay hardened over his behavior in his car. She waved back with two discreet fingers. He nodded and mouthed, *See you later.*

She didn't answer because her heart might have softened, but it was not quite the naive idiot it had once been.

Aaron was outside with his camera locked down on a tripod. His single text the previous evening had said he drew the short straw. That and he would not be attending the reception because he planned to fly to San Diego to attend Melanie's funeral, scheduled for Saturday morning. His usual evening and morning texts had been missing. Nothing since their phone conversation in Rick's car. It wasn't like him. When she walked by into the church, he hadn't met her gaze. Separating personal and professional?

Serena Cochrane would be buried in her hometown of Port Arthur on Monday. Aaron had been excused from covering that funeral in order to make the trip to California.

It was an unsettling time for everyone. Three people whose lives had been cut short in dramatic, unpoetic ways. Three different funerals reflecting how disparate those lives had been.

Nina heaved a breath and took another look around as they plodded down the aisle. The wooden pews with cushy red pillows for seats were packed in the cavernous sanctuary. Dad's colleagues from the judiciary and law enforcement had turned out en masse. Judges from the district courts, court reporters, bailiffs, and attorneys sat by county commissioners and city council members. How much was respect and how much curiosity remained a mystery. Still, Dad would be pleased with the turnout.

Except for Detective Matt King, who sat fourth row from the back. His brown hair was slicked back. His blue suit stood at attention, not daring to wrinkle at a funeral. His expression inscrutable, he nodded as she passed.

Checking out the crowd for suspects? Watching her every move? Reminding her she was still a suspect in at least two murders?

Grace gasped and stumbled. Her grip tightened on Nina's upper arm.

"Hang in there. We're almost done here," Nina whispered as she put her arm around the other woman's waist and leaned close. "You can rest on the drive to the burial ground."

Dad would be buried in a private ceremony next to his parents in the historic San Jose Burial Grounds south of downtown. Not much time to recover, but a little, for them all before the reception started.

"I can't believe she's here." Grace's face turned white despite a layer of peach foundation already marred by tears. "After all these years."

Nina surveyed the crowd to her right. Dozens of people she didn't recognize stood, respectful, waiting for the procession to pass. Her gaze zipped down the back row. Then back again, more slowly. A woman with a half smile out of place in this moment of shared misery stared back at her. The pale-blue eyes were familiar. They were the ones Nina saw in the mirror every time she brushed her teeth. Despite wrinkles and sun damage, the woman still resembled Nina with her high cheekbones and long chin. The blonde hair streaked with gray like unintentional highlights had been cut in a page boy meant for a younger woman.

The woman moved. She squeezed past the couple standing between her and the aisle.

Dragging Grace with her, Nina picked up her pace. She had nowhere to go. The pallbearers minced along, carrying Dad to his last resting place with all the dignity due to a judge and pillar of the community.

Jan's startled cry marked the moment she realized who the woman was.

Sun burst through robust clouds just as Nina and Grace started down the long steps in front of the church.

"Nina. Jannie."

No one called Jan Jannie. Not anymore.

"We have to stop. We have to talk to her." Grace tugged her arm free. She craned her head and looked back. "Lizzie?"

"Not here. Not now." Nina grabbed her arm again. "This isn't the place." She swept them toward the waiting black limousine.

"Gracie, please." Her biological mother had acquired a southern accent. South of Dallas maybe. Or Louisiana. "Just stop for one second."

"She's your dad's only sister." Grace pulled free and halted. "She's your mother."

"You're my mother."

Liz Fischer grabbed Grace and pulled her into a hug. "I'm so sorry for your loss, Gracie."

"When did you get here? How did you know?"

"Just got here. Saw it on Facebook." Her voice quivered. She drew back and turned to Nina. "Baby, you're a beautiful woman."

"Don't *baby* me." Nina's arms argued with her heart. Hug or no hug? Her arms refused to move. Her heart did handstands. Her brain might explode. "Where have you been? Doing what? Not getting in touch with your family? Then you saw a post on Facebook and decided Dad's funeral would be the best time to talk?"

"You call him Dad. That's so sweet." Liz—she was Liz now, not Mom or Mommy or anything in the vicinity of parent—crept closer. "Do you call Gracie Mom?"

"Not here and not now." Nina made a show of looking over Liz's shoulder. "You didn't bring our brother? Or is it a sister?"

"I know you hate me." Liz smiled. Her teeth were yellowed from tobacco and coffee. How could she smile at a time like this? "But I wrote you. I tried to stay in touch. You know that. Geoff was the one—"

"Just stop." Nina didn't hate her. She'd read the letters. She knew the story. She knew her mother just as if she'd spent the last eighteen years following her around from one bad motel to the next dingy apartment with no AC, roaches, and water that came from the kitchen sink, cloudy and full of sediment. "Not here."

"Is this my granddaughter?"

She leaned down and patted Brooklyn's face. "She looks just like you, Jannie, when you were little."

"Get in the limo, Brooklyn." Jan nudged Brooklyn forward. Her sniper-Army-sergeant voice was in full force. "We need to get going."

"I need to talk to you." Liz grabbed the open door and held on. "We need to talk."

"Not here." Nina tugged the door from her grasp. "You know where we live."

They piled into the funeral-home limo.

Her pixie face white and stained with tears, Brooklyn snuggled against Jan in the deep, cushioned leather seat across from Nina. "Who was that, Mommy?"

Jan put her arm around her daughter. "Just someone Aunt Nina and I used to know."

"She smelled funny. Like dirty clothes." Brooklyn wrinkled her nose. "And cigarettes."

Unable to turn away, like a spectator at a train wreck, Nina stared through the tinted window. Liz turned and melted into the throng of people milling about on the sidewalk. King approached her. Their conversation appeared animated. As the limo pulled from the curb, Nina leaned forward. The two turned and walked toward the parking lot. Liz's hands moved. Tie her hands and she wouldn't be able to speak.

She would be forty-five now. She looked sixty. Even though she was thin to the point of emaciation, she walked in that ponderous way old women had when their hips hurt. She probably told people she knew when it would rain because her sciatica flared up.

What were they talking about?

It didn't matter. Liz didn't live in the house. She knew nothing about any of the murders. King could milk her for information all he wanted.

Liz couldn't tell King anything because she wasn't family anymore. She hadn't been for a long time.

*   *   *

Funerals were the worst. Aaron had once arrived at an accident scene where a little old lady lay in the middle of the street. Her knitting needles and red yarn had catapulted into the neighbor's yard after she was hit coming home from Wednesday night Bible study by a teenager on his way home after a date. He once shot a story about twenty abused, emaciated, sore-covered horses. He'd shot video of a body stabbed sixty-eight times. Another time he arrived at the scene of a head-on highway collision before the first responders. Two children lay dying yards apart on the asphalt. He had to decide which one to comfort. Fortunately, others stopped as well.

Still, funerals were worse. The public display of agony wrapped up in a neat package for all those vicarious ghouls watching the six o'clock news.

Add to the torture that this involved Nina, and it was excruciating. Watching her suffer. Knowing how much she hated public speaking. They shared that phobia. His hands sweat just thinking about it as he slipped into the area at the back of the church reserved for the media. Her voice had been steady and clear.

He was proud of her—at least he would be if he weren't busy extricating himself from her life.

Time to back away, to get back to the station. Time not to think about that lip-lock between Nina and Rick. He'd driven up to the house just in time to see them in the front seat of Rick's car.

Just in time to drive away.

Nina didn't need him. She had Rick. She'd always had Rick.

How long could Aaron go on knocking his head against this particular brick wall?

He unclipped the camera from the tripod, rested it on one shoulder, and picked up the tripod. The burial was private. His work here was done, if Kelly Moran would stop schmoozing with the mayor and get her rear in the vehicle.

Too many of the mourners in the crowd were there to see and be seen, but at least it was over. Geoffrey Fischer wasn't who he said he was. Neither was Rick Zavala. He was using Nina. Another man who deceived and lied.

Aaron would never lie to her.

Yet she kept choosing Rick over and over again.

Detective King exited the church at that moment, right behind Councilman Leon Murphy and County Commissioner Joe Beltran. The detective didn't seem happy. He ducked between two court reporters and touched the arm of a skinny, gray-haired woman dressed in wrinkled, faded black pants and a black short-sleeved blouse, who had stopped to light a cigarette.

She turned. The woman in Nina's Christmas picture faced King. Older, gray, wrinkles around the eyes and mouth, a lot of sun damage, but still the same skinny, tanned woman with pale-blue eyes. Once she and Nina had looked alike. Now the mother looked old beyond her years.

Whatever King said, Liz Fischer didn't seem happy to hear it. Aaron squeezed past his buddies from Channels 4 and 5. He started rolling. King had his back to Aaron. Liz shook her head. King said something, and she shook her head more vehemently now. They walked down the steps and headed across the street, still talking.

It would be obvious if Aaron headed after them. He stopped at the corner, camera still hot. A man in a black sweatshirt followed King a few yards behind. Maybe he was headed to the bus stop at the park.

King looked back. The man turned and cut diagonally across the park. King motioned to Liz. They sat on a park bench usually reserved for homeless folks waiting for the Travis Park United Methodist Church's soup kitchen to open.

Sweatshirt man circled back around. He leaned against a massive heritage pecan tree, head down, arms crossed over his chest as if he were taking a nap.

"What are you doing?"

Aaron jumped three feet. He turned. Kelly laughed. "Sneaking around much?"

"It's broad daylight. I'm spying on Detective King." He saw no need to tell the reporter King was interviewing Nina's biological mother. "You got everything you need for the package?"

"Who is he talking to?"

"A family member."

"Which one?"

She was a reporter. Not as good as Melanie. "Her name is Liz Fischer. She's the judge's sister."

Liz threw her cigarette on the ground and stubbed it out with her black pump. King stood and shook her hand. Even at a distance it was easy to see the discussion had not gone well.

King headed directly at Aaron and Kelly.

"You ready to go?"

"I think it's too late for that."

King halted between Aaron and his illegally parked station unit. The detective's hands rested on his hips. Inches from his service weapon. "Are you spying on me?"

Seriously? "It's a public event and a public park. I was just waiting for Kelly so we can go back and put our package together."

"Were you filming the whole time?"

"Dude, no one films anymore."

"You know what I mean." King's frown deepened. "Did you shoot my interview with Liz Fischer?"

"I was just getting a weather shot for the five o'clock forecast."

"Was the guy in the black hoodie in your weather shot?"

Aaron handed his tripod to Kelly, who took it without complaint. "You saw him too?"

"Yeah, I saw him and I want that video."

"You sure want a lot of our video lately." Aaron hit the Record button again. "Maybe in return, you'll give us an update on the investigation into the murders of Melanie Martinez, Serena Cochrane, and Geoffrey Fischer. Have you made any progress at all?"

"If you cooperate now, maybe I won't haul your butt over to PSHQ for another interview regarding your presence at a murder scene." King didn't look the least bit hot and bothered. "Maybe I won't get a warrant to search your apartment."

Aaron sighed loudly, just for show. He wanted the mystery of these deaths solved as much as King. Maybe more. So Nina could move on with her life. And so could he. "I'll put the video in Dropbox for you when I get back to the station."

"I'd appreciate that."

"Who do you think he is?"

"I don't know, but I plan to find out."

King's expression said hoodie man would not find their first encounter pleasant.

25

The roar of the industrial-size dishwasher helped Nina block out the questions that whirled around in her mind. Around and around. She concentrated on wiping down the counters. The final meal of the day had been served at Haven for Hope. The San Antonio Food Bank served more than one thousand meals a day, seven days a week, to homeless folks receiving services from Haven for Hope. All the servers for breakfast, lunch, and dinner each day were volunteers. Simple meals when compared to the fancy china serving dishes filled with New York strip steak, baked potatoes, green beans, Caesar salad, and four kinds of dessert cake served at her father's funeral reception.

Her family had pronounced her crazy for refusing to miss her turn serving food on the day of her father's funeral and the reception afterward. She needed this. Not volunteering meant the killer took yet another piece of her life and threw it in the trash. It had been almost five o'clock before she could slip away from her mother's side. Grace was a wreck. She needed her daughters. Once she lay down to rest, Nina had slipped out. Too late to get to the bank. Now it was closed until Monday. Aaron was gone. Who knew what Detective King was up to.

She rinsed the washcloth and started on the stove tops. Monday she would go to the reading of the will and from there to the bank. If only Aaron would go with her. He'd promised to help her solve this. Instead, he seemed to be avoiding her. At the funeral, he'd been working. She understood that, trying to separate work and personal feelings. It couldn't have been easy. Maybe it had been too much for him. Melanie's death, Serena's death. Maybe he needed space too. She would give him until tomorrow. If texting didn't work, she'd track him down.

She would offer him comfort.

She inhaled the lingering scent of baking chicken thighs marinated in barbecue sauce and tried to piece the events together. Could Serena's death have been an accident followed by a scared driver making a run for it? Could Melanie's murder have been the result of a home invasion in which the burglar had been caught in the act and fled before he could steal anything?

Coincidental? Ridiculous. They had to be related.

"All the trays are washed and put up." Deb Washington, another longtime volunteer, sang out as she chugged by with a huge bag of paper napkins. "I restocked the shelves."

She settled the bag on the shelf next to a box of salt and pepper packets. "Hey, I wanted to say how sorry I am about your father." Deb slung her beaded braids over her shoulder and smiled. She wore red lipstick even when she volunteered. "It was awful. My whole church has been praying for your family."

"Thank you. I appreciate that."

"Have the police found the killer?"

"No—"

"Nina Fischer." The volunteer coordinator from the front office marched through the double doors to the kitchen, Liz right behind her. "You have a visitor. A very insistent visitor."

Visitors weren't generally allowed, and they couldn't access the grounds unescorted.

"What are you doing here?" The same question as before. Only more so. Liz had failed to materialize at the reception. No surprise.

She'd always liked to pick and choose when to show up. She could be counted on to pick the least opportune moment. "You shouldn't be back here."

The volunteer coordinator gave Nina a pained smile. "She wouldn't take no for answer."

"I'm her mother." Liz directed that outrageous statement to Deb. "Pleased to meet you."

"I'm so sorry. I'll escort her out when I leave."

The coordinator nodded, but her backward glance at Liz was anything but friendly.

"Do you mind if I step out for a minute?" Nina shot Deb an apologetic look. "I promise not to leave you holding the bag with all these cucumbers."

"No worries. Go, go." Debbie made shooing motions with her voluminous apron. "I'll keep an eye on the chicken."

Nina nudged Liz from the serving area and across the long room filled with orange-topped tables with attached benches. She didn't stop until they reached the commons area with its half-grown trees that did their best to shade picnic tables a stone's throw from the chapel.

She took a seat and motioned for Liz to sit across from her. "How did you find me this time?"

"I went home. Pearl told me. She wasn't happy about it. She wouldn't let me in. She said everyone else was napping. I told her I'd sit on the steps and wait for you if she didn't tell me where you were."

Home. Sometimes Nina forgot her biological mother once had lived in the Fischer house. "Why?"

"You're my daughter. I came back to San Antonio because I missed you and Jannie. I want to see you. And Brooklyn too."

"Missed us? After eighteen years, you suddenly missed us? Weren't you busy raising my half sister or brother? He or she must be about thirteen now."

"Hudson is thirteen. Emma is ten."

"Hudson. Emma." Dizziness swept over Nina. Accompanied by a strange sense of the surreal. Her mother had replaced Nina and Jan with new kids. New kids who had no uncle to swoop down and save them. How had they survived? Were they surviving? "Where are they?"

"Hudson took Emma to the library. She likes the library. And it's free." She shrugged as if her daughter's fondness for the library was a mystery to her. "I know you don't understand—"

"Of course I don't understand. You kept having kids, even though you couldn't take care of the ones you had."

"It's not like I planned it that way. Besides, I think I've done a decent job with these two."

"Did Dad know there were two more?"

"Yes. He said he wasn't going to take them. Which was rich, because I never offered them to him."

"Offered them? I guess you never abandoned them in the middle of a tent city filled with strangers, many of whom live on the street because they have untreated mental illnesses. Some suffer from psychotic breaks. Some, like people who live *in* houses, are simply mean."

"I meant to come back for you and Jannie. I did come back, but you were already gone."

"You meant to come back? Mom, I was nine years old. Jan was seven."

"You think I don't understand what I did to you? I was messed up. You know I was."

"The adult me knows that. But the little girl me was terrified, hungry, and afraid to close her eyes at night."

Nina refused to unearth old memories with Liz. A few people had been kind. Annie let them Dumpster-dive for food with her and gave Jan the least rotten pieces of fruit found in the bin behind the grocery store. Keith, an Iraq war vet with a prosthesis on one arm, let them sleep

in his tent a few nights while he kept watch. Tippy showed them how to
sneak into the YMCA locker room to take showers. Good times.

"I know it was hard."

Liz pulled a cigarette pack from her faded denim shirt pocket. The
sound of the cellophane crumpling and the smell of phosphorus when
she struck the match sent Nina down another memory lane. She'd
opened her eyes one morning to see snake tattoos slithering up both
arms of a man slumped in a chair next to the motel room bed where she
and Jan slept. He wore a black T-shirt and faded jean shorts. His legs
were covered with black hair. He smiled at her, stubbed out the cigarette,
and smoothed her hair. He smelled like beer. "Morning, sunshine."

She'd never seen him before in her life. Liz was nowhere in sight.

"Hard?"

Liz sucked a long draw on her cigarette and let the smoke escape
through her nose. She flipped the matchbook through her fingers like
a card shark doing a trick. "I'm here now. I'm asking you to forgive
me. Isn't that what Christians do?"

They did. Another of Nina's failings. The inability to forgive.

Nina's heart beat in her ears. Her pulse pounded. Yes, she wanted
to forgive. Her mother. And her father. Was she capable of forgiving?
Dad had been partially to blame for their long separation. Her mother
had tried, albeit not very hard, to contact them. She'd given up after
her letters went unanswered. Did that mean Nina had to welcome
this virtual stranger back into her life?

She tugged her Leica from her bag and slid the strap over her
head. "Why didn't you come to the reception? You could've talked to
everyone then."

And no one would've made a scene.

"I was . . . I didn't feel good." Liz tilted her head and smiled,
suddenly flirtatious. Her teeth were stained with coffee and tobacco.
The sun backlit her face, giving her an ethereal look. She was skin and

bones. She looked like a biker babe without the Harley and the biker. "That's right. You're a photographer."

The camera had its usual medicinal effect. It created a fortress wall between Nina and a painful past. The crashing waves in her ears receded. "What were you talking to Detective King about after the funeral? I saw you as we were driving away."

Liz pursed her lips and formed perfect smoke rings, a technique she'd perfected years ago to the delight of two little girls who didn't know better. "King? Oh, King the cop. He knew who I was. The guy had done his homework. I guess he recognized me from . . . you know, a mug shot."

From one of the many arrests for public intoxication, panhandling, trespassing, pot possession, or fighting. Nina focused and snapped shot after shot. The commons created a soft, peaceful backdrop to the hard lines around her mother's mouth and the crow's feet around her eyes. Her denim shirt was a size too big and missing the top button so her wrinkled cleavage was displayed. She wore green Army pants and black tattered Converse sneakers. Living from the Salvation Army store or a church homeless closet/pantry.

"He wanted to know when I'd last seen Geoffrey. He wanted to know where I'm staying. Why I came back to town. If I knew some reporter named Melanie something. And if I knew Serena, which of course I did, although I barely remember her."

"Where are you staying?"

"With a friend."

She still had friends in San Antonio? More likely another seedy motel room. How did she feed this half brother and half sister? Where were their fathers? Same father or different fathers? A person had to have an address to get food stamps. "The church down on the access road gave me some vouchers. I have some money from a waitressing gig back in Baton Rouge."

As if she read minds.

"What were you doing in Baton Rouge?"

"Earning money to get here."

"Did King ask you about me?"

"Sure. Did I know what a pain you are? To which I said, if you're anything like me, I would imagine so."

"But you wouldn't know because you abandoned me years ago."

"I did one good thing. I asked Geoffrey to adopt you and Sissy."

One good thing. It had been one good thing. And it had been her idea and not Dad's. The letters proved that. "Did you ever get married?"

"What is this? Twenty questions?"

"I just want to know something about my biological mother."

"Biological mother. That's what adopted kids call them."

"Yes, it is."

Liz snorted. She stubbed out the cigarette on the bench and lit another one. She took her time as if concocting an answer. "No. I wasn't into that. I don't need to be tied down by some jerk who tells me what to do and wants dinner on the table by six. Most men are jerks in my experience."

She never expected better so she never received it. A wave of sadness enveloped Nina. Liz wasn't just her biological mother. She was also a woman—a depleted, sad, disappointed woman who'd never loved with abandon, never been truly loved.

Trying to hold back tears, Nina chewed her lower lip. She and Jan had pinky sworn that they would never be like their mother. Never drink. Never abandon their children. While Jan had conceived a child out of wedlock, she had loved and cherished that child and married her father. She'd asked for forgiveness and received it.

Nina had feared being burned by love. Being so afraid of love, she might never have it. The failure to trust in love. She would not be her mother. She would learn to trust and learn to love. All-in, all-cards-on-the-table love.

Aaron's kind of love. God's kind of love.

She swallowed against the lump in her throat. Was it as simple as that? Aaron claimed it was.

God?

Would He understand the entreaty when she called His name?

Aaron claimed prayers didn't have to be elaborate. He said God understood her pain.

He loved her despite her flaws.

Good thing, because her doubt was at the top of the list.

"Earth to Nina!" Liz waved her cigarette in Nina's face. "Where'd you go? Am I boring you?"

"No. Nowhere." Forgiveness started with Liz. At least an effort at forgiveness. Feelings of abandonment stored up for eighteen years couldn't be erased in a day. She could try. Maybe God would give her an E for effort. Liz's letters represented her best effort at love. She wasn't responsible for Dad's unwillingness to hand the letters over to Nina and Jan that proved their mother had been willing to try again. They would put their cards on the table and start over. "Did you know Dad never gave us your letters?"

"I figured as much. We agreed that no contact would be best, but I couldn't help myself. I thought of you and Sissy every day. Every single day."

"He kept them. I found them and read them after he died."

"Which means you know I never stopped loving you. I did the hardest thing a mother can do. I gave you up to someone who could do right by you."

"You make it sound so noble now. You wanted to have your life without feeling guilty about it." Her stomach suddenly rocking, Nina waved away the stench of tobacco. "You chose alcohol and pot and men over your children. There's nothing noble about that."

"You have no idea what I've been doing since Geoffrey brought you here."

"Whose fault is that?"

"His."

"Seriously. You're trying to blame him for your failings as a parent. He raised us. He loved us. He gave us a roof over our heads and food and clothing. He paid for my college education and made sure I went."

"He was a saint, I know." For the first time, Liz's words had an edge. She stubbed out the cigarette smoked down to the filter and lit yet another one. Her hands shook. "I lived with Saint Geoffrey for a lot of years. Mister bachelor's degree in three years, Harvard Law, Mister Do-No-Wrong. You never knew our father and mother."

Grandma and Grandpa Fischer died in a car accident in New York City the year before Dad adopted Nina and Jan. Grace's parents were divorced. Her mother died of breast cancer, her father of prostate cancer on opposite coasts.

"I know Dad loved them and missed them."

"Of course he did. They worshipped the ground their son walked on." She coughed, the loose hack of a longtime smoker, swiveled, and spit in the grass. "I can tell you this about them. When I got knocked up with you, they didn't get all huggy and kissy like Grace and Geoffrey did with Jannie."

Nina swallowed against nausea. "There was no huggy kissy—"

"They wanted me to give you up for adoption then. I said no. I wanted you. They kicked me to the curb with the clothes on my back. I was eighteen. I had enough money for a bus ticket to Tampa."

"Dad said you got kicked out after they caught you drinking in the cellar and smoking pot after they'd just paid for rehab."

"It was all part of the same." Her tone turned defensive. "I didn't drink or smoke while I was pregnant with you, if that's what you're thinking."

The one thing that kept her from vices. "Why Tampa?"

"I thought your daddy was there."

Nina wouldn't call this man whom she never knew *Dad*. That was reserved for Geoffrey Fischer, whatever his failings might have been. "Who was he?"

"A guy I knew. Just a kid from my class. He and a friend drove his Camaro to Florida right after graduation. They thought they could get jobs there."

"Did you find him?"

"Sure. Shacked up with a waitress he met at a club."

No superhero.

"What about Jan? Who was her biological father?"

"You want the truth?" Liz's gaze dropped to the table for a second. She looked up, her blue eyes brilliant and hard as stone. "I have no idea. Men came and went in those days."

Nina put her hand to her mouth. She swallowed bitter bile in the back of her throat. *Inhale, exhale.* She let her hand drop. "Why did you come back here?"

"I told you. To ask for your forgiveness." Liz motioned with one finger with its nail chewed down to a painful nub. "Let me take your photo."

Nina glanced at her phone. Almost time to serve dinner. "I have to go." She stood. "Do me a favor. Don't ever tell Jan what you just told me."

"My lips are sealed." Liz pulled her fingers across her thin lips, turned them, and tossed away the imaginary key. "It's not like it's something I'm proud of."

She grunted, stood, and smashed the cigarette butt with her ragged tennis shoe. "I'd like to come to the house tonight. I want to see Jannie before she heads back to Afghanistan."

"I'll give you a tip." Nina forced herself to soften her voice. "Call first. Make sure she's there and she wants to see you."

"I haven't had a drink in three months." Liz dug around in a coffee-stained canvas bag. "I got my chip in here to prove it."

A step in the right direction on a long road to redemption.

"I have to get back to the kitchen."

"I wondered if you could spot me a twenty for the bus and some groceries for the kids."

She wanted money. Of course. Twenty bucks would be an eighteen pack or a couple of bottles of cheap wine. Nina worked to keep her expression neutral. "My shift will be over in half an hour. Wait and I'll give you a ride. I'd like to meet my half brother and half sister."

"Sure, sure." Liz slumped on the picnic bench. "I got nothing better to do than sit around and wait while you feed a bunch of bums and hoboes."

"It's your call." People who were homeless like Liz had once been. "If you're not going to wait, tell me. I'll escort you to the gate. Or you can come with me and sit at one of the tables until I get done with serving."

"I can't smoke in there. I'd rather sit here in the sun." She sounded like a child who'd missed her nap. "Besides, I've done my time hanging around the down-and-out."

So had Nina. Enough to feel nothing but compassion for people who were trying to dig themselves out of deep holes. "Don't go anywhere. Stay put. Do you understand?"

"I'm not a kid."

When she returned thirty minutes later, Liz was gone. Nothing left behind but cigarette butts.

26

The seventh-floor law offices of Gomez, Gomez, Barkley, and Benavides featured a conference room with an impossibly large mahogany table with at least two dozen leather chairs, each tucked in at the exact same angle. Nina shivered. The AC blasted from overhead vents. Glad for the warmth of the mug of coffee Tamera Gomez had offered her, Nina sipped the dark brew and tried to ignore her empty stomach's protest. Floor-to-ceiling windows offered a spectacular view of downtown San Antonio's Riverwalk. In the distance stood the Tower of the Americas and the Alamodome framed against low-lying gray clouds.

Pulling her cardigan closer, she glanced at her phone for the fortieth time. Not a single return text or call from Aaron. He should've returned from San Diego yesterday. He usually worked Mondays. Why the silent treatment? It had been a long weekend without him. Two days of waiting and wondering what the week would bring. What was King doing? Where was Rick, also missing in action?

"You left the TV on again last night." Grace had chosen a black tea-length dress for the occasion with lacy black gloves and a black box hat. Very Jackie Kennedy. She sipped her espresso with a dainty slurp. "I heard you snoring on the couch and covered you up with a blanket. A Spencer Tracy/ Katharine Hepburn movie was on: *Guess Who's Coming to Dinner?* I love Sidney Poitier. I love that movie."

228

Unable to sleep in her own bed, Nina had camped out both nights in the living room, watching old movies and retracing the events of the previous week over and over again. Both mornings, she'd awakened to the sun doing its best to seep through clouds outside the bay window, a crick in her neck, and Peanuts sleeping on her bare feet. Dreamless sleep. Sleep so deep and dark could only result in a grogginess that three cups of coffee couldn't shake. "Me too. I couldn't sleep."

"Me neither. I keep thinking your father will come through the door. Or call me." Dark circles around her eyes gave Grace a hollow look. "It's hard to know what to do next, so I seem to do nothing. I have a book deadline, but I don't seem to be able to focus on anything."

Nina squeezed her hand. "Your editor will understand."

Jan glanced up from her phone. "Brooklyn is texting me her wish list for her birthday. It's still two months away." And Jan would not be here when it happened. "She wants a real stethoscope and microscope. The kid is bizarre."

"Forward her text to me—"

The door banged open and Trevor stormed in. "You started without me?"

"We did not. Where have you been?" Grace frowned. Her muted pink lipstick stained her upper teeth. "You left after the reception and didn't come back."

"The police picked me up Friday after the reception and kept me in an interview room half the night." Coffee stained the sleeve of his wrinkled white shirt. His khaki pants were a shade too long. They bunched up over his brown leather loafers. Trevor's eyes were bloodshot and he needed to blow his nose. "King is ridiculous. He insisted I had a reason to shoot Dad. Like Vicky is a reason to shoot my own father."

"Who is Vicky?"

"My . . . a friend."

"Girlfriend." Jan did her best redneck impression, drawing the word out in several syllables. "Tattoos and all."

"Shut up. She's an artist. She does body art. She has a master's in Eastern religions."

"That was two days ago—"

"Could I have your attention?" A sheaf of paper in her hands, Tamera Gomez stopped at the head of the mahogany table. She looked like a model for a shampoo ad. Every shiny black hair on her head knew its place. Her tawny complexion wouldn't dare to have a flaw. Her blue pinstripe suit shouted professional. When she'd met them at the front door and escorted them to the conference room, she'd been cool enough to ignore the cuts and bruises on Nina's face. "My father apologizes for not being able to be with us today. His health hasn't been good—"

"Send him our best." Grace interrupted. "He was always such a dear. I'm sure you'll do fine, sweetheart."

Tamera laid the sheets of paper in front of her and slid into the luxuriously soft leather chair. She adjusted glasses with large tortoiseshell rims and red temples and pulled at a gold knot earring. "I have before me the last will and testament of Geoffrey Samuel Fischer. It was signed with witnesses attesting to its validity, dated, and notarized on said date and placed in the care of attorney Fidel H. Gomez, whom Judge Fischer named as his executor." Tamera's voice hesitated over the date, then strengthened. "My father then filed the will with the Bexar County Clerk. Although it is not a requirement in Texas, he felt it would reduce any confusion over the legitimacy of this, his most recent will."

This will had been drawn up six weeks before Dad's death.

Grace's gasp stopped the flow of words.

"Are you all right, Mrs. Fischer?"

Her skin mottled red under a layer of pale-peach foundation,

Grace nodded. Nina slid her hand across the table and covered Grace's. "Are you sure? Do you want some water?"

The words had such ringing finality. It was hard for Nina to grasp. It must be so much harder for Grace, who'd been married to him for thirty-five years. "No. I'm fine. It's just that date. Are you sure that date is correct?"

Tamera perused the papers for a second. Her enormous brown eyes behind the glasses' thick lenses held compassion and a touch of something else. Pity? "The records show that this will was drawn up six weeks ago. It replaces an earlier will entered into the record in 2010."

Shortly after their argument and Grace's decision to divorce him.

Grace's soft sigh gave the young attorney permission to continue.

"It was Judge Fischer's wish that the will be read immediately or as soon as reasonably possible upon his passing. We will submit it to the probate court to be probated, as required by law. I won't read all the fine print, but rather go to that section of interest to his loved ones. That is, the bequeathals."

Again, her gaze made the rounds at the table. Nina did the same. Jan studied her fingernails. Trevor scowled. Grace picked at a tissue until it disintegrated in a heap of tiny pieces.

"To my wife, Grace Abigail Fischer, I leave our cabin in Puerto Vallarta, the time-share in Maui, the 2015 Mercedes, and all the artwork displayed in the house. An inventory is attached as a codicil."

Her forehead wrinkled, mouth drawn down in a perplexed frown, Grace shook her head. She turned to Nina. "I don't understand."

"Wait, let her finish." Nina squeezed her hand. "Let's hear it all, then we'll talk."

It didn't make sense. Texas was a community property state. Everything that belonged to Dad belonged to Grace.

"Judge Fischer knew you would have questions. He wanted to make it clear that these were his wishes and he asked that you abide by

them. He assured my father that you would understand and you would
do it. He mentioned you had your own income. He also reminded you
of the agreement that you signed when you married."

"That was thirty-five years ago, and it only pertained to the
house—"

"Grace." Nina rubbed her hand. "This is hard for everyone. Let's
just get through it, okay?"

Miserable. The divvying up of a man's life. Geoffrey had been
more than the sum of his stuff. He was a man, a human being. He
made mistakes. Terrible mistakes.

Her parents had a prenup. An unbelievable fact. It was unheard
of in that day and age, surely. And neither had been rich. Dad had
been a junior partner at a law firm. He inherited some money from
his parents, but not a fortune by any means. Why on earth would he
want a prenuptial?

Tamera put one manicured nail on the paper in front of her as if
finding her place. "To Trevor James Fischer, my only son, I leave my
2016 Prius, my book collection, my gun collection, my computers,
and seventy-five thousand dollars."

Trevor leaned forward. His skin turned bright red. His hand
slammed on the table. "That's it? That's all? The man had assets up
the wazoo and he left me a bunch of law books and guns he knows I
wouldn't touch with a ten-foot pole—"

"Mr. Fischer, please, if we could just get through this. I know you
have questions, but I'd like to get it all out on the table first."

Jan scooted her chair closer to Trevor and put her arm around
him. "Do you really want his money? You've made your own life. You
can be proud of that."

Jan was a smart woman.

Trevor subsided in his chair, but his breathing came in noisy
bursts. Grace started on another tissue.

"To my sister, Elizabeth Marie Fischer, I leave nothing."

No surprise there. Still a tiny pinprick stung a place close to Nina's heart. The if-onlys sang in her ears. If only they'd been allowed to answer those letters. If only he could forgive his sister for her weaknesses, her addiction, for running away. If only some of his wealth could've gone to rescuing his sister and making her whole again instead of feeding his own addiction.

If only he could recognize that he was no better than his sister.

Reconciliation. Maybe Nina could find her. Maybe.

"To my granddaughter, Brooklyn Grace Shelton, I leave a fund of three hundred thousand dollars to be held in trust for her college education. If she chooses not to attend college, the money shall be given to the San Antonio chapter of the American Society for the Prevention of Cruelty to Animals."

"He never gave up on trying to manage lives, did he?" Jan drank from the tall bottle of Dasani she'd brought with her. Tears rolled down her cheeks. She did nothing to stop them. "Brooklyn will go to college. She'll make him proud."

"To my daughters, Nina Simone Fischer and Janis Lyn Shelton, I leave the remainder of my estate, to include my family home and all my remaining assets, to be shared fifty-fifty with the proviso that one of them must live in the house at all times with my granddaughter. The house must be maintained in good standing in the King William District. Pearl Safire and Abel Martinez must continue in their employment as long as they are willing and able. In addition, Pearl and Abel each shall receive honorariums of five thousand dollars. These are my wishes, and I ask that you follow them down to the last letter. Failure to do so, and all assets will be sold, and the proceeds will go to the San Antonio chapter of the ASPCA, with the exception of the house, which would be deeded to the San Antonio Conservation Society to be maintained as a museum in perpetuity."

Trevor lurched. His chair flew back and hit the wall with a resounding *thwack*. He smacked the cup of coffee. Liquid spilled in all directions. "I can't believe he would be such a jerk to you and me, Mom." Spittle sprayed from his open mouth. "They aren't even really his kids. But they get it all. They get it *all*."

Knocking empty chairs left and right, he slammed from the room. Blessed silence followed.

Not really his kids. After all this time, her brother's true feelings were revealed. Not really his kids. A true statement that hurt more than broken bones. Their father had left them that which he valued most—his family home. Not to the son who would carry on not only his bloodline, but his name.

Trevor had a right to be angry, but the audaciousness of Geoffrey Fischer's generosity toward two little girls who'd grown up continued to astound Nina.

Or was it his way of apologizing for keeping something so monumental from them? He couldn't forgive his sister. He never gave her children a chance to do it.

Jan laid her head on the table and sobbed.

Grace rose and trotted to her. "It's okay, sweetie. He knew I had my own money. I didn't need his. He also knew I intended to leave him, to divorce him. To be honest I'm relieved."

"But surprised." Nina sucked in a breath. Her legs weren't working or she would go to Jan too. "You didn't know about this, did you?"

"No, but I never wanted the family mausoleum. The truth is, I already put a deposit down on a condo in New York City. I did it right after I discovered your father's deceit."

"New York."

"To be close to my agent and my publisher and to the world."

"Are there any questions?" Her expression unperturbed by these family admissions, Tamera removed her glasses and rubbed her eyes.

She looked about sixteen. "Anything I can do to help? When my father gets out of the hospital, he'll meet with you again to go through the details."

Grace shook her head. "Thank you for being so kind and for putting up with our histrionics."

"It's a difficult time. It always is." Tamera tapped a stack of papers against the table until they were perfectly aligned. "You have my number if there's anything we can do for you in the meantime."

Nina smoothed her fingers over the scarred leather of her backpack purse. It held her Leica, her billfold, and the key Serena had given her. "Did my father say anything about a safe-deposit box?"

"No. A spreadsheet of his assets is attached to the will. You'll have a complete copy of everything before you go." Tamera stood. "I'm sorry for your loss. We're at your disposal as you work through the legalities of the judge's passing."

Nina offered her thanks and waited until the lawyer left the room. "Do you know anything about a safe-deposit box?"

Grace shrugged. "Your dad didn't talk about things like that. Why?"

"I just wondered if everything had been covered."

"The will's only six weeks old. You think there's something more recent?"

"No. No, it's nothing."

"We should go home." Jan blew her nose. "Sorry I got all mushy. As much as I fought with him, I still—"

"Loved him." Grace patted her head. "He loved you both. No matter what else he did, he loved his children."

"So why cut Trevor out?"

"Geoffrey felt the need to take care of you two. He always did. From the minute he saw you in that awful foster home in Miami. He wanted Trevor to learn to take care of himself. To stand on his own two feet." She turned and went to the windows overlooking downtown San Antonio. The Tower of the Americas stood in the distance, a monument to far thinkers and the 1968 World's Fair. She moved toward the door. "Maybe I'll take him to New York with me. I think he'd like that."

And he would never have to learn to stand on his own.

Grace looked back. "Are you coming?"

"Jan will go with you. I'll try to find Trevor, try to talk to him."

But first, she would find Aaron and find out why he had stopped talking to her for no apparent reason. If it was grief, they could work their way through it together.

She needed him. She hoped he needed her too.

27

When all else failed, work. Aaron grabbed his gear and shoved through the station's double glass doors. Sporadic fat drops of rain hit his face. Great. Nothing like shooting in a downpour. September was one of the few months when San Antonio received a decent amount of rain. He shouldn't complain. The aquifer that fed their water supply needed refilling after a long summer. At least his assignment did not involve a funeral. He'd had his fill of shooting family members filled with agony and despair over the sudden, premature loss of a loved one.

First Nina—he was not thinking about her. Of course, that meant he could think of nothing else the entire trip to and from San Diego. And in between he thought about the frailty of Melanie's mother, who'd fainted on the church steps after the ceremony.

This assignment was simple. Shoot a protest at the Federal Courthouse over the SB 4 sanctuary city bill. The mayor and the county commissioner's court judge would be there. Spray the crowd. Sound bites with whomever.

"Wait for me." Kimberly Jenkins ambled after him. She was a decent reporter with a fair eye for detail. She was also seven months pregnant, miserable, and trying not to show it.

"Sorry." He leaned against the door with his body while she squeezed through. "Do you have an umbrella?"

She shook her head. "It's gonna be a bad-hair day."

Her obligatory reporter 'do frizzed on her shoulders. No amount of product could withstand South Texas humidity. "I keep a couple in the truck."

A good place for them when a person needed to make a dash from a building to the truck.

Kimberly laughed. "Good place for them."

At least she still had a sense of humor. His was missing in action. Kimberly had just come off the evening shift and didn't know Melanie well. She could still laugh.

"Aaron."

Two syllables and he would recognize that voice anywhere. He forced himself to turn. Nina strode across the parking lot toward him. No umbrella. Her face and hair damp. Her smile questioning. "Hey."

"Why haven't you been answering my texts? Or my calls? I thought you would call me as soon as you got in from San Diego. How did it go? How are Melanie's parents doing?"

"As well as can be expected." He glanced at Kimberly. She clearly expected him to introduce this person. "Can you give me a minute?" He tossed her the keys. She caught them despite the enormous watermelon belly that preceded her every move. "Thanks."

"Sure, but we don't have much time." Her curious gaze went to Nina. "If it starts to rain hard, the protesters may scatter."

"Not these folks. They're a determined bunch."

With a murmur of assent, she put her bag over her head to shield it from the rain and waddled toward the marked unit that sat three rows over, wedged between a Dodge Ram and a Toyota Corolla.

Aaron turned to Nina. "It was tough. Her mother ended up in the emergency room."

"Poor thing, I feel so bad for them—"

His stomach twisted at the image of Rick's hands all over Nina's face and neck and arms. "I have to work."

"I can understand that. I don't understand you not calling or answering my texts." Her voice went flat. She didn't seem to notice the rain that wet her pink cheeks or soaked her thin, silky blouse. "We have to go to the bank to see what's in that deposit box. It may tell us who had a reason to murder my father."

"I have to work."

"Why are you being so short with me?"

To protect his heart. To keep from saying things he couldn't take back. To keep from exploding. "You heard Kimberly. We're headed to a story. Miss story, lose job. That's the way it works."

"I thought you wanted to help me figure out who killed my dad."

"You seem to have this under control. I figured Rick was helping you."

The confusion on her pretty face fled. "You saw us on Wednesday, didn't you?"

"You said you wanted me to come over." He whirled and headed toward the truck. "My gear's getting wet."

"It's not what you think." She scampered alongside him. Her hand grabbed his arm. "Aaron, stop. He kissed me."

"That was hard to miss." Aaron tugged away and kept walking. "Looked to me like you kissed him back."

"We have a lot of baggage. You know that."

"Does baggage include letting him stick his tongue down your throat and grope you?"

"Don't be a jerk."

He opened the hatch and shoved his camera inside. "Me? I know I'm just your sidekick, but I don't go around kissing all the girls." It had been years, literally, since he'd kissed a woman. Since he fell in love with the one standing in front of him. "I thought you knew that—knew me. When I do, it means something."

"I know that. Believe me I do. I was overwrought." She wiped strands of hair from her face. Her eyes were bright with unshed tears. "A mess from the interview with King. From seeing Melanie's body. I needed you."

"But you figured you'd take Rick instead. I get that. A lawyer with a BMW." Bitterness welled up in his voice like acid. The feelings had been simmering all weekend. Now they boiled over, engulfing him and her. "He's a way better catch than a photographer living in a one-bedroom apartment and driving a fifteen-year-old SUV on its last leg."

She looked as if he'd slapped her. "You know I'm not like that." Shaking her head, she backed away. "Whatever."

She whirled and ran to her VW Bug.

Banging his head on the 4Runner seemed the best option.

Kimberly stuck her head out the window. "We need to go. I'd like to get the story before I have this baby."

"Coming." He grabbed his yellow rain slicker and hustled into the driver's seat.

"Was that Nina Fischer?"

"Yah."

"Isn't she a suspect in that judge's murder?" Kimberly rubbed her stomach and winced. "Baby thinks it is. She thinks it's a big story."

"No. Yes. I don't know."

"What happened to her face?"

"It's a long story."

She grabbed a bottle of water from her bag and took a swig. "Baby's thirsty." Did all pregnant women talk like that? "Did you get an interview?"

"No."

"Why not?" Kimberly's eyes widened. She shook her head. "You're dead meat if Claire finds out, or Greg. Even worse, karate-chopped dead meat."

"She's a friend."

"Oh." She giggled. Apparently baby thought that was funny. "It didn't look like it."

"We had a disagreement."

"Where I come from, we call that a fight."

Where Aaron came from, they called it jealousy. The truth of the matter smacked him between the eyes. It didn't matter if she kissed Rick Zavala or Rick kissed her. Aaron loved Nina Fischer. Nothing would change that.

She needed him. He would settle for that any day of the week.

Because he had no choice.

*　　*　　*

Men were stupid, stupid, stupid. Of course, this could not be classified as a breaking news story. Nina slammed the car door and grabbed a tissue from the box on her front seat. She sopped the rain from her face. Just rain, nothing else. Aaron could sit on his high horse and ride off into the sunset for all she cared. A mangled sob died in her throat. She had work to do. She would solve Dad's murder and, in the process, figure out who killed Melanie. She did not need a man to do that.

With a gargantuan sniff, she pushed the Start button and gunned her little VW's engine. Dad called it a poor excuse for a car. He wanted her to drive something big and safe, not something that would crumple in the path of the Ford F-350s favored by Texans—even those who lived in the city and had no reason to drive pickups. She called it Lady Bug and it suited her fine.

She turned onto North St. Mary's headed south. Her dad always banked at the Frost Bank downtown location closest to the King William District. The one on Houston Street was only minutes away if traffic cooperated. Which it never did, but particularly not in the rain. After months of drought, autumn seemed determined to fill up the aquifer in one month. People in South Texas did not know how to drive in the rain. Lack of practice.

The notes of "Band on the Run," which today should be "Man on the Run," told her Trevor was calling. She pushed the button on her steering column.

"We have to talk."

The voice loud on Bluetooth filled the car. It was barely recognizable as her brother's. "I'm so sorry. I know you're disappointed."

"I don't give a flip about his money."

Not true, but Nina understood the desire to believe it. She never cared about money, but Dad had made it possible for her not to care. Wanting independence and having it were two different things. She'd done her best to make it on her own. So had Trevor. But Dad had found ways to take care of her. Trevor, he'd shoved out the door as soon as possible. "You know Jan and I will do anything we can to help you. It's a big house. Jan is deployed half the time. We'll share."

"I don't want to live in his house."

"Then what do you want?"

"I want to feel like my own father respected me. That he loved me."

"Dad loved and respected you enough to know you could make it on your own." The painful truth loomed large. "He obviously didn't think Jan and I could. We needed to be taken care of. You don't."

"That's one way to look at it. The other is he didn't want to reward his worthless son by giving him something he hadn't earned."

"He disapproved of my photography. He disapproved of Jan's career in the military. He fought for what he thought was best because he cared about us. He was wrong in many ways, but the fact that he loved us enough to fight for it is something not everyone gets from their parents."

"Why did he have to make us feel like failures in the process?"

"He was flawed. I don't know about you, but so am I. Do you want to cast the first stone?"

A long pause. "No. I should've told y'all about Vicky."

"I'd like to meet her. She sounds great."

"You'll like her. She's a free spirit. She kind of reminds me of you."

"That's a big compliment."

He cleared his throat. "I'm sorry about what I said before."

"I know. Why did you say you were in Dallas the night Dad died?"

"Because I was drunk when I got the call. I had words with Dad that day."

"Everyone did, it seems."

"A bill came to the house. He opened it. I'm behind on my school loans."

"A lot of people are."

"Yah, but a lot of people don't go on to get their doctorate when they still owe on their master's and their bachelor's."

She hung a right on East Martin. Traffic bunched up even though the light ahead had turned green. Two guys pushed a stalled car with orange Tamaulipas plates out of the intersection in the pouring rain. Nina sighed and turned up the windshield wipers. "You really think Dad thought a degree in journalism and a career in photography and writing poetry deserved his hard-earned money? Grace writes romances and he didn't leave her a dime."

A sound caught somewhere between a strangled sob and a cough beat against her ear. "I just wanted him to love me."

The heart of what any child wanted from a parent. "If anyone understands that, I do, and I'm so deeply sorry." Nina waited a few seconds for her voice to steady. "Both my parents abandoned me. Dad never gave up on you. He wanted you to be a man who stood on your own two feet."

Silence.

"Trevor?"

"I'm here." Raw emotion turned his voice into an old's man raspy mutter.

"Where are you? Let me come get you after I get done at the bank. I'm almost to Frost downtown now. We'll go someplace, get some food, talk. You can come home with me—"

"It's not my home anymore. It's yours. Don't you get that?" He disconnected.

Nina hit redial. Eventually Trevor's voice-mail message picked up. She disconnected. He would see that she had called. Maybe he would change his mind and come to the house.

Trevor had a right to his feelings. Geoffrey had taken his desire to manage his children's lives too far. Even beyond his life. It would have cost him nothing to evenly divide his substantial estate among his children. All his children. But he had to make one last statement, one last I-know-best-you-don't.

Ten minutes later Nina stood shivering and soaking wet in an air-conditioned room at Frost Bank filled with safe-deposit boxes. With a smile, the clerk, who'd been too polite to stare at Nina's face, pointed out the correct box and left her to her own devices.

Her heartbeat ratcheted up a notch. *Get it over with, Fischer.* The revelations the box held couldn't be any worse than knowing her father was a gambler who led a double life. Gritting her teeth, she fumbled with the metal box and opened the lid.

A manila envelope. The shiver that went through her had nothing to do with the AC. She lifted it out. A slim ivory-bond envelope from the stationery her dad kept on his desk in his chambers lay underneath. No writing on the outside. It was sealed. She undid the clasp of the bigger envelope first and looked inside. A stack of newspaper clippings. She sifted through them. Nothing.

Nothing else. Just seven newspaper articles. The air fizzled from her lungs. Yellow lights danced in her eyes. She grabbed the table and leaned over. "One, eight, seven, four, eleven. One, eight, seven, four, eleven. One, eight, seven, four, eleven."

Her breathing began to even out. She inhaled, exhaled. "Easy, in and out, in and out."

All this for some newspaper clippings. Serena Cochrane dead in a hit-and-run. Melanie Martinez dead, shot in the head in her own bedroom.

Dad dead, shot in the chest in his own study.

Okay. The smaller envelope. Not having a letter opener in her bag, she used a nail file to cut a thin slit on the narrow side. Gloves were another thing she could've used.

Hindsight.

With the tips of her fingers, she shook the letter open and laid it on the table.

Three paragraphs written in her dad's perfect cursive. He was resigning from the bench to take a position with Coggins, Gonzalez, and Pope, attorneys-at-law.

She plopped onto the chair and read it again, then a third time. The words never changed. Her father planned to give up his judgeship and become a civil litigator with Rick's firm. The letter had no date and it wasn't signed.

Not yet. He was waiting for something, but what?

Why hide the letter in a safe-deposit box? Why write it at all until such time as he was ready to make the move?

She reached for her phone. Aaron. He was good at puzzles. He shot news stories about politics and court cases all the time. He hated it because it was nonvisual, but he did it.

She dropped the phone back in her bag. Aaron was mad. He was an idiot.

She would figure this out on her own.

The articles had to mean something. She settled back and began to read.

Ten minutes later she slid the articles back into the envelope and rubbed her temples. All the articles reported on civil cases in her dad's court. All the cases had resulted in huge monetary settlements for the plaintiffs. All the plaintiffs were represented by attorneys from CG&P.

A fatality helicopter crash in which the families of the victim received a $14-million settlement. An amusement-park ride accident that resulted in a child's death: $21.5 million. A food-poisoning death resulting from a chain restaurant meal: $12 million. And so on.

What did they have in common? Her dad's court. Big settlements. CG&P. What did it mean? Why was it so important that these articles had to be kept in the box? Why not bookmark them on his computer where he could print them out anytime he wanted? She needed to look at his computer to see if they were bookmarked, but the police had his desktop and the thief had his laptop. The advantage of having these articles in this box meant no one would see or know he had some sort of interest in these cases aside from being the presiding judge.

But what?

She groaned and raked her limp hair back in a ponytail, using a scrunchie she found in her bag. Aaron would have ideas.

She rolled her shoulders and cranked her neck side to side. It popped. No new thoughts came to mind. She slid the articles back into the envelope, added the letter to it as well, and stood. Maybe fresh air would help.

Maybe fresh air would sweep away the dizzying disappointment and her dashed hope. A hope she hadn't even realized she harbored. She wanted the box to hold a letter addressed to each one of her dad's children, explaining what happened to him. Pledging his undying love. Explaining how he took the plunge off the straight and narrow directly into the canyon of deceit.

It wasn't his way. She'd have to be satisfied with the symbolic gesture. He gave Jan and Nina his home. His estate. To him, that said it all.

She slipped the envelopes into her bag and returned the box to its slot. A few minutes later she pulled from her parking space in the ground lot and headed for I-10. Dark, rolling clouds dumped a steady rain, washing away the grime of San Antonio's historic grid of one-way meandering streets that followed the old Spanish acequias.

Trevor lived in an apartment not far from the UTSA campus on Loop 1604. Nina had no idea where his girlfriend lived, so she could only hope he'd gone home to nurse his wounds. And not to a bar, his go-to remedy after fights with Dad.

Lunch-hour traffic hemmed her in until she made it to the East Martin Street entrance ramp. From there it thinned a little as I-35 and 10 intersected beyond the purple Finesilver Building. Her mind reviewing the article headlines in a loop, she tapped her fingers on the wheel to the tune of her thumping windshield wipers smearing the rain. She needed new blades. Jury awards $14 million in helicopter crash. Jury awards $21.5 million in amusement park death. The juries had determined the amount of the settlement. They'd found in favor of the plaintiffs. Her dad's involvement included ruling on pretrial motions in hearings held in his court in all seven cases. Nothing was unusual about it.

Traffic had thinned, yet a dark-blue SUV with tinted windows continued to ride her back bumper. He had plenty of room to go around. She glanced at her speedometer. The speed limit was fifty-five on this stretch. No one drove that slow. But it didn't rise to seventy-five for a while yet.

She let her speed creep up to sixty-five. The highway was slick with rain mixed with oil. She didn't need a ticket. She had dealt with police enough in the past week and a half. She let up on the gas a tad.

The guy behind her didn't. "What's your problem? Go around."

Now she was talking to herself.

He had plenty of room to pass.

His bumper came within inches of her back end as if taunting her. He held steady.

"What are you doing?" Adrenaline shot through her body like mainlining a gallon of coffee. The shakes enveloped her. *Breathe. Breathe.* She forced herself to look in the rearview mirror. The other driver was a man with a dark face, dark hair. No one she knew. "Back off, buddy."

Her voice quivered. She swallowed. "Back off." Louder, stronger. That was better.

They hit the spot where the upper and lower freeway levels reconnected. She moved across rain-slicked lanes crowded with traffic. The SUV pulled up alongside her. She moved over two more lanes until she hugged the right lane, better known in Texas as the slow lane. The SUV followed.

She jabbed the call button on her wheel. "Call 911."

"Calling 911."

A second later a calm female voice flowed into the car. "911, what's your emergency?"

"A man is trying to run into me with his car."

"Are you on foot, ma'am?"

Nina worked to keep the panic from her voice. "No, I'm in my car on I-10 West. I just passed the West Avenue exit. I'm driving a 2015 red VW Bug. He's in a dark-blue SUV of some kind."

That didn't narrow it down much, but cars were not Nina's forte.

"Is this a domestic dispute?"

"No, I don't know the person. I don't recognize the car."

"We have officers in route. Can you pull over?"

"I'm afraid to stop."

"Understood. Just stay on the line. Stay calm and focus on driving safely."

What did she think Nina was doing? The SUV sped up and crept closer to the line. They were neck and neck now. Nina hazarded a glance in that direction. The tint in the side windows was too dark. She couldn't tell if there was a passenger in the front seat. Nothing stood out about the SUV.

"How far away are—?"

The SUV smashed into her. She lost control.

The VW swerved, rocked, and careened into the barrier.

She slammed on the brakes. Still, momentum flung her forward.

The side curtain air bag exploded. Her head banged it and then against the headrest.

Tires squealed. Metal screamed. The VW slid along the concrete barrier. Sparks flew.

So this was what they meant by seeing stars.

28

A moan broke the silence. Nina opened her eyes. She was alone in her VW. The moan belonged to her. She straightened. The seat belt refused to budge. She winced. Pain radiated along her sternum.

And in her neck.

And up and down her spine.

The windshield wipers had stopped.

The 2015 VW Bug had a four-star rating in government tests involving side-impact crashes. That fact rambled around in Nina's throbbing head. She'd done battle with a much bigger SUV and survived. Her dad had hated the VW—no match for the diesel-spewing monster pickup trucks favored by so many hard-core Texans. Might as well get a Mini, he said.

But he grudgingly conceded the safety features were good.

She tried to lean forward. Her locked seat belt held her in place. A smell like gunpowder overpowered her. Smoke filled the air. Or powder. She couldn't be sure.

Not moving was good. Very good. Her stomach rocked. The smell nauseated her.

Sirens wailed.

Now they decided to show up.

She forced her eyes open again. Her left temple hurt. The whole side of her face hurt.

The bruises from her encounter with the intruder in her front hallway hadn't even begun to turn yellow and fade yet. Now there would be more.

Why did she feel so calm?

She hadn't died. She'd been certain she would. But she hadn't.

The side curtain air bag had deflated a second after exploding. Her door hung open. Had she opened it?

A stranger—a man—leaned over her.

"I'm okay. I'm okay."

"Uh-huh. Lean back. Close your eyes." Rain dripped on her face. A dark hood hung around his head. His arm reached past her. Black rain jacket. He smelled like Paco Rabanne cologne. Dad's favorite. Good. He smelled like her dad. She closed her eyes against the pounding in her head. Something brushed against her. His hand? "Rest. I'll get help."

The scream of the sirens grew louder and louder. She covered her ears.

A fire truck rolled to a stop next to her, followed quickly by an ambulance. Their sirens mingled in a cacophonous song that set her nerves jangling.

She should get out. She turned her head. Pain ricocheted down her spine.

More sirens. Police units.

Two or three.

One stopped in the slow lane. An officer clad in a yellow rain slicker left his lights running, exited the Crown Victoria, and set up flares to block traffic from getting too close to the accident scene. Now they were blocking traffic. San Antonio motorists hated that.

"Ma'am, can you hear me?" A firefighter in full regalia tapped on the shattered windshield. "Ma'am?"

"I hear you." She struggled but the seat belt had her pinned to the seat like a butterfly pinned to a collector's board. Her shaking fingers refused to cooperate long enough to release the seat belt. "I'm fine."

"Don't move. We want to check you out first. Then we'll get you out of there in a jiffy."

"I'm good. I'm fine. I just need help getting this seat belt off."

"Sit tight, miss." His gear in one hand, a paramedic squeezed between two firefighters. He made quick work of examining her pupil responses, checking her blood pressure and respiration, and thoroughly examining her arms and legs.

Yes, she had some chest pain, but the seat belt was responsible. Her neck hurt, but a simple case of whiplash. The paramedic, an older, grizzled-looking man with a short, trim beard, agreed she would have some bruising from the seat belt.

Everything still worked.

He undid the seat belt and helped her pull her legs from the foot well. "Easy. Easy."

Strong, sure hands patted, pressed, appraised. A gurney appeared, pushed by another paramedic. "It would be best if we transport you to an ER to get checked out." He touched the bruise on her cheek. "This looks older."

"I'm not getting on that gurney and I'm not going to the ER."

"Are you refusing to be transported?"

"I'm saying it's not necessary."

"We can't make you go if you refuse treatment." His expression was kind, his tone placatory. "I strongly suggest you go to your own doctor and get checked out, for your own sake."

"I will. I promise."

She had her fingers crossed.

A police officer strode forward. "Let's get you over to my vehicle where you can sit and I can ask you some questions."

Nina grabbed her bag and her camera. It didn't look any worse for wear. The officer guided her to his unit, now parked on the other side of the concrete barrier in the grass-and-mud median that separated the highway from the access road. He squatted and shoved his hat in its plastic rain protector back on his head. "If you're feeling up to it, let's talk about what happened."

She tugged the blanket provided by the first responder tighter around her shoulders and eased onto the seat. "The driver was following too close. The next thing I knew he pulled up, swerved, and slammed into me."

"Two witnesses confirm your story. The SUV hit you and kept going. They both thought it was a case of road rage. You didn't have any prior interaction with this SUV?"

"Witnesses stopped? Did they get a license plate?"

"No."

"Was one of them a man wearing a black rain jacket?"

"Yep. Him and another man. They gave their accounts to one of the other officers and then went on their ways."

"Do you have their contact information? I'll need it for my insurance."

"It'll be in my report."

"The man opened my door. He told me help was on the way." The hand brushing across her face surfaced. He wore gloves. Gloves in September in San Antonio? "He smelled like my dad."

"People for the most part are good."

The officer, whose name tag read RODRIGUEZ, was young. Probably fresh out of the academy. Hispanic. Big smile in a dark, handsome face. In ten years would he still say that? In two years? "I didn't recognize the SUV. The windows were tinted. I couldn't see the driver. He came out of nowhere and started tailgating me—"

"Let me through. I'm a friend! Nina!"

She swiveled and glanced beyond the cruiser. Aaron fought to do an end run around an officer who stood next to a second cruiser squeezed against the highway access road. He had no camera on his shoulder. He'd jumped the curb in his 4Runner and parked at an angle behind the Crown Vic. She could use a friend right now, even one who'd been crazy enough to think she liked Rick more than him. That she loved Rick. She did in her own way—just not like that. "He is a friend. Can they let him through?"

The officer put his finger and thumb between his lips and wolf whistled. His colleague glanced back. Rodriguez gave a backward wave. The other officer stepped out of Aaron's way.

He raced toward her in a stride that would've done an Olympian proud. "Are you okay?" Rain dripped from his sodden copper curls. He seemed ready to do battle. Ignoring the rain puddles and the mud, he dropped to his knees next to the officer and grabbed both Nina's hands. "Claire heard an accident go out over the scanner. She told me to head this direction. I saw your car and freaked."

"Slow down. Slow down. I'm fine."

"You don't look fine." Aaron turned to the officer. "She doesn't look fine. Did EMS check her out?"

"Yeah, they did. Take it easy before I have to call them over for a cardiac event." The officer's phone beeped. "I'm gonna take this. Don't go anywhere."

The last words were directed to Nina. His phone to his ear, his gaze on the access road traffic, he ambled toward the other officer.

"I'm sorry about earlier. I don't care who you kiss. Okay, so I do care, but I shouldn't have been such a jerk about it. You don't owe me anything. You're a free agent—"

Nina put her fingers over his lips. "Chill, McClure. We have bigger issues here. I opened the safe-deposit box."

His hand closed over her fingers and pulled them away, but he didn't let go. His fingers were warm, and the ice inside her began to melt. His Adam's apple bobbed. He blinked. "What was in it?"

"Seven newspaper clippings in an envelope." She leaned toward him. His warmth drew her like a fireplace on a winter morning. Or was it a moth to a flame? "I'm such an idiot. I grabbed my bag and my camera, but not the envelope. It's in my car. We need to get it before they tow it away."

Glancing toward Officer Rodriguez, who had his back to them, Aaron helped her from the seat. She stared at her sweet little Lady Bug. Crumpled. Likely totaled. Lady Bug was the first car she picked out and made payments on herself. Her beautiful Lady Bug was DRT, as they liked to say in the news business. DOTR. Dead Right There or Dead On The Road. Her legs buckled.

Aaron's arm went around her waist. "Easy. Are you sure you shouldn't let them take you to the ER?"

"I'm fine." Carless. She still owed money on Lady Bug and she wasn't totally sure how much insurance would cover. Cars were the least of her problems right now. Someone had tried to kill her. "Hurry. They're getting ready to push the car up on the tow truck. Tell them to wait."

It was one of those tow trucks that carried the dead and maimed cars on a flatbed instead of hooking it up and lifting in on its rear tires. Aaron leaned on the barrier and waved at the tow truck driver as he walked past, his head ducked down in his yellow slicker. The driver growled something about traffic tie-ups.

"Give us one minute, please."

"Get whatever you need and get out. Thirty seconds."

"Hey, didn't I tell you to sit tight?" Officer Rodriguez strode toward them.

"I need stuff from my car before they take it. My house keys are in there."

A true statement.

"You can't go on the highway."

Police had two lanes shut down. Traffic crept through the bottle-neck beyond their units. "We'll stay on this side of the car. I'm not giving permission to tow my car until I have my stuff."

Rodriguez wavered. "I'll get it for you."

"It'll be faster if I did it. I know where everything is."

His scowl as big as his earlier grin, Rodriguez crossed his arms. "Like the guy said, fifteen seconds. It's too dangerous out here."

"It's a parking lot out there."

Nina led the way. They scampered around the barrier and squeezed onto the passenger side between the car and the concrete. The rain came down harder. A steady *rat-a-tat-tat* against the cracked windshield. The door had been shoved into the frame. Paint and primer were gone and sheer metal exposed. The side window had shattered in the process. Which made access somewhat easier.

Aaron poked his arm through the open space and tugged. The door squealed and budged a few inches. He squeezed around until he could wedge himself between the car and the barrier and move the door a few more inches. "I don't see an envelope."

"Let me in. I'm skinnier than you are." Aaron moved out and Nina squeezed in. She eased down until her line of sight allowed her to peruse the front seat. Nothing. Not surprising, considering the force of the collision. "I'm sure it's on the floor. Help me get the door open wider."

Together they wrestled it open far enough for her to kneel and squeeze her arm and shoulder through the opening. She felt around. A brush. Her favorite ink pen. Two rolls of film. She grabbed those and tucked them in her pocket. Film was expensive. A *Writer's Digest* renewal notice. She bent forward, her neck protesting, and peered into the foot well. She craned her head to search under the seat.

The envelope was gone.

29

Aaron stood guard. Nina would stay on the Fischers' living room couch for the next twelve hours if he had to get Pearl to hold her down. The Fischers' cook-slash-maid was a giant of a woman built like a king-size bed, who ran the household like it belonged to her.

Nina's nose had started bleeding on the way home and Aaron practically carried her into the house. Pearl had taken one look at them and rushed into "her" room for a first-aid kit, hot water bottle, and heating pad. Then she added ice packs and a cup of hot tea to the prescription. After twenty years, people were used to taking orders from her.

Pearl had tugged a crocheted comforter over Nina and insisted she not move a muscle. Not even twitch an eye. After taking ibuprofen for what she described as a teeth-rattling headache, Nina went to sleep with an ice pack on her cheek. She'd been asleep for almost four hours.

Grace wasn't there. Neither was Jan. According to Pearl they'd returned after the reading of the will and then gone out again. No, she did not know where they went. Nor was it her job to keep track. "I ain't no secretary and I ain't no receptionist. I got work to do."

And she did it very well.

Nina moaned. Her eyes opened. Her hand went to her forehead. She sat up. "You let me sleep. You shouldn't have let me sleep. We need to find copies of those articles online. We need—"

"Do not move. Period. You can't keep getting beat up and not take five minutes to recover." He plopped down in the overstuffed chair across from the couch. "If you lie still until Pearl brings you some soup and a grilled cheese, I'll let you run through what happened. We'll plot next steps. Steps to be taken when you feel better."

"I'm fine."

"You're not fine."

She stuck her tongue out at him. "My neck hurts when I lay down. I feel better sitting up."

Her face, already battered by not one but two intruders, was black and blue and purple in some places, green and yellow in others. She looked like a boxer who'd gone ten rounds and then been KO'd by a muscle-bound heavyweight.

The thought of food—even Pearl's famous homemade three-cheese-and-focaccia-bread sandwiches—made Aaron's stomach twitch. He hadn't eaten much since Melanie's death. A steady diet of Dunkin' Donuts coffee and crunchy peanut butter from a jar kept him upright. He couldn't remember the last time he'd slept. "You can sit up as long as you don't get up."

"You're not the boss of me."

"No, but I'm your friend and friends don't let friends wander around wounded. Tell me about the articles."

She ran through it quickly at first, then more slowly as her remaining energy dissipated. Her head bobbed. She plucked at the comforter. "Rick's firm has something to do with this."

"That worries you."

"Yes."

"I know he means something to you, but—"

"He's a friend too."

A friend who wanted more. Something he and Aaron had in common. "I guess what it comes down to is whether discovering the truth and finding your dad's killer are the two most important things to you." He chose his words with great care. "Or are protecting your dad's reputation and your friend's future in politics more important?"

"Too bad we can't have both." She gazed beyond him to the windows. "Nothing is more important than the truth. We both know that. Three people are dead. Two, at least, were innocent bystanders who didn't deserve to be caught up in a tempest of my father's making. We have to figure out who did it. Melanie and Serena deserve justice."

"Okay. Let's start with what you remember about the articles—"

Pounding on the front door made them both jump.

"I'll get it." Wiping her hands on her apron, Pearl marched by. "What is wrong with these people? Don't they know how to ring a doorbell? Heathens."

A second later King bolted into the living room.

*   *   *

Rick gritted his teeth and pasted a smile on his face. This fund-raiser-slash-hand-gripper was well under way. The smell of barbecue smoke from the big pit clung to his suit. His hair drooped. His hand hurt from the grip-and-grin. His jaw hurt from the grin-and-grip. The Tejano music reached a crescendo as the men whirled their partners on the makeshift dance floor. The party had rented a closed used-car dealership building and turned it into a campaign headquarters.

Here came another contributor. An attorney who went to school with Peter. The wife, who was at least fifteen years younger, worked in the mayor's office. Good connection. He widened his grin and made sure his grip remained firm. "How's it going, Louis? Dineen. Thanks for coming. How's your daughter? Still being scouted by UT's basketball team?" He prided himself on remembering every big contributor. Ten thousand and up. "Did you get enough to eat? Can I get you a beer?"

Dineen, who'd had some work done on her face and her chest, gushed and went off to get a beer for her man.

Louis slipped onto the stool at the round, high table and surveyed the crowd. The Tejano band finished the Emilio Navaira song and immediately started an old Selena tune. Sad to think they were both dead. Sadder about Selena, shot down by her fan-club president just as her career was taking off. Emilio's brush with fame lasted much longer, but his star had been dying long before he succumbed to the grave. With a shout the dancers headed back to the floor.

"Are you making inroads against that scum Benavides?" Louis had to shout to be heard over the accordion, bajo sexto, keyboard, and drums. "If we don't trounce that guy, we'll look bad to the entire party."

"Polls look good."

"Sure they do. You're a newbie." The sarcasm in his voice matched the curl of Louis's upper lip. "He's a five-term rep in the Texas House. You're trying to skip up the ladder without doing your due diligence on the local level."

"Why are you supporting me then?"

"Because Peter asked me to and I owe him a favor."

"I can take Benavides. I've shaken more hands and walked more blocks and kissed more babies and done more TV interviews and run more ads. We just need a little more capital to make it to the finish line."

The finish line being election day in November. It loomed far too close. Too much ground to make up.

"Peter seems convinced."

"Peter's right."

The object of their conversation ambled their direction, his high-society wife, Tiffany, on one arm and his lovely daughter

Cicely—newly divorced, a junior partner, and new member of the bar—on the other. She looked like the beauty-pageant queen she'd once been. High cheekbones, perfect skin and teeth, an amazing body clad in skinny jeans and a tight, white *Vote for Zavala* T-shirt, shiny strawberry-blonde hair, and blue eyes reminiscent of her dad's. She also looked three sheets to the wind.

Peter flashed that self-satisfied smile he got when they won a court case.

"You look happy. Why the smile?"

Peter draped Cicely over a stool. Tiffany drifted away. A contributor with a gut the size of an enormous beach ball bulging over a silver-and-turquoise belt buckle shaped like the state of Texas immediately asked her to dance. She took him up on the offer without a backward glance.

"Can I borrow Rick for a minute?" Peter directed the question to Louis. "Business."

"No problem." Louis patted Cicely's hand. "I'll make do here."

Cicely curled her fingers around his and released the smile of someone who had a huge headache and worship of the porcelain throne in her future.

"What's going on?" Rick followed Peter into one of the offices and closed the door. "Did we get a break? Did they solve Fischer's murder?"

"No. However, we did nip another problem in the bud. Mr. Miles performed his tasks with extraordinary finesse." His nose wrinkled. "Unlike you."

"What tasks?"

"With the help of his associates—"

"What associates? More people know about our little problem?"

"If you'll let me finish. Mr. Miles has, shall we say, a security firm. I've hired him and the firm to assist us with security needs."

Peter eased into a chair and leaned back, arms behind his head. He seemed far too happy. "With the help of his associates, he surveilled Nina Fischer. She visited a safe-deposit box at Frost Bank. He was able to retrieve the contents of that box."

White-hot anxiety hit Rick in the chest with the force of a cattle prod. It was hard to breathe. He tried to pace, but the room was too small. "How? How did he retrieve the stuff? When? He didn't hurt Nina, did he?"

"You are such a wuss. You need to get over it. Her car—if you want to call that Bug a car—is totaled, but she only has a few bumps and bruises. She'll live."

"Get over it?" Rick stomped around the desk and grabbed Peter by his two-hundred-dollar red silk tie and jerked. "You endangered her life with a car accident? I'll kill you and then I'll kill him."

Peter grabbed Rick's tie and brought him closer. His face was so close, Rick could see the shape of his contacts in his icy-blue eyes. He had a tiny scar over his left eye. A mole hidden in his frosted-silver bangs. He smelled of barbecued ribs and Dewar's. "You better think real hard about what you do next. You can be an ambulance chaser on the south side or you can be the next representative of this area in the Texas legislature. Is some girl you've got the hots for worth your future, your career with the firm? You get elected to the legislature, women will be hanging all over you. Nina Fischer has made it clear she'd rather avoid the limelight. Her mother has to drag her to social events. She doesn't bother to hide her boredom. You need someone like my daughter who understands how to work a crowd."

Rick breathed. He let go of the tie.

"Good choice."

He whirled and stormed to the door.

"Use a breath mint before you shake any more hands."

"I'm not shaking any hands. I'm going to Nina's."

"She's fine. Hardly a scratch."

"Nobody touches her but me."

"Fine. But if push comes to shove, that means you finish the job Mr. Miles started. Are you man enough to do that, or are you just a loser from the barrio? You mess this up and you'll end up right where you started."

He couldn't let that happen. He was destined to be somebody important. Nothing would stand in his way. And no one. Not even the woman he loved.

*   *   *

The ibuprofen hadn't helped. Neither had the soup and sandwich. Nina rubbed her forehead. Maybe King would get the hint. The detective had pulled up a straight-back chair from the bay window and seated himself directly in front of the coffee table that separated them. He appeared to be settling in for the night. He seemed to enjoy the meal much more than Aaron, who picked at his sandwich until Pearl finally removed it with a *harrumph* punctuated by a swish of her long skirt.

At least King seemed finished with his earlier tirade. His monologue. Why hadn't she called him after the accident? Why did he have to find out from a uni? Did she think it was related to her father's death, or was it simply another bad San Antonio driver? The rapid-fire delivery of the questions didn't leave much time to assemble answers.

"So you're okay?" Despite the question, King's expression remained hard, tense, and irritated. "Did the EMTs check you out?"

"I made sure." Aaron shifted in his chair. Had King intentionally set his chair up so Aaron had to look at his back? "She refused to go to the hospital. She's banged up. Her nose hurts, her head hurts, her back and neck hurt. You probably should come back tomorrow."

"I can speak for myself." A spurt of anger gave her new energy. "Let's just get this over. What do you want? Why are you here? Again?"

"You got run off the road today. Are you seriously suggesting that it's unrelated to your father's murder? To the deaths of Melanie Martinez and Serena Cochrane?" He jabbed his finger at her. "You told me you weren't stupid. Neither am I. Tell me why someone would try to run you off the road."

"It all happened so fast." True. Not the whole truth, but true. "One minute he was riding my bumper. The next my car hit the barrier. It was raining. The road was wet."

Behind King, Aaron scowled and mouthed the words *Tell him.*

Uh-uh. Not yet. Not before she figured out what the connection was between the articles and her father's life. Then she would turn the entire thing over to King. She just needed a head start. If he would leave, she and Aaron could get into her laptop and start searching that virtual archive known as the World Wide Web.

"You think it was an accident?"

"No." She wouldn't lie. It was no accident. Besides, he could pull the 911 tape and know what she said to the dispatcher. "He intentionally swerved, forcing me into the barrier."

"You keep saying he."

"It was a man. The windows were tinted so I didn't get a good look at him."

"The report says—"

"If you saw the police report you know all of this."

"I also talked to the traffic investigator on the scene. I want to hear it from your lips, *señorita.*"

"Don't *señorita* me. I'm tired. I'm in pain. Go reread the report."

"Are you refusing to cooperate? I could arrest you for impeding an investigation."

"I could sue you for harassment."

"It doesn't help your cause to be snippy with me." A thoughtful expression on his face, he leaned back in his chair. "There has to be a connection. And there's something you're not telling me."

"Nina."

Aaron's voice held a note of warning. He would explode any second, and it would all come cascading out of him. He didn't dissemble. He didn't lie. That was what made him so lovable.

She froze. No, no, no. Yes. He was lovable. So much more so than that fledgling politician in her life. She didn't want to love anyone, but the barriers were weakening.

Drive-bys and intruders weren't the only dangers in her life.

"Nina?" King had bags under his bloodshot eyes. He rubbed his five-o'clock shadow with both hands. "Are you planning to share, or should I get out the handcuffs?"

"Fine—"

Pounding on the door.

Again.

Shaking her head, Pearl marched by. "Like a train station around here."

A second later Rick bounded into the room.

30

The living room was getting too crowded. The men in Nina's life were crowding her space. She rubbed her temples and stared at the floor. Maybe they would go away. Rick stormed across the carpet to the couch where he plopped down next to her and grabbed her arm. His gaze bordered on frantic.

"Why didn't you call me, *mi amor*?" He swore in Spanish as he touched her face. His fingers grasped her chin and moved her head from one side to the other. Horror registered. More swearing. "I will kill the hombre who did this to you."

"I don't recommend that." His expression neutral, King intervened. "Did you drive here?"

"Why?" Rick's fingers tightened on her chin. Nina pulled away. His hands shook. His gaze darted from her face to the ceiling and back. "It has nothing to do with you."

"It seems to me you might have been drinking." King's tone didn't change. "That would have something to do with me."

"I'm fine." Nina could take care of herself. As she had told Aaron and King—repeatedly. She couldn't tell King about the box of receipts, the stolen newspaper articles, or the neon notebooks in front of Rick. He had nothing to do with her dad's death. She'd swear to that. But his firm did. CG&P was mentioned in every article. Serena had died over that safe-deposit box key. "You do smell like a brewery. Uber home and get some sleep. I'm beat and I'm going to bed."

She stood. The three men in the room stayed put. She sat. "What would it take to get the three of you to go home and save the inquisition for tomorrow? When we're all fresh."

The warring emotions in the room tired her more than the letdown from the car wreck. Unconditional love from Aaron. Rick's version of love. Similar to what he felt for his BMW or his fancy sound system. Impatience from King. Trying to be patient but not quite making it.

"This can't wait."

"Whatever it is, it will have to wait." Her jacket slung over one arm, Grace marched into the room. "Pearl tells me my daughter was in car accident today. She needs to rest. If you want to talk to her, make an appointment with her lawyer for tomorrow." She cocked her head toward the foyer. "All of you. Now."

"Fine. Miss Fischer, 10:00 a.m. at headquarters. That will give you time to recuperate. Bring your lawyer." His expression morose, King stood. He jerked his head toward the door. "Mr. Zavala, I'd like to talk to you outside."

Rick scowled. His hand covered Nina's and squeezed until it hurt. "Do *I* need a lawyer?"

"That's totally your call."

His hand slipped away. Nina rubbed her fingers over the white indentations. He'd cut off the blood circulation for a split second. She'd never seen him so riled up, so jittery. "He's tired and he's been drinking. Let him set up an Uber. He'll come downtown tomorrow. Won't you, Rick?"

"I'd rather get it over with now."

Smelling of alcohol and barbecue, he leaned in close. She jerked back. The kiss landed on her cheek. His frown smoldered. He shrugged and stomped over to Grace. "If you need anything, just say the word. I'm your man." His glance traveled to Aaron, who hadn't moved. "She's tired, man. Give it a break."

Aaron didn't respond. He looked dead on his feet. His gaze traveled to Nina. She nodded. "Go home. I'll call you in the morning."

He stood and squeezed around the table. His lips brushed her forehead. His fingers touched her cheek for a brief second. He nodded to King, said good night to Grace and Jan, and then all three of them were suddenly gone.

"What was that all about?" Grace put her hands on her hips and glowered. "What aren't you telling the detective? What aren't you telling me?"

Daffy hopped up on the couch and climbed daintily into Nina's lap. She wrapped her arms around the purring ball of fur and breathed. "Did Dad ever talk to you about resigning from the bench? Going into private practice?"

"Never." Grace drew the two syllables out with all the southern flair she could muster. And soaked them in scorn. "He loved his job."

"So we thought. But what if he got so entangled in gambling debt that he needed to make more money, a lot more money?"

Frowning, Grace plucked at her skirt. "He should've talked to me. I'm his wife. And I had money."

"Then he would've had to admit he had a problem." Nina laid her head on a pile of pillows. "I don't think Dad wanted to quit gambling. I think he wanted to gamble more."

Like any addict, he was willing to do whatever it took to satiate the ever-growing desire, even if it meant giving up his job. His wife. His family.

Even if it meant breaking the law.

Geoffrey Fischer was no better than his sister.

*   *   *

King's cool stare didn't bother Nina. Not this time. She was an old pro. A veteran. She should bring her sleeping bag and jammies to the police station next time. She wrapped her hands around the cup of water he'd brought at her request and stared at the wall behind the detective. Fred Teeter was getting his exercise representing her.

"Detective, what am I doing here?"

"I thought we were waiting for your attorney."

"That doesn't mean I can't ask you questions, only the other way around."

"I'd rather not have to repeat myself."

"Suit yourself."

A few more minutes passed in silence. Nina used the time to surreptitiously study her aggressor. He seemed even more tired than he had the previous night. Bags under his bloodshot eyes. A wrinkle or two in his shirt. His doodles on the yellow pad lying on the table that separated them suggested impatience. And a love of ice cream cones. Nina longed for her camera. They'd taken her bag at the door.

He dropped the pen and leaned forward, both elbows on the table. "How did the reunion with your mother go?"

"How do you know about that?" The man who drove her off the highway wasn't the only one following her. "Don't you have anything better to do than follow me around?"

King looked momentarily confused. "I saw you talking at the funeral."

"Right." She was losing it. "And I saw you talking to her. What did she—?"

Fred Teeter burst into the room. Using the word *burst* loosely. His elegantly old-fashioned leather briefcase under one arm, he patted Nina's shoulder as he squeezed behind her chair. "Detective, we've been patient with your shenanigans, but it's time to stop. This amounts to harassment of my client." He slapped the briefcase on the table and wiped his forehead with a handkerchief. "We have every intention of lodging a complaint with the chief. We'll go to the city manager if necessary."

"Do what you have to do." King leaned back in his chair. His yawn displayed a set of perfect teeth with nary a filling. "But first I'd like to ask your client why she had breakfast with Serena Cochrane on the day she died."

"We're back to that. You have something against breakfast?" Nina straightened in her chair. Good posture was everything. "It's the most important meal of the day."

"What was in the safe-deposit box?"

"What box?"

"You really want to lie to a police officer?"

She didn't. Lying was never a good ploy. "How do you know about the box?"

King pulled a manila folder from underneath the notepad. "Emails exchanged by Mrs. Cochrane and your father's court reporter. She found his behavior odd and said so in an email to Tabitha Rainier."

"Okay. But what makes you think she gave the key to me?"

"Because you had breakfast with her and fifteen minutes later she was dead. Melanie Martinez knew about it. You went to see her and voilà, she's dead. Why else?"

King could turn *why* into a four-syllable word. It was an art form created in East Texas.

"How do you know Melanie knew about the key?"

"Texts between her and Mrs. Cochrane. The fact that you don't want to tell me about it makes me think there was something really important in that box and you don't want anyone to know about it."

"It's a private matter." One that would destroy her family's reputation and decimate her mother.

"How about I just arrest you for three counts of homicide?"

"No GSR on her the night of her father's murder or the day of Melanie Martinez's death." Fred managed to get a word in edgewise. "You've seen the video of the intruder who killed Ms. Martinez."

"That doesn't mean Miss Fischer wasn't in on it. She might not have pulled the trigger, but she had something to do with it. Her presence in these three related cases was no coincidence."

"I—"

"Don't answer." Fred waved his stubby fingers like a frenetic fan.

"I want the murderer caught and held accountable." Nina gripped her hands to still their shaking. "Newspaper clippings and a letter. That's it."

"Elaborate."

Nina ran through every detail she could remember from the seven articles.

"High-dollar settlements in your father's court, clients all represented by CG&P." He tapped the pen on the folder, his gaze fixed over her shoulder. "Where are the articles?"

A shudder ran through Nina. She took a breath. "Gone."

"Gone?"

"Someone took the envelope from my car."

"Someone?"

She explained in as few words as possible.

"A perfect example of why civilians should not meddle in murder investigations. Did you not think to bring that key to me? Did you not think to bring the envelope directly to me?" With each question, King's voice rose. He stood and began to pace. "Obviously not. Did you see why I'm so tempted to arrest you even if the DA's office says I don't have enough evidence to make it stick?"

"I would have, eventually. My concern was with protecting my dad's reputation." And her mother and her family's reputation. And Rick's reputation. What did he have to do with her dad's death? Nothing, surely. He cared about her dad. He cared about Nina. "He was a good man with a long record of public service. He deserves the benefit of the doubt."

"Which is why you failed to divulge his gambling addiction, that Grace Fischer planned to divorce him, and that he planned to retire from the bench to become a partner in CG&P."

"My father was a judge for twenty-plus years. Maybe he was ready for new challenges. That's not a crime." Nina's voice rose to match his. She took a breath and reined it in. Staying calm was half the battle. "My father loved being a judge. He loved lording it over others. As a partner in CG&P he would've been a great lawyer with huge resources at his fingertips."

More money for gambling.

King marched to the table, leaned over, and stabbed his finger in her face. "But you don't deny he had a gambling addiction."

"I don't deny it, no." Nina leaned away. "I'd appreciate if you didn't spit on me."

"Sorry." He whirled and began to pace again. "There's nothing you know that we don't already know. You need to understand that. We have your father's computer and access to all his emails and his search history. We have access to the texts on his phone and all his phone records. We have his financial records. Our IT folks are combing through them right now. Including the accounts in a bank in Las Vegas."

The technology age had made solving crimes easier and harder. "Did it occur to you that maybe he had gambling debts he didn't pay so some debt collector came looking for him?" Nina stared at King. He stared back. A game of chicken in which both refused to give. "They fought and he ended up dead."

King shoved a yellow notebook at her and a pen. "Write down everything you can remember about those articles. Everything."

She did as she was told, but only after giving him her most withering glare.

"Your father had almost a million in his Las Vegas account. He could afford to pay up." A million dollars. The penny-pinching Prius driver who constantly turned off the AC was a millionaire. "More likely his daughter wanted the money for her art gallery and photography business and didn't want to wait until he died of old age."

She slapped the pen on the notebook and shoved it back at the detective. "I didn't know Jan and I were the primary beneficiaries in his last will."

"All things considered, I'm worried about your sister reaching old age."

"You're crazy. I'm done listening to these ridiculous suppositions." She stumbled from her chair. "If you plan to arrest me, do it, and stop wasting my time."

"All he has is circumstantial evidence." Fred stood with more aplomb. "If he had enough to arrest you, you'd be behind bars right now."

"Then why read me my rights?"

"It's an intimidation tactic. Or in case his constant harassment and interrogation cause you to bless him with a confession." Fred slipped his arm under hers in an elegant gesture. "Come along, my dear, you look tired."

King slipped between them and the door. He put one hand on the knob. "Let's be very clear, shall we? The second I find a piece of evidence that connects you to these murders, I'm throwing your bony behind in jail."

"You, you, that's just—"

"Let's go." Fred hustled her out the door.

"He did not just call me bony."

"He's trying to get your goat."

"It's working."

She still hadn't told him about the neon notebooks.

31

Internet search engines were a thing of beauty. Horror making a nasty nest in the pit of her stomach, Nina stared at her laptop screen. In every case mentioned in the newspaper articles, her dad had heard pretrial motions. The motions had gone the way of Coggins, Gonzalez, and Pope. The dates of the newspaper articles corresponded to the dates in the neon notebooks. CG&P had paid her dad to rule in their favor, paving the way for more firepower to force settlements or winning jury trials. Low thunder rumbled in the distance. The bushes scraped against the house. It creaked in the wind. She slapped the laptop shut, shoved her chair away from her dad's desk, and stared up at Aaron.

"He was crooked."

Aaron paced the length of the study, did an about-face, and marched back to the desk that separated them. "It's circumstantial evidence, at best."

She grabbed a pen and made check marks next to each case on the new list she'd made of what she was able to recall from the stolen newspaper articles. It was better than the list she made for King because she wasn't under duress—much—when she made it. By searching the cases, she'd found the articles online and printed them. She and Aaron had been around and around about what to do with them.

Now it was ten o'clock at night, what was left of her family was asleep, and something had to be done about this newfound knowledge.

The connection had become apparent. The reason Dad had kept the articles in the safe-deposit box was also apparent. He needed money to pay his gambling debts and to finance more gambling. The money fueled his addiction. The money allowed him to create his alter ego in an alternate universe. Peter Coggins leveraged her father's weakness to get favorable judgments. In exchange for favorable rulings on motions entered by Coggins on big-dollar cases, Coggins paid her dad a percentage of the final judgment. Simple. Beautifully evil. "To top it off, my father was planning to blackmail Peter Coggins into giving him a piece of the partnership. That's what the letter of resignation was about."

"You don't know that for a fact."

"Why are you defending him? He was a liar." How would she tell Grace, who slept in the master suite upstairs, unaware of how far her husband's treachery had gone? How would she tell Jan, who deployed to Afghanistan in less than two weeks? And Trevor. He'd already imploded and disappeared to Austin with his tattoo-artist girlfriend. "He was a criminal."

"Because I know it's killing you." Aaron leaned over the desk. He slid his hand over hers and squeezed. "Which is killing me. Your father has let you down. He was murdered. You're treated like a suspect. Your biological mother shows up. You have a half brother and a sister you didn't know about. I don't know how much more one person can take."

She tugged her hand away. "I'm not a hothouse orchid. I can handle it."

"Believe me, I know you're one tough dude—"

"Aaron." She stood and grabbed her coffee mug. After three cups of Aaron's diesel-strength muddy brew, she should be able to leap buildings in a single bound. Instead, she felt like a wet dishcloth. "I need to talk to Rick."

"You can't. He's got to be in on it." Aaron stepped between her and the door. "We need to talk to King."

"He's well on his way to figuring this out. If he has financial records and phone records and Dad's emails, it's not going to be circumstantial. He'll follow the money trail."

"Then let him do his job and stay out of it. Three people are dead."

"I can't." She inhaled and swallowed against the lump in her throat. "I need to know what Rick's role in all this was. I can't believe he would stoop to murder. He's going to be the next state representative from our district. He worked so hard for that. So long. Why would he throw it all away?"

"What if it was Rick? What if the firm didn't like the idea of being blackmailed by the judge they corrupted?"

"There's no way Rick knows about this. He's a good guy." She did an end run around Aaron and headed down the hallway to the kitchen. Rick couldn't know. She had trusted her father. He was a liar and cheat. Not Rick too. She needed to be able to trust a childhood friend. "A little egotistical, but he's good. He wants to serve the public like my dad did. He wants to make a difference. He'll go with me to tell King. I know he will."

"He wants to be somebody and that can do weird stuff to people. You know that. He's a politician and politicians get in over their heads all the time."

"You're a cynical journalist."

"So are you, usually."

She set her coffee cup on the granite counter and tugged her phone from her hip pocket. "I'm calling him."

"Don't call him." Aaron reached for the phone. Nina danced back. He shook his head, his blue-gray eyes dark with concern. "Call King. Tell him our theory."

"I won't blindside Rick. I've known him—"

"Since you were nine. I know. He threw you a lifeline when you needed it. I know."

"Then let me do what I need to do." She went to the windows that overlooked the backyard. A full moon reigned. Stars twinkled. Light in the dark. She placed the call.

Rick answered on the first ring. *"Mi amor."*

He only let Spanish, rooted in his childhood, intrude when he was drinking or incredibly stressed or both. "Have you been drinking?"

"I had a couple of beers, that's all. It's Saturday night, after all." No slur in his voice, but still he sounded different. Amped up. "What's up?"

"I need you to come over." Nina turned from the window. The kitchen seemed no warmer or friendlier. "I need to talk to you about something, and I don't want to do it over the phone."

"I don't know. It's late and I've got court in the morning."

Confident Rick was gone, replaced by a guy with a hitch in his voice she hadn't heard since his stepdad smacked him around for stealing a Baby Ruth candy bar from the convenience store. The candy bar had been for his mama. Rick had always walked on moral thin ice. The ends justified the means. In relationships, in work, in life. "What's wrong?"

"Nothing. Nothing besides, you know, life in general."

"Before my dad died, you would be here 24/7 if I let you. Now I need you and you don't want to come." Nina turned her back on Aaron and his wildly gesticulating hands telling her to hang up. Careful to keep her voice low, she marched back down the hall to the office. "Is it because you know something about my dad's death?"

"No. No, of course not." The more he protested, the guiltier he sounded. "No, that's not it. I'll be there in ten." He disconnected.

Nina laid the phone on the desk. She leaned over and slapped both hands on the cool, slick varnished wood. Her stomach knotted. She swallowed against acrid bile. "He's coming."

"So I gathered." Aaron flopped into the overstuffed chair by the window. He swiped at his face with both hands. His eyes were blood-shot with exhaustion. "I hope you know what you're doing."

Nina did too.

Eight minutes later his knock—more of a pounding—sounded on the door.

Nina opened it and Rick shoved past her. He brought with him a cold wind. His dark hair was tousled and curled to his head. "I don't know anything about your dad's death, okay, nothing."

"Shush! Everyone is sleeping, and I'd like to keep it that way. They've been through a lot."

"You didn't tell me this jerk was here." He gestured at Aaron, who rose from his chair, his burly frame bristling. "What do you need me for? You've got golden boy photog. He speaks your language."

"Calm down. I found some things—Aaron and I found some things. I need to know . . . what you know. An envelope was stolen from my car after the accident yesterday. An envelope from Dad's safe-deposit box. It had articles—"

"Why are you telling me this now? Why didn't you let me help you with the safe-deposit box?" He threw his hands up. "I'm a lawyer, for crying out loud."

"Quiet! I was trying to protect my dad's reputation. I knew how much you respected him, revered him. You were like a second son to him. I thought maybe it wouldn't have to all come out."

Rick gave a bitter, half-strangled laugh. "But not anymore?"

"I think my dad's double life got Melanie and Serena killed." She couldn't live with that. No matter what it meant for Judge Geoffrey Fischer. Or for Rick Zavala. "I want their murders solved too. It all has to come out."

"You're playing with fire, both of you. Please, please, let it go." He backed away from the desk, away from Aaron. "Let the police figure it out. You should leave for a while, both of you. Go skiing. Go mountain climbing. Go to the Caribbean."

"You want Aaron and me to go somewhere together?"

"I do."

"You are drunk."

"Not drunk."

He didn't sound drunk. He sounded terrified. Nina moved toward him. She reached out her hand, touched his sleeve. "What is it? What is wrong? Please tell me."

Rick shoved her hand away. Slowly, he stepped back. He pulled a small black gun from his pocket. "I didn't want it to come to this. You have to believe me. I love you. *Te amo, mi amor.* Always have. Always will."

The gun loomed, bigger and bigger, until it filled Nina's vision. "Rick."

"Don't say a word. Please don't scream. Don't yell. I don't want Brooklyn to come down. Or Grace. You have to believe me, I love you all like family." He flashed the gun at Aaron. "Both of you move. *Move.*" His sob broke her heart. "I don't want to hurt you."

A parade of three, they made their way in silence to the hallway, then to the front door. "Move." He jerked the gun. "Up against the wall."

"Rick—"

"Shut up, *por favor.* Please." He backed toward the door, grabbed the knob, and pulled.

In walked Mr. Five-O'clock Shadow. The gun in his hand made Rick's look like a kid's water gun.

32

Seeing the events through the lens of a camera. Sharp. In focus. Low light. Flash needed. But Nina had no camera in her hands. Nothing separated her and Aaron from two men with guns. One of them her best friend for years.

Not anymore.

"If you scream, I'll kill every one of the people in this house." Mr. Five-O'clock Shadow's cannon dipped toward Nina. "Anyone you wake up is dead." His lazy smile broadened, but his eyes left no doubt he meant it. "You remember me, don't you, beautiful?"

"I recognize you, yes. You took the envelope from my car under the guise of being a good Samaritan." She also recognized his smell. Paco Rabanne. "Why are you doing this?"

"Because you're too nosy for your own good." Five-O'clock Shadow reached into his pocket and pulled out a set of keys on a glittery key chain. Grace's keys. He tossed them on the floor. "I also paid you a visit in the middle of the night, if you'll recall. Who knew Peter could be so sneaky as to steal them right under your noses."

A trusted family friend's mask ripped away. Peter had let this man into her house. He molded Rick into someone she didn't recognize. "Rick, please don't do this. Stop it. Stop him."

Rick didn't move. He didn't speak, but his face crumpled.

"Shut up, beautiful." Five-O'clock Shadow motioned toward

Rick. "Point the way to her darkroom. Then get out. You did your thing, let me do mine."

"You don't get to call her beautiful." Rick's gun wavered. He no longer looked like an up-and-coming politician, a polished attorney, a man with a purpose. He looked like the scared elementary school kid waiting to get jumped by the gang who sold meth on his street every day after school. "You don't get to call her anything."

"Shut up, little Peter." Five O'clock jammed the gun in Nina's chest. His smile never changed. "Hey, cupcake, let's take a little tour of your darkroom."

"You stole something from me. I want it back. Do you work for Peter Coggins? Did you kill Serena Cochrane?" It took every ounce of strength, but Nina kept her voice to a whisper. Aaron's hand crept into hers. She squeezed but never took her gaze from the intruder. "Or were you too busy killing Melanie Martinez? Did you kill my dad?"

"That's a lot of questions. 'Course you used to work for the newspaper, didn't you?" He hadn't bothered to hide his face. He didn't intend for them to describe him to anyone. His smile punctuated that fact. "This is no story, pretty lady, at least not one you'll be telling. You can call me Skeeter or Skeet for short. I'm a friend of a friend, you might say."

"Why are you doing this?"

"Money."

Her heart thudded. Cold sweat trickled between her shoulder blades. Nausea gagged her. "You kill people for money."

"And kicks sometimes. This time it's mostly money. I don't dig killing beautiful chicks." He talked like a bad movie script. "Move. Zavala, get out now."

Rick stumbled forward. "No, I changed my mind. You can't do this."

"Are you gonna do it?"

"No, but—"

"Think, buddy. Do you want to make Peter mad? No, I don't think you do. Are you willing to give up your career, your law license, your future because you have the hots for this lady?"

Rick shook his head. "I'm sorry, I'm so sorry, Nina. I didn't mean for this to happen." His voice trembled. Tears leaked down his cheeks. "If you'd just let things alone, none of this would've happened."

"You selfish sack of crapola. You're crying instead of doing the right thing." Aaron lunged at Rick. "Go ahead, shoot me, you coward."

Rick didn't shoot him. He smashed the gun in Aaron's face. The blow knocked him back into Nina's arms. The breath knocked from her lungs, she staggered under his weight and hit the wall. "Get away from us. Get away now."

"You have to believe me, Nina, I didn't want to hurt anyone. I didn't kill your dad." Rick's voice rose. "I told you that."

"Keep your voice down." *Don't wake up, Brooklyn. Don't wake up, Jan. Please Grace—Mom—don't wake up. Please.* Nina sank to the floor, Aaron in her lap. He groaned and struggled to sit up. Nina wiped blood from his nose and lips with her sleeve. "It's okay, we're together," she whispered. She glared up at Rick, who was more of a stranger than Skeeter. "Maybe you didn't do it personally, but you had it done by a baboon like this."

"No, I didn't. We didn't. We were as surprised as you were—"

"Enough small talk." Skeet pointed the gun at Rick. "Go, now, while you still can. Or you can join the party in the darkroom as one of her victims. A love triangle, how does that sound?"

Rick backed toward the door. "What are you going to do to them?"

"Miss Thing here is despondent. Terribly despondent over her father's death. She can't bear to live. She takes her boyfriend with her when she goes."

"No one will believe that. No one." Nina scrambled to her feet and helped Aaron up. He grabbed her arm and planted himself in front of her. "I would never hurt him."

"And I'd never hurt her."

"Just like your buddy Rick. Haven't you learned? It's amazing what people do under duress. Let's go. Where's the darkroom?"

"Upstairs." Rick had his hand on the doorknob. He jerked the door open. "Third floor."

"Of course it is."

"Good-bye, Nina. Good-bye." Rick whirled and stumbled through the door. He closed it gently behind him.

Nina entwined her fingers with Aaron's. Together they plodded up the stairs. His nose dripped blood on the front of his shirt and the carpet. Like red bread crumbs. The murder-suicide scenario would never work. Not with Aaron's injuries. Surely Skeet would see that. Did he have a Plan B? Her body shook. She stumbled. Aaron's grip tightened.

"Why the darkroom?" She tried to keep her voice conversational. Wasn't that what they did in the movies? They kept the killer talking to buy time to figure out the big escape.

"Because it's poetic. That place of creation became a place of destruction."

A killer with a sense of poetry.

At the top of the stairs, Nina paused. Daffy hopped from the couch and meandered their direction. She stopped. Her back arched. She hissed.

"A black cat crosses your path. Nice." Skeet's laugh rumbled in his throat. "Not your lucky day."

Daffy streaked past them down the stairs. Peanuts and Mango would be in Grace's room where she always shut the door. Runner had retired to Brooklyn's room as usual. The door was shut to keep grown-up noise out. One small thing for which Nina could be thankful. *Please God, let them sleep through this.*

The three of them squeezed into a room that once had been her sanctuary.

"Hmmm. Nice." Skeet tapped the photos of Liz clipped to the clothesline rope. "Friend of yours? Auntie Em?"

"Mother."

"No wonder you're about to kill yourself."

"I'm not."

"Keep your voice down. Remember, you don't want poor little Brooklyn to get caught up in this."

"Would you really kill a little girl?"

"I charge more for minors since it's a death-penalty offense in this state."

"So is killing two or more at the same time."

"I'm aware. Which is why I don't plan to get caught." When he smiled, he resembled a wolf. A ravenous, rabid wolf. "Have a seat, photographer guy. It was so nice of you to be here. You saved me a trip to that rat trap you call an apartment." He gestured at the floor. "Side by side."

The gun flicked across Aaron's forehead, ruffled his hair. "We need just the right angle to make this scenario fly." Frowning, Skeeter stepped back and tilted his head. "I'm not seeing it. Are you seeing it? Stand up. Over by the counter. I think we need to reverse the scenario. Photog man is despondent because you want nothing to do with him. He decides to kill you and then himself. You fight back. He's wounded but determined. He gets the job done."

"I would never hurt her." Glaring at Skeet, Aaron helped her to her feet. His hands fisted. "You're crazy if you think anyone would buy that. They all know I've been in love with her for a hundred years."

"A hundred years—"

"Now is not the time." Aaron's blue-gray eyes were luminous in the soft darkroom lights. "But let's just say it was love at first sight six years ago."

Tears clogged Nina's throat. They had wasted so much time. She had wasted so much time with Rick. So much time not trusting the man standing next to her. *God, please forgive me for taking so long to trust You and him.*

"I'm sorry." She managed a whisper. "I'm sorry I didn't see. I love you too. No matter what happens now."

Aaron sighed. "Would it sound stupid if I said I'm insanely happy right now?"

Skeeter laughed so hard he coughed, but the cannon never wavered. "You two are ridiculous. Man, is the joke on poor Ricky boy. He didn't have a chance with wonder boy here." Skeeter pretended to stick his free finger down his throat. "You two lovebirds are killing me with this mushy stuff. Let's get down to business before I lose my supper all over your shoes."

Nina wanted to live. For the first time in years, she wanted to live the life on the other side of her camera. A long life or however long God intended. With Aaron. Nina cast a glance around the darkroom. The enlarger. Chemicals. She edged toward the gray tubs on the counter. "Did you kill my dad?"

"No, ma'am, I did not."

"There's no reason to lie." She glanced at Aaron. His gaze drifted toward the counter. His nod was infinitesimal. They had nothing to lose. "It's not like I'll be able to tell someone."

"I'm not lying. I didn't have nothing to do with it. My boss is as stumped as you are."

Aaron edged toward the counter. "Peter Coggins, you mean."

"I signed a confidentiality agreement."

"You signed an agreement for murder?" Aaron snorted, more of a groan than a laugh. "You put it in writing? That's a lawyer for you."

"Figuratively speaking."

Together they grabbed the tub of developer and hurled its acidic, toxic contents at Skeet.

He threw an arm up to cover his face, ducked, and staggered back.

"Drop it. Police."

Skeet whirled.

The boom of shots fired filled the air. Nina dove to the floor. Aaron's weight told her his body covered hers.

It was over. That fast and that slow.

33

"Are you hit? Nina, are you hit?"

She tried to answer Aaron's frantic questions, but she couldn't get enough air to breathe, let alone talk. "Get off me," she gasped. "Get off."

Aaron stumbled to his feet and held out his hand. She grabbed it. Her legs wobbled, but she managed to stand upright. "Are you hurt?" She patted his blood-speckled shirt. His hands touched her cheeks, her shoulders, her hands. She looked down. She was speckled too.

The blood wasn't Aaron's.

Or hers.

Skeet lay on the floor, facedown. Detective Cavazos squatted next to him. He touched his fingers to the man's neck. He glanced up at King and shook his head.

King sighed and turned back to Nina. "That's what they call a squeaker."

"How did you know?"

"Rick Zavala called the station looking for me."

She leaned into Aaron. Chills ran through her mixed with white heat. Sweat rolled down Aaron's face. His hair was damp. So were his eyes. "I told you he wasn't a bad man."

King sighed again. "He also admitted he murdered Melanie Martinez." He motioned for them to follow him from the darkroom. "Careful where you step, please. What did you throw on him?"

"Developer. It's an irritant for skin and eyes."

"I gathered that."

"Is it over? Someone talk to me. What is going on?" Grace's high-pitched demands wafted through the open door to the stairs. "Somebody, please!"

Nina wobbled toward the stairs. King grabbed her arm. "They're fine. I need you to stay put for a minute, okay?"

His phone went to his ear. He asked for an ambulance. Paramedics. CSU.

She didn't need an ambulance. She needed to see her family. "I'm fine. Is everyone all right?"

"I checked on everyone." King's partner appeared at the top of the stairs. "They're fine. I'll meet CSU at the door."

King nodded and gave Cavazos a thumbs-up. They seemed to be getting along better. "Your friend Rick gave us the lay of the land."

"He's not my friend."

"I'm sorry about that." He did seem sorry. "What were you thinking? Are you that naive or truly morons?"

"Hey." Aaron tottered as if he might make a run at King. Nina took his hand. "Name calling isn't necessary."

"You couldn't trust the professionals to do their jobs? You had to get in our way."

"You were busy looking at me, interrogating me and Aaron and Jan and Trevor. Instead of finding out who really killed my dad. I had no choice."

"Says you." He sounded like a fifth grader. "We had the money trail. We had the electronic trail of texts and emails. We needed to cross a few more t's, that's all. Police work takes time. It's not guns blazing. It's methodical evidence collection that solves cases."

"Are you done?"

"I'm done."

"Rick killed my dad because he tried to blackmail Peter Coggins into taking him on as a partner?"

"The conversation was fast and furious and slightly garbled, but he says no."

Nina strangled the urge to scream. "Seriously? He'll admit to killing Melanie but not my dad?"

"I haven't had a chance to interrogate him. This was a ninety-second phone call. We were more concerned with getting here before we had two more murders—or more—on my hands. Don't worry, before this is over, he'll admit it."

"What about Peter Coggins and the others?" Aaron's words were slurred as if the reality of the last thirty minutes—had it only been thirty minutes?—had stunned him. "Do they know it's over?"

"My folks are rousting them from bed as we speak. We need to grab them before they realize what went down here." King grinned happily. "They won't know old Skeet here is dead for a while. It gives us a chance to milk them. They'll think we know more than we do."

"He was the guy in the park." Aaron swiped at his nose. Blood soaked his sleeve. "The guy following you and Liz."

Nina snatched a tissue from the box on her coffee table. "He was the guy who reached over me after the accident and grabbed the envelope from my car. I could smell the Paco Rabanne on him."

Aaron took her offering. "Who was driving the SUV that hit Nina?"

"We don't know everything. Possibly Jerome Solomon, your dad's bailiff, or one of Skeet Miles's thugs from his so-called security firm. It's a work in progress—one we would've finished if two amateurs playing with fire hadn't gotten in our way." King shrugged. "We do know this guy was a bad dude who hired himself out as a hit man. His real name is Marcus Miles."

"Where's Rick now?"

"He said he was on his way downtown to turn himself in."

King stood back to let a paramedic pass. The woman glanced from Nina to Aaron and then back. "He looks a little worse for wear. I'll start with him."

"I hate to do this to you, but I need both of you to come downtown one more time to be interviewed." King yawned and checked his watch. "Cavazos will handle it."

"Not you?" Nina was too tired for sarcasm. She wanted to sleep. She wanted to think. She needed to think about Aaron's words and what she'd said to him. They needed to talk before the light of day made them both too scared to admit they'd spoken the truth under duress. It wasn't fear of dying. It was fear of living. "Are you headed home to catch up on your beauty sleep or something?"

"I imagine I'll be tied up with the officer-involved shooting team for quite a while. Again."

34

Brooklyn looked so peaceful when she slept, her stuffed giraffe tucked under the sheet with her. Perpetual motion stilled by exhaustion. Nina stood in the doorway and watched in the soft glow of a nightlight while Jan pulled up the pink-and-purple comforter, patted Runner's knobby head, and slipped away from the bed.

A soft *woof* hummed in the dog's throat as he settled down, head on paws, on the fluffy pink rug next to the bed. One of the three amigos—her gerbils—stretched and curled up again around his buddies. The wheel in their cage squeaked, then stilled.

"She never woke up." Rubbing red-rimmed eyes, Jan smiled. "Runner never left her side. If an intruder came in here, he'd make mincemeat out of him."

Runner stood guard over the most precious, innocent, defenseless person in the house. "Good dog. We need to give him extra rations."

Nina led the way down the hall to the kitchen. The crime-scene folks were still working upstairs. Aaron sat with Grace in the living room, alternately holding her hand and filling her coffee mug. "We need to talk."

"I know." Jan selected a coffee pod and stuck it in the Keurig. "I can't believe Rick and CG&P were behind this. Coggins always gave me the creeps, but Rick? Dad did so much for him. He took a maid's son and gave him an education and helped him get a position at a good law firm. Plus Rick's been in love with you forever."

"Rick couldn't separate his feelings for me from his desire to be somebody. I knew he was ambitious, but I never saw this coming. Who would've?" Nina collapsed on a stool at the island. The muscles in her legs and arms still trembled hours later. She had given her sister the high points—or in this case, the low points—after the detectives finished grilling her. She and Aaron would have to go downtown yet again for formal statements later in the day. "I want you to know I tried hard—so hard—to protect his name. Our name. Now it's all going to come out."

"It's not your fault. It's on him." Jan's tone was hard, but pain and exhaustion etched lines around her mouth and eyes. "I understand wanting to protect him, but he blew it. Not you. He was so pious and sanctimonious about Liz's addiction. Come to find out he had his own. One he let destroy him."

Jan had always been the clear thinker, the logical one in the family. The knots in Nina's stomach tightened. There would be a firestorm of stories on every outlet in town and beyond for days to come. Everything she'd wanted to avoid for her family's sake would come to pass now. She couldn't control it. She never could. If she'd learned anything from the past few weeks, it was that fact. She was not in control.

Eventually this story would become old news. It would be replaced by another story of a cheating politician or another celebrity who used his position to abuse a woman. Life would go on. The media would leave the Fischer family alone to heal and to learn from the mistakes they'd made. "Addiction runs in families."

"It does, so we always have to be on guard." Jan added skim milk to her coffee and stirred with more vigor than necessary. "You and me and Trevor. And we have to set the example for Brooklyn."

"Always." Which brought them around to Liz and what Nina had not shared with Jan. No more secrets. Her sister needed to know everything before she deployed. "We need to talk about Liz."

"She abandoned us. I don't know why she's here now, but she can't just hop on the bandwagon now that Dad's gone."

"I need to show you something." Nina picked up the stack of letters from the island. King hadn't objected to her bringing them downstairs, the letters and the box where she kept her mementos. "We know Dad hid many things from us—"

"Lied to us, you mean." Jan plucked her mug from the Keurig and moved to the island. She cupped it in both hands. Her eyes were bloodshot and her hair a tangled mess. The purple-striped terry cloth robe hung open, revealing her favorite Mickey Mouse nightshirt. "Pretended to be a Christian. Pretended to be a law-abiding judge."

"It's true. I'm still trying to absorb all this too. He was a flawed human being, but that doesn't change the fact that he loved us. He was our father, the only one we'll ever have." Nina touched the yellowed envelope on top with its loopy handwriting in faded ink. Postmark Miami, Florida. "Dad loved us so much he didn't want us to know he wasn't perfect. He made mistakes. Big mistakes. Not showing us these letters was one."

Jan pushed away her cup and picked up the first envelope. "Letters from whom?"

"From Mom."

"From Liz, you mean."

"Yes. She wrote to us. I don't know what was going through his head. Maybe he didn't want us to be let down by her again." Mango strolled into the room and made a beeline for Nina. He wound himself around the wooden stool leg. Nina hopped down and scooped him up. She needed pet therapy like never before. His warm body and throbbing purr eased the tension in her shoulders and arms. "He knew he was giving us a better life, one she could never give us. I don't know, but he did what he thought was best."

"She wrote us?" Jan ran her fingers over the envelope and looked up at Nina. "Where were they? You've read these?"

"I have." Running her hands across Mango's soft orange fur over and over, Nina explained how the letters came into her possession. "She wanted us back. Dad didn't want us to know. I was waiting for the right time to tell you. So much has happened, I didn't want to heap more coals on the fire."

"Are they going to make me even sadder?"

"Probably."

"I can't take that right now." Jan dropped the envelope. "I'm getting ready to deploy to a country where you can expect to be served an IED with breakfast. I'm spending three days with a husband I haven't seen in six months before I go. I'm leaving my seven-year-old daughter, who just lost her grandpa, again. I don't need this."

"I understand. But I couldn't let you go without you knowing that our mother cared enough to write us. Sixteen times. She sent us photos. She remembered good times." Nina settled Mango on her lap so she could pull the photos from her rose-covered memento box. She held them out. "She wanted us back. That's something to hang on to when you think about her. Grace will always be our mother, but we can have two moms."

Jan examined the two photos, one at the motel, the other on Christmas Day. Her face crumpled. "I loved that doll."

"Me too."

"There were good times, now and then, weren't there?" Sweet resignation colored Jan's face. Gone was the military sniper, the platoon commander. For a second she looked like that little girl who wanted McDonald's chicken nuggets, french fries, and ice cream for her sixth birthday but settled for hot dogs and beans drenched in barbecue sauce at the soup kitchen. "Or do I just pretend that to make myself feel better?"

"Good times are relative when you're homeless." A fresh orange. Soap. Clean underwear. Socks. An air-conditioned library with free books and a clean bathroom fully stocked with toilet paper. Nina held up her single seashell. "Only Liz could make it sound normal not to be able to keep all the seashells we collected because there wasn't room for them in the car where we lived."

"I loved going to the beach."

"She remembers that. She remembers how fearless you were. How she had to drag you from the waves."

"She does?" Tears trickled down Jan's face. She didn't seem to notice. "Remember those new sneakers we got that Christmas? They had lights on the soles that lit up when we walked. I loved those shoes."

"We have to hang on to the good memories." Nina slid from her chair, gave Mango one last pat, and settled him on the floor. He stretched and strolled to his water bowl. Nina slipped closer to her sister and opened her arms for a hug. Jan returned the favor with a ferocity that could only come from having walked through those years together and survived. Because they had each other. "Aaron always says that forgiving lifts a huge burden. It lets you move on with your life. It frees you from the past. That's what I want now. To let it go and be free. If I can forgive Dad for everything he did, I guess I can forgive Mom for not caring enough. Or being unable to care. Do you think you can?"

"I'll try. I just know I never want Brooklyn to feel like I feel right now." Jan's voice broke. "If I don't come back, she'll need all the family she can get."

"You're coming back. You're good at what you do. Brooklyn knows you love her. She's proud of you." Nina grabbed a tissue, handed it to Jan, and then snatched one for herself. "She has a great mom and a great dad, a grandma, and an aunt and an uncle who love her like crazy."

"Because they are crazy." Jan hiccupped the laugh of exhaustion and near hysteria. "They'll find us in the dictionary next to the word *dysfunctional*."

Nina sucked in a breath. If only this conversation could end here. One more revelation had to be made. "That's not all."

Jan groaned. "You're kidding, right? Why not lower the boom all at once? Rip the bandage off. It hurts less."

"We have a sister and a brother. Half sister and half brother."

"She had more kids?" Jan closed her eyes and opened them. "How old? Living with her all this time? Where have they been? On the street?"

"Thirteen and ten. It's a horrifying thought, isn't it?"

"What they've been through." Shaking her head, Jan wadded up the tissue in a ball. "I don't have to imagine. Neither of us do. We know. She wanted us back, she didn't get us, so she replaced us."

"I'm trying not to look at it like that. I sincerely doubt it was a conscious decision, any more than having us was." Nina rubbed Jan's back the way she used to do at night when they first moved into this house. Jan would slip from her bunk bed and climb into bed with Nina "just this once." Every night. "They're the reason I want to make peace with her. They need our help. Dad isn't around anymore to save them."

"She's not handing them over."

"No, but she came back for a reason. I'm hoping it's because she knows they need family. They need us. She needs us."

Jan ducked away from Nina. She took her coffee cup to the sink, rinsed it, and placed it in the dishwasher. She stood for several seconds, her back to Nina. Finally, she turned. She looked far too sad and old for a woman her age. The expression would be the one Nina saw in the mirror in the morning. "I agree. I'm sorry I won't be here to help you with this. Send me pictures. I'll skype when I can."

"I will. I promise."

"I want to know everything. I need to take a shower. I feel dirty." Jan started for the door, then reversed directions and headed to the island where she scooped up the letters. "May I take these for a few days?"

"They're as much yours as they are mine."

Jan held them against her chest. She sighed. "Does she say who your dad is? Or mine?"

Nina shook her head. Some things were better off left unsaid. She would not send her sister off to war with the knowledge that her mother didn't know who her father was. It wasn't a lie. Nowhere in the letters did Liz talk about their fathers. Let the Superman theory go with Jan. She would need it. "No, but she makes it very clear that she wanted us back. And she's here now. She wants to be a part of our lives now."

"I can live with that. Like I have a choice." Her smile was grim. The career Army woman was back. "Of course, I'll take the easy way out and go to Afghanistan and let you deal with this entire mess. Liz. Mom. The siblings. Trevor."

"You'll be busy serving your country. We're even."

She saluted Nina and strode from the room with the same determined stride that had taken her to the recruiting office not long after Brooklyn's birth.

Making peace with the past took time, but they were both headed in the right direction. Nina went to find Aaron.

35

The doorbell rang. Nina jumped and shrieked. "Get a grip."

Talking to herself wasn't a good sign, even though every day the anxiety and the sense of walking on the razor's edge lessened a little. Day by day, she thought a little less about those moments in the darkroom with the man she loved and the man who planned to kill them both. The night when she had been certain she would never have the chance to live. Yet she still jumped at every noise, flinched at every backfire. Her therapist said it would take time. Give it time.

Strangely, the panic attacks had stopped. Simply stopped. As if given a true reason to panic, she'd learned not to do it for smaller, less earth-shattering crises. Time would heal the other wounds.

That was one thing she would never take for granted again. Time. No one had as much as they thought they did. People walked around like they were immortal. She'd said those words, her voice filled with despair, at her last session.

"It'll get easier. One day at a time." Dr. Wallace said so and Nina believed it. With Aaron in her life, anything was possible.

She had a chance at a fresh start. Honed by the fire, like silver. No one said it would be easy, but she had God and Aaron in her life. First, she had unfinished business. Liz and her half brother and half sister. She wanted a clean slate with her biological mother. They would somehow become a family.

Starting with a simple dinner. Nina wiped her hands on the dish towel and glanced at the table. Everything looked perfect. Sunflowers for a centerpiece. Place settings for four. Liz, Hudson, Emma, and herself. Aaron had wanted to come as moral support, but Nina preferred to do this on her own. She would welcome her mother and her half siblings into her life. Starting with homemade lasagna, garlic bread, fresh tossed salad, and Dutch apple pie, her specialty. Food made everything better. The aromas mingled in a homey scent that calmed her stomach and her spirit.

The doorbell jangled a second time.

"Here we go." This she directed to Daffy and Mango, who ducked under the table, ready to attack any unwelcome intruders. Peanuts took the lead down the hallway. Runner, the big baby, headed for Brooklyn's empty room. "Coming."

Nina opened the door. A six-pack of Diet Dr Pepper in one hand and a brown paper bag tucked against her chest, Liz swept past her. "Took you long enough." She chuckled as if to underline an attempt at humor. "This is Hudson and Emma. Hudson is the shy one." She kept walking. "I brought the drinks."

A brother and sister Nina never knew she had. Nothing seemed familiar in Hudson's dark-brown hair, amber eyes, and bronze skin. He needed a haircut. Emma had a peaches-and-cream complexion. She wore thick, curly blonde hair past her shoulders. She needed a brush. Except for her blue eyes, she didn't look much like her mother. Did they have the same father? Did Liz know who their father was? Again, the questions pursued her, giving her a strange sense of déjà vu.

Not sure how to proceed with these newfound relatives, Nina held out her hand. Hudson shook but his gaze bounced from the floor to the ceiling. Emma ignored the hand and threw both arms around Nina in the kind of hug a person gave to her favorite aunt. "Are you really my sister?"

"I really am."

"Half sister." Hudson had that adolescent boy voice teetering on the edge of puberty.

"Right. Come in the kitchen. I have ice for the sodas. We can sit on the patio for a few minutes while I heat the garlic bread. The lasagna has to sit for a few minutes before I cut it."

She was babbling. Liz didn't seem to notice. She headed straight for the island in the middle of the kitchen. She deposited the sodas and fumbled with the paper sack. It held a bottle of red wine.

Nina froze in the middle of the kitchen. "I thought you quit drinking."

Hudson snorted and Emma opened her mouth. Liz pointed one finger at them. Emma's mouth closed. "I did. I did." Liz's pasty cheeks darkened. "That doesn't mean you can't have a glass of wine with dinner."

"I don't drink."

"You are the smart girl. I'll leave it for Grace. She always liked a decent merlot."

Grace never drank anything stronger than ginger ale. *Breathe.* Nina pulled the lasagna from the oven. With any luck the kids would think the heat was the reason for her red face.

Liz made a beeline for the cabinet. She found the glasses on the first try. Helped herself to the veggie tray and dip on the island. Picked up Peanuts and scratched his favorite spot behind his ears. All as if she'd lived in this house forever.

Nina scooped up her camera and led the way out the back door. Small plates in hand, they trailed out to the deck where Grace had artfully arranged rattan chairs with palm tree-print pillows around a glass-top table. An early October breeze lifted the leaves in the live oaks and pecans. Gray and heavy, clouds scudded across the sky, making the sun play hide-and-seek as it set in the west. The air felt heavy,

like rain. The kids stood stiffly until Liz ordered them to sit. They sat
on either side of their mother, who seemed oblivious to their discomfort. Their silence unnerved Nina. "Have you started school?"

"Yes." They answered in unison.

"Do you like it?"

"No." That was Hudson.

"Yes." Emma cracked her first smile. "I like to read. A lot."

Nina smiled back. "Me too."

Going slow like a photographer on an African savannah, she
eased the camera to her face.

"Always the photographer." Liz frowned. "What's up with that?"

"It's how I get to know people."

"Whatever." Liz lit a cigarette.

Neither child moved as the smoke drifted into their faces. Liz
draped one arm around Emma. The girl coughed behind one thin
hand. She was short and skinny for a ten-year-old. Pearl would want
to fatten her up. She wore a faded cotton shirt and baggy khaki pants
a size too big. Wrinkled but clean. Hudson, who was tall and gangly,
wore a green T-shirt and jeans that were a little too tight. Like he'd
suddenly outgrown them.

"Do the cops think this Rick Zavala guy killed Geoffrey, but he
won't confess to it?"

Nina let the camera lean against her chest. "We don't have to talk
about that right now."

"Don't worry about the kids." Liz rested the cigarette on the plate
and snagged a carrot. She doused it in dill dip. The sound of crunch-
ing followed. "They know. They live in the real world."

She didn't wait to swallow before talking. Geoffrey's parents had
taught them manners. Liz had attended excellent private schools. She
chose her mode of existence. She chose to be this person.

The question was why. The answer flummoxed Nina. Shock

value? Sour grapes? Too many drugs? Too much alcohol? All of the above?

"Rick confessed to killing Melanie Martinez to keep her from finding out about the firm's involvement in bribery and corruption. His boss, Peter Coggins, is charged with hiring the man who killed Serena Cochrane and tried to kill me, but neither one of them will admit to killing Dad. They're all charged with conspiracy to commit murder, public corruption, racketeering, and anything else the district attorney can come up with."

"I guess they're trying to avoid the death penalty."

"Maybe." This was a fresh start night. Not a night for discussing murder and corruption. Nina snapped a few more photos in rapid succession. "Give me a smile, you two, come on. Let's have a nice family photo."

Hudson's smirk would have to do. "How about a funny outtake? Give me your best cheesy looks."

This they did well. All three of them hammed it up for the camera. Tongues sticking out, cross-eyed, eyes shut, mouths open. "Good, this is good. You guys are great."

Feeling more relaxed for the first time in days, Nina lowered the camera. "The bread should be warm by now. Who's ready to eat?"

"Me!" Emma dashed for the door.

Hudson followed at a pace more suited for a teenager in the making.

"I hope you like lasagna." Nina used mitten potholders to carry the main attraction into the dining room. "It's hamburger and spicy sausage."

"My mouth is watering. I'm so hungry." Emma carried the bread basket. She scooted into the first chair. "I could eat a horse."

"I thought you wanted to be a vegan." Hudson snorted. "Like you can afford to be picky."

"Okay, you two. Eat and keep your mouths shut like civilized human beings." Liz plopped down in the chair at the end of the table. Where her brother once sat. And before him, her father. "I get so sick of listening to them bicker."

"It's okay. Jan and I did plenty of that growing up." Liz had missed that part of their life. But that was behind them now. Now they would make up for lost time. "Emma, what grade are you in?"

"Third." She glanced at her mother, then at her empty plate. Her earlier effervescence dissipated. "We changed schools a few times. I got behind—"

"I wish Jan and Brooklyn could be here. I really wanted to spend some time with my grandbaby." The bite in Liz's tone didn't match her words. "And Trevor, you never did say where he went."

"Brooklyn needed to spend some time with her dad after his being deployed for seven months. And it's tough on her when her mom deploys immediately after him." Why did she feel like she had to make excuses? Will and Brooklyn always went camping to ease the ache during Jan's first week of deployment. Their lives had been like this long before Liz decided to return. "Trevor is moving this weekend. To Austin. He got a job teaching at a private college up there. He needed a fresh start."

"Good for him." Again, her tone said the opposite. "And, of course, Gracie is off writing somewhere. They both have to recover from getting shafted in the will."

"Grace doesn't feel shafted. She decided a retreat with some writing friends in Wyoming would be a good way to get her fresh start."

Liz dumped ranch dressing on her salad and picked up her fork.

"Let's say grace before we eat."

Hudson and Emma stared at Nina with startled expressions as if she'd just asked them to undress in public.

"Sure. Sure. You go ahead." Liz dropped her fork. Her gaze swiveled toward her children. "Don't act like heathens. Bow your heads."

Nina prayed over the food and added a silent request for the right words to make this a fresh start for everyone in the room. "What about you, Hudson, what do you like to do for fun?"

"Basketball, soccer, baseball. Anything that involves a ball." The boy dug into the extra-large piece of lasagna Nina had served him. "I've made some friends this summer at the Y and they go to the same school so we play pickup basketball every day—"

"You were here this summer?" Nina's hand froze over the bread basket. Her hunger receded, replaced with faint nausea. "When did you get to San Antonio?"

"Fourth of July weekend. We watched the fireworks at Woodlawn Lake, 'cuz they were free. Who knew there was a place in Texas hotter than Houston?"

"I thought you came here from Baton Rouge." A few days after Dad's death, according to Liz.

"What is this, the third degree?" Liz stuffed a chunk of bread in her mouth, chewed, and swallowed. "We were in Baton Rouge, we stopped in Houston. We were here and there. It's not like I kept a diary. I don't know exactly what day we got here."

"It was the day after my birthday." Emma chimed in. She had sauce on her chin. "Remember, Grandpa bought me an ice cream that day we saw him in the park."

Grandpa could only be one person in these children's lives. Geoffrey Fischer.

"You said you arrived right after Dad died." The smell of lasagna turned Nina's stomach. Her mouth went dry. She took a sip of water and swallowed the lump of sawdust in the back of her throat. "You said you wished you had a chance to talk to him before he died."

"You misunderstood." Liz took a long swallow of soda. She burped behind her hand. "You heard what you wanted to hear."

The aroma of bread mingled with the pie's cinnamon and brown sugar no longer smelled enticing. "My hearing is excellent."

"Why are you making such a big deal about this?"

"Because you lied." Just like her brother. "You lied about everything. Why?"

Liz dumped her napkin on her plate. "I don't have to sit here and take this from my own daughter. Show some respect."

Another liar. Dad lied. Liz lied. She couldn't trust this person. Grace was her mother. Would always be her only real mother. "For a person who's a pathological liar? You have to earn respect."

"That's what Mom always tells us." Emma piped up. At least her appetite didn't seem affected by the tension at the table. Hudson had given up any semblance of trying to eat. "Could I have some more lasagna?"

"Sure, sweetie." Nina reached for the spatula.

"We gotta go." Liz shoved back her chair. "I just remembered I got a job interview at the Hyatt tomorrow. Nothing fancy like being an art photographer but it'll pay the rent."

"We haven't had dessert yet." Emma's face crumpled. "It's apple pie."

"Don't punish the kids because you got caught in a lie." Nina followed Liz to the kitchen where she picked up her bag and stuffed the bottle of wine in it. "Don't start drinking because of this."

"Don't think so highly of yourself that you think you could drive me to drink."

"I'm sorry if I offended you, but you did lie and you know it." She forced herself to lower her voice. Emma and Hudson didn't need to hear anymore. "What I can't understand is why. Why did it matter when you arrived in San Antonio? Why lie about seeing Dad? Why not come to the house and see the rest of us—Jan and me? Why wait until the funeral? It doesn't make any sense."

"He's not your dad."

"Then who is?"

"Beats me, but I *am* your mother."

"Not in any way that counts."

Liz bulldozed past Nina. "Come on, you two, let's go. It's a school night. Move it."

"Liz! Mom!" There. She'd said it. For Hudson's and Emma's sakes. They needed family in their lives. They needed someone who didn't smoke in their faces. Someone who made sure they had haircuts and toothbrushes. Someone who went with them to the library and watched those basketball games. She could swallow her pride for them. She grabbed the apple pie and a plastic bag. Along with her card. It had her cell phone number on it. Trying to slip the pie in the bag without dropping it, she strode after Liz. "At least take the pie with you."

Liz already had the front door open. The sauce still smeared on her chin, Emma struggled with her thin Windbreaker. Hudson grabbed the jacket's arm and jerked it around her. "Mom said to hurry."

"I'm trying."

"Easy. Take this with you." Nina handed the pie to Hudson, who handled it as if it might explode. She tucked the card in his jeans jacket pocket. "I'm sorry you didn't get to stay longer. I hope to see you again soon. You're welcome here. Anytime. If you need anything, call me. I mean that. Anytime."

"Sure." Hudson shook his shaggy head. "Someday."

"He isn't going to need anything from you." Liz stomped down the front steps without looking back. "Get a move on, you two. Now."

"Thank you for the pie." Emma doled out another sweet hug. The words were whispered. "It was nice to meet you."

Good manners. She hadn't learned those from Liz. Who had raised this little girl? And her big brother. Nina wanted to know more. She wanted to know this girl. She wanted to know Hudson. They needed help. They needed big sisters. Even if it meant putting up with Liz. "I promise to see you again," she whispered in Emma's ear. "Soon."

Emma's wan smile reflected all the times promises had been made and broken.

They swept out the door and were gone.

Silence.

"That went well." The *ticky-tackity* on the tile announced that Peanuts had followed. Nina scooped him up and buried her face in his fur. "What just happened?"

Peanuts whined and snuggled closer. "Exactly, lovie."

The adrenaline of an entire day of anticipation and preparation fizzled, leaving her flat and tired. The darkroom called to her. The only place where anything made any sense. The kitchen had to be cleaned first. Pearl would have a conniption fit if she saw her pristine, hallowed grounds treated in such a despicable fashion.

Nina worked fast, driven by thoughts that went around and around. Maybe Liz really didn't remember when she had arrived, but she couldn't have forgotten a reunion with Dad. Why would she deny it? Why didn't he say anything about it? Why lie?

Despite her best efforts it took almost forty-five minutes to clean the kitchen and store the food. Aaron would be happy with the plethora of leftovers as promised. Of course, she would have to make more pie. Her own plate of food went the way of the garbage disposal. The smell made gorge rise in her throat.

Her cell phone, plugged into the charger by the cellar door, played "Born to Run" by Bruce Springsteen. Her ringtone for Aaron. Maybe he could make something of Liz's erratic behavior.

"Are they still there? How did it go? I just had to make sure you saved me a big slice of pie—"

"They're gone." Unplugging the phone so she could pace, Nina launched into a description of the evening. She went to the window and stared out. The rain announced its arrival with *pitter-patter* on the glass. "It was a disaster of epic proportions."

"You exaggerate."

"No, really, it was." She turned and found herself face-to-face with Liz.

And a small black gun.

Again.

At least it wasn't the cannon.

36

Liz held the handgun to Peanuts's head. She shook her head and whispered, "Say a word, he dies, then you die. Politely say good night to your boyfriend."

"You're too hard on yourself." Aaron's voice continued, husky and concerned, in Nina's ear. "I'll come over and we'll work on the exhibit. You can tell me all the gory details."

Peanuts wiggled and whined. Liz's fingers turned white as she clenched the dog to her chest in a one-handed grip.

"I'm exhausted." Nina didn't have a problem sounding exhausted. Not sounding terrified, a little more difficult. "Can we talk about this in the morning?"

"I thought you wanted to work tonight."

"It's been a long day."

"No kidding. I worked a three-car accident—"

"Can you tell me about it in the morning?"

"Sure. Text me when you wake up. I'll bring you a bagel and a double espresso."

Nina's stomach heaved. She sidestepped toward the island. It held a wooden block filled with knives. Would she really consider stabbing her own mother?

Grace was her mother.

"Stop." So much evil in one snarled syllable. Peanuts barked. "Hang up."

"Did you hear me? What's wrong with Peanuts?" Aaron sounded confused. "Unless you'd rather have donuts."

"Nothing. Whole wheat bagels with that chipotle cream cheese sound good. Talk to you tomorrow."

"I love you."

"Ditto."

"What?"

She hung up. "How did you get in?"

The gun left Peanuts's head. Its barrel pointed at Nina. Liz dropped Peanuts. He landed on his feet and skittered under the table. She tugged keys from her pocket. Keys on a UT Longhorns key chain. She swung them back and forth so they made a jiggly tune. "I snagged these on the way out the door."

Liz jerked her head toward the cellar door. "Open it."

"There's no wine down there anymore. We use it for storage of canned goods and paper goods."

"Go."

Nina tore her gaze from the gun. She peered over Liz's shoulder. "Where are Hudson and Emma? Do they know what you're doing?"

"Don't be stupid. I put them on a bus back to the motel. They know how to take care of themselves. They know better than to ask questions." She took a step forward. Her sneakers squeaked on the tile. "They just don't know when to shut up."

"Why are you doing this?"

"You couldn't leave it alone. You had to ask twenty questions. They're stupid, stupid kids who open their mouths and spew information."

"I don't care that you lied. Okay, I care. But it doesn't matter."

"It matters to a certain detective. He asked me the same questions you did. I lied to him. Now you know."

"You lied to the police." Not a smart thing to do. "And you're afraid I'll tell him."

"I know you will. In a heartbeat. Because you're a good little girl. I'm proud of that, you know. I know I didn't have anything to do with it, but still. You're a good girl."

"Go on, say it. You killed your brother."

Liz's smile said it all. Nina's stomach lurched. She grabbed the doorknob to keep from falling. Blackness flowed, then ebbed. Purple lights flashed. No panic attack. *Not now, not now.*

"You killed Daddy? Why? Why kill him?"

"He's not your daddy." Liz jabbed Nina in the ribs. The physical pain didn't touch the depth of the agony of knowing Liz killed her own brother. "Stop stalling. Open the door."

Her throat tight with tears she refused to shed, Nina gritted her teeth and did as she was told.

God, please. Please. Don't let her do this to Aaron. Please don't let Grace or Jan find me dead in the basement. Or Brooklyn.

Better her dead than Aaron or the girls. *He's a good man. God, give him a good life, please. Help him find love again.*

She eased the door open. The musky scent of dust and humidity wafted from below.

A second later a shove sent her sailing into the darkness.

37

Pain.

Nina gasped. She curled into a fetal position. Her hip hurt. Her ribs. Her head.

Everything hurt.

A smell. The stench of cheap wine and mustiness enveloped her. Her stomach rocked. She moaned. *Get up. Get up. Move. Now. Nobody gets to lie here and die.*

She forced her eyes open. Darkness.

The cellar.

Then a sliver of light. No, a flicker. A candle.

Nina raised her head. Pain exploded behind her ear. She tried to sit up. More pain throbbed in her arm. She stifled another moan.

"Sorry. I was hoping the fall would take care of business and we wouldn't be sitting here now." Liz crouched on the floor next to a cluster of candles on old saucers. Tiny flames barely illuminated the corner where she huddled, gun in her hand, a few feet from where Nina lay at the foot of the wooden stairs leading from the kitchen to the cellar. "You shouldn't have said anything about me drinking. It's your fault. You sounded just like him. Just like them. I've had enough of that stuffed in my craw to last me a lifetime."

"Why didn't you shoot me then?" Nina inhaled a ragged breath. "Why push me down the stairs?"

"Turns out it's harder to kill your own daughter than a person would think." She chuckled, a bitter sound that reverberated against the thick cement walls.

Her meaning hit Nina with the force of a cannon ball. "Yet you killed your own brother."

"It was his fault. Mr. High and Mighty." Liz laughed so hard she snorted, which only made her laugh more. "I wanted to come home. I wanted my share of the money Mom and Dad left when they died. He owed it to me. It was mine. I thought seeing his niece and nephew playing in the park where we used to play when we were kids would soften him up. He loved the paddleboats and the sky tram and the carousel at Brackenridge Park when we were kids. Mom used to take us there. Now they're all gone, of course. The kids fed the ducks, though. They wanted to go to the zoo, but who wants to pay those prices to look at animals?"

Money. This was about money.

She rambled on, the flames making dark shadows on her angular face. Nina eased into a seated position. Pain tore through her chest. Her breath caught. Broken ribs? The talking was good. It bought her time. Again. "He would've paid, if you'd asked. Dad liked the zoo. He liked the hippo. And the giraffes. The giraffes are Jan's favorite. Brooklyn wants to be a veterinarian."

"Too bad I won't meet her. He called me Dizzy Lizzy, you know." A match flared, revealing her frown. The smell of phosphorus and tobacco filled the air. The end of the cigarette glowed and bobbed. "He shouldn't have done that."

"He could be mean." Trying to remember when she'd last been in the cellar, Nina scanned the darkness without moving. Shelves of canned goods lined a far wall. Dad had bordered on being a prepper. He kept extra bottled water, paper goods, and other staples from Costco in the cellar, once the home to his father's renowned wine collection. A collection Dad never revived after Liz's stints in rehab and his parents' deaths. "It was his way or the highway."

"But not to his little princesses."

"He was strict." No baseball bats. No weapons. Toilet paper and baby wipes. "He wanted what he thought was best for us."

"He shouldn't have gotten all righteous with me. How could I expect him to raise two more of my kids? Only he didn't call them kids. He knew how to hit under the belt. He got plenty nasty with me. Mr. Self-Righteous Christian. Just like Mom and Dad. He deserved what he got."

Dad had a righteous streak. In the end it had killed him. He lied, cheated, deceived, and gambled away his marriage and his family. But his hypocrisy killed him. *God, can You forgive him? He lost his way. I'm so sorry he lost his way.*

And then his sister killed him before he had a chance to find it.

"You killed him over money?"

"I didn't come here to kill him. I came here to reason with him, but he made me so mad, I couldn't help myself. I wanted to shut him up so I shut him up for good."

"How did you do it? Get in the house and out without being seen?"

"The same way I did as a kid." Liz waved the gun. It made bizarre shadows dance on the wall behind her, reminding Nina of the games they used to play while camping in a tent in the backyard. "I came through the back entrance to the cellar."

"It's been sealed up for years."

"So you thought. So Geoffrey thought. This was my favorite place to hide as a kid. Where do you think I got my first taste of wine? I used to hide my pot stash down here and my cigs. It was perfect. Quiet. I could go upstairs stoned out of my mind and they never even noticed. Good times."

Keep her talking. "Where did you get the gun?"

"Stole it off my ex Joel."

"Were you married? Is he Hudson and Emma's father?"

"No to both questions. I thought about marrying him. Not that he ever asked. I thought he was a keeper at first. He always had money in his pocket and he didn't mind that I had two kids. Turns out he earned his money by robbing gas stations and convenience stores." She patted the gun and cackled. "Using this gun. After I found out, I took the proceeds from his last job and this gun and got out of Dodge. It was a nice little nest egg until I could get Geoff to ante up. It's not like he could report the theft to the police."

"Don't do this. Just leave me here and disappear. I won't tell anyone."

"And let you have what should've been mine? You're crazy."

"You'll never have it now."

"So. Neither will you."

Liz was the insane one. She could plead insanity and get the help she needed. "I know Detective King. I can call him. You can turn yourself in. They'll get you some help."

"I'm not going to jail. No way. What do you think rehab was like? Like jail. I ain't doing that again."

"What about Hudson and Emma? Don't do this to them. How can you kill their half sister? What kind of mother does that?"

"Just shut up, *shut up*." The cigarette dangling from her lip, Liz stood and staggered toward Nina. "I'll leave here just like I did after I killed Mr. Hoity-Toity Judge. Slip away. Nobody has to know. I'll be here to comfort Jannie and Grace. They'll welcome Hudson and Emma to the family. We'll be one big, happy family again. Before they know it, I'll control all that money that should've been mine to start with."

"You'll get caught. They'll figure it out. Aaron will never let it go. If you leave, disappear. I'll take care of Hudson and Emma. Both of them. I have the means to do it. Please, Liz, let me take care of them."

"I wish I could. You grew up good. A decent human being. Better than Geoffrey." She edged closer until she stood at the bottom of the stairs. "It's too late for that."

Liz raised the gun.

"Don't."

The door opened. Liz whirled. She fired.

Aaron tumbled down the stairs.

38

Nina hurled herself at Liz. Their bodies collided.

Liz's head snapped back. She hit the cement floor. The gun went off again. The noise exploded in Nina's left ear.

An acrid smell like fireworks exploding burned her nose for a second. Clanging reverberated inside her head. Chunks of ceiling descended. Dust burned her eyes.

No time to think. No time to mourn. No time to fear. "You shot him, you shot Aaron."

Grunts met the hurled accusation. Followed by a stream of obscenities so vile they soiled the air.

Half blinded, Nina grabbed at the gun. They wrestled and writhed on the floor.

One of the candles tipped over. Hot wax touched Liz's face. She screamed again. More obscenities. Liz was old and weakened by debauchery. Nina had youth and muscle on her side, but her injuries shackled her.

She smacked Liz's arm against the floor again and again.

The gun skittered across the floor. She nailed Liz's arms to the floor with her knees and hands.

Liz ceased to struggle. She began to cry big, ugly sobs.

"I'm not hit." Aaron's hoarse voice gasped in the semidarkness. "I'm here. Are you hurt?"

Same song. Second verse. Or was it the third time?

"Aaron, are you really okay?"

"I ducked and rolled down the stairs. I felt the bullet singe my ear." Still gasping for air, he crawled toward the gun. "I really hate these things, you know."

"I know." Nina stared at her mother. Liz's chest heaved. Her wrinkled face contorted until Nina no longer recognized her. A stranger who had sneaked in and out of her life.

"Let her up, Nina, I've got her." Aaron rose to his knees. He held the gun with both hands, pointed squarely at the woman on the floor. "The police are on their way. King is on his way."

Nina eased to her feet on weak legs. Every muscle throbbed. A pain stabbed her in the chest every time she inhaled and exhaled. Two fingers felt broken on her left hand. The bongos performed in her head again.

Liz rolled onto her side and covered her face. Nina tensed, waiting. Nothing. Just sobs.

She backed up until she stood next to Aaron, but she never took her gaze from the woman on the floor. "How did you know?"

"Ditto. You've never said ditto in your life."

"It's a line from a movie."

"I know. *Ghost.* Patrick Swayze says it to Demi Moore. She can never get him to say, 'I love you.'"

Nina's legs trembled. Her mouth didn't seem to want to form words. She leaned over and put her hands on her knees. "I didn't know if you would get it."

"I got that something was wrong. You didn't answer my texts after we hung up. When I got here the front door was unlocked."

"She killed Daddy."

"I know." He put one arm around her and squeezed. The gun never wavered. "She'll get justice now."

"No, no, no, I can't go to jail. I can't be in a cell." Liz crawled to her knees. She held up her clasped hands as if praying. "I'm your mother. Don't make me go. Please. They made me insane. I heard voices. They told me what to do."

"She's got the insanity plea down." Aaron's tone waxed philosophical. "That's one trial I don't plan to shoot."

"Me neither."

Instead, she would be the star witness in her own mother's murder trial.

Sirens screamed.

Again.

*   *   *

Aaron didn't move. Not even when King pounded down the stairs, his Smith & Wesson in hand.

"Gun, gun!" King shouted as he hit the bottom of the stairs. His partner followed close behind. "Lower the gun, Aaron, now."

"She killed Judge Fischer." He couldn't seem to make his arms move. His fingers were frozen around the trigger. "She tried to kill Nina. She would've killed me."

"I know, but it's over now." King's voice dropped to a low, soothing bass. "We've got it from here. You can lower the weapon. Now."

Command reverberated in that last syllable.

Aaron wanted to comply, but his body wouldn't cooperate.

"Aaron, it's okay. King can't cuff her until you put the gun down." Nina had that same soothing touch in her voice. Her thumb rubbed the skin on the back of his hand in a soft, circular motion. "We have to go find Hudson and Emma. They'll be waiting for her and she's never coming home."

"You leave my kids alone." Snarling, Liz rose halfway up on her knees. "They're mine, not yours."

"Don't you move or I will kill you." Aaron took a step toward her. "I'm not kidding. It will be self-defense, won't it, King?"

"You need to stand down."

"Please, Aaron."

The ugly, black, stinking gun lowered of its own accord. He squatted and laid it with all the gentleness he could muster on the cement floor.

Cops swarmed Liz. Two seconds later she was cuffed and dragged up the stairs. She refused to move her feet, so Cavazos and a uni carried her between them.

Nina leaned into Aaron. She was warm. *Thank You, God, she's warm and alive.* He wrapped his arms around her and lowered his head so it rested in her hair. "I thought you were dead," he whispered. "I cannot live without you. You get that, right?"

"I thought you were dead." She tightened her grip around his waist. "I love you. I don't want to live without you."

"Ditto."

They both laughed, the hysterical sound of two people who'd gone around the bend.

"This is getting to be a habit." King holstered his weapon and seated himself on the steps. He scratched his chin. "I don't really need this kind of excitement every other day."

"You live for it."

Aaron and Nina spoke at the same time. They laughed again. More hysteria.

Nina's laugh cracked and quivered. "My mother killed the man I treated like my dad. How will I tell Jan?"

"I'm sorry." Aaron rubbed her back and kissed her hair. "I'm so sorry."

Nothing else could be said. It couldn't be made right. Justice would not change Nina's family history. But it didn't hurt either. "She has something wrong with her. Something somewhere in her psyche got messed up. Maybe it can be fixed."

King snorted. "Sorry. I'm a cynic. But you could be right. Tell me from the beginning."

Nina told her story. Aaron picked up where she left off.

King scratched his chin some more. "So you knew something was wrong because she said 'Ditto.'"

"Yep."

"Huh." He sighed and stood to make way for the EMTs. Again. "I don't get it, but I'm glad you two do."

So was Aaron.

39

Exhibit receptions used to make Nina crazy. Not anymore. Compared to murder and mayhem, they were tame affairs. She picked up a glass of club soda decorated with a wedge of lime and traversed a wide path around an old acquaintance from the *Express-News* who likely was more interested in a story than in the exhibit. A sax, trumpet, and keyboard blended in a soft, jazzy melody in the main room at the Blue Star Gallery. No blues tonight. Joe, Samuel, and Ralphie, three Haven for Hope residents fresh from the drug rehab program, provided the music.

More than two hundred people munched on fresh fruit, veggies, dip, crackers, and cheese provided by San Antonio Food Bank chefs-in-training. The event had a luminous fairy-tale story quality that made her fearful she would lose her glass slipper and the carriage would turn into a pumpkin.

As far as she was concerned, the other story was over. Her ribs only twinged occasionally, her headaches from the concussion had dissipated, and the bruises faded. Rick had made a deal. He would testify against Peter Coggins, but he was still going to jail for murder. Coggins would be tried on bribery, public corruption, racketeering, and conspiracy to commit murder. A half dozen of his colleagues at the firm would go to jail with him.

Everyone except Skeet. A good Christian would pray for his

soul. Nina tried. God would forgive her for needing to try so hard to forgive. Liz continued to hug her insanity defense like a long-lost friend. She claimed childhood abuse in all forms from parents and her brother. Nina hadn't seen her since that night in the wine cellar.

Tonight was a night to leave those horrifying memories behind. To start fresh. At least that's what Dr. Wallace kept insisting. Nina's true family was here for her. Including Hudson and Emma, who seemed less shell-shocked each day, just like their half sister. Her friends from Haven. The staff and the guests of honor, the former homeless individuals who'd been helped by the organization and now had jobs and apartments. Aaron. All his colleagues from the news business. Melanie's friends and coworkers. Serena's friends and coworkers. The important people.

Nina took a breath and relished that thought. Only Jan was missing. Deployed. Still in the danger zone of a different sort. *God, protect her and bring her home safely. This family has suffered so much loss. Please.*

Jan hadn't said much when Nina shared the news via Skype. She shrugged and offered a resigned smile. Then went back to her job. Healing work needed to be done. Life's loose ends could not be tied up neatly. Fairy-tale endings were for Grace's romance novels and Lifetime movies.

In the meantime Nina honed her rusty prayer skills every night. For Jan, for Hudson, for Emma, for Brooklyn, for Grace. A long, long list of people hurt by a selfish, psychotic woman.

Nina was still working on praying for Liz.

She turned to the enormous black-and-white photos that adorned the walls. These were her heroes tonight. People who experienced homelessness and found ways to survive.

The frail man with his shopping cart. The men gathered around the trash fire with their bottle in a paper sack. The pregnant woman curled up on a filthy blanket under the I-10 at the Martin Street highway overpass. The toothless, grizzled man in overalls, barefoot, pulling a red Radio Flyer wagon filled with all his earthly possessions. A little girl with a dirty face and runny nose in a diaper riding a tricycle dwarfed by a passing semi on the highway behind her.

On and on they went. In each area video vignettes ran on a continuous loop. The interviews she and Aaron had conducted over the last year. Stories of jobs lost, health deteriorated, wars that didn't stay overseas but came home with a soldier who couldn't close his eyes at night without seeing and hearing and reliving the explosion that killed his buddies. Stories of women abused by husbands, homes repossessed, children living in cars, and men driven into the street by voices that couldn't be stilled, no matter how much they drank.

Aaron had done a masterful job of editing digital images to look like black-and-white film, giving them a beautiful Vietnam-newsreel-era feel. Stories that needed to be told and that Nina and Aaron needed to tell.

"There you are."

Looking sharp in the only suit he owned, Aaron approached. He carried an armful of red, pink, and yellow roses. "For you, my lady." He kissed her gently on the lips and handed them over. "You look gorgeous."

"Thank you. This old thing?"

They grinned at each other. What she would wear to the reception had been a topic in dispute for nearly two weeks. She wanted to wear black slacks and a white blouse. Grace objected. One day her mother had appeared at her bedroom door with a box from Dillard's. A beautiful electric-blue sheath with a lacy overlay that fit like a glove and flared gently just about the knee. Along with matching ballerina flats, a nod to Nina's staunch refusal to wear heels.

"Every girl needs a party frock," Grace said before settling into a chair to watch her daughter try it on.

"Are you sure you're okay?"

"I'm fine." She inhaled the roses' heavenly sweet scent. "More than fine. Content. Come what may. The best is yet to come."

They were clichés. But every cliché had at its core an eternal truth that made people say it over and over until it lost its burnish. She wasn't a writer tonight. She was a bruised, battered survivor. Just like her Haven for Hope friends. She'd weathered the storm and still stood firm. Better than ever. Her faith had emerged from the storm, as unsteady as a toddler's just learning to walk, but on the right path.

"People love the photos."

"I don't want them to love them. I want them to be up in arms. I want them to notice these people and really see them for the first time in their lives." She tried to tether her emotions, but they chomped at the bit. "I want them to stop and say hello and offer to take them to dinner when they see them on the street instead of ducking their heads and hiding their eyes."

"Preaching to the choir, my friend."

"I know." If anyone understood, Aaron did. Because he understood her like no other man ever had or ever would. Like the fairy tales, she was allowed her knight in shining armor. Together they had saved their world. No princess in a tower, she had been on the battlefield with him. A mighty team.

"I'm glad Hudson and Emma were okay with including photos of their mom." His hand rubbed Nina's back. She closed her eyes and let the comfort of his touch ease the tension that held her captive. "I'm glad you decided to include them."

Swallowing against sudden tears that tended to appear out of nowhere, she took a breath and nodded. She couldn't talk about it. Not yet. Not even to the therapist. Emma and Hudson now had their own child psychologist recommended by Nina's. They needed a neutral party to whom they could talk. They needed time to become a part of this new family and accept that their mother, a murderer, had given up their custody to Nina without a fight.

One photo of Liz captured the desperation mingled with bravado that was her mother at Haven that day in the commons. The smoke rings hung in the air. Her lips were puckered as if she might give Nina a kiss. But she didn't.

She never had. Not in her entire life. That the present tense should be no different should not surprise Nina. It didn't.

Another photo captured the moment she had ruffled Emma's curls that night in the backyard before she tried to kill Nina. She had the most maternal of smiles on her thin lips. She looked like every mother Nina had ever known. In the outtake group photo her skinny arms flailed, fingers splayed, her head thrown back, mouth open, as if she'd erupted with laughter at the very moment the shutter clicked. Hudson had rabbit-ear fingers behind Emma's head. Little Emma crossed her eyes and stuck out her tongue.

They looked happy.

Photos might be worth a thousand words, but sometimes photos lied. They told stories that didn't exist, had never existed, would never exist.

Nina had scanned Liz's letters and created captions with excerpts in her biological mother's handwriting. They hung below each of the five photos on display. The juxtaposition of optimism and reality made Nina stare into the darkness every night, unable to sleep. No audio vignette existed for this story.

The thought of her mother's voice blaring in this exhibit at this moment was unbearable.

"Are you sure you're okay?" Aaron's hand crept around her shoulders and squeezed her tight against him. He had such strength, such broad shoulders. "You're shivering."

"Here comes trouble."

Dressed in his usual natty blue suit, Matt King strode toward them. For once he smiled. "Congratulations. It looks like your exhibit is a hit, if the lack of parking spaces means anything."

"I'm surprised you're here." Aaron shook the detective's hand. "You don't strike me as the art exhibit type."

"Actually, I just bought a loft condo north of downtown. Right there on Madison Square Park." He grinned. "I need something to hang in the living room. And this is a good cause. Cops see what homelessness does to people every day."

Proceeds from the sale went to Haven for Hope. Another reason to like this man who'd saved Aaron and her lives that night in the darkroom. "Which one did you pick?"

"The little girl in a diaper riding her tricycle under the overpass."

"That should make for some interesting conversations when you bring home dates."

"I don't bring home dates. I'm a good Christian boy."

Another thing she hadn't known about Detective Matt King. "How are you?"

"Cleared by the officer-involved shooting team and back on full duty."

"I know, but how are you?"

"If you're asking me if I regret shooting Skeeter Miles, the answer is I sleep just fine. I hope you do too."

"I'm working on it."

"So how is your partner—your real partner?" Aaron threw in the question.

"I forgot for a second that you're in the news business. Always on the job." King chuckled. "Off the record? He's asked for a new partner. He says I'm trigger happy. I say the guy committed suicide-by-cop. The shooting team agrees. Looks like Manny Cavazos and I will be paired up from now on."

Until the next incident. Maybe she should introduce him to her counselor. "Try to be careful. Next time it could be you who takes the bullet."

"Yes, ma'am." He saluted. "I'll be by tomorrow to pick up my piece. Don't let anyone else grab it."

"No worries."

He strode away, another hit-and-run completed. He probably intended to go home to that condo and make notes on a new case or back to HQ to comb through evidence.

"I think you made a new friend." Aaron shook his head. "I hope you're up for that."

She shrugged. King needed a woman in his life. Nina needed to do some matchmaking. A person couldn't have too many friends. "Absolutely."

Aaron's arm tightened around her waist. "Before we get into the speeches and all that jazz, there's something I want to ask you. It's important."

"Of course."

He turned to face her. With great care he took the roses from her arms and laid them on the closest white-linen covered table. She longed for her camera to capture that moment. He dropped to one knee.

"Aaron, are you all right?" She glanced around. Grace, Trevor, Will, and the children were drifting their direction. Her friends from Haven right behind them. His buddies from the news business. They all had grins the size of Texas on their faces. A wave of anticipation crowded her. The music faded. The room grew quiet. "What's going on?"

Aaron plucked a small black velvet box from his suitcoat pocket. He cleared his throat. "I had this whole speech prepared. I can't remember any of it. I have loved you since the day I met you. We both know how short time can be, and I don't want to waste another minute of it." He snapped the lid open. A simple solitaire diamond glistened in the gallery lights. "I know how hard it is for you to trust. I can be trusted. I will love, honor, and cherish you. I promise never to leave you of my own accord. You can trust me, and even more, you can trust God. Nina, will you marry me?"

A thrill ran through Nina. For a second it seemed as if her ballet flats lifted from the burnished tile floor and she floated in the air. That kind of thing didn't happen to a woman like her. Until now.

No waiting. No more wasted time. No fear. Smiling, she knelt. "Yes, I'll marry you. Will you marry me?"

Aaron let out a whoop. One fist pumped. His newsroom buddies Snoopy-danced around the room. An intricate series of high and low fives followed by fist bumps commenced.

A flash caught her by surprise. Emma used her new camera, a gift from Grace, to take photos of this special moment. Aaron's best photog buddy was shooting the proposal. Likely it would be seen on Channel 29's nine o'clock newscast. News families were like that. She would be a part of that family now.

"We better give them something to talk about." Aaron slipped the ring on her finger. He took her hand and together they stood. "Seal it with a kiss?"

He leaned in. Nina stretched up to meet him halfway. The kiss went on and on. Catcalls sounded and more applause.

Eyes closed, Nina captured the image in her mind. No need for a camera. No need for a lens to filter the view. She could see their future clearly. Always together as long as they both shall live. God was in charge of how long that would be. She could live with that too. Their new story had begun.

A NOTE FROM THE AUTHOR

While *Tell Her No Lies* is a work of fiction, the plight of people experiencing homelessness is not. Haven for Hope is a real place in San Antonio, Texas. Haven serves the needs of thousands of men, women, and children every year. They come from all walks of life. Many are veterans who have served their country honorably. Many suffer from mental illness. All need our prayers. Financial help is also appreciated. If you're interested in learning more about Haven for Hope, visit the nonprofit organization's website at http://www.havenforhope.org.

I take joy in every book I write, but *Tell Her No Lies* has a special place in my heart. Early in my fiction-writing career, I published two romantic suspense novels. Then I switched genres to Amish romances. I love writing those books, but romantic suspense was my first love. It's been my dream to be able to share the story in *Tell Her No Lies* for several years. My dear editor and friend, Becky Monds, stepped up and presented the manuscript to her HarperCollins Christian Publishing team. She encouraged her colleagues to take a chance on it. Her efforts helped make my dream come true. My heartfelt thanks go to Becky for her support and her fantastic job of editing the manuscript. I also want to thank my agent, Julie Gwinn, for her hard work in diligently searching for the right home for it. As always, line editor Julee Schwarzburg has saved me from a deluge of errors. Her patience is monumental.

A huge thanks goes to retired San Antonio Police Detective Richard Urbanek. Richard tweaked Detective King's homicide investigation techniques. His knowledge of police procedures was invaluable. Richard was a good sport in reading a romantic suspense novel, and he also caught a couple of historical inaccuracies that would have been embarrassing for me. His observation that, in the end, this is a work of fiction reminded me that sometimes writers are allowed a little poetic license.

I'm also in debt to my husband, Tim Irvin, for his expertise regarding the profession of news photography and the TV news business in general. His insight garnered from twenty-five years in the business helped to give an authentic ring to those scenes in this novel. His expertise regarding digital video cameras was particularly helpful. Any remaining factual errors are all mine.

I thoroughly enjoyed setting this book in my adopted hometown of San Antonio. Readers, please know that while I've used the names of real businesses, particularly media outlets, in this story, all the characters and crimes are figments of my overactive imagination. If I've fudged on locations or descriptions for my own purposes, please forgive me. I take full responsibility for any inaccuracies.

Finally, my deepest appreciation goes to my readers. May you be blessed by our Lord Jesus Christ.

DISCUSSION QUESTIONS

1. Sometimes the people who should love us the most are the ones who also hurt us the most. How do you deal with hurt and strife caused by family members?

2. Nina has a hard time seeing God the Father as someone she can trust after she realizes that her adopted father has been lying to her for years. What would you say to her to help her understand how different her heavenly Father is from her earthly father?

3. Nina spent part of her early life being homeless and coping with the stark realities of her situation. As an adult she volunteers to help homeless people in her community. She incorporates their struggles into her art. What does Scripture say about helping those who are poor or hungry? Do you incorporate good works into your life? How?

4. Rick overcame poverty to attend law school and run for public office. Then he allows his desire for power and acclaim to send him down a path of crime and self-destruction. Is power or public acclaim important to you? Do we sometimes get carried away, trying to make our dreams come true? How do you make sure you're walking the path God has chosen for you?

5. Aaron cares deeply for Nina, but he's never stepped up and told her that he has feelings beyond friendship for her. Do you think he's right to keep his feelings to himself in favor of friendship? Is friendship sometimes more important than romance? Was he right to act on his feelings in the midst of the turmoil in Nina's life?

6. Nina's mother, Liz, takes revenge on Geoffrey out of bitterness and anger that she has stored up for years. While the great majority of us will never commit a heinous act of murder the way Liz did, we are guilty of harboring bitterness and anger. Sometimes we let it show through smaller, petty acts and words. How do you let go of these feelings? What do you do with negative thoughts? What does Scripture tell us to do?

7. Nina says she has forgiven her adoptive father for his deceit, but she's still working on forgiving her mother for murdering him. What does Scripture say about forgiveness? Is there someone in your life you need to forgive? What keeps you from doing it? What would you say to Nina to help her forgive Liz? Could you forgive her?

8. When life is hard and keeps getting harder, we often wonder why God would allow us to suffer so much. Scripture says in everything God works for our good. How do you see God at work in the difficult times in your life? What are the blessings that come to mind when you think of God's grace?

9. Geoffrey's decision not to tell Nina and Jan about the letters from Liz was a lie of omission. He may have felt it was best for them not to know. Is there ever a time that lying—such as little white lies—can be justified? Do you think Nina's feelings of betrayal are justified? What do you think would be a better way of handling the situation?

10. Nina says Geoffrey was a Christian. He went to church, served as an usher, and participated in church activities. She puzzles over how he ended up with a second hidden life that involved gambling and engaging in criminal activity to support his addiction. Do you think church attendance is a sign that a person is a Christian? How can Christians help each other be accountable for their behavior outside the church walls? What ultimately makes a person a true Christian?

Don't miss the next romantic suspense novel from Kelly Irvin!

OVER
THE LINE

When a college student dies at Gabriella's feet after muttering her
brother's name in the parking lot, vicious gun smugglers believe
she knows more than she should. And they're determined to make
sure she suffers the same fate.

Coming June 2019!

THOMAS NELSON
Since 1798

Bestselling author Kelly Irvin also writes
Amish romances. Escape with her to
these intriguing communities.

Every Amish Season Novels
Upon a Spring Breeze
Beneath the Summer Sun
Through the Autumn Air

The Amish of Bee County Novels
The Beekeeper's Son
The Bishop's Son
The Saddle Maker's Son

Novellas by Kelly Irvin
A Christmas Visitor in *An Amish Christmas Gift*
Sweeter than Honey in *An Amish Market*
One Sweet Kiss in *An Amish Summer*
Snow Angels in *An Amish Christmas Love*
A Midwife's Dream in *An Amish Heirloom*

ABOUT THE AUTHOR

Photo by Tim Irvin

Bestseller Kelly Irvin is the author of fourteen books, including Amish romance and romantic suspense. *Publishers Weekly* called *A Deadly Wilderness* "a solid romantic suspense debut." She followed up with *No Child of Mine*. The two-time ACFW Carol finalist worked as a newspaper reporter for six years writing stories on the Texas-Mexico border. Those experiences fuel her romantic suspense novels set in Texas. A retired public relations professional, Kelly now writes fiction full-time. She lives with her husband, photographer Tim Irvin, in San Antonio. They are the parents of two children, two grandchildren, and two ornery cats.

Visit her online at KellyIrvin.com
Facebook: Kelly.Irvin.Author
Twitter: @Kelly_S_Irvin